Prophecy Decoded

A Systematic Approach to End-Time Theology

by

DR. RODNEY E. HARRIGAN, Th.D., Ed.D., BCPP

Contents

Foreword by Dr. John WS Howard, Ph.D,. D.Psy, N.D.

President & Founder – Guilford School of Theology

President of the International Association of Pastoral Psychologists

הפירוש הנכון של תוכנית הגאולה של אלוהים נמצא בכל התורה, התנ"ך וכתבי
היד היווניים העתיקים שלך

Published by: Robert Graham

Paperback ISBN: 978-1-964551-32-6

Library of Congress Control Number: 2024921827

Case ID #: 1-14290408771

Dedications

To my mother, Emily Peterson Harrigan, and father, Alpheus J. Harrigan, who gave me unwavering love, inspiration, and roots. Every "good" that I tried to do was because I wanted to make my mother and father proud.

To my wife for her strength, loving personality, and intelligence, she made me the person that I am. Elaine led me to Christ and gave us two wonderful daughters. There are no greater treasures in life. She continues to inspire me through her debilitating illness, where she can barely talk and is totally blind, but she still sees and inspires.

To our daughters, Pamela & Sherrice, who make me proud to be a father and who lead me in the path of righteousness with their husbands, Isaac and Bryan.

To our only grandchild, Sophia, who is the light of my life and hope for the future. She is an amazing glimpse of who and what her generation is becoming.

To my brother Jimmy, sister Pat, and all the relatives on both sides, who seem to look beyond the moments and see who I am still becoming.

To my Harlem friends who were my oasis in the desert. Life was wonderful with them in those early formative years.

To Dr. John W.S. Howard, founder of the Guilford School of Theology, who made it possible to achieve my lifelong dream, and who empowered me to pursue another passion that I did not realize I had.

Forward by Dr. John WS Howard

My name is John W.S. Howard I am the president of Guilford School of Theology located in Greensboro, NC. I hold a Bachelor of Arts degree in philosophy and religion, a Master of Divinity degree in theology, a Doctor of Philosophy in philosophy, and a Doctor of Psychology in general psychology. I met the author approximately three years ago while he was a doctoral student at GST pursuing a doctorate in theology. I know him to be a gentle and kind man with a strong commitment to public service. He has a long history of service in the corporate arena as well as in the field of Christian Education.

The author has demonstrated that he is indeed a researcher who does not always accept tradition, orthodoxy, or superficiality. He prefers to get to the root of the meaning of words and the core of their history. This includes the cultural perspectives and the language of origin. The author of this fine work has spent a tremendous amount of time in developing it for his readers' understanding and application.

While the author pursued his doctorate degree at GST, I had the opportunity to meet his family which was a joy to see them interact with each other. I observed him being attentive to his wife as well as seeing how much his daughters and sons-in-law loved him. He is a family man who holds true to the ideals of family values which are central to the core values that make this nation great. After getting to know this author and his family, and upon his graduation, the Board of Trustees scheduled a meeting and decided to vote him in as Dean of Academic Affairs. It was a vote by an overwhelming majority.

What I love about this book is the author's insight into decoding prophetic messages in the Scriptures. The Bible has a number of hidden messages, which requires a scholarly and perspicacious approach to reveal the actual meaning for practical application. In this book, one cannot help but feel the genuine motivation and commitment of the author to get at the meaning and practical use of the end time prophecy or the eschatological understanding of God's intention for human existence. The author certainly has an appetite, a spiritual calling, and an inward yearning of the soul for such an undertaking.

As one reads this great work, you can expect to have many of your questions answered as it relate to an understanding of the end time prophecy. The reader will learn how the teaching of the end times relates personally to his/her life in the here and now. In addition, you can expect this book to prepare you to live out your life as a Christian for our soon coming King, who is Jesus Christ.

John W.S. Howard, Ph.D., Psy.D

President and Professor of the Hebrew Language

at Guilford School of Theology

Forward by Robert Graham

My name is Robert Graham; I am a senior manager publishing in a multinational publishing company with the privilege of working with over 700+ authors in my career. Dr. Rodney is an intellectual individual with a strong sense of morality, ethics and care for other humans. It is an honor to give me a forward insight into the book "Prophecy Decoded: A Systematic Approach to End Time Theology".

Dr. Rodney E. Harrigan's "Prophecy Decoded: A Systematic Approach to End Time Theology" is quite an impressive read. The way he dives into the complexities of eschatology is really something. He breaks down different theological methods—exegesis, biblical history, systematic theology—so thoroughly that it gives you a complete understanding of end-time prophecy.

This book presents a comprehensive exploration of eschatology from a Christian perspective, aiming to clarify misconceptions about end-time prophecy through systematic theological methods. Dr. Harrigan leverages his extensive background in theology and counseling psychology to offer readers a deeply researched and well-structured analysis of biblical prophecy.

The book is notable for its exhaustive coverage of eschatological topics, spanning from definitions and historical context to detailed theological arguments. The meticulous categorization of terms and events aids in the reader's understanding of complex eschatological concepts.

Dr. Harrigan employs a systematic theological methodology, incorporating exegesis, biblical history, and practical theology. This structured approach ensures that readers are guided logically through the intricacies of eschatology.

The integration of biblical scripture with historical context enriches the narrative, providing a well-rounded understanding of eschatological events. The book's emphasis on Hebrew hermeneutics highlights the importance of original scriptural languages in interpreting prophecy.

The inclusion of personal reflections and autobiographical elements adds a unique and relatable dimension to the text. These sections serve to humanize the academic content, making it more accessible and engaging for readers.

The extensive use of charts and visual aids helps to summarize and clarify complex information. This is particularly useful for visual learners and those new to the study of eschatology.

The book includes a robust bibliography, providing readers with numerous sources for further study. This reflects the author's thorough research and dedication to the subject matter

Robert Graham

Forward

At the time of this publication, I hold doctoral degrees in theology and counseling psychology. I am putting the final changes on a second book to be published in a few months. My goal in authoring this book is to clarify the misconceptions about end-time prophecy, to leave a legacy of the importance of education, and to document snips of my life at the request of my children, and for generations to know how God took care of me, in spite of me.

I experienced growing up in the ghetto of Harlem in New York City in the 1950s and 60s in a loving family of father, mother, sister, and brother. Despite living in an apartment building infested with mice and roaches in an environment of gangs, numbers, prostitution, and teenage pregnancy, unaware of what God was doing in my life, I was born into a God-fearing, loving family. Although we did not attend Church regularly or talk a lot about God, we acknowledged God and tried to live morally.

Fortunately, I survived the ghetto when friends in my neighborhood dropped out before attending high school, and some did not live beyond their twenties. Yet I experienced "success" in Corporate America, academia, religious institutions, and even music. To God be the glory for the things He has done in the lives of my family and me.

I began to document some of my life's experiences by writing excerpts at the end of each chapter. However, with the final edit, I combined them into one section of this book, which can be found in the appendix.

Preface

My theological method, argument for the existence of God, and the relationship of doctrine and theology are the cornerstones of my eschatological study. Theological Method: I utilize the methods of theology: exegesis, biblical, historical, systematic, and practical. However, my primary method is systematic theology.

Theological Argument: My argument for the existence of God is ontological, that which no greater can be conceived, although I touch on the two other arguments: teleological, beginning with the sensation of nature, there must be a design, and cosmological, first-cause argument and the argument from contingency.

Doctrine & Theology: I see the relationship between doctrine and theology as theology starts with doctrine. The doctrine states the scripture. Theology explores ways in which the doctrine is understood, what should be taught, and how. John 10:30 says that Jesus is one with the Father; that's doctrine. Theology explores subjects like, in what way is Jesus one with the Father? What are the implications of that oneness?

Christian eschatology is the specific area I focus on because discussion, preaching, teaching, and study of end time are often avoided in the pulpit and Bible study. Eschatology is the study of death, judgment, and the final destiny of the soul. It answers the fundamental questions of systematic theology. In Anthropology, the question is how sin is completely overcome. In Christology how the work of Christ is crowned in perfect victory. In Soteriology, how the work of the Holy Spirit is manifested in the redemption and glorification of God's people. In Ecclesiology, the final pinnacle of the Church (Charles River Editors, 2020).

There are several reasons for studying eschatology. First, researching and reporting God's Word brings us closer to Him. Eschatology offers a deeper understanding of the Scriptures.

Second, examining eschatology brings a more in-depth understanding of end-time prophecy. This book incorporates a primer for a general study of Bible history, culture, and language. Understanding eschatology is more than just looking at the work of the Apostle John,

Daniel, and a few other prophets. Eschatology is the fiber that weaves throughout the entire Bible. This theology of end-time prophecy proclaims God's Plan of Redemption.

Third, it clarifies the confusion about the different views of eschatology, showing that there is only one correct view of end-time prophecies.

Fourth, this position may stimulate dialog among eschatological theologians to flush out the confusion. While it is instructional to study eschatological views and arguments throughout the ages, God is not the author of confusion, so there cannot be several ways the eschaton will happen.

Finally, because of a desire and commitment to family to write about my legacy, which I did in terms of my reflection on family, friends, and life. These reflections are identified in the appendix titled "**Becoming Me.**"

The chronology of eschatological events has continued to be a debate among theologians, philosophers, deists, and atheists throughout history. The book explains why the pretribulation-premillennium (PTPM) eschatological chronology is the only correct interpretation of end-time prophecy. The proof is in the Scripture as it is illuminated in the Old Testament prophets, the Jewish marriage process, God's covenant, the Passover, and the Feasts. It is also illuminated in the New Testament by the early Church fathers, writers of the gospels, and the epistle of the New Testament writers, and even parallels the birth of a child.

The key to understanding the correct interpretation of end-time prophecy is to trace God's Plan of Redemption articulated throughout the Bible and to investigate the writings of Old and New Testament prophets, early church fathers, and Greek scholars.

This book contains fourteen chapters divided into five sections. Section One articulates vital definitions of terms critical for understanding eschatology. Additional terms defined throughout this book provide a valuable primer for eschatological study and a general understanding of the Scriptures. Ideology and Hebrew biblical history, culture, and language discussion are essential elements for interpreting God's Word.

Section Two details evidence for PTPM based on God's Plan of Redemption as revealed in The Marriage Covenant, the Seven Annual Covenants, the Passover Haggadah, the Seven Annual Feasts, and Bar and Bat Mitzvah ceremonies.

Section Three highlights the evidence and thoughts of Early Church Fathers, Greek Scholars, Early Church Leaders, and other thinkers.

Section Four addresses the motivations and fallacies of other eschatological views and the problems with the historical criticism methodology for interpreting Scripture.

Finally, Section Five culminates with interpreting the book of Revelation from the Hebrew perspective. The diagram below is the systematic structure of this book in the flow of five sections containing 14 chapters.

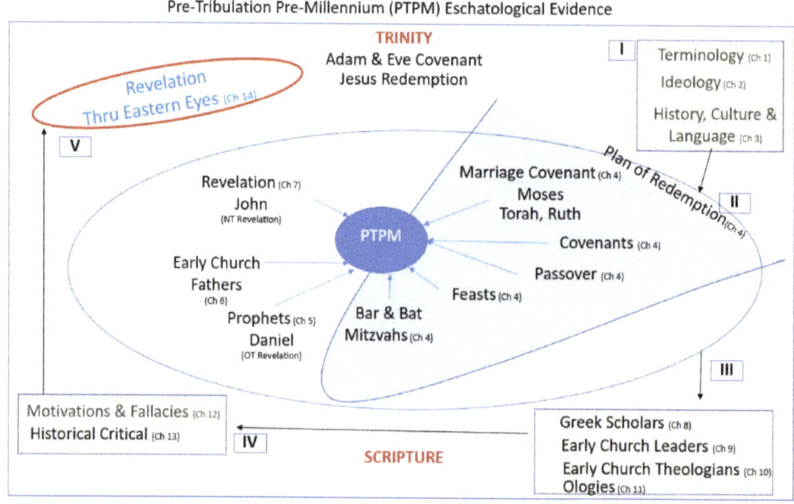

Four elements of my personal writing style for this paper are extensive use of charts, Scripture in red, definitions of basic biblical terms, and chapter headings stated in English and Hebrew. Extensive use of charts summarize content and is an index for quick access to information. All charts anchor on four chronological ages of history: the ancient age, the medieval age, the modern age, and the contemporary age. All dates are for approximate guideposts, not exact times.

"Scriptures in red" highlight that Scriptures are the definitive Word of truth. Scripture references emphasize the importance of the Word of God as the only source of truth and proof when interpreted correctly.

The use of chapter names in English and Hebrew with Hebrew pronunciations are a reminder that the original Scriptures are written in Hebrew and are the best source for understanding God's communications. Biblical figures of speech, particularly idioms and metaphors, are defined in terms of Hebrew culture and language.

Scripture translated into Greek or English can be misleading when translating Hebrew into the Greek or English languages. A related cause of misunderstanding is using terms interchangeably when each has separate meanings. The "time of the Gentiles," "the time of Jacob's Trouble," and "the day of the Lord" are examples of terms used interchangeably. However, "the day of the Lord' refers to the time of God's final judgment. The "time of Jacob's Trouble" refers to the time that God judges the Jews for refusing to acknowledge that Jesus is the Messiah—that time specifically refers to the second half of the Tribulation period. The time of the Gentiles refers to the time that the Gentiles rule on earth and the Jews did not. These times are not simultaneous. The "time of the Gentiles" is this present age. It ends when a certain number of Gentiles turn to the Lord. Only God knows that number. When that time ends, God will judge the Jews. The "day of the Lord" refers to the time of the Second Coming of Christ. He rules during the Millennium and throughout eternity.

Chapter titles in Hebrew are reminders that the trustworthy source of Scripture is written in Hebrew, not Greek, Aramaic, English, or any other translation. Often, translations use the context of the target language's historical perspective and culture, leading to errors in interpretation. Often, the errors occur in substituting target language expressions that do not properly interpret the meaning of Scripture in Hebrew.

SECTION I: Background

Section I contains the background of definitions of key terms used in this document (Chapter 1), a personal theological ideology that guides perspective (Chapter 2) , and an explanation of the influence of history, culture, language, and Bible translations which shape the interpretations of Scripture (Chapter 3).

Chapter 1: Terminology מינוח (minuakh)
{ בראשית }

The terms used throughout this document are defined in four groups. Group one defines the terms used in the thesis statement of the Th.D. dissertation upon which this book was written. Group two defines the events in the pretribulation-premillennial (PTPM) view. Group three defines the major eschatological views that will be analyzed. Group four describes the types of calendars, dates, and times used in Christian history.

Group One: Meaning of thesis statement: Eschatological Hermeneutical Apologetic: Defending the Faith by correctly interpreting end-time prophecy.

Reading left to right, as in English, eschatology is the study of end times. The word "eschatology" is derived from the Ancient Greek term ἔσχατος (eschaton), meaning "last," and ology meaning the study of. It was first used around 1844 CE. Hermeneutics interprets the meaning of Scripture. While hermeneutics seeks to understand Scripture, exegete interprets, and homiletics is the art of delivering the message of Scripture. Apologetic is reasoned arguments in justifying the Faith. It is defending the Faith. Therefore "eschatological hermeneutical apologetics" means the end times (eschatology) study of the meaning of Scripture (hermeneutics) to defend the Faith (apologetics).

The second line of the thesis is the translation of the first, read right to left as in Hebrew. The statement is "defending the Faith (apologetics) by interpreting (hermeneutics) end time (eschatology) prophecy." Thus, the thesis is defending the Faith by correctly interpreting end-time prophecy. The word 'correctly' is used to convey that only one interpretation is right.

Hebrew Hermeneutics.

Hebrew hermeneutics is a comprehensive approach to biblical exegesis. Hebrew hermeneutics interprets Scripture using a system of logic that has been used for thousands of years. Scripture is interpreted on four levels simultaneously: *p'shat, remez, darash,* and *sod.* Each level is more intense than the previous (Klein & Spears, 2016, p. 16).

P'shat understands scripture using the meanings of the words in the passage. It is a literal interpretation. *Remez* means hint. *Remez* interprets Scripture as hinting at a deeper truth. *Darash* – interprets Scripture as allegorical, typological, or homiletical. *Sod* means hidden. At the *Sod* level of interpretation, a hidden, secret, or mystic or wisdom meaning is realized. (Klein & Spears, 2016, p. 128). An example of a *Sod* interpretation is Revelation 13:18 (Wansbrough, 2019), where the identity of the Beast is expressed by the number six-sixty-six (Klein & Spears, 2009, p. 16).

Applying this layered method of interpreting Scripture to the seven Churches of Asia Minor, existing in the book of Revelation, the literal interpretation is that seven actual churches existed when John authored the book, *p'shat.* The Scripture hints that the seven churches are the seven ages of the church, *remez.* A typological interpretation is that there are seven churches in the last days, *drash.* Lastly, the passage can be interpreted as seven types of people during the last days, *sod* (Klein & Spears, 2016, p. 16).

This cyclical approach to interpreting Scripture can explain why the Preterists do not believe that there will be a literal one-thousand-year reign of Christ, even when the Book of Revelation states it clearly. Preterists are interpreting Revelation allegorically, *darash.*

Hebrew Hermeneutics is a distinctly different approach to interpreting Scriptures from the Greek Hermeneutics method.

Greek Hermeneutics

Greek hermeneutics interprets the writing translated by the Hebrew text on two levels, either literal or allegorical, but not at the same time. Sometimes, the interpretation is referred to as spiritual or literal. The Greek interpreters developed their interpretations by working with mythological text, and they assumed that the truth of the Scripture was seventy-five percent imagination and twenty-five percent truth. (Klein & Spears, 2016, p. 15). Hence, when referring to the Septuagint translation of the Torah, it limits the interpretation to one of the four Hebrew interpretations.

Group Two: Theology and Doctrine

Theology is the study of doctrine. Doctrine is a statement of fundamental beliefs about God, His creatures, and their relationship to Him. Theology is the study of God through systematic analysis and Coherent statements of Christian doctrine. It is biblical and studied in the context of human culture (Erickson, 2015, p. 19).

There are several ways to approach theology, Natural Theology, Tradition, Scriptures, and Experience. Natural Theology studies truths about God and human nature. Tradition inquiries about what has been held and taught by Christian individuals and organizations. The Scriptures are held to be the confirmation of truth. Experience as an approach relies on Christian experience as authority (Ibid., pp.23-24).

The methodology of theology requires collecting biblical materials, organizing them in a meaningful way, and examining history and language. It is also important to consult other cultural perspectives and sources beyond the Bible. This process culminates in determining the essence of the doctrine, inquiring what questions are being asked by the contemporary age to develop a central interpretive idea or theme (Ibid., pp. 25-34).

ESM focuses on the Scripture from an ancient and contemporary interpretation of Scripture, reinforced by considering the perspectives of various disciplines outside religion that are labeled "ologies."

Group Three: Events in God's Plan of Redemption

The events illustrating God's redemptive work to restore the broken relationship between humanity and Himself that culminate in eternal life for believers provide a path to end time events. **Creation**: God created the world and humanity, intending a perfect relationship with His creation. **The Fall**: Humanity's disobedience in the Garden of Eden, which introduced sin and separation from God. **Covenant with Abraham**: God's promise to Abraham to make his descendants a great nation through which all nations would be blessed. **The Exodus**: The deliverance of the Israelites from slavery in Egypt, symbolizing God's power to save and His commitment to His people. **The Law Given to Moses**: The giving of the Ten Commandments and the Law at Mount Sinai provides a moral and spiritual framework for the Israelites. **The Prophets**: Prophets like Isaiah, Jeremiah, and others foretold the coming of a Messiah and called for repentance and faithfulness to God. **The Incarnation**: The birth of Jesus Christ, God becoming human, to live among humanity. **The Ministry of Jesus**: Jesus' life, teachings, miracles, and demonstration of the Kingdom of God. **The Crucifixion**: Jesus' sacrificial death on the cross to atone for humanity's sins. **The Resurrection**: Jesus rising from the dead, defeating sin and death, and proving His divinity.

The Ascension: Jesus' return to heaven, promising to send the Holy Spirit to guide and empower His followers. **Pentecost**: The coming of the Holy Spirit upon the early believers, empowering them for mission and spreading the gospel. **The Church Age**: The period in which the Church conducts the mission of spreading the gospel and living out God's kingdom on earth. **The Second Coming**: The anticipated return of Jesus Christ to fully establish God's kingdom, judge the living and the dead, and bring about the new heaven and new earth.

Group Four: Eschatological Events: Rapture, Tribulation, Second Coming of Christ (Parousia), Marriage in Heaven, Armageddon, the Millennium Kingdom, the Great White Throne Judgement, and the New Heaven and New Earth (Eternity).

The Rapture: Jesus Christ will return to gather His believers, both the living and the dead, taking them up to heaven (1 Thessalonians 4:16-17), 1 Corinthians 15:51-52).

Tribulation: Jesus Christ will return to gather His believers, both the living and the dead, taking them up to heaven (Matthew 24:21-22, Revelation 6:-18).

The 2nd Coming (Parousia) The visible return of Jesus Christ to Earth at the end of the Tribulation. Christ will come in glory to defeat the forces of evil and establish His kingdom (Matthew 24:30, Revelation 19:11-16).

Marriage in Heaven: The union of Christ (the bridegroom) with His Church (the bride) in a heavenly celebration (Revelation 19:7-9). This event symbolizes the intimate and eternal relationship between Jesus and His followers.

Armageddon: The visible return of Jesus Christ to Earth at the end of the Tribulation. Christ will come in glory to defeat the forces of evil and establish His kingdom (Revelation 16:16; 19:19-21).

Millennium: A thousand-year reign of Christ on Earth, characterized by peace, righteousness, and the binding of Satan. During this time, Christ will rule with His saints (Revelation 20:1-6).

Great White Throne Judgment: The final judgment of all people, where the dead are resurrected and judged according to their deeds. Those not found in the Book of Life are cast into the lake of fire (Revelation 20:11-15).

New Heaven and New Earth: The creation of a new, perfect state of existence where God dwells with His people forever. The old heaven and earth pass away, and God makes everything new (Revelation 21:1-4, Isaiah 65:17).

Proper interpretation of end-time prophecy begins with the fundamental belief that the Bible is literal, not allegorical. Dissimilarities center around the timing and the timing of when end times will come and the sequence of the two events, the rapture and the 2nd Coming of Christ. The Rapture is the return of Christ in the clouds (1 Thessalonians 4:13-16). It may occur before or after the Tribulation or not at all. Tribulation is the end-time event of judgment from God lasting seven years. It will affect the entire world with unprecedented affliction, culminating with the return of Jesus Christ. At this Second Coming, Christ returns to earth to rule His earthy kingdom and judge the world. (Luke 4:21, Isaiah 61:2).

Group Five: Eschatological Views: Covenantism, Preterism, Amillennium, Post-millennium, Dispensationalism, Pretribulation, Midtribulation, and Posttribulation.

Awareness of the meaning of eschatology and how eschatology was perceived in the Old Testament provides insight into the development of eschatological views in the New Testament. Eschatology comes from the Greek words eschaton (last things) and logos (word or doctrine) meaning the word concerning last things. Eschatology is the study of the end of things: the end of conflict, end of individual life, end of the age, end of the world, end of the cosmos, end of time, and most importantly, the end of evil. It is also the beginning of unhindered love, peace, joy, gentleness, goodness, and a new heaven and new earth to last for eternity.

While the term "eschatology" did not exist until the New Testament period, the thoughts of Old Testament writers expressed their theologies of last things. Old Testament writers expressed eschatology in terms of distinctive elements and focused on the destination of Israel, not on all mankind. In fact, the focus of Old Testament eschatology was how to live right, not how to go to heaven.

Old Testament Eschatology

Old Testament eschatology is primarily about the destiny of Israel and the world. Secondarily, it is about the future of the individual. It refers to the imminent restoration of Israel from exile and the establishment of the perfect kingdom. It was aimed at stopping the present crisis of captivity and enslavement.

Israel expected the messiah to come to judge their enemies and end exile (Isaiah 11). Divine judgment was on the wicked nations and Israel (Zechariah 14). Belief in resurrection developed in the second century BCE (Daniel 12:2). Before that, the belief was that the dead led to a shadowy existence in the underworld (*Sheol*) (Isaiah 14). The belief changed when individual retribution after death developed in Judaism. It changed to the wicked being tormented in *Sheol,* but the good would have joy in paradise.

Eschatological thoughts gave rise to the doctrine of the Theology of Hope, a phrase devised by Moltmann. Moltmann defines hope as the affirmation that there will be a New Heaven and New Earth through the redeeming work of Jesus Christ. (Moltmann, 1993). Hope is one of the three theological virtues, the others being faith and charity (love). Love is distinct from the latter two because it is directed exclusively toward the future, as confident expectation. When hope has attained its objective, it ceases to be hope and becomes a possession (Encyclopedia, 2022).

Metaphysically, the essence of eschatology is understood by looking at the essence of the subjects of eschatology: life, death, and resurrection of things.

The Essence of Eschatology (Metaphysics) הברית הישנה (esshatology haberitt hayeshenah)

The essence of eschatology is the metaphysics of death, judgment, and the final destiny of the soul and the cosmos.

A personal view of the metaphysics of eschatology is that it is the eschaton of God's redemptive process that culminates in the Lordship of Jesus Christ. Although the book is often titled The Revelation of John, the true nature of eschatology is how God redeemed His people through Jesus Christ. That is why the Revelation was given to Jesus, and Jesus revealed it to John to share it with the seven churches and all humankind. Also, that essence is consistent with the understanding that every book in the Bible is about Jesus. New Testament eschatology incorporated much of the Old Testament eschatology in the context of the revealed Christ, the Messiah.

Covenant Theology

Covenant theology (also known as Covenantalism, Federal theology, or Federalism) is a conceptual overview and interpretive framework for understanding the overall structure of the Bible. It uses the theological concept of a covenant as an organizing principle for Christian theology. Covenant Theology teaches the understanding of God's ontological participation through the covenants He established. In harmony with Historical Premillennialism, it teaches that God uses His covenants to communicate with His people. It differed from Dispensationalism, which was established much later in the ninth century by John Nelson Darby (Ashley, 2023). In Covenant Theology, Israel and the Church are one people of God. The Church is grafted into the Israel people. Covenant Theology existed during the early church period and continues to be a topic of theology today. Although Covenant Theology is not an eschatological view, it has implications for eschatology.

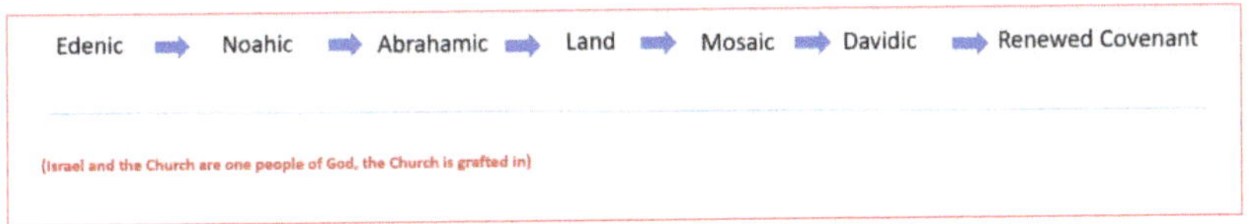

Figure 1: Covenant Theology

Covenant Theology History

During the medieval church period (c. 500-1500 CE), Covenant Theology was distinct but harmonious with the early church fathers. Because of criticism that Christianity caused immorality, the early church spoke about redemption as a story of two laws: the old law of Moses and the new law of Christ. Grace had the power to keep the law to be justified. It was widely held that covenant theology was created in the middle of the 17th Century; however, it existed in the early church period. The elements of Covenant Theology are the covenant of redemption, the covenant of works, and the covenant of grace. The renewed covenant is often called the New Covenant. It is both new and separate. At the same time, it is a renewal of the Abrahamic and Mosaic covenants (Ashley, 2023). Figure 1 summarizes the seven covenants in the order God made them with the Israelites and Christians.

Covenant Theology and God's Plan of Redemption

God's covenants attest to His order of redemption. Covenant Theology sees the Bible as one continuous story, contrasted with dispensational theology, which sees the Bible story as periods in history. God's Plan of Redemption unfolds in His covenants in various forms throughout time. The covenants establish the framework and backbone for the entire Bible storyline (Gentry & Wellum, 2018). An analysis of the covenants reveals that there is order and sequence to God's plan of redemption.

New Testament Eschatology

Figure 2 depicts the eight major eschatological interpretations, which span from literal to allegorical interpretations that arose through the history of Christianity. The key differences in interpretations are based on two events: whether the millennium will occur before or after the Second Coming of Christ and whether the Rapture will happen before, in the middle, or after the Tribulation. The" Historic-Premillennial-Pretribulation" interpretation is highlighted to identify it as the only view that existed for the first two hundred years of Christianity (Larkin, 1920). The eight eschatological views emerged over the two thousand years of Christianity.

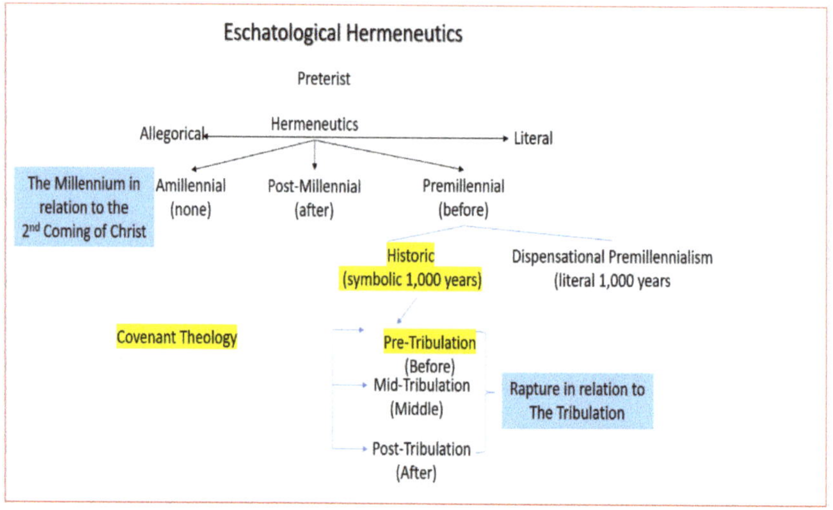

Figure 2: Exchatological Hermeneutics

Preterist View

There are two views on preterism: partial and full preterism. Partial preterism contends that only part but not all of Bible prophecy, including prophecy in Matthew 24, Daniel 9, and Revelation 19-20, has already been fulfilled when Jerusalem fell. It conforms to the early Christian creeds that believe in a future physical Second Coming of Christ, the resurrection of the dead, and the last judgment.

Full preterism declares that 70 CE fulfilled all biblical prophecy. It does not hold to a future judgment, return of Christ, or resurrection of the dead. It is sometimes considered "radical" and usually described as "unorthodox" because it goes against the ecumenical creeds of early Christianity.

The Full Preterists believe the eschatological events in the Olivet discourse (Matthew 24:1-25; Mark 13:1-37; Luke 21:5-36) already happened during the first century of the early Church. This view asserts that the resurrection of believers has passed, and believers are in the new heaven and new earth are here right now. God's people have already been spiritually resurrected. At death, the believer will live eternally with spiritual bodies (Ice & Gentry, 2009).

Ice and Gentry describe three forms of preterism: mild, moderate, and extreme. Mild preterism states that the Tribulation was fulfilled when God judged the Jews in 70 CE, and He judged the world when Rome collapsed in 313 AD. However, they still look for the future coming of Christ. (Toussaint, 2004, pp.469-490). Moderate preterism sees prophecy fulfilled, but they hold to the future Second Coming, physical resurrection of the dead, an end to temporal history, and establishment of the new heaven and new earth. Extreme preterists see prophecy as fulfilled, and believers are now in the new heaven and new earth (Ice & Gentry, 2009).

In 1614 CE, at the time of the Counter-Reformation, the Spanish Jesuit Alcazar first published his thesis on preterism. He advocated that the preterist period began with the life of John and extended to the destruction of Jerusalem by Titus in 70 CE. The Preterist view provided a Catholic defense against the Protestant historicists who associated symbols of biblical prophecies with historical people, nations, or events. The historicists associated the Harlot in Revelation 17 with the Roman Catholic Church, identifying the Church as a persecuting apostasy. Shifting the identification of the Antichrist to a previous Roman emperor, Nero conveniently cleared the Catholic Church and the current Roman emperor. This view appears to be politically and arbitrarily motivated, not spiritually inspired.

In support of their view, Preterists argued that Nero was the beast in Revelation 13, and therefore, there was no future fulfillment of the time prophecy; the prophecy was already fulfilled. There were four elements to the argument. First, the number of the beast is six-hundred-sixty-six, and Nero's name involves a form of gematria (a calculator for finding the value of a word or phrase). Second, Nero's number is also the variant number of six-hundred-sixty six that appears in ancient manuscripts. Third, all who dwelt on the earth worshiped the beast, and all the earth worshiped Nero. Finally, the beast's head received a mortal blow from the sword, and so did Nero. Hitchcock rejected this argument (Hitchcock, 2007). The Preterist view is contrary to the commonly held understanding in Revelation. The Preterist view continues to be promoted. Figure 3 is a diagram of the Preterist Chronology events that already occurred in the first century.

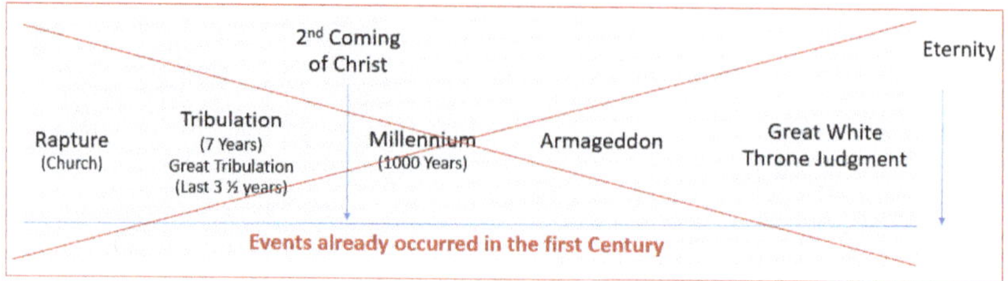

Figure 3: Preterist Chronology

Preterist Historical Perspective

The Preterist view was slow in gaining acceptance outside the Roman Catholic Church. Russell, a nineteenth-century author, declared that the events of the Book of Revelation were only of interest to the first-century audience. The apocalypse was a transfigured form of the prophecy on the Mount of Olives that allegorized and dramatized the Parousia. A Dutch Protestant, Hugo Grotius (1583-1645), wrote his "Commentary on certain Texts Which Deal with Antichrist" in 1640 (Newport, 2000). Noe attempted to find common ground between Protestants and the Roman Catholic Church (Noe, 2006). However, acceptance of the Preterist view continued to struggle (Russell, 1878).

Amillennialists View

Hoeksema says the amillennialists interpret Revelation 20:4-6 (Wansbrough, 2019) as describing the present reign of the deceased believers in heaven ruled by the victorious Christ. Amillennialists do not believe that Christ will rule on earth for a thousand years. The kingdom of evil will continue to exist alongside the kingdom of God until the end of the world. This condition is called "inaugurated eschatology." They are looking forward to the Second Coming of Christ and a future, glorious, perfect kingdom eschatology." (Hoekema, 1979, p. 261). Since there is no earthly millennium, a millennium is often described incorrectly as no millennium period (Hoeksema, 1951). Although Hoeksema agrees with the amillennialists' view, Missler finds problems with this view.

He argues that Israel has a prophetic destiny. That destiny is in God's Covenant, specifically in the Davidic covenant, confirming that Christ will rule on earth during the Millennium period. These messianic promises are found throughout the Bible. For example, the angel Gabriel promised Mary that Jesus would sit on the throne of David. The throne of David did not exist at that time; therefore, the Millennium could not have already taken place. Additionally, there are confirmations of Christ's reign in the New Testament (Missler & Missler, 2009). The Amillennium chronology is pictured in Figure 4.

Amillennialism Chronology

2nd Coming of Christ

Eternity

Rapture (Church)

Tribulation (7 Years)

Great Tribulation (Last 3 ½ years)

Millennium (1000 Years)

Armageddon

Great White Throne Judgment

Deceased believers are ruling with Christ in Heaven

Figure 4: Amillennialism Chronology

Premillennialism

Premillennialists believe that Christ will return before the Millennium, the one-thousand-year period of righteousness and peace. The Church was Premillennial for over two hundred years until the Church father Origen conceived the idea that Scripture was the "husk" of Biblical truth. The "kernel" of scriptural truth was the spiritual part of truth. His spiritual conception led him to allegorize the interpretation of Scripture. Allegorizing the scripture led the Church away from looking for the Lord to return to set up an earthly kingdom. (Daley, 1991, pp. 47-59)

Postmillennialists View

Postmillennialists agree with amillennialists in that there will be no millennium reign on earth but in heaven. The millennium is not exactly one thousand years, and Christ will return after the millennium (Hoekema, 1979, p. 262).

According to the postmillennialism, described by Boettner, a proponent of postmillennialism, there will be a prolonged period of righteousness as more people are converted to Christianity, peace will prevail and that is the millennium period. It will be a gradual merging into the millennial age (Hoekema, 1979). Figure 5 summarizes the Postmillennium chronology.

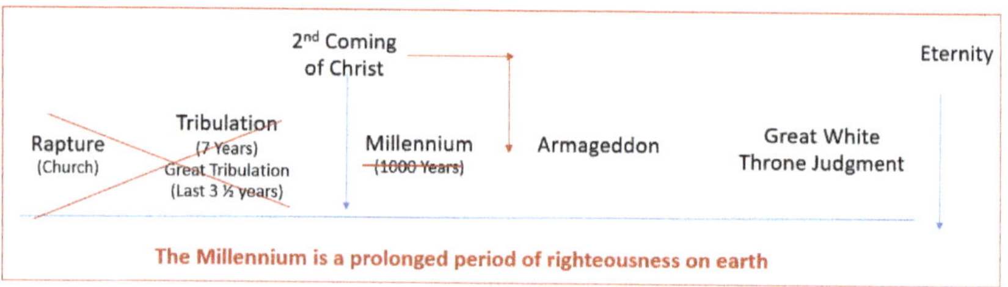

Figure 5: Post Millennium Chronology

Historical Premillennialism

Historical Premillennialism is a view that the Second coming of Christ will occur after the tribulation and before the thousand-year period of righteousness, the Millennium. The chronology of events is the Rapture, Tribulation, Second coming of Christ, Millennium, Armageddon, the Create White Throne Judgment, and the Eternal State. Figure 6 summarizes this view. Premillennialism was supported by the early church fathers, Papias, Irenaeus, Justin Martyr, Tertullian, and others (Daley, 1991).

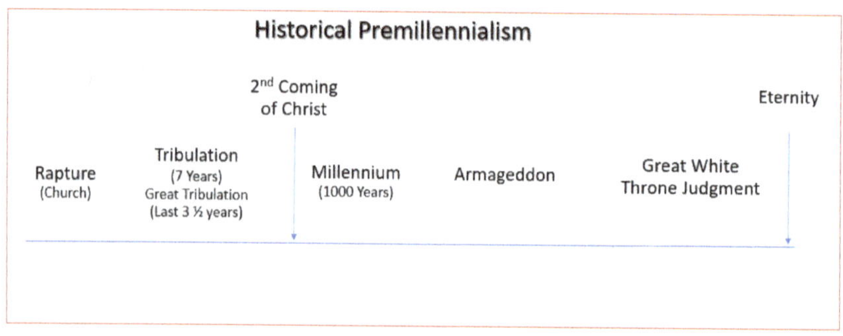

Figure 6: Historical Premillennialism

Covenant Theology supports this view and was prominent during the period of the early church.

Dispensational Premillennialism

The Dispensational view is antithetical to the Historical Premillennial view. Dispensational Premillennialists believe God deals with people differently at different dispensations (periods of history) until Christ returns. The key difference is that dispensationalists believe that Israel and the Church are separate people of God. Covenant Theology believes that Israel and the Church are one people of God. The Church is grafted in.

The Dispensational view was a Christian fundamentalist movement in American Protestantism in the late nineteenth century. Dwight L. Moody spearheaded it. It focused on core Christian beliefs that included historical accuracy and inerrancy of the Bible, the imminent and physical Second Coming of Jesus Christ, virgin birth, resurrection, and atonement.

The view was a reaction to the theological modernism that was attempting to revise traditional Christian beliefs. Theological modernism focused on incorporating new developments in the natural and social sciences, especially the theory of biological evolution. Figure 7 shows the historical periods of Dispensationalism.

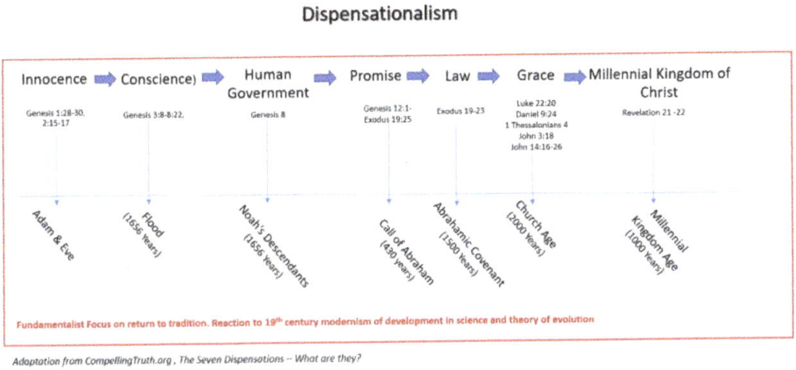

Adaptation from CompellingTruth.org , The Seven Dispensations – What are they?

Figure 7: Dispensationalism

Premillennial-Posttribulation View

Premillennial-Posttribulation believers think the rapture will occur after the great Tribulation before Christ returns to rule on the earth for a thousand years, the Millennium period, Figure 11. Midtribulation believers think that rapture will occur during the Tribulation, Figure 12, and Pretribulation believers think that rapture will occur before the Tribulation, Figure 13. The Tribulation period starts with the second abomination of desolation (Matthew 24:15) and ends at the Second Coming of Christ (Matthew 24:29). The first abomination of desolation occurred in the second century BCE when the Greek King

Antiochus IV Epiphanes replaced the alter on which offerings were made with a pagan god. (Daniel 9:27; 11:31). Jesus referred to the abomination of desolation as a future event that will occur when the Temple is rebuilt in Jerusalem during end times. Figure 8 shows the chronology of the events in the Premillennial-Posttribulation view.

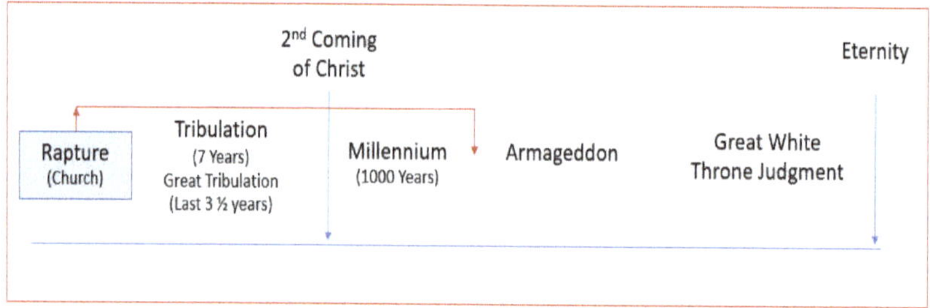

Figure 8: Premillennium Posttribulation Chronology

The eight eschatological hermeneutical views and the dates they were perceived are shown in Figure 2. While it could be argued that dates may or may not be exact, they still have an especially useful purpose. They show the relative distance between the time of development and the beginning of the early church. Notice that there was one view for more than two hundred years before other views arose. The significance of the gaps between views will be explored in Chapter Eleven. Figure 9 shows the events of the development of eschatological views.

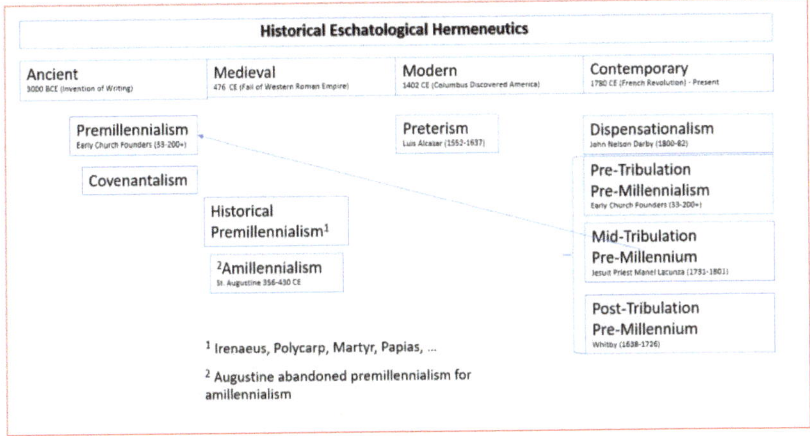

Figure 9: Timeline of Development of Eschatological Views

Premillennial-Midtribulation View

Premillennial-Midtribulation believes the Rapture will occur in the middle of the tribulation when Christ has returned and is ruling on the earth for a thousand years. Figure 7 shows the Premillennium-Midtribulation chronology.

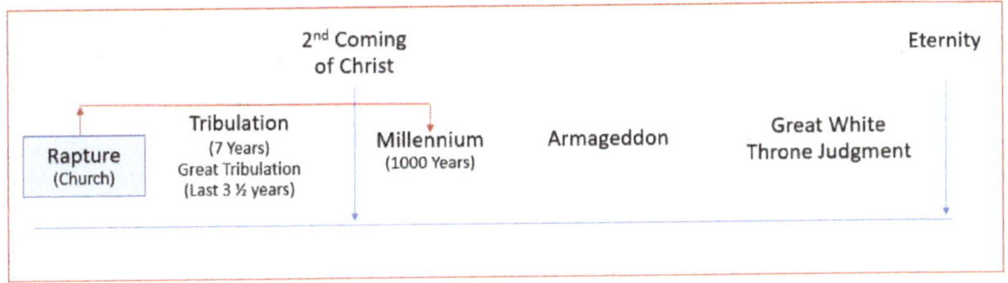

Figure 10: Premillennium Midtribulation Chronology

The Premillennial-Pretribulation View (PTPM)

Premillennialists believe that Christ will come after the world decays to a state of crisis, which is the end of the Tribulation (Wilcox, 1991). The sequence of the events will be the Rapture, Tribulation, Return of Christ, the Millennium Rule, Armageddon, the Great White Throne Judgement, and the New Heaven and New Earth (Schwertley, 1999).

The events of the Pretribulation-Premillennium (PTPM) view are summarized in Figure 8

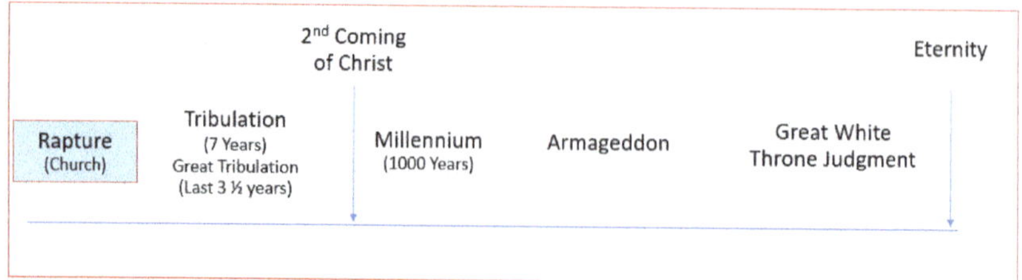

Figure 11: PTPM Chronology

The eight views are summarized in Figures 9.

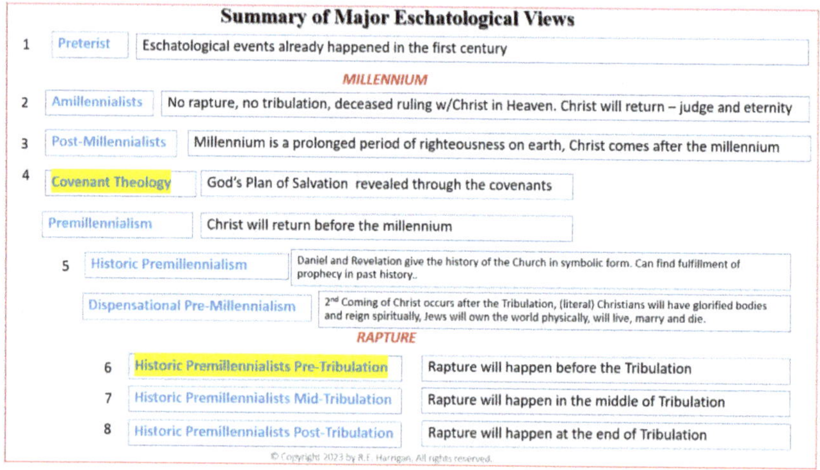

Figure 12: Summary of Major Eschatological Views

These are not the only views. There are views that are not included in mainstream discussions about eschatology. Heiser states that beliefs about end time prophecy lack certainty, particularly the nature of the kingdom of God, the unconditional promises of Abraham, and the rapture (Heiser, 2022). He says Paul viewed Christians as already in the kingdom (Colossians 1:13), the apostles linked the gospel with the kingdom of God (Acts 8:12; 28:30-31), and in Revelation, the kingdom is already present before the millennium (Revelation 20:1-6). Also, the unconditional promises of Abraham described to him (Genesis 15:18-19; Exodus 23:31) are very closely aligned with the land brought under the domination of Israel during the reign of King Saul. This implies that the land promised to Abraham was already fulfilled. However, there are different boundary descriptions of the land. Finally, he says references to rapture are not consistent. Jesus touches down on earth (Zechariah 14:4) and comes as a warrior (Revelation 19:11-16). In other references, Jesus comes in the air during the Rapture to take His Church home (1 Thessalonians 4:16-18), and He comes as a warrior in His second coming (Revelation 19:11-16). He says there is ambiguity about whether Jesus returns once or twice (Heiser, 2022).

Sometimes, views are characterized as idealism, futurism, and historicism.

Idealist, Futurism, and Historicism (Dimock, 2018)

Idealist sees no evidence of timing of prophetic events in the Bible. Thus, they conclude that their timing cannot be determined in advance. Idealists see prophetic passages as being of value in teaching truths about God to be applied to present life. Idealism is not a major factor in current evangelical Christian discussion about when prophecy will be fulfilled.

Futurism claims that ancient Rome fulfilled apocalypse prophecies. The rest is restricted to a literal Antichrist who will reign for three-and-a-half literal years. Futurism further claims that the Antichrist will be an individual and not a system.

Historicism considers that most prophecy has been or will be fulfilled during the present church age. It was the chief view of Protestants from the Reformation until the mid-nineteenth century. Historical Premillennialists find fulfillment of prophecy in the history of the past. Daniel and Revelation give the history of the Church in symbolic form. However, Adventist historicism is the belief that the primary purpose of the biblical books of Daniel and Revelation is to foretell selective notable events from their times until the second coming and beyond.

Departures and Commonalities

Disagreements in the eschatological views after the first two hundred years of the Church centered around five areas. First, the time of the end of the world ranged from immediate expectations of the Apostolic Fathers to the sixth-century commentators on John's Apocalypse (Daley, 1991, p. 221), Jesus said the end may come sooner, or it may come later (Matthew 25). Second, there were different views on the materiality and physical character of the resurrection. Origen expressed that the risen body would be spiritually different from the physical body. It was opposed by the Justinian's Councils of 543 and 553. Third, the extent of eschatological salvation varied significantly. Origen hoped for the salvation of all spiritual creatures. Augustine argued that at least all Christian believers will experience the final mercy of God (Daley, 1991, p. 222). Fourth, there were differences in the possibility of change and progress for those whose final destiny had been determined. Most ancient writers assumed that the end of life in the body was the end of human change. Origen suggested that souls, after death, continue to grow in knowledge and desire for God. Last, the views on the possibility of being purged from sin after death were different. In the pre-Christian experience, both Greeks and Jews considered suffering to be a way to wisdom and a personal means of sin. Origen saw human suffering as a medicinal process to restore all souls to their original union with God. Despite the differences, there were commonalities in the views (Daley, 1991, pp. 222-223).

Central to the views is the idea of a linear view of history, the conviction that history has a beginning and an ending, rooted in the plan of God. Equally central to Patristic eschatological thought is that the fulfillment of human history must include the resurrection of the body. Christian writers saw the need to have the promise of bodily resurrection. They also agreed on the ideas of God's universal judgment (Daley, 1991, p. 220).

From the end of the second century with Tertullian, Patristic writers began to suggest a judgment at the end of everyone's life. The idea began to germinate about what modern theology calls an "interim state" between death and resurrection. In this state, the dead will begin to experience the fate that will be theirs in fullness when history ends ((Daley, 1991, p. 200).

Early Christian writers universally assumed the final state of existence would be permanent, perfect happiness for the good and permanent misery for the wicked. Theologians also shared the general sense that the dead were still involved in the life of the Church. This is the concept of "communion of saints" (Daley, 1991, pp. 221-222).

Group Six: Calendars, Dates, and Time

When considering calendars, dates, and times there are three areas to be cognizant of. One area is the number of Jewish, Christian, and secular calendars used during the span of time covered in the Bible. The second area is the understanding of chronos and kairos time which separate Western from Eastern thought. Finally, there needs to be an understanding of what time really means.

Jewish and Christian Calendars & Dates

Calendars and clocks are used universally as tools for recording dates and times. While God's time is accurate, calendars and clocks are not. Dates and time were first determined by observing the sun and the moon. Eventually, they changed from observation to calculation. There were the ancient Jewish calendars and rabbinic calendars, solar calendars and lunar calendars, the Julian calendar, and the Gregorian calendar. Jewish communities in Palestine and the diaspora established their lunar calendar independently from one another and would often celebrate the same festivals at various times (Stern, 2001).

The Biblical Lunar Calendar used by ancient civilizations has twelve months of thirty days or three-hundred-sixty days a year. Official Jewish civilian calendars are based on lunar cycles of twenty-eight days. Months in the calendar were expressed as alternating days of twenty-nine days and thirty days, having twelve months per year. A thirteenth month was added seven times in each nineteen-year cycle called *Adar Beit*. It follows "*Adar*" and lasts twenty-nine days (Gill, 2019). Not all dates were known. On the other hand, the Jewish religious calendar is used to calculate the dates of the feasts and festivals. It is four days shorter than the civilian calendar.

Julian Calendar

The **Julian calendar** was also called the **Old Style calendar or the Ancient Calendar.** It was established in forty-six BCE by Julius Caesar as a reform of the calendar of the Roman Republic. It had three hundred sixty-five days in a year, with a day added every four years, the leap year. Caesar, advised by the Alexandrian astronomer Sosigenes, introduced the Egyptian solar calendar, taking the length of the solar year as three-hundred-sixty-five and one-fourth days. The year was divided into twelve months, all of which had either thirty or thirty-one days except February, which contained twenty-eight days in common years and twenty-nine in every fourth year (a leap year). The Julian calendar was gradually abandoned in favor of the Gregorian calendar in one thousand five hundred and eighty-two CE.

Gregorian Calendar

The Gregorian calendar is the calendar used in most parts of the world. It went into effect in one thousand five hundred and eight-two CE when Pope Gregory the Thirteenth replaced the Julian calendar. The main change was to space leap years differently to make the average calendar year a different length that more closely approximated the solar year that is determined by the Earth's revolution around the Sun.

Weeks

Weeks in the Bible are used as figures of speech. The Sabbath on the seventh day is also called a week of days (Genesis 2:2; Exodus 20:11) (Wansbrough, 2019). Feast of weeks are called weeks of weeks (Leviticus 23:15-16) (Wansbrough, 2019). The period of the months of Nisan to Tishri is called the weeks of months (Exodus 12:2; Leviticus 23:24) (Wansbrough, 2019). Sabbatical Years for the Land are also called weeks of years. Daniel's seventieth week is forty-nine years.

In summary of this discussion on calendars, the time and periods in the Bible may vary depending on which calendar is used and when. They are not included in debate; rather, they provide a reasonable approximation of the relationships between events and people. Figure 13 summarizes the calendars used throughout Christian history.

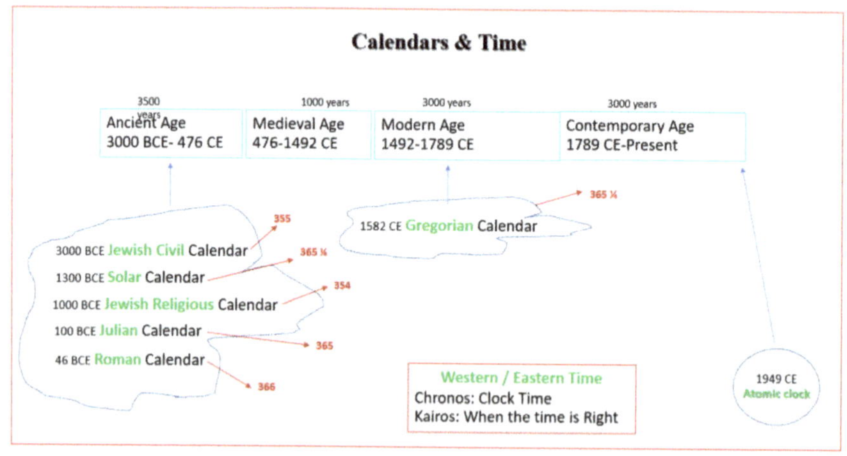

Figure 13: Calendars & Time

Chronos and Kairos Time

Chronos time and *Kairos* time used by Greek writers were, typically translated to the English single word "time," with no distinction between Chronos and Kairos time. Chronos described quantitative time such as a chronology or a sequence measured by clocks and calendars. *Kairos* was used qualitatively to mean just the right time, as in the fullness of time, God sent His Son, Jesus. It was not a precise date on the calendar or time on the clock. In reading Scripture, it is important to know what kind of time is being discussed (Richards & O'Brien, 2012)

Biblical authors were more concerned with kairos time, the appropriateness and fitting of events. They were more concerned with timing (kairos) and as much with time (chronos). The 'day of the Lord' is kairos time. Westerners are oriented and make sense of circumstances and plans for the future by *Chronos time*. As they see it, there is no meaning without sequence. This paper relies on chronos time because order and sequence are important for organizing the ways people, places, and things related to one another. However, when interpreting Scripture, awareness of which kind of time is being discussed and which unit of measurement is utilized will clarify the meaning of the passage. Then again, events in the Bible are not always presented historically or chronologically. Sometimes, they appear to be arbitrary and even contradictory when, in fact, they are emphasizing different things. Consider the story of the temptations of Christ.

In Matthew, the order of temptations was stone to bread, jumping off the pinnacle of the temple and worshiping Satan (Matthew 4:1-11) (Wansbrough, 2019). In Luke, the order was stone to bread, worship Satan, and jump off the mountain (Luke 4:1-1) (Wansbrough, 2019). Interpreting these stories as one is right and the other is wrong is misunderstanding the passages. The chronological sequence is unimportant. Luke used the temple as a theme in organizing his Gospel, so he ended up jumping off a mountain. Matthew had every major event in the life of Jesus occur on a mountain, so his sequence ended with being taken to a high mountain and tempted to worship Satan. Both accounts are correct, although the sequences are different. Another consideration is the essence or metaphysics of time.

Metaphysics of Time

Metaphysics is a branch of philosophy that attempts to explain the reality of all things. Metaphysics inquiry goes beyond physical and human science. The metaphysics of time is the explanation of the nature of temporal reality. There are two prevailing theories about the essence of time: whether time passes or flows or whether it has a dynamic aspect. The A-theorists surmise that the only time that exists is the present time (presentism), or the past and present exist (growing block), or as time passes, current times come into existence (spotlight). The B-theorists take all times to exist (externalism) (Natalij, n.d.).

Clearly, there is much to consider about time when studying Scripture, particularly what the Scripture says about time in the context of the verse. My metaphysical view of time is that time is a gift of God that allows humankind to "order our steps in thy Word" (Psalm 119:113). It exists to help humankind comprehend the path to eternity. In the eternal state, there is no time. Tom Bradford exegetes that eternity means timelessness because time is decay, and there is no decay in heaven. Eternity is not an expression of an endless period of time. It is an expression of a place, a kingdom in which time does not exist (Bradford & Korman, Accessed: 2023).

Group Seven: Theologies, Exegetes, and Homiletics

Theology is the professional study of the nature of God and religious beliefs. It is "faith, seeking understanding" (Wright IV & Martin, 2019). A theologian's purpose is to help the Church understand God in a deep and richer manner. Theology is vital to even the believer drinking milk. Without proper theology, believers can have a misunderstanding of salvation and their relationship to Christ. An example of misunderstanding is once saved, always saved. People believe that they can lose their salvation. Paul explains that this is not so (Ephesians 1:13) (Wansbrough, 2019). A theologian would use scriptures throughout the Bible to support the conclusion.

Exegete is the interpretation and exposition of the biblical text. Biblical exegesis is a careful, systematic study of scriptures to discover the original intended meaning of a passage in the Bible. Exegeting might involve studying theology. Unfortunately, pastors may not have time to study theology while shepherding the Church, especially since they must set up programs for the church, determine direction and ministries, and minister to individuals in the congregation while preparing and delivering instructions every Sunday.

Delivering or writing sermons is the practice of homiletics. It is the art of preaching. It requires the study, understanding, and application of rhetoric to the art of public preaching. These methods of learning and teaching Scripture will help the recipient get a clear appreciation. Believers can enhance their understanding if they learn to discern the various methodologies.

Behind these methodologies are the beliefs that guide thoughts, which become ideologies. Embedded in ideologies are axioms of reasoning. They are fundamentally understood without question. They are the basic building blocks of how Scriptures are reasoned.

Chapter 2: Ideology אידיאולוגיה (ide'ologya) {ברא }

The guiding ideology in this paper is an adaptation of the beliefs, theological, and philosophical principles of interpretation of Scripture expressed by Wright & Martin: Scripture is the doorway to living and life-giving contact with God. The separation of God and His creation through <u>ontological participation</u> is the foundation for thinking effectively about Scripture. God is separate and outside of Creation, communicating with His Creation when He deems it is needed. Scripture and Creation provide an open system of communication between God and humankind. Humankind is endowed with an intelligible nature from God. The nature of human beings in Creation has a natural tendency to communicate intelligently by action with God and each other. The intelligence communicated by God in the Bible is the revelation of salvation through His incarnation of Jesus Christ, who establishes an understanding of God and all things related to Him. The Holy Spirit impresses the truth and reality of the divine mystery of Jesus and salvation to the human spirit. <u>Relationality,</u> humans existing in relation to each other, is an essential structure in God's Creation. God created humans to be in active communication with each other. This is the essence of existing (Wright IV & Martin, 2019, p. 12).

Chapter 3: History, Culture, Language, Translations: היסטוריה, תרבות, שפה, תרגומים (hissetoreyah, tarebutt, safah, tiregumim)

There are four perspectives that contribute to understanding Scripture in general and particularly eschatology. The historical perspective sheds light on when and how culture changes over time. Culture shapes how scriptures are interpreted. Language identifies the meanings of words, phrases, and sentences. Sometimes, there are unique features of language that have no equivalent in the target language. Syntax and figures of speech like metaphors, similes, idioms, and hyperboles have different meanings in the targeted language and need to be translated correctly.

Biblical translations, especially English translations, have different purposes and objectives for translating biblical text. The purpose of the King James Version (KJV) was to make the Geneva translation of the Bible, which was a good and popular version, better. The purpose of the Good News Bible (GNB) was to provide a clear and simple translation for non-native-speaking readers. The purpose of the Expanded Bible (EXB) is to allow readers to see multiple possibilities for words, phrases, and interpretations embedded in the test.

History

Timelines and dates used in this paper are connected to the ages of world history. Whenever practical, timelines are displayed relative to the history of the ages of the world. By hanging other histories and timetables under the ages of world history, everything is tied together in one whole picture, and that is easier to track what was happening at various points in time. While admittedly the tendency of putting things in sequences and lists and timelines is a Western cultural characteristic not shared by Eastern cultures, it is particularly useful. The history of the Jews, for example, can be explained in each of the ages of world history from the ancient to the contemporary ages.

World History of the Ages

The timeline of the ages of world history is summarized in Figure 14. There are four segments in the timeline: the ancient age, the medieval age, the modern age, and the contemporary age. The Ancient Age covers the period from the invention of writing in three thousand BCE to the fall of the Western Roman Empire in four-hundred-seventy-six CE. After the Ancient Age, the Medieval Age lasted until Columbus arrived in the Americas in one-thousand, four-hundred seventy-two. Next came the Modern age, which lasted until the Contemporary Age at the end of the French Revolution in one-thousand seven hundred eighty-nine. The Contemporary age includes the age of Renaissance and the Age of Enlightenment (Baker & Andrews, 2020). While these periods of history have been described in terms of clearly defined events, it is understood that the transitions from one stage to another were only realized looking back, not at the moment of transition.

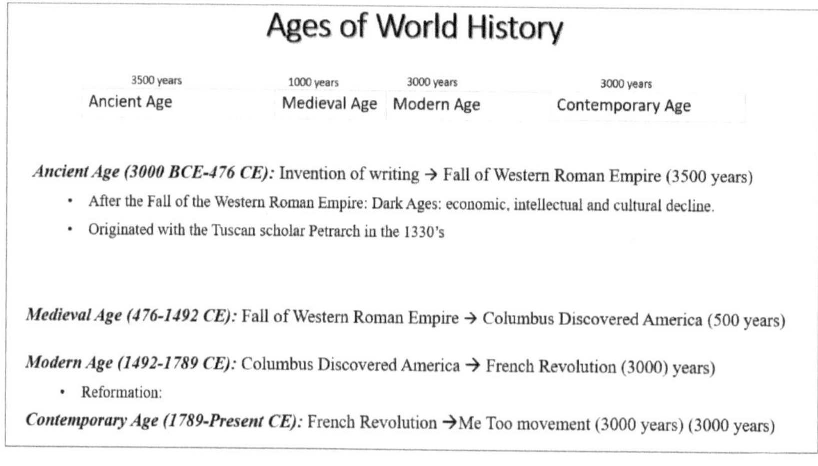

Figure 14: Ages of World History

Nation of Israel

Utilizing this context of the ages of world history, the development of the history of the Israel nation through the early church period happened in the ancient and medieval ages. However, Israel continues to play a role in God's redemption, especially in the eschaton. Israel has a role in the end-time prophecy even after the Church is raptured. This will be discussed in Chapter nine.

Figure 16 shows the major periods of Israel's history in the context of the ancient and Medieval ages. During the Ancient Age, the events of the emergence of Israel as a nation follow the stories of the early world in Genesis 1.

Israel's history continues through the period of the Old Testament and the New Testament events of the Messiah and the Early Church. This period was broadly referred to as the first time period during the reign of King Solomon. The second temple period began with the destruction of the first temple during the Babylonian conquest of Judah and the rebuilding of the temple when the Jews returned to Judea and rebuilt by decree of King Cyrus of Persia. The period ended with the destruction of the second temple in seventy CE during the Maccabean Revolt.

Jewish history after the second temple period can be divided into three periods: Early, Middle, and Late third centuries CE. The chart also shows the timeline of the dominance of the four empires that ruled Israel and the world: the Babylonians, Medo-Persians, Greeks, and the Romans. The Byzantine Period of the fourth and fifth centuries was the name given to the Eastern Region of the Roman Empire after Western Roman was dissolved. In the seventh century the Muslims conquered the Israel territory. Israel gained statehood in 1949.

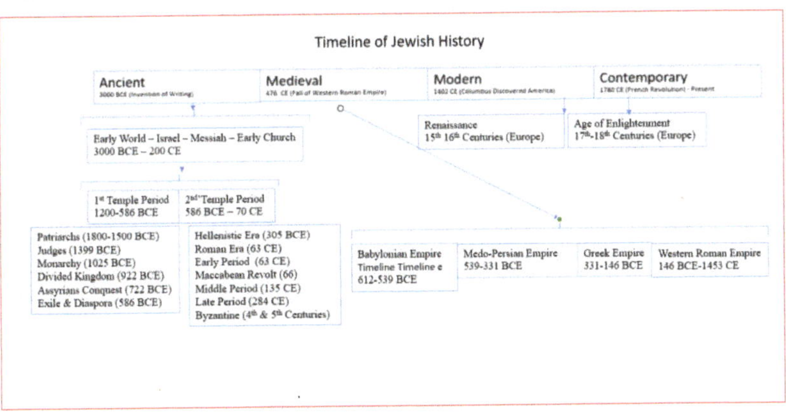

Figure 15: Timeline of Jewish History

Hebrew People

Historically eschatology is grounded in faith and hope of God's promises and fulfillments (Genesis 12:1-3) (Wansbrough, 2019). God promised Abraham that all nations would be blessed through him and his descendants would be in a land flowing with milk and honey (Exodus 3:8) (Wansbrough, 2019). His people will increase in number and possessions, and God will be in their presence (Genesis 49:8-12; Numbers 23; Deuteronomy 33:13-17 (Wansbrough, 2019). The journey of the pathway to promise and hope is the subject of eschatology. The events of eschatology evolved over time, culminating in the clear path understood in over two hundred years of the history of the Church. Over the next two thousand years, various understandings of eschatology emerged because of the thoughts of church leaders, philosophers, and theologians. Those various thinkers and their thoughts, 'ologies,' are surveyed in chapters six, seven, eight, and ten.

Hebrew people were also referred to as Israelites and Jews in the Bible. The names reflected the historical periods of God's chosen people. However, the names are used interchangeably and only sometimes refer to a time. The Hebrews were a tribe of nomads and slaves until the end of the time of judges, in approximately one thousand BCE. The Israelites were a sovereign united nation and then a divided nation until the return to their land in Judah. In approximately five-hundred-sixteen BCE, when the nation was divided into the North and South, ten tribes became known as the Northern Kingdom of Israel under the rule of King Jeroboam I, located in Shechem. The remaining two tribes became known as the Southern Kingdom of Judah under King Rehoboam, located in Jerusalem. From that time until the end of the history recorded in the Bible, they were known as a religious group called the Jews. Figure 16 is a chronological depiction of the names of God's chosen people from ancient to contemporary times.

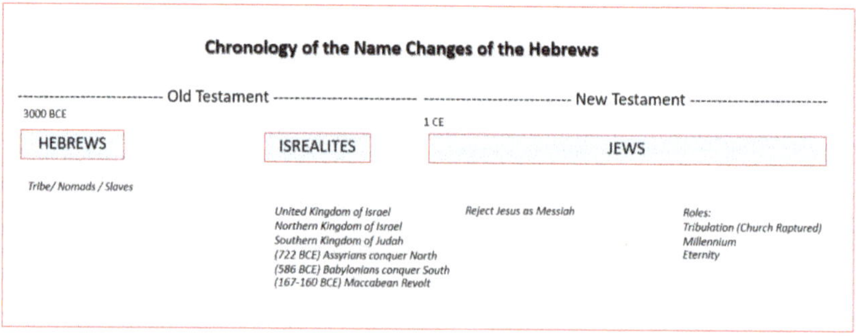

Chronology of the Name Changes of the Hebrews
Old Testament
New Testament
3000 BCE
1 CE
HEBREWS
ISREALITES
JEWS
Tribe/ Nomads / Slaves
United Kingdom of Israel
Northern Kingdom of Israel
Southern Kingdom of Judah
(722 BCE) Assyrians conquer North
(586 BCE) Babylonians conquer South
(167-160 BCE) Maccabean Revolt
Reject Jesus as Messiah
Roles:
Tribulation (Church Raptured)
Millennium
Eternity

Figure 16: Chronology of the Name Changes of the Hebrews

When God made himself known to Moses and the Israelites on Mt. Sinai and said He would be their God, they became a unique, distinct people. Unlike all other tribes and nations who worshiped multiple gods, the Hebrews served the one true God.

A history of the Hebrew people as told in the Scriptures is described throughout sixty-six books of the Bible, including their role in the eschaton. The Bible is organized by subject and not always chronological. Seventeen books, Genesis 11 (Wansbrough, 2019) through Esther, provide the history in chronological order. The twenty-two remaining books, Psalms through Malachi, fill in the details of the first seventeen books. While the Old Testament focused on the Jews, the New Testament was focused on Christ and the spread of Christianity and the early church. However, Hebrew history was embedded into the one hundred years of the New Testament.

Figure 17 outlines the historical periods in the Bible. The Bible can be divided into five historical segments: the history of the Early Word, the History of Israel, the history of the thirty-three years of the Messiah, the history of the Early Church, and the Eternal future. Each of these segments can be further divided. The Early World is about events before and after the Flood (Genesis 1-11a) (Wansbrough, 2019).

Israel's Old Testament history can be divided into the development of the people from the patriarchs, Abraham, Isaac and Jacob, the conquering of the Land under Joshua, the creation of the United Kingdom of Israel under Saul, David, and Solomon, and its separation into the Northern Kingdom of Israel and the Southern Kingdom of Judah, ending with the conquering of the Northern Kingdom by King Sennacherib of Assyria in 722 BCE and the conquering of Judah by King Nebuchadnezzar in 586 and their return to Judah 70 years later (Genesis 11b-Malachi) (Wansbrough, 2019)..

The history of the Messiah can be divided into His Birth, Early Childhood, the Great Galilean Ministry, the Late Judean Ministry, the Perean Ministry, the Last Week, and the Resurrection. (Mathew, Mark, Luke, and John) (Wansbrough, 2019).

The history of the Early Church began at Pentecost during the Feast of the Unleavened Bread, covering the Acts of the Apostles, deacons, other disciples, and Paul (Acts – Jude) (Wansbrough, 2019).

The book of Revelation describes the events of the Rapture, the Tribulation, the Second Coming of Christ, the One-thousand-year Millennium, Armageddon, the Great White Throne Judgment, and the eternity of the New Heaven and the New Earth, the PTPM view of eschatology.

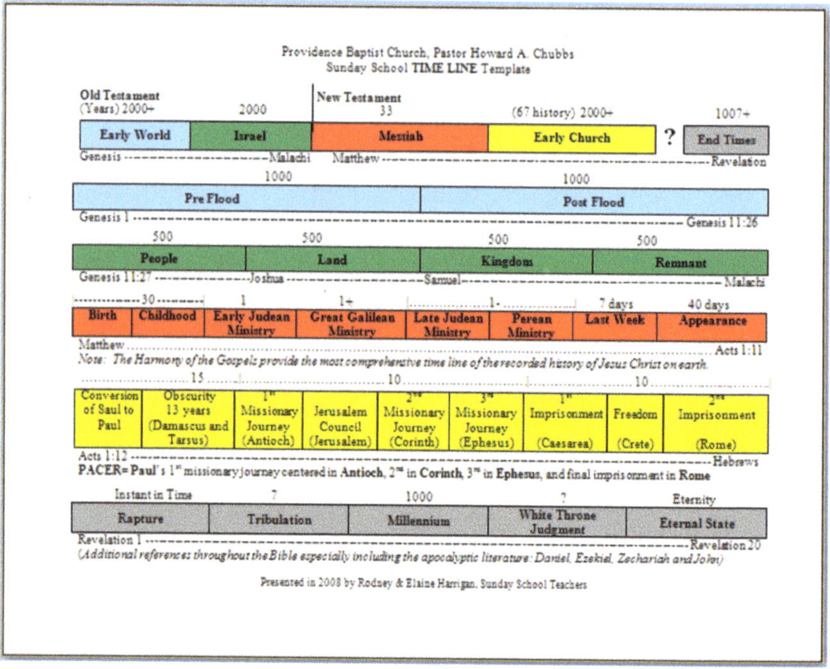

Figure 17: History of Israel in the Books of the Bible

Beginning in the New Testament with the assembly of the Sanhedrin Court, the governing body of the Church, the Christian councils assembled to address global and fundamental matters of the Church. The Sanhedrin was the supreme council of Israel located in Jerusalem. It was the legislative body in all matters of Torah law. After the First Jewish-Roman War (55-73 CE) fought in Judea, Jewish towns were destroyed, people were displaced, the Temple was destroyed, and the land was appropriated for Roman military use. This ended the Sanhedrin Court. Ecumenical councils were established as early as 325 CE to establish consensus among the Churches.

Ecumenical Councils

Ecumenical is derived from the Latin word oecumenicus, meaning "general, universal," and from the Greek word oikoumenikos, meaning "from the whole world," In Greek means the entire world (oikoumene). Beginning with the Sanhedrin court, Christian churches established councils to consider and rule on questions of Christian doctrine, administration, and matters that affect the whole Church. The intention was to reach an orthodox consensus. As Paul said, "Keep the unity of the Spirit (Church) in the bond of peace" (Ephesians 4:3) (Wansbrough, 2019).

The first few centuries of Christianity did not know large-scale councils, which became feasible after the Church gained freedom from persecution under the Edict of Milan by Emperor Constantine in 313 A.D. The first seven councils were meetings of several hundred Christian leaders representing the Western, Eastern Orthodox, and Catholic churches. The meetings were convened by Roman Emperors and convened for about a duration of a month each. The purpose was to reach a consensus on Christological doctrines and church problems. The topics in chronological by the date of the councils included:

1. **Arianism:** an influential heresy denying the divinity of Christ, originating with the Alexandrian priest Arius (c.250–c.336). Arianism maintained that the Son of God was created by the Father and was, therefore, neither coeternal with the Father nor consubstantial.

2. **Nature of Christ**: an influential heresy denying the divinity of Christ, originating with the Alexandrian priest Arius (c.250–c.336). Arianism maintained that the Son of God was created by the Father and was, therefore, neither coeternal with the Father nor consubstantial.

3. **Passover Celebration**.

4. **Ordination of eunuchs**.

5. **Kneeling on Sunday and Easter to Pentecost prohibition**.

6. **Validity of baptism by heretics** (belief or opinion contrary to Christian orthodox religion).

7. **Lapsed Christians**.

8. Apollinarianism is a heretical doctrine[1] that taught that Christ had a human body but not a human mind or will. Instead, he had the Logos, or the divine word of God, as his rational soul. It was named after Apollinaris, a bishop of Laodicea in the fourth century , and condemned by the First Council of Constantinople.

9. Sabellianism: relating to the teachings of Sabellius (fl. c.220 in North Africa), who developed a form of the Modalism doctrine that the Father, Son, and Holy Spirit are not truly distinct but merely aspects of one divine being.

10. Holy Spirit.

11. Successor to Meletius: Melitius, or Meletius (died 327), was **bishop of Lycopolis in Egypt.** He is known as the founder and namesake of the Melitians (c. 305), one of several schismatic sects in early church history that were concerned about the ease with which lapsed Christians reentered the Church.

12. Nestorianism: the doctrine that there were two separate persons, one human and one divine, in the incarnate Christ. It is named after Nestorius, patriarch of Constantinople (428–431), and was maintained by some ancient churches of the Middle East. A small Nestorian Church still exists in Iraq.

13. Monophysitism: a person who holds that in the person of Jesus Christ, there is only one nature (wholly divine or only subordinately human), not two.

14. Origenism: Origenism refers to **a set of beliefs attributed to the Christian theologian Origen.** The main principles of Origenism include allegorical interpretation of scripture, pre-existence, and subordinationism. Philo the Jew, Platonism, and Clement of Alexandria influenced Origen's thought.

15. Monothelitism: a theological doctrine in Christianity, which holds Christ as having only one will. The doctrine is thus contrary to dyothelitism, a Christological doctrine that holds Christ as having two wills (divine and human).

16. The Human and divine wills of Jesus.

17. Iconoclasm: the rejection or destruction of religious images as heretical; the doctrine of iconoclasts

The First Seven United Christian Ecumenical Councils (before the Split) (Davis, 1990)

COUNCIL	DATE (A.D.)	CONVENING EMPEROR	DOCTIRINAL & THEOLOGICAL ISSUES (Matters or faith & practice)	HIGHLIGHTS OF PROCLAMATIONS
First Council of Nicaea	325 May – June	Constantine I	Arianism .Nature of Christ .Passover Celebration .Ordination of eunuchs .Kneeling on Sunday and Easter to Pentecost prohibition .Validity of baptism by heretics .Lapsed Christians.& other matters	Formulated the original Nicene Creed. Defined the equality of God the Father and Christ, his son.
First Council of Constantinople	381 May - July	Theodosius I	.Arianism .Apollinarism .Sabellianism .Holy Spirit .Successor to Meletius	Defined the divinity of the Holy Spirit.
Council of Ephesus	431 June - July	Theodosius II	.Nestorianism .Theotokos .Pelagianism	Proclaimed the Virgin Mary as the "Most of God"
Council of Chalcedon	451 October- November	Marcian	.The judgement issued at the Second Council of Ephesus in 449 .The alleged offences of Bishop Dioscorus of Alexandria .The relationship between the presbyter Boniface .Formal Presidency	Defined two natures of Jesus Christ, divine and human. It condemned chapters of Nestorian writings.
Second Council of Constantinople	553 May – June	Justinian I	.Nestorianism .Monophysitism .Origenism	Dealt with the issue of the two natures of Chrity, human and divine because in spite of the previous Council of Chalcedon Monothelitism was spreading.
Third Council of Constantinople	680-681 November- September	Constantine IV	.Monothelitism .The Human and divine wills of Jesus	Repudiated Monothelitism and reaffirmed Christ being both human and divine with bother human and divine wills.
Second Council of Nicaea	787 September- October	Constantine VI & Empress Irene (as regent)	.Iconoclasm	Emperor outlawed pictorial presentations of Christ and the saints. This was the last ecumenical council accepted by both Eastern and Western churches

Figure 18: The First Seven Christian Ecumenical Councils

The Catholic Church held 21 ecumenical councils throughout its history. The Second Vatican Council took place from 1962 to 1965 for the purpose of bringing bishops from around the world to discuss and make decisions on important Christian matters (Encyclopedia Britannica Editors, 2020).

The Catholic and Eastern Orthodox churches rejected the Council in Trullo (692), a.k.a. the Quinisext/Penthekte Council, which was accepted by the Eastern Orthodox Church.

Some Christian denominations do not accept all proclamations. The church of the East accepts the first two councils. Oriental Orthodox accepts the first three. Both the Eastern Orthodox Church and the Catholic Church recognize the first seven councils. The first four ecumenical councils are recognized by some Lutheran Churches, Anglican Communion, and Reformed Churches, but they are considered subordinate to Scripture (Olson, 1999, p. 158), see Figure 19.

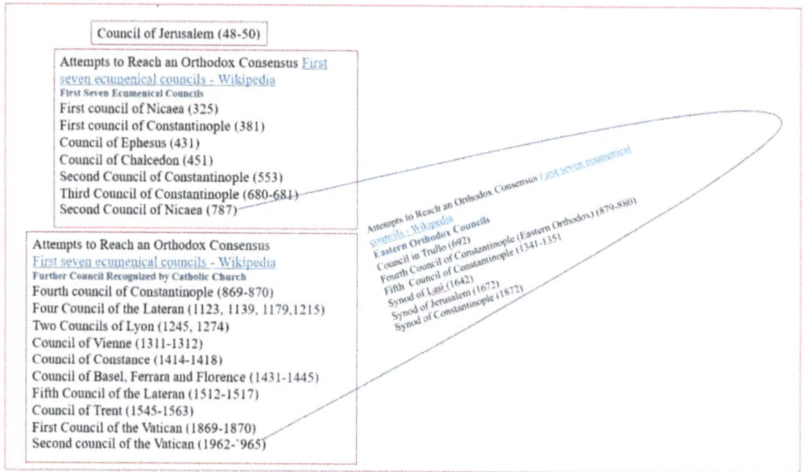

Figure 19: Ecumenical Councils

History of Eschatological Views

During the Early Church period, the premillenium was the prevailing view. This view persisted as the only view of the end time for more than two hundred years. Over the following two thousand years, other views emerged. There was no indication that these views were inspired by God and based on Scripture. For the most part, they were reasoned in the minds of philosophers, theologians, and church leaders. This notion is explored in Chapter 11. In fact, they were often thoughts based on political motivations, as covered in chapters 7, 8, and 10. The other views gradually emerged; see Figure 20.

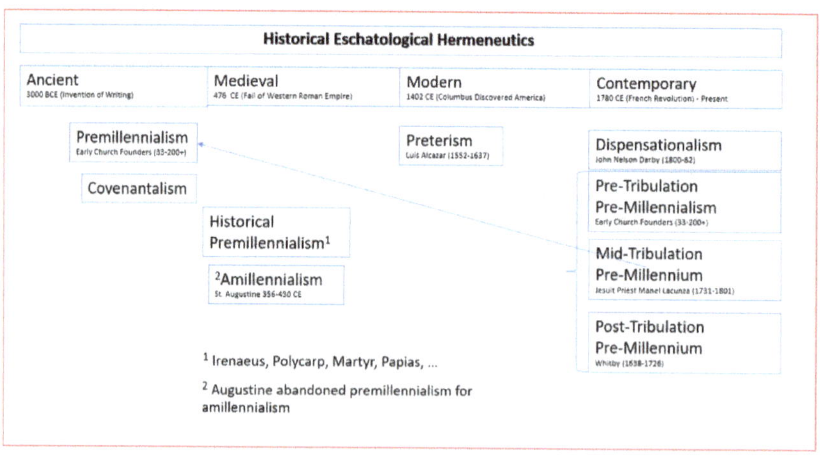

Figure 20: Historical Eschatological Hermeneutics

Hebrew history described in the Bible testaments authenticates the PTPM eschatological view, especially Daniel's seventh-week vision in the ancient times in the Old Testament and God's revelation to Jesus, who revealed it to John Revelation in the New Testament medieval age. Thus, history validates the sequence of the events of eschatology. Culture further validates the PTPM interpretation of eschatology.

Culture

Culture is shaped and reflected in ways of thinking and mindsets that result in world views. Thinking is deliberating, pondering, planning, debating, and logically figuring out things. Thinking is a *process*. Mindset is the *resulting conclusions* from thinking. Mindset is the opinions, judgments, and beliefs. Collections of these views and beliefs form a worldview, which is an understanding of how the world works. That understanding fuels a way of life, which is culture.

A culture will change throughout history because thinking, mindset, and worldview change. Think about how views on religion, marriage, sex, values, and the like have changed each generation: Baby Boomers, Generation X, Millennials, and Generation Z.

The culture that existed in the early church period and today in the East is quite different from the culture that gradually developed in the West almost eighteen hundred years later. Richards and O'Brien define the Western region as Europeans, Canadians, and residents of the United States of America, and they define the Eastern region as everything else, non-western. The danger in generalizing about Western and Eastern cultures is to try to account for the cultural, ethnic, social, and political diversity of cultures between the West and the East and the diversity of cultures within the West and within the Eastern cultures. Although generalizations are always wrong, they are usually helpful (Richards & O'Brien, 2012, p. 19).

Culture is an integral part of understanding scripture. For example, the word Shalom is translated to mean hello or goodbye. Even the transliteration of the Hebrew alef-bet to the English alphabet renders the hello or goodbye meaning. Yet, the cultural intent of Shalom was to wish order and wellness with God and wholeness for family and neighbors. Shalom is spoken while hands are in a praying position and bowing repeatedly when speaking (Robinson, Essential Torah: A Complete Guide to the Five Books of Moses, 2006).

Order is how God communicates throughout the Bible and what He expects from His people. God told Job, "If thou canst answer me, set they words in order before me, stand up" (Job 3:5) (Wansbrough, 2019).

 Moses wrote that in the beginning, God created the heaven and the earth (Genesis 1). In Exodus, God said, "And thou shalt bring in the table, and set in order the things that are to be set in order upon it" (Exodus 40:4) (Wansbrough, 2019). The psalmist invoked the reader and hearer to order steps by the Word (Psalms 119:133) (Wansbrough, 2019). Paul told the Corinthians 'Let all things be done decently and in order" (1 Corinthians 14:40) (Wansbrough, 2019). The scriptures on order are extensive throughout the Bible.

These are the guiding principles that provide a deeper understanding of Scripture. Figure 21 highlights the differences between Eastern and Western cultures. The list is in order of increasingly difficult to detect. The more difficult it is to detect the difference in culture, the higher the likelihood of differences and misinterpretations of Scripture. The Eastern Culture reflects the Early Church Culture and much of the East today. Western culture reflects the culture that has developed over centuries in the West, especially in North America. Eastern culture is defined as everywhere else for the purpose of this paper.

Eastern/Western Cultures Compared

Eastern Culture	Western Culture
Differences in Language	
Differences in Social Customs (Mores)	
Karis (Quality) Time	Cronos (Quantity)Time
Relationships override rules	Rules applied equally to everyone
Patron-Client Relationship	Contractual Obligations
Honor & Shame	Innocent or Guilt
Differences in Virtues	

Figure 21: Eastern/Western Cultures Compared

Eastern and Western Cultures

Early Christians believed in collectivism, the principle of the community having priority over the individual. Harmony was everyone's primary goal. Preserving harmony was much more important than self-expression or self-fulfillment. A person's identity comes from faithfully fulfilling his place in the community. The most important characteristic of community living was collectivism. The group was given priority over the individual. The Council of Elders makes decisions. Arranged marriages are common because the community should decide what is best for the young couple to protect them. The marriage was between two families. In the West, a person's identity comes from distinguishing himself from the community. The goal was to move beyond the community (Klein & Spears, 2016, p. 96). The contrast was "we" versus "me," "public" versus "private."

Differences in Language

Language is the most obvious cultural difference that can cause misreading of Scripture. Meaning of words, rules of grammar, structure of syntax, and figures of speech are ways that languages differ. The Bible was written originally mostly in Hebrew. Exceedingly, small parts of the Bible were written in Aramaic. Then, the Bible was translated into Greek, English, and other world languages. When reading an English Translation of the New Testament, it usually has been translated from Greek, which was translated from Hebrew. Translations can be misrepresented and misunderstood. This is especially true since translators are using their cultural perspectives and worldviews to interpret the Greek worldviews, which interpreted Hebrew worldviews. That is why the meaning of Scripture is more accurate when it is read in Hebrew with an understanding of Hebrew culture. Consider the Galatians 5:22-23 (Wansbrough, 2019), the fruit of the spirit. There was no English equivalent for the Hebrew word being translated. Therefore, the Hebrew word was translated with an English description: love, joy, peace, longsuffering, gentleness, goodness, meekness, faith, and temperance. That is also why ministers will say there is only one fruit ((Richards & O'Brien, 2012, p. 74).

Greeks have four different words for love: *agape* (God's love), *phila*, (brotherly love), *eros* (romantic love), *and storage* (bond or affection between family members), The English translation for each of those Greek words is love. English descriptions then must use and adjectives and descriptions to define the kind of love it is.

In the Sermon on the Mount, in the book of Matthew, Jesus said if you are a peacemaker, then you are *makarios*. *Makarios* is a feeling one has when one is happy, a feeling of contentment when one knows one's place when life has been fortunate. There is no single word for *makarios* in English. English translations substitute a word like happy or blessed.

An English translation may use an idiom like "My life has really come together" (Richards & O'Brien, 2012, p. 75).

Differences in Social Conventions (Mores)

Paul followed a Greek custom of listing things in groups of give with a summary word at the end. Paul said in Colossians 3:5, "Mortify therefore your members which are upon the earth; fornication, uncleanness, inordinate affection, evil concupiscence, and covetousness, which is idolatry." His message was speaking against idolatry. The five words were not in any order. They were not the only five kinds of idolatry. They were not the most important words. That was just a custom that could be misunderstood to mean not doing these specific things. If the Greek culture were not understood, the correct meaning could not be clear. If the English culture were assumed in the reading, it could be interpreted as these are the most important sins in order.

Kairos and Chronos Time

Time was viewed mostly as Cronos time in the west and mostly *kairos* time in the east. Western time was focused on clock time, calendar time, and time of day. It was the Greek word *Cronos* time. Eastern time was focused on *Kairos* time, that is, when the time is right, quality of time versus quantity of time. God created the world when He felt like it. God sent his son, Jesus, Yeshua, when the time was right (Richards & O'Brien, 2012, p. 142).

Kairos also describes a situation or circumstance. Paul said to the Ephesians, "See that you walk circumspectly, not as fools, but as wise, Redeeming the time, because the days are evil" (Ephesians 5:15-16) (Wansbrough, 2019). To understand *kairos* time, look at the Christmas story. The Christmas story often compresses the narrative so that the angels, shepherds, and wise men all come to see baby Jesus in a manger in a stable at the same time. However, the story of Jesus goes through His toddler years. It appears that Joseph and Mary stayed in Bethlehem for nearly two years because when the wise men arrived, they went to a house where Joseph, Mary, and baby Jesus were living (Matthew 2:11) (Wansbrough, 2019). During that period Joseph was following work opportunities, which was customary to do at that time. This was the time (*kairos*) for work.

Jesus gave the parable of the kingdom of heaven being like a king who prepared a wedding banquet for his son who sent his servants to the invitees who refused. This story could be misinterpreted to mean that the wedding guests were ungrateful or they were too busy and did not have the time. However, the focus of the parable was on timing. Understanding the culture at that time gives a distinct perspective on the story. When a banquet was announced, it was an event that would happen soon. The exact date was not really known. The banquet would depend on the timing. The weather may not be conducive. Supplies had to arrive from out of town. The fatted calf had to be killed on the day of the feast because there was no refrigeration. When all the preparations were made, the feast happened on the right day (*kairos* time). The Western interpretation assumes the guests will not come because they do not have the time or they feel the banquet is a waste of time because banquet invitations note the day and time. The issue was not refusing to come to the banquet at the calendar time (*chronos*). It was refusing to come when the timing was right (*kairos*) (Richards & O'Brien, 2012, p. 146).

Westerners think of *Chronos* time when reading a passage of scripture. The assumption is that the passage refers to a discrete, measurable moment in history. However, the Bible writers describe *kairos* time more often than *chronos* time (Richards & O'Brien, 2012, p. 141). The biblical authors were more often concerned with *timing* rather than *time*.

Focusing on *chronos* time tends to seek an order of events. The charts in this paper are a Western way of describing things. This focus on order can sometimes cause confusion about passages of scripture. Gospel writers did not always compose their stories in chronological order. Sometimes, they had a different focus that would make two different accounts of the same story seem like one is right and the other is wrong. There are no contradictions in the Bible. In the story of the three temptations of Jesus, Matthew's sequence of events is different from Luke's. Matthew has every major event in the life of Jesus that occurs on a mountain, so his story ends on a mountain. Luke uses references to the temple as a theme, so his story ends on the pinnacle of the temple. Both stories are correct. Chronological time is not important. Biblical writers were intentional about the sequence of events they presented. Focusing on the time without considering the timing may cause the meaning of the sequence to be misinterpreted (Richards & O'Brien, 2012, p. 148).

Relationships and Rules

In the Eastern culture relationships were more important than rules. Paul told the Galatians Christ would not profit them if they let themselves be circumcised (Galatians 5:2) (Wansbrough, 2019). Then Paul circumcised Timothy Lystra because they knew Timothy was a Gentile (Acts 16:3) (Wansbrough, 2019). Paul wanted Timothy to be accepted by the Jews in Lystra. The relationship was more important than the rules. Westerns would see this as showing favoritism; rules should apply to everyone equally (Klein & Spears, 2016, p. 154).

The Patron-Client Relationship

Another difference between Easter/Western cultures is the way business is conducted. It is a relationship agreement, not a contract. The relationship is understood between the patron and the client. It is not documented. It is understood. Everyone knows what is expected of the patron and the client. Patrons solved problems for the clients. Problems could be trouble with the local grade guilds, refinancing a loan, or smoothing over tensions with city leaders. The patron provides services for the client in return for their loyalty. The client is obligated to honor the patron's request. The patron is obligated to meet the needs of the client. The client was a friend of the patron but not a peer. In return, the client was expected to reciprocate with public praise, readiness to help, and gratitude (Klein & Spears, 2009, pp. 80-83). When the patron gave an unmerited gift, the client was obligated to be loyal in return. In the New Testament, the Roman world conducted business through this system of patrons and clients (Klein & Spears, 2016, p. 82).

This relationship was described as *charis,* meaning grace, and *pastis,* meaning faith. In fact, when Paul explained the new relationship with God in salvation, He used words everyone understood. He borrowed those terms because they were familiar to people in New Testament times so they could understand the relationship between God's grace and living by faith (Klein & Spears, 2009, p. 82). Paul worked for himself rather than accepting gifts that would oblige him to the giver. He could not be obligated to come to his patron on request because he traveled so much and needed to remain flexible. Although Paul accepted a gift from the Philippian Church, he tied it to God. He said he was not accepting the gift out of need because he learned to be content. Paul interpreted the gift as an offering to God, not himself.

Later, if the Philippians had a need, they would look to Paul's God (Philippians 4:19) (Wansbrough, 2019). Thereby Paul was not obligated to the Philippians.

Paul also used this patron-client system to obligate the Jerusalem Church to the Gentile Churches by gathering funds from them for the poor saints in Jerusalem. The Jerusalem Church became obligated to the Gentile Churches by saying others will praise God for their obedience to the faith, tying the hearts of the Jewish Christians in Jerusalem who needed the gift to the Gentile Christians, who gave the gift (2 Corinthians 8-9) (Wansbrough, 2019) ((Klein & Spears, 2016, p. 165).

Honor/Shame and Innocent/Guilt

The culture of the East is an honor/shame culture, while the Western culture is an innocent/guilt culture. In the innocent/guilty culture, the laws of society, the rules of the church, and the local codes of the home are all internalized. A person's conscience will discourage them from breaking any of these. The battle is inside.

In the honor-shame culture. The individual was not to bring shame on themselves or their family, church, village, tribe, or faith. Shame comes when the expectations of the community are not met (Klein & Spears, 2016, p. 118). Paul stated that his life was blameless according to the law before and after the Damascus Road experience (Philippians 3:4-6) (Wansbrough, 2019).

Even the culture of the Old Testament was an honor/shame culture. The Holy Spirit convicted unrepentant sinners. In the story of David and Bathsheba, honor/shame permeates the story. Although it is assumed that David stubbornly refused to repent, that was not the reason for his apparent resistance because he did not have an innocent/guilt conscience. He repented because the prophet Nathan shamed him. David was not concerned about the right or wrong of adultery. He was concerned about protecting his honor as the king. When Uriah, Bathsheba's husband, would not give David an honorable way out. He shamed David, who retaliated by having Uriah killed in battle. As far as David was concerned, the matter was settled. (Klein & Spears, 2016, pp. 123-125). Virtues and vices are also culturally ingrained into the interpretation of Scripture.

Differences in Virtues and Vices

Virtues and vices are the moral standards of morality. They are the things we value. Virtues and vices profoundly influence behaviors. There are biblical virtues and vices that should guide our thoughts and actions. There are cultural virtues and vices that may be good or bad but are not biblical. Culture shapes the understanding of virtues and vices. There are virtues and vices that guide behavior that are contrary to Christian morals. When they are referenced in the Bible, it is instructive to know the types in order the properly interpret scripture.

Biblical values are often expressed in a list, as discussed earlier. See Figure 22 for a representative list of Biblical Virtues.

Biblical Virtues

Scripture Reference	Biblical Virtue List	Summary
Colossians 3:5	Put to death whatever belongs to your earthly nature:	Idolatry
	Sexual immorality	
	Impurity	
	Lust	
	Evil desires	
	Greed	
Colossians 3::8-9	Rid yourselves of:	Stop lying to each other
	Anger	
	Rage	
	Malice	
	Slander	
	Filthy Language	
Colossians 3:12	Clothe yourself with:	Love
	Compassion	
	Kindness	
	Humility	
	Gentleness	
	Patience	

Figure 22: Biblical Virtues

Cultural and non-biblical virtues are listed in Figure 23. Self-sufficiency is a Western virtue. North Americans value those who make way for themselves without help or handouts. It has a ring of wisdom. However, the Bible expresses the opposite value. James warns against putting too much faith in our own plans and dishonoring God (James 4:15) (Wansbrough, 2019). Paul says to carry each other's burdens (Galatians 6:2) (Wansbrough, 2019).

Around the world, people are fighting for freedom. Jesus says to turn the other cheek. When a soldier wants to carry his equipment one mile, carry it two (Matthew 5:39) (Wansbrough, 2019).

Pax American, a state of international peace regarded as overseen by the United States of America or the United Kingdom, is based on the strength of military might. Pax Romania was the practice of the Roman Empire. It brought peace to that part of the world. Ships could sail the Mediterranean without fear of pirates. Travelers could move along the roads without fear of bandits. Yet America and the Romans used force and military might to achieve peace. Jesus said His peace is not the peace that the world gives. Paul said to the extent that it is possible to live in peace with one another (Romans 1:18) (Wansbrough, 2019). The Psalmist said that he had lived too long among those who hate peace. He was for peace, and they were for war (Psalm 120:7) (Wansbrough, 2019).

Leadership is a Western virtue. A follower indicates a weakness in a character who lacks ambition and creativity. Leadership implies that a person is efficient, creative, productive, and charismatic. However, the Bible urges fellowship and followers of Jesus (Matthew 4:19) (Wansbrough, 2019)..

Tolerance is not a biblical virtue. God declared that he would bring disaster to his people for their tolerance of idol gods (Jeremiah 44:11) (Wansbrough, 2019). Westerners tend to be tolerant of all religions (Richards & O'Brien, 2012, p. 184).

Cultural Non-Biblical Virtues

Virtue	West	Biblical
Self Sufficiency	Virtue: make a way for yourself – ring of wisdom	Vice: putting too much faith in our own plans dishonors God (James 4:15) – if God wills
Fighting for freedom	Virtue: freedom is worth fighting for	Vice: turn to other cheek (Matthew 5:39, 41) (Matthew 24:16) – flee to the mountains.
Pax Americana (Peace)	Bring peace by force with war if necessary Romans: peace through war	Vice: Lead quite lives (1 Thessalonians 4:11)
Leadership	Virtue	Vice: Follower
Tolerance	Virtue: don't criticize anyone's religion	Vice: God declared He would bring disaster on them and destroy Judah because of their tolerance of idolatry (Jeremiah 44:11)
Plan	a survival skill, not a virtue	Not explicit
Procrastination	Vice	Not explicit
Plagiarism	Vice	Not explicit
Frugality	Virtue: a penny served is a penny earned	
Hard Work	Virtue: God helps those who help themselves	
Savings	Virtue: Financial independence – importance of saving – good stewardship and delayed gratification	Vice: greed (parable of man who built newer and bigger barns for their grain) – did not share his excess

Figure 23: Cultural Values

Evolution of the Western Culture

The Western worldview, mindset, and cultural norms evolved from the historical thoughts of noted philosophers like Plato and Church leaders like St. Augustine. Before Plato, the views were Eastern. There was no distinction in Christian views. Plato set the Western world on the path toward the inner voice being capable of choosing between right and wrong. He wrote that humans do right only when others are watching but they could and should resist the temptation to do wrong. They had an inner motivation for moral conduct (Richards & O'Brien, 2012, p. 114)

Beginning with St. Augustine, Christians understood Paul's conversion as a troubled conscience of guilt of sinning but transformed by the message of Christ's forgiveness. Paul "saw the light," not so much literally as internally. Luther encouraged Western Christians to come to Christ by their own consciences, convicted from reading God's laws (Philippians 3:4-6) (Wansbrough, 2019).

Scholars agree that the Holy Spirit convicted biblical characters through external, not internal, voices (Klein & Spears, 2016, p. 120).

Jewish (Hebrew, Israel) Sects

Culture may be defined as 'the way we do things around here,' or 'the difference between us and them,' or the language, customs, symbols, norms, values, beliefs, rituals, artifacts, and dialect, accent, slang, and ethnicity of a people.' Culture changes over time but there are unique features that remain constant throughout history.

Hebrew culture is built on the foundation of the one true God and his Torah, the book of instruction. Torah more accurately means 'instruction' although 'law' is an appropriate translation. Three distinct groupings/sects of Hebrew cultures developed throughout the years, which were fueled by diasporas resulting from enslavement in Egypt and later domination by conquering nations. See Figure 24.

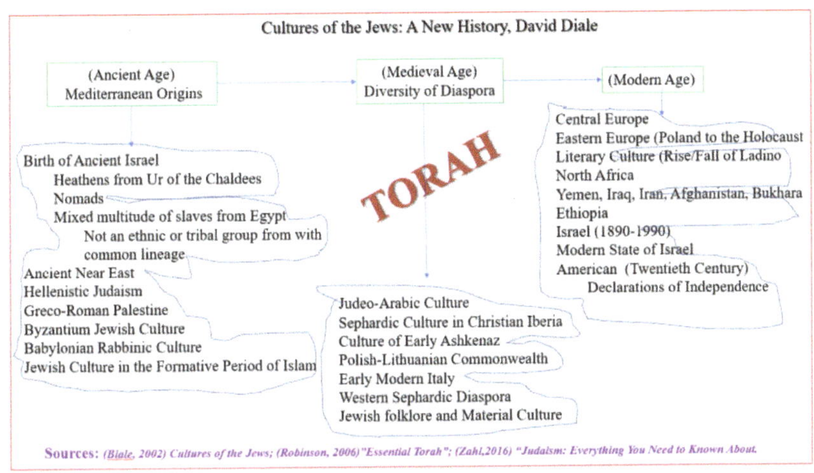

Figure 24: Jewish Sects

Uniqueness of the Hebrew Language

The uniqueness of the culture is reflected in the language. Language is an intricate part of culture. Language expresses, facilitates, and shapes culture. Old Testament Hebrew language is unique in its relationship to the Bible, survival as a language, and its word forms. God spoke the Bible in Hebrew. Moses wrote in Hebrew primarily and truly little Aramaic. The Bible was addressed to Hebrew people. Even the Septuagint is a translation of Hebrew into Greek. Hebrew is the only large-scale example of an ancient language to survive.

Hebrew was spoken and written until the destruction of the First Temple in five-hundred-eighty-six BCE. After that, Hebrew was used primarily as a literary and liturgical language. At the end of the nineteenth century, European Jews began a cultural renaissance in Palestine to resurrect the language. In one thousand nine hundred twenty-two, the language became the official language of the British Mandate for Palestine. Today, it is a modern language spoken by Israeli citizens and Jews around the world. This happened after Hebrew had not been a spoken language for two millennia. It is one of two Northwest Semitic languages still spoken. Aramaic is the other spoken language still existing today (Grenoble, 2005, p. 63).

All languages today are either textual or pictographic, but not both. Hebrew is both. The twenty-two letters of the 'alef-bet' have textual and pictural meanings. As an illustration, the word 'love' אהב is *ahav* in Hebrew. It is made of two Hebrew letters. A*lef (א)* is a picture of an ox or bull, meaning strength, leader, or first. The word *father (הב)* is a picture of a man holding up his hand, meaning reveal, and a picture of a house, meaning household or family, that says, 'love is the father's heart revealed (Seekins, 1999, p. 183).'

Two things contributed to its survival. First, the Torah was always the center point of the language. Last, when the Hebrews had to adapt their language to that of the conquering nations, they did not completely enculturate. In fact, they impacted the language to which they were subject.

A Greek translation of Hebrew in the New Testament gave rise to two distinct cultural worldviews because of the different mindsets. The Hebrew mindset that drives the culture of the early church provides the original meaning of Scripture. The Greek mindset of the Septuagint shapes contemporary translations and can lead to misinterpretations.

God spoke Hebrew to Abraham and the prophets. It is also the only language that has survived time intact. When the Hebrews were scattered in the diasporas created by the conquering world powers (Babylonians, Medo-Persians, Greeks, and Romans), they were not completely culturized. Hebrews adopted a foreign language into their culture, but they also adapted the foreign language to Hebrew culture as well. This resulted in the dialects of Hebrew around the world.

Hebrew and Greek Languages

The Old Testament is written in Hebrew and a little Aramaic. The New Testament is written in koine Greek, the Greek of the common people. However, the New Testament Greek translation is a translation of the Hebrew Tanakh. Therefore, the Bible is written primarily in Hebrew. At least ninety percent of the Bible is written in Hebrew (Klein & Spears, 2016, p. 145) (citation).

Old Testament Hebrew was translated to Greek by seventy-two scholars commissioned by Ptolemy II Philadelphus. That translation is named the Septuagint. Septuagint is the name seventy, sometimes named LXX, the Roman numeral for seventy. It was written years after the Old Testament Tanakh. A problem arises in interpreting the meaning of New Testament Scripture because the Old Testament was written with a Hebrew mindset, but the New Testament was written with a Greek mindset. The mindsets are quite different. In fact, the New Testament is written with a Greek mindset using the Septuagint as a basis instead of the Hebrew Tanakh. The Septuagint was used to translate the contemporary English versions using an English mindset. Therefore, the correct way to understand the full meaning of the original text is to read the Hebrew Tanakh or an English translation of the Tanakh with the Hebrew mindset. One such translation is the Revised New Jerusalem Bible (RJMB). The purest translation of the Tanakh is the Jewish Publication Society Tanakh of 1917 (Tanakh Jewish Bible: Jewish Publication Society 1917 Translation, 1919). Language shapes the inner thought process, which is a mindset. A mindset shapes the worldview. Greek and Hebrew Mindsets and World Views are different.

Greek and Hebrew Mindsets

A mindset is a frame of mind, the set of attitudes held by someone, a way of thinking. A mindset has more to do with personality, influences, and motivations. A biblical mindset is characterized by striving to be transformed by the renewal of your mind (Ephesians 5:26) (Wansbrough, 2019). It means agreeing with God, obeying Him, and worshiping Him. A person's mindset shapes their world view, a perspective on what a person sees and interprets about the world. A worldview is a philosophy of life and the understanding of the world. World views are learned and passed on by culture and education.

A biblical worldview is based on God's revealed truth, the Bible. It directs our life in the world. A mindset is how one thinks, and a worldview is what one thinks. Figure 25 summarizes the different mindsets.

MINDSET

Greek (Western) Mindset	Hebrew (Easter) Mindset
Life analyzed in precise categories	Everything blurs into everything else
A split between natural and supernatural	Supernatural affects everything
Linear logic	Contextual or "block" logic
"Rugged Individualism"	Importance of being part of group
Equality of persons	Value comes from place in hierarchies
Freedom orientation	Security orientation
Competition is good	Competition is evil (cooperation better)
Man-centered universe	God/tribe/family-centered universe
Worth of person based on money/material possessions/power	Worth derived from family relationships
Biological life sacred	Social life supremely important
Chang e+ cause & effect limit what can happen	God cause everything in the universe
Man, rules nature through understanding and apply laws of science	God rules everything, so relationships
Power over others achieved thru bus., politics, and human orgs.	Power over others is structured by social patterns ordained by God
All that exists is the material	The universe is filled with powerful spirit beings
Linear time is divided into neat segments. Each event is new	Cyclical or spiraling time. Similar events constantly reoccur
Orientation to the near future	Everything blurs into everything else
History is recording facts objectively and chronologically	Supernatural affects everything
Change is good = progress	Contextual or "block" logic
Universe evolved by change	Importance of being part of group
Material goods = measure of personal achievement	Value comes from place in hierarchies
Blind faith	Knowledge-based faith
Time as points on straight line)"at this point in time …")	Time determined by content ("In the day that the Lord did …")

Figure 25: Greek and Hebrew Mindsets

The differences in mindset were developed gradually over centuries as a function of history, culture, and language, beginning with Greek philosophers. The influence of Greek philosophers will be discussed in chapter eight.

Those mindsets led to different world views, as outlined in Figure 26.

Greek and Hebrew World Views

	Greek (Western) World View	Hebrew (Eastern) World View
Perspective	Man's temporary	God's eternal perspective
Mentality	Snapshot	Full movie
Example: Listen	Means pay attention, do what you are told	Means attention, do, incorporate into life, adopt in speaking and conduct, trust it is good, teach it
Senses	Sight- visible things static, images	Dynamic of hearing and feeling
Relation to God	Many Gods – unclear, changing	One God, clear right and wrong, moral behavior, does not change, works in cycles
Relation to man	Flesh and soul, physical man	Unity of spirit, soul and body, strive for righteousness, redemption, sanctification, spiritual man
Thoughts	Abstract	concrete
Description of objects	In relations to its appearance	In relations to its function
Verb Congregation	I am, you are, he is	He is, your are, I am
Time	Day – midnight to midnight	Day -sunset to sunset
	Week – named after pagan gods	Week – first, second …day, Sabbath
Distinction	Knowing, theory, spontaneous and luminous play of the intelligence	Doing, practice, duty and strictness of conscience

Figure 26: Greek and Hebrew World View

Figure 27 summarizes key elements of the Greek and Hebrew cultures.

CULTURE

Greek (Western) Culture	Hebrew (Eastern) Culture
Distinction	Harmony
Me	We
Private	Public
Time (Chronos)	Timely (Kairos)
Innocent or Guilt	Honor & Shame
Rules applied equally to everyone	Relationships override rules
Contract	Patron-Client
Virtues & Vices Western vs Ancient Culture	
Virtue: Individualism, Self-Reliant Vise: Conformity, failure to recognize full potential	Virtue: Conformity Vice: Individualism, Self-Reliance
Victorian English customs and practices were virtues: Teeth, Tall, Slender, Hair	Missing teeth, fat_,, normal and natural
Wealth: more than enough to go around: save, keep	Wealth: limited resource , share excess, there were always those in need
Virtue: Highest goal - Be true to yourself Vice: Conformity	Virtue: highest goal – Supporting the community Vice: Seeks only glory, doesn't get along
Virtue: why put off to tomorrow what you can do today	Virtue: why do today what you can put off until tomorrow

Figure 27: Culture

Hebrew Language Linguistics

The Hebrew alphabet is written with consonants. Words had to be spoken orally to understand how to pronounce them until vowels were added. Masoretic Text is a system of dots and dashes called vowel sounds developed by a Jewish tribe called the Masorites. They developed the system about six hundred years after the Septuagint in the tenth century CE. These vowels codified the pronunciations of words, making it unnecessary to depend on orally communicating the pronunciation.

Other translations included the canon of the Old and New Testaments. They emerged in abundance during the contemporary age. The Revised New Jerusalem Bible (RNJB) applies archaeological, linguistic, literary, and theological studies in its translation. RNJB is closer to the original Hebrew than Greek and English translations (Wansbrough, 2019).

Idioms and Metaphors.

The context of the ancient Hebrew culture enlightens and informs the Scripture, particularly as it applies to the interpretation of Hebrew idioms and metaphors. Interpreting original Scripture using modern language, idioms, customs, and culture undoubtedly leads to error. For example, the modern idiom "what's up" is interpreted as "how are you doing," not what is above you in the sky. "Destroy the Law" and "fulfill the Law" does not mean the law is terminated or no longer valid. The proper interpretation in the context of this Hebrew idiom is discovered in the practice of rabbinic argument.

"Destroying the Law' was an idiom for misinterpreting the Law. Jesus was accused of misinterpreting the Law, not destroying the Law. His system of interpretation was being called into question. "Fulfilling the Law' was thoroughly and correctly interpreting the Torah (Klein & Spears, 2009).

In Revelation, Jesus says, "Behold I am coming like a thief in the night" (Revelation 16:15; 1 Thessalonians 5:2) (Wansbrough, 2019). The modern interpretation of the "thief" idiom refers to a quiet and sly infiltration. The Hebrew idiom means coming like an armed intruder who comes boldly and makes His presence known. (Klein & Spears, 2009, p. 14)

In Romans, Paul says, "For Christ is the end of the Law" (Romans 10:4) (Wansbrough, 2019). The "end" does not mean termination, conclusion, or finalization. It means focus or goal (Klein & Spears, 2009, p. 14). The goal and purpose of the Torah is said to lead humankind to righteousness through Yeshua. This interpretation of "end" can be applied to a broader meaning of end times. "End times" in eschatology can mean the study of the focus and goal of God's plan for humankind.

In the Davidic age, the hope became the hope of the future messiah (2 Samuel 7) (Wansbrough, 2019). Isaiah prophesied the millennialism in David's day during the ninth century BCE (Isaiah 2:4) (Wansbrough, 2019). In the eighth century BCE, the prophets spoke of the "day of the Lord" (Amos 5:18) (Wansbrough, 2019). proclaiming a day of Judgment in fulfillment of the promises to Abraham. The oppression of Assyria and Babylon in the seventh and sixth centuries BCE was not because of the might of empires but rather a punishment for Israel's disobedience of the laws of God.

The richness of Hebrew words can be seen by observing the dual representations of letters as textual and pictographic; see Figure 28 for examples.

The richness of Hebrew Phonics and Pictographic

The Richness of Hebrew Words

ENGLISH WORD	HEBREW WORD	HEBREW LETTERS	PHONIC / PICTOGRAPHIC MEANING	Reference
God	Elohim	אלוהים	The first, strong controller	Seekins, p.169
Grace	Khesed	חסד	To fence or protect life.	Seekins, p.169
Jesus	Yeshua	ישוע		Reverso
Messiah	Mashiach	Le'ehovמשיח		Reverso
Holy Spirit				
Faithful	hamaaminim	המאמינים	The life of a mother (always ther, always faithful)	Seekins, p. 164
Hope	gee-va	קווה	What comes after the nail.	Seekins, p.172
Love	v. Le'ehov nf. Ahava	לאהוב אהבה		Reverso
Peace	Shalom	שלום	Destroy the authority that establishes chaos.	Seekins, p.193
Satan	v. Lekhate v. Lakhato	לחטא שטן	The snake that devours life (or) The teeth that surrounds life.	Seekins, p.203

Figure 28: The Richness of Hebrew Words

Language is an additional consideration for proper interpretation. Up to ninety-four percent of the Bible was written in Hebrew first. It was written by ordinary people using Hebrew idioms and reflecting Hebrew customs, practices, and preferences (Klein & Spears, 2009, p. 9).

The historical changes in the cultural developments of the Church contribute to understanding the development of eschatological views. From the ancient age of the early church to the age of Enlightenment, eschatological thoughts have been influenced by culture. Keller observed that the culture of the early church was characterized by unity across ethnic boundaries, forgiveness, and reconciliation, hospitality to the poor and suffering, the sanctity of life, and a sexual counterculture. The description of the leadership of the Antioch church in Acts 13 and the importance of racial reconciliation in Ephesians 2 (Wansbrough, 2019) are examples of unity across ethical boundaries. Forgiveness and reconciliation were strong cultural norms. Christians taught forgiveness and withheld retaliation against Roman and Jewish persecution, imprisonment, attacks, and murder. This was unheard of in the shame-and-honor culture in which vengeance was expected. (Keller, 2020).

Keller explained that the Christians helped all poor regardless of race or religious beliefs. Jesus' parable of the Good Samaritan (Luke 10:25-37) (Wansbrough, 2019) was unprecedented. Christians rescued and took in unwanted infants who were commonly thrown onto garbage heaps to die or be taken by traders into slavery and prostitution. According to Keller's findings, the Christian norms were different. The Church believed in heterosexual marriage and forbade sex outside marriage. Clearly, the culture of the Church was different from the prescribed culture of the time. Bennett described how culture changed over the ages. (Bennett, 2011)

Bennett explained that theologians described the early Church period as a time of 'corporate eschatology,' that is, the culture affected the entire body of Christian believers and even all of humanity. Theological speculations occurred throughout the history of Christian thought and resulted in countless apocalyptic scenarios of the world being violently destroyed, the righteous saved, and the unrighteous condemned. Bennett holds Augustine of Hippo accountable for this change. As a highly influential Church leader in the fifth century, Augustine changed the definition of death. His perception of death was changed from a final extinction to one of eternal terrible torment in hell (Hughes, 1989).

By the late seventeenth and early eighteenth centuries of enlightenment, corporate eschatology changed to the optimistic conviction that humankind was moving toward moral and societal perfection in the current and future worlds. These theories continued to develop into the nineteenth century with the theory of evolution. The eschatological vision of the optimism of hope changed back to the corporate eschatology of eternal torment for unbelievers because of the two world wars, industrial-scale slaughter, and the threat of nuclear annihilation of the twentieth century (Bennett, 2011). "Christianity is eschatology; eschatology is hope (McGraft, 2007). Therefore, the influence of the historical, cultural context of the eschatological beliefs of the Preterist, Historical Premillennialism, Amillennialism, Dispensationalism, Mid, and Post Tribulation as Bennett suggests, is more speculative, not motivational or the inspirational direction of the Holy Spirit. The Hebrew history and culture are properly interpreted through the Hebrew language of the Hebrew Bible.

Hebrew Language. The original language of the Word of God in the Bible was given to Moses who was a Hebrew, spoken to him in Hebrew, intended for the Hebrew people. It was called the Torah. The Torah contains five books: Genesis, Exodus, Leviticus, Numbers, and Deuteronomy. Torah means instruction, although it is often called the law. Understanding and interpreting the Word of God deepens with an understanding of the Hebrew history, culture, and language.

Most languages are phonic or pictographic. Kang and Nelson discovered that most contemporary-age languages in the East are pictographic, while Western languages are phonic. The Hebrew language is the only ancient language that has survived in the world that is pictographic and phonetic. Words and meanings are represented simultaneously in different but complementary ways (Klein & Spears, 2016, pp. 21-23). This combination provides a richer, more thorough understanding of the Scriptures.

Words commonly used throughout the Bible were selected based on personal preferences. Each word is identified by the English word, the equivalent Hebrew word, the Hebrew word written in block Hebrew letters, and the phonic/pictographic meaning. The cultural interpretations have not been added. Shalom, for example, was usually spoken while hands were in front of the cheek and bowing. Shalom means wishing you wholeness in your relationships with God, your family, and your neighbors.

The words that appear in various Bible translations use the basic meanings without the original context of history, culture, and the nuances of language, like idioms and metaphors. However, they are strong starting points. Over the years, the most stable and authentic Hebrew Bibles have been the Tanakh and the Talmud.

The Hebrew Bible Translations

The enduring foundation of the Hebrew culture is the Torah. The Tanakh, Talmud, and Septuagint are the earliest translations of Jewish Scripture. These documents are the central, most important text of Judaism.

Torah

The Torah is the Hebrew book containing the instructions God gave to Moses on scrolls at Mt. Sinai during the 13th Century BCE. It consists of the first five books of the Bible: Genesis, Exodus, Leviticus, Numbers, and Deuteronomy, also known as the Pentateuch, the Greek meaning "five scrolls," and the Chumash, from the Hebrew meaning "five-fold entry." The term Torah was eventually used to describe the entire body of Jewish learning and its continuing expansion in this present day. Although the word Torah is commonly translated to the word "Law" when it was first translated into Greek, the word is best translated to the word "instruction." Unfortunately, the Torah is the least understood book. The Torah is neither a book of science nor history. It is the sacred epic of a community in the making chosen by God for a destiny that is not it has not yet fulfilled (Rabbi Mariner, 1996, p. 7).

Tanakh

The Tanakh is the closest printed version of the original Torah. It consists of three parts: the Torah, the Prophets, and eleven Writings, as shown in Figure 29.

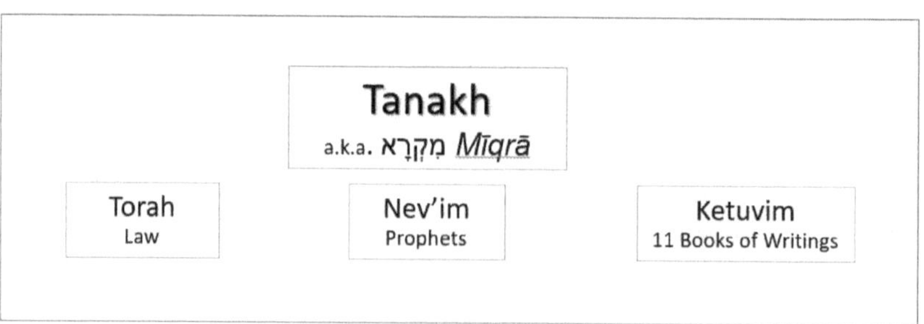

Figure 29: Tanakh

Talmud

The Talmud is the only other authentic Hebrew Bible. It is useful, but it is not the Torah. It contains the written collection of oral Law. It is more like a commentary on the Torah. It has two divisions: the *Mishnah,* which is the application of the Torah, and the *Gemara,* further detail on the teachings in the Torah, see Figure 30. Since the Tanakh is written in the original ancient Hebrew, it is the best source for the meanings of original Scripture.

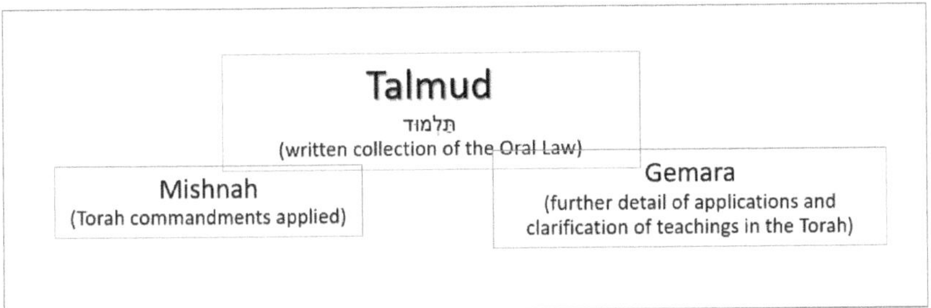

Figure 30: Talmud

Septuagint

The Septuagint is the oldest Greek translation of the Hebrew Old Testament. Septuagint means seventy and is also referred to by the Roman numeral LXX. The name derives from the tradition that seventy (or seventy-two) Jewish scholars in Alexandria were commissioned by Ptolemy Philadelphus (285-247 BCE) to translate the Hebrew Bible into Koine Greek, the common language of the time. It was written during the Hellenistic period for the Jewish diaspora who were culturalized to speak Greek and did not know Hebrew. Contemporary translations of the Septuagint added the apocrypha, biblical writings not accepted as part of the canon of Scriptures.

Notice that it was a translation of the Hebrew Torah into Greek, by Greek-speaking scholars, for Hebrews who only spoke Greek. Therefore, the translation interpreted through the Greek culture, mindset, and worldview was filtered through the lens of Greek culture, history, and language.

That filtering says something about the modern English translations of Bibles. Modern translations use filtered koine Greek that is further filtered through the English culture, mindset, and worldview. The

Western culture, mindset and world view is different and often opposite of the Eastern culture of the early church period. This is why it is important to understand the original Hebrew Scripture, an arduous task being confined by the Western perspective. See Figure 31 for an outline of the content of the Septuagint.

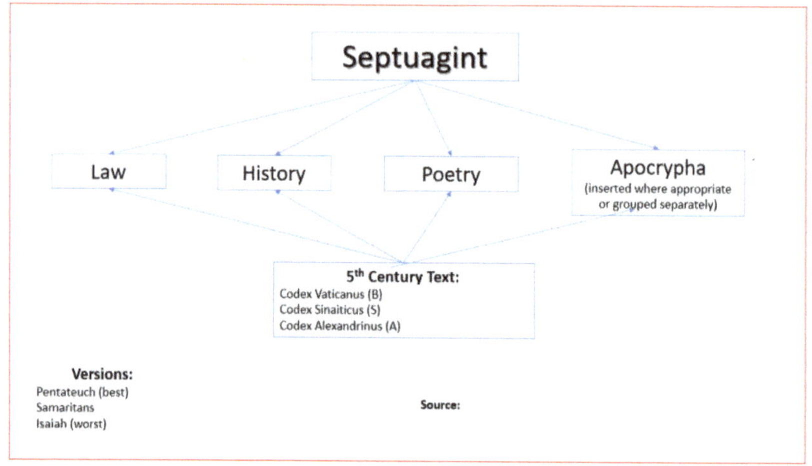

Figure 31: Septuagint

Superiority of the Talmud

Early Church Fathers made it clear that the Tanakh was the superior preferred source of understanding scripture (Klein & Spears, 2016, pp. 20-21). Papias, Bishop of Hierapolis in Asia Minor (mid-second century AD), is one of the early witnesses. Concerning the Hebrew origin of the Gospels, he states: Matthew wrote the words of the Lord in the Hebrew language, and others have translated them, each as best he could like Irenaeus, Origen, and Eusebius (Eusebius, Ecclesiastical History III 39, 16).

Irenaeus (AD 120-202) was Bishop of Lyons in France. His literary endeavors were undertaken in the last quarter of the second century AD. Irenaeus states: Matthew, indeed, produced his gospel written among the Hebrews in their own dialect (Eusebius, Ecclesiastical History VI 8, 2).

Origen (first quarter of the third century), in his commentary on Matthew, states: The first [gospel], composed in the Hebrew language, was written by Matthew… for those who came to faith from Judaism (Eusebius, Ecclesiastical History VI 25, 4).

Eusebius, Bishop of Caesarea (circa AD 325), writes: Matthew had first preached to the Hebrews, and when he was about to go to others also, he transmitted his gospel in writing in his native language (Ecclesiastical History III 24,6).

When original Scriptures and context are not used, misinterpretations can occur, particularly in translating Hebrew metaphors and Idioms.

Misinterpretations of Hebrew Metaphors and Idioms

Hebrew metaphors and idioms may be misinterpreted if the interpreter does not consider the original Hebrew text in the context of culture, history, and language. Torah, for example, is better translated as instruction. Although 'law' is an appropriate translation, the Torah is more than the law. In fact, the Torah is the marriage contract between God and His people. Examples of Greek mistranslations of Hebrew idioms are identified in Figure 32.

Hebrew Metaphors and Idioms

Scripture	Greek Translation	Hebrew Idiom
Torah	Law	Instruction
Book of Revelation	Revelations	Revelation
Matthew 5:17-18	Abolish the Law	Rabbinic Discourse Technical Terms: destroy & fulfill
Revelation 16:15	Nakedness: lack of physical garments	Protective covering: eternal covenant with God
1 Thessalonians 5:2	Like a thief in the night: soundless, sly, cat-burglar infiltration	Comes boldly, like an armed intruder who kicks in the door and makes sure everyone knows in the neighborhood.
Romans 10:4	Christ is the end	
Genesis 30:22	Remember	Intervene

Figure 32: Hebrew Metaphors and Idioms

The timeline of key translations of the Hebrew Bible are identified in Figure 33.

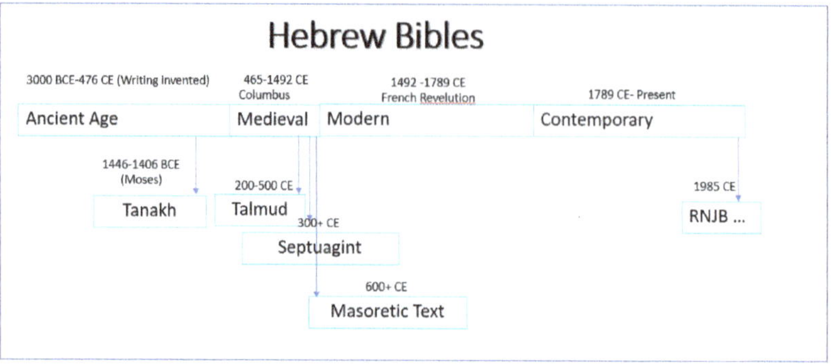

Figure 33: History of Hebrew Bibles

Taking into consideration the factors of history, culture, and language, the interpretation of Scripture can be rightly divided.

Rightly Dividing the Word (Larkin, 1920)

Rightly dividing the Word requires an awareness of the audience addressed in the scriptural passage, the role of Jesus at the time of the interpretation, and the timeline of the passage. The reader, listener, and interpreter must be conscious of the humanity of the audience. Classes of humanity described in the Bible are Jews, Gentiles, and the Church. Each classification has a development of culture and language based on experiences through history. Isaiah spoke of them as Jews in Judah and Jerusalem without reference to Israel or the Church. Paul spoke of the Jews as the twelve tribes of Israel in the Book of Hebrews, connecting the Jews and Israelites as the same people. James spoke of them in relation to the Israelites and the Church, distinguishing between the Israelites and the Church. Anyone who was not a Jew/Israelite was a Gentile. Hence, there were three groups of people in the Bible: Jews, Gentiles, and Christians.

The four thousand years of the biblical history of the Jewish people originated with God's call to Abraham. For the next two thousand years, they evolved from a family of Abraham to a clan, to twelve tribes, to more than four hundred years of slavery in Egypt, to over three hundred years as an independent nation, to slaves again by the conquering world powers of Babylon, the Medo-Persians, the Greeks, and the Romans for over one thousand years.

Concerning awareness of the role of Jesus, He was identified in His role as a prophet from the time of Eden to the Cross, symbolized by the altar. He is identified in His role as the High Priest during the period of the Cross to the Crown, symbolized by the table. Finally, Jesus will be identified as king in his role when he surrenders his crown to the Kingdom of God, symbolized by the throne.

Rightly dividing the Word requires being able to distinguish when God is speaking about the past, present, or future times. The times and seasons are the dispensations and age. Dispensation is a moral or probationary period in the history of the World. The form of administration is different in each disposition. Administration of the Jewish dispensation was the Law. The administration of the present dispensation is Grace. Administration of the future is righteousness. The Biblical ages are the Antediluvian Ages from the fall to the flood, the present ages from the flood to the second coming, and the ages of ages, the millennial time, and the perfect age.

God changes the times and the seasons (Daniel 2:21) (Wansbrough, 2019), It is not to know the time or the season of His return (Acts 1:7) (Wansbrough, 2019). Recognize the times of ignorance (Acts 17:30) (Wansbrough, 2019), the time of the Gentiles (Luke 21:24) (Wansbrough, 2019), and the times of refreshing (Acts 3:9) (Wansbrough, 2019), the times of restitution (Acts 3:12) (Wansbrough, 2019), and the fulness of time (Ephesians 1:10) (Wansbrough, 2019).

Be mindful of the things that are joined together in time and should not be separated: the Word of God and the Spirit of God, Christ and Salvation, Faith and Works. Be mindful of not joining together what God has separated: Heaven and Hell, Baptism and Regeneration, Natural Heredity and Spiritual Heredity, The Church and the Kingdom.

Fundamental to proving that PTPM is the true and only correct view of end time prophecy is understanding the nature/metaphysics of the Bible. The Bible is summarized in the first words of Genesis. In the beginning, God created the heaven and the earth (Genesis 1:1) (Wansbrough, 2019). The entire Bible rests on these words. Two concepts bring meaning to these words. "God created the heaven and the earth" means that God exists independently of everything and anything. He has no beginning and no end. When He was ready, He created earth, and He intervened in His creation. God does whenever

He likes for whatever reason He determines. This concept is ontological participation (Wright IV & Martin, 2019, pp. 135-140).

The second concept is relationality. Creative beings exist in relation to each other. It is an essential structure of created beings. Creative beings act by communicating their actions. (Wright IV & Martin, 2019, pp. 140-147). There is nothing else besides God and His Creation. The only things that exist are God and His Creation.

The Bible is the instructive story of who God is and how He interacts with His creation. God created everything when He created Creation. He created time, and He is outside of time. He created beings and redemption before humankind sinned. God created everything that is.

SECTION II: Evidence of PTPM

Section II provides evidence that the Pretribulation Premillennium (PTPM) view is the proper interpretation of the eschatological events. The evidence is in God's Plan of Redemption with His fiats of the Passover, the Covenants and the Feasts (Chapter 4), the Old Testament prophecies (Chapter 5), the history of positions of the Early Christian Fathers (Chapter 6), the New Testament Writings (Chapter 7), the writings of the Greek Scholars beginning in the nineteenth century until the present (Chapter 8), and the Book of Revelation (Chapter 9).

God frequently declared His Plan of Redemption. It can be seen in His marriage ceremony, in His eight covenants with Israel, in His instructions for the Passover service, the Haggadah, in the Seven Annual Feasts of Israel, and the Bar and Bat Mitzvah process and celebration described throughout this document, summarized in Figure 37.

Chapter 4: Plan of Redemption תכנית הגאולה takhenitt hageulah) {את}

In God's Plan of Redemption, there are fundamental truths about the Bible that can be reflected in groups of three, like a tripod that has three legs. God is present as the Father, the Son, and the Holy Spirit. Man is made in God's image as body, spirit, and soul. The Soul of man is made of intellect, emotions, and will. Marriage is the union of husband, wife, and God. The process of Salvation is regeneration, sanctification, and glorification, see Figure 36.

Fundament Truth Triads

Tripod	1	2	3
Plane/Tripod	Point A/Leg 1	Point B/Leg 2	Point C/Leg 3
God	Father	Son	Holy Spirit
Revelation	Hebraicness	Menorah	4 Covenant Types
Man in God's image	Body	Spirit	Soul
Soul	Intellect	Emotions	Will
Marriage	Husband	Wife	God
Salvation	Regeneration	Sanctification	Glorification

Figure 34: Fundamental Truths Triads

God revealed His Plan of Redemption in at least ten manifestations of His Word. First, the Plan of Redemption through the marriage covenant with Adam and Eve. Second, in His covenants with Israel. Third, in His annual Passover celebration, the Haggadah. Fourth, in His fiats concerning annual feats conducted through the priest, and fifth, in the male and female mitzvahs He continued to proclaim His plan. Sixth, His plan is in the prophetic messages of the prophets; seventh, through the early Church fathers; eighth, through Jesus and the New Testament writers; ninth, through the Greek scholars; and tenth, through the book of Revelation.

The first five manifestations can be expressed metaphorically and literally as drinking from four cups representing the types of covenants, and the last five manifestations as the PTPM chronological sequence of the redemption plan. All ten manifestations illustrate that God's Plan of Redemption is consistent and unchangeable throughout the whole counsel of God. Figure 38 shows the parallelism in nine of the manifestations. Figure 44 shows the alignment with the Bar and Bat Mitzvah's.

Evidence of PTPM

Marriage (Adam & Eve)	Covenants (Moses)	Passover Haggadah (Abraham)	Feasts (Priest)	Prophets & Early Church Fathers	NT Writers & Greek Scholars	Revelation (John)
Cup of (Sanctification)	Blood (Service)	Cup of (Praise)	[1]Passover (Crucifixion)	Rapture	Birth	Rapture
			Unleavened Bread (Burial)	Tribulation	Crucifixion	Tribulation
Cup of (Beginning)	Salt (Friendship)	Cup of (Elijah)	First Fruits (Resurrection)	Parousia	Resurrection	Parousia
			[2]Harvest (Pentecost)	Millennium	Pentecost (Paraclete)	Millennium
Cup of (Redemption)	Sandal (Inheritance)	Cup of (Redemption)	[3]Trumpets (Rapture)	Armageddon	Rapture	Armageddon
Cup of (Praise)	Betrothal (Acceptance)	Cup of (Acceptance)	Day of Atonement (Parousia)	Great White Throne Judgment	Parousia	Great White Throne Judgment
			Tabernacle (The Kingdom Age)	New Heaven & New Earth	New Heaven & New Earth	New Heaven & New Earth

*(4) Whole = all, entire
(7) Complete = end, finished

[1] First Coming
[2] Birth of the Church
[3] 2nd Coming

Figure 35: Evidence of PTPM

Marriage Evidence ראיה (re'aya)

The marriage relationship is central to everything God proclaims. God is love. He loves humankind and wants love in return. God's desire is expressed in the marriage covenant. God sketches himself in the first sixty-five books of the Bible (Klein & Spears, 2009). That is why it is said that each book of the Bible is about Jesus (Nation, 2022).

God instituted the marriage covenant with Adam and Eve. There are two types of marriage: metaphorical and literal. Metaphorical marriage symbolism is found in Hosea, Isaiah, Jeremiah, and Ezekiel. Hosea symbolizes the relationship of God as the bridegroom and Israel as His bride. "Help meet" and "ruler" are the roles God gave to Adam and Eve. They define the covenant relationship between husband and wife. God identifies himself as the Bridegroom throughout Scripture (Benson, 2003, Introduction).

Literal examples of marriage are seen in the story of Adam and Eve, Abraham and Sarah, Isaac and Rebekah, and Ruth, in Hebrew marriages, and in the Torah (Ibid, p77-83).

Torah takes the form of the Hebrew marriage contract called the Ketubah. The contract is established between two families during the meal they have together. They bring in a scribe or a rabbi to write the document, which has five parts. First is a combined family history of the bride and groom. It contains detailed the combined history of the two families. Second, it is the personal and family history of the bride. Third, it is the personal and family history of the groom. Fourth, it contains the responsibilities of the groom. Last, it must be witnessed with seven signatures (Klein & Spears, 2009, p. 7).

The five books of the Torah are about the marriage contract. Genesis combines the family histories of the bride and groom. Exodus identifies the personal and family history of the Bible. Leviticus is the history of God's family. Numbers is the story of God's love affair with His people in the wilderness. Deuteronomy specifies the responsibilities that the bride and groom must fulfill. Finally, the seven signatures are identified throughout the Bible. Adam and Noah are the two witnesses. Abraham is the father of the groom. Jacob is the father of the bride. Moses is the scribe who wrote down the Torah as directed by God. David is the bride, God's beloved, and Yeshua is the groom, representing salvation (Klein et al., 2012, p. 8). Figure 38 shows the relationship between the Ketubah and the Torah.

The Torah Marriage Contract

Marriage Contract	Torah
Family Histories (Combined)	**Genesis:** combined family history of the Bride and Groom
Bride's Personal & Family History	**Exodus:** Personal and family history of the Bible
Groom's Personal & Family History	**Leviticus:** history of God's "family," Levites
Story & Anecdotes of Meeting of Bride & Groom	**Numbers:** story of God's love affair with His people in the wilderness
Responsibilities of Bride and Groom	**Deuteronomy:** specifies the responsibilities that the Bride and Groom must fulfill
Seven Signatures	**Adam and Noah:** two witnesses **Abraham:** father of the groom **Jacob:** father of the bride **Moses:** the scribe, he wrote down the Torah. **David:** the bride, God's beloved **Yeshua:** the groom, representing salvation.

Figure 36: Torah Marriage Contract

The redemptive story of Jesus is a story of the marriage covenant. The Bible begins with the marriage contract in the Torah and ends with the betrothal in the book of Revelation.

Ancient Hebrew Marriage, A Process

Ancient Hebrew marriages were part of a "process" of commitment and covenant that often took years. It involved both sides of the family, friends, and the rest of the community. Matches were "arranged" even years in advance, but not legally binding. The potential bride and groom often initiated the interest, but parents had to approve. The potential bride had final approval. When there was general agreement, the prospective groom and his father leaked to the bride's family that a formal proposal was coming.

The first official move was for the bridegroom and his father to go to the bride's house with a betrothal cup, wine, and the bride price in a pouch and knock on the door. The bride's father opened the door only if the bride approved the marriage. This meant that the marriage could take place if the terms could be worked out. In Revelation 3:20 (Wansbrough, 2019) when Yeshua said He stood at the door knocking, He was asking if there is a willingness to have a deep, loving relationship with Him. Opening the door is accepting Him as our redeemer and forming a lasting relationship with Him. We have to grow into a loving relationship of marriage, which is Yeshua's invitation. It requires a commitment to walk in a loving relationship with Him. (Klein & Spears, 2016, pp. 52-54). Once the initial agreement to be married was worked out, often through intense discussion, a formal contract was written.

As the fathers worked out the details of the wedding, they would eat dinner together with her family. In Revelation 3:20 (Wansbrough, 2019) the Scripture invites you to "sup with Him." Throughout the negotiation process the two families would also drink three of four betrothal cups at well-established points. These cups represented the progressive relationships leading to the marriage and signified exactly where the betrothal parties were in their negotiations. Each cup identified the commitment of the families. The process would break down if no person participated mentally and spiritually in the steps.

The first cup was the Cup of Sanctification equating to a servant covenant between the two families. The second cup was the Cup of Bargaining, consumed by the bride and groom and their fathers only, covenanting to become eternal friends. The third cup was the Cup of Redemption or the Cup of Inheritance, signifying the shared inheritance of the marriage partners. Only the bride and groom drank it at the end of the meal to symbolize their exclusive commitment to each other and their growing level of intimacy. This officially sealed the marriage agreement. Usually, a scribe wrote the formal agreement called a *Ketubah*. At that point, the young men of the families would go into the street blowing rams' horn trumpets (shofars) to announce the signing of the marriage contract. Although the ceremony nor the consummation had occurred, they were officially married.

Until the final consummation of the marriage, only the bride could back out with just a statement. The groom would only be able to back out with a writ of divorce on extremely limited grounds. Torah's unconditional requirement that a man and a woman may live together only with the formal sanction of *Kiddushin*. The *Kiddushin* process may take years, and the bride could end the process without justification at any time (Klein & Spears, 2016, pp. 51-73)

Before the Torah was given, if a man and a woman wanted to marry, the man would bring her into his home and have intercourse privately without the testimony of witnesses, and she would become his wife (Simon, 1999).

Potential bride and groom usually initiate first. When all signals are gone, the prospective groom and his father let it leak out to the bride's family.

The Details: The groom brings his father to the bride's house, carrying a betrothal cup, wine, and the anticipated bride prize, the mohar, in a pouch. The father knocks on the door, establishing the covenant: The bride's father looks at the bride, "Should he open the door?" The bride nodes yes and the door is opened: "We can have a marriage if we can work out the terms." There are intense negotiations by the families because marriage is an agreement between two families: a progress identified by four covenant relationships (four cups of wine milestones). The families eat dinner together in the bride's father's home. The Cup of Sanctification is equated to a servant (blood) covenant, consumed by every member of the families as soon as the door is closed, in an agreement for families to serve each other. The Cup of Beginning negotiates the terms. Upon agreement, the family enters the covenant of friendship. The Cup of Inheritance or Redemption is consumed at the end of the meal by the bride and groom only. Officially, the marriage agreement scribe came in and wrote the marriage covenant. The groom's father pays the mohar to the bride's father as a purchase and a gift.

It was customary for a good father to give the whole or a generous portion of the mohar to his daughter. A father who appropriated the whole mohar for himself was considered unkind and harsh. The bride received the *mohar,* and the *mattan* that the groom presented to her. A rich father sometimes gave his daughter a field or other landed property as well as female slaves. Young men of the family went to the streets and blew the horn announcing the marriage contract. They are legally married. Anyone who cohabits with her is guilty of capital punishment. If the husband wishes to separate, he must have a divorce.

The groom goes away and prepares a place for him and his bride in his father's house and returns at an unexpected time. Time passes. When it is time for *nisu'in* (nuptials), the *kiddushin* and the *nisu'in* are accomplished through" *chupah.*" The rabbi holds a cup of wine and recites the *hagafen,* a standard blessing on the wine; that is followed by the *kiddushin* blessing, thanking God for sanctifying them with the mitzvah of betrothal. The bride and groom sip from the cup, the fourth Cup of Praise. The groom places the wedding band on the bride's right index finger while saying in Hebrew and the vernacular, "with this ring, you are consecrated to me according to the law of Moses and Israel." If the bride wants to give a ring, she must do it later, not under the *chupah.* First came a combined family history of the bride and groom, which included detailed family trees and anecdote. Second there was the personal and family history of the bride, with a detailed family tree and anecdotes. Third came a personal and family history of the groom, also with a family tree and anecdotes. Fourth came the story of how the bride and groom met, with related anecdotes. Fifth came a concluding section detailing both the bride's and the groom's responsibilities before and after the wedding (Klein & Spears, 2016).

The Wedding Party

As the groom finalized his preparations, he would let word slip out that the wedding day was near. Meanwhile, the bride's family and friends would begin preparing for a feast. The bride and bridesmaids would buy enough oil to keep their lamps lit for at least two weeks. The bridesmaids' job was to watch for the groom's arrival. When they saw him coming for his bride, their lamps would show the way. They were also expected to warn the bride, a small but especially important job (Matthew 25:1–13) (Wansbrough, 2019). The groom could come anytime between six pm and midnight on the second through the fourth day of the week. When he did so, he had to see his bride's welcoming light in her window. If she let it burn out, he would take that as a sign that she had either changed her mind or simply did not care anymore, and he would turn away and leave her in darkness.

The Mikveh (Bath)

Hours before dawn, the groom and his men would leave the bride with her bridesmaids. Her friends would lead her to the mikveh, a ceremonial bath where she would be bathed in running ("living") water. As in every Hebrew *mikveh*, or baptism, she would bow forward into the oncoming stream, facing the source as an act of love and submission to God, the source of all life. The ancient Hebrews knew where life came from. Therefore, by honoring God through the *mikveh*, by submitting and subjugating their lives to Him, they brought into play another major symbol of covenant and purification.

Modern Hebrew Marriage The Torah is the five parts of the ancient *Kiddushin*.

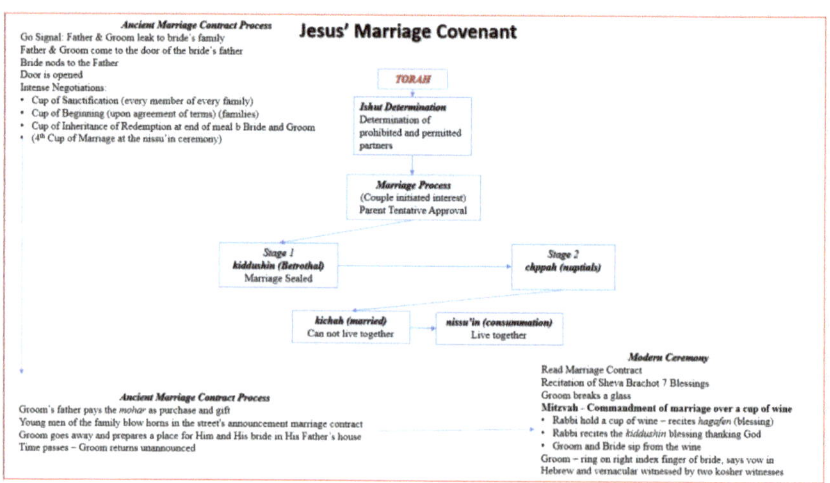

Figure 37: Marriage Covenant

Marriage Covenant: Jews, Church & Eschatology		
Jewish Marriage Covenant	*Jesus Marriage Covenant*	*Revelation*
Parents select the couple	God's elect	
Groom left his father's house to travel to the home of the bride	Jesus left His father's house and came to earth	
Marriage contract (betrothal)	This sup is the new covenant 1 Cor 11:25	
Sealed with purchase and gift to bride's father	Crucifixion and Resurrection Jesus paid for his bride 1 Cor 6:19-20	
Bride set aside	Eph 5:25; 1 Cor 1:2; 6-11 Heb 10:10; 12:12	
Groom departs to his father's house to prepare a place	John 14:2-3;	
Groom back for bride, unannounced	Rapture – Jesus came for his bride	Marriage super of the lamb
Back to Father's house		Eternity with the Father

Figure 38: Marriage Covenant, Jesus, and Revelation

Missler compares the Jewish wedding to a pattern of Jesus as the bridegroom and the marriage supper of the Lamb. The Jewish wedding begins with the betrothal, the engagement. The engagement is sealed with a contract, the marriage contract *ketubah*. After payment was made of the purchase price for the bride, the bride and bridegroom are set apart and sanctified (Isaiah 61:10; Judges 14:10-11; Jeremiah 2:32; Isaiah 49:18; Psalm 45:8-15) (Wansbrough, 2019). The bridegroom departs to his father's house to prepare an additional room for his bride. The bride prepares for his return, but she does not know when. The wedding, the *chuppah,* is a surprise gathering (Jeremiah 7:34; 16:9, 25:10; Psalm 45:8-15; Matthew 25:1-13) (Wansbrough, 2019). A marriage supper lasts for seven days (Judges 14:12; Matthew 9:15; 22:11-14; John 2:1) (Wansbrough, 2019).

Fulfillment of the marriage by Jesus begins with establishing a covenant. The cup is the new covenant in His blood (1 Corinthians 11:25) (Wansbrough, 2019). The purchase price means ownership (1 Corinthians 6:19-20). The bride is set apart ((Ephesian 5:25-27; 1 Corinthians 11:1:2; 6:11; Hebrews 10:10; 13:12) (Wansbrough, 2019). There is a reminder of the covenant during communion (1 Corinthians 11:25-26) (Wansbrough, 2019). After the bridegroom returns from his father's house, he is escorted to gather his bride (1 Thessalonians 4:16-17) (Wansbrough, 2019). (Missler, The Book of Revelation: Commentary Handbook, 2020)

Evidence in Covenants ראיה (re'aya)

God's Plan of Redemption can be considered a covenant that is an overview of the covenants. However, there are usually eight covenants that are considered God's covenants established with and through His people. God's covenants proclaim the path of fulfillment of God's plans for the redemption of believers.

Eight Covenants

The Bible identifies eight different covenants God made with and through His people, Israel. Covenants are conditional and unconditional. Unconditional covenants are fulfilled regardless of Israel's obedience or disobedience. Unconditional covenants will bring curses if not obeyed.

The Edenic Covenant

The Edenic Covenant is a time of innocence. God made a conditional covenant with Adam in the Garden of Eden. The Edenic Covenant defined man's responsibility toward creation and God's directive regarding the tree of the knowledge of good and evil. Adam was to obey God's command to not eat from the tree of the knowledge of good and evil, and he would have eternal life. He rebelled and was punished with death and condemnation for himself and all mankind (Genesis 1:26-30; 2:16-17) (Wansbrough, 2019).

The Adamic Covenant

The unconditional covenant of grace, the Adamic Covenant, included the curses pronounced against mankind for the sin of Adam and Eve, as well as God's provision for that sin (Genesis 3:16-19) (Wansbrough, 2019). God promises that a savior will come who will crush the head of the serpent (i.e., Satan). In the covenant of grace, people are saved by God's grace through faith in Christ alone because of Christ's perfect keeping of the law and his perfect and complete sacrifice once and for all for sin (Genesis 3:15) (Wansbrough, 2019).

Noahic Covenant

The Noahic Covenant was an unconditional covenant between God and Noah specifically and humanity generally. After the Flood, God promised humanity that He would never again destroy all life on earth with a Flood. God gave the rainbow as the sign of the covenant, a promise that the entire earth would never again flood (Genesis 9) (Wansbrough, 2019).

Abrahamic Covenant

In the unconditional Abrahamic Covenant, God promised many things to Abraham. He personally promised that He would make Abraham's name great (Genesis 12:2) (Wansbrough, 2019)., that Abraham would have numerous physical descendants (Genesis 13:16) (Wansbrough, 2019)., and that he would be the father of a multitude of nations (Genesis 17:4-5) (Wansbrough, 2019). God also made promises regarding a nation called Israel. Another provision in the Abrahamic Covenant is that the families of the world will be blessed through the physical line of Abraham (Genesis 12:3; 22:18) (Wansbrough, 2019). The Messiah would come from the line of Abraham.

The Land Covenant

The unconditional Land Covenant, or Palestinian Covenant, gave more detail about the land in the Abrahamic Covenant. According to the terms of this covenant, if the people disobeyed, God would cause them to be scattered around the world, but He would eventually restore the nation (Deuteronomy 30:3-5) (Wansbrough, 2019). When the nation is restored, they will obey Him perfectly (v.8), and God will cause them to prosper (v.9).

The Mosaic Covenant

The Mosaic Covenant was a conditional covenant that either brought God's direct blessing for obedience or God's direct cursing for disobedience upon the nation of Israel. Part of the Mosaic Covenant was the Ten Commandments (Exodus 20) (Wansbrough, 2019) and the rest of the Law, which contained over six hundred commands, approximately three hundred positive and three hundred negative. The history books Joshua through Esther detail how Israel succeeded at obeying the Law or how Israel failed. Deuteronomy 11:26-28 (Wansbrough, 2019) details the blessing and cursing.

The Davidic Covenant

The unconditional Davidic Covenant amplifies the "seed" aspect of the Abrahamic Covenant. God promised that David's lineage would last forever and that his kingdom would never pass away permanently

(2 Samuel 7:8-16) (Wansbrough, 2019). The Davidic throne has not always been in place. There will be a time, however, when Jesus from the line of David will again sit on the throne and rule as king (Luke 1:32-33) (Wansbrough, 2019).

Renewed Covenant (New Covenant)

The Renewed Covenant (New Covenant) is a covenant made first with the nation of Israel and with all humankind. In the Renewed Covenant, God promises to forgive sin, and there will be universal knowledge of the Lord. Jesus Christ came to fulfill the Law of Moses and renew the covenant between God and His people. Under the Renewed Covenant, Jews and Gentiles can be free from the penalty of the Law. Sinners can receive salvation as a gift (Ephesians 2:8-9) (Wansbrough, 2019)..

A biblical covenant (*b'rit*) is an everlasting agreement establishing a relationship between God and His chosen people. God made eight covenants with Israel: Edenic, Adamic, Noahic, Abrahamic, Land, Mosaic, Davidic, and the New Covenants (Figure 16). Although the eighth covenant is often referred to as new, it is not new. It is a renewal of God's covenant. The Hebrew name for the New Testament is *B'rit Hadashah* means renewed covenant. Covenants are not contracts.

Fruchtenbaum described the covenants in his paper "The Eight Covenants of the Bible." (Fruchtenbaum, Israel and the Messianic Kingdom, 2005). God's Edenic covenant with Adam (Genesis 1:28-30; 2:15-17; Hosea 6:7) (Wansbrough, 2019). established the dispensation of Innocence and works in the paradise of the Garden of Eden. Life was promised to Adam and his posterity on condition of his obedience (Westminister Divines, 2021). This was the age of Conscience (Ibid, pp.9-11).

God's covenant with Adam (Genesis 3:14-19) is the judgment on Adam for all humanity because Adam and Eve disobeyed God by eating from the knowledge of good and evil and because Satan deceived them. This was the age of conscience and the promise of redemption through Christ (Ibid, pp. 7-9).

God's covenant with Noah for all humankind (Genesis 9:1-17) was to repopulate the earth after God destroyed it with a flood. God preserved the earth. This was the age of Human government (Ibid, pp. 11-13).

The covenant with Abraham (Genesis 12:1-3; 12:7; 13:14-17; 15:1-21; 17:1-21) (Wansbrough, 2019). was for the whole Jewish nation, not for all of humanity. There were provisions for Abraham, Israel, and Gentiles. This was the promise that all nations would be blessed through Abraham and his seed. This was the age of promise (Ibid, pp.13-17).

The Scriptural account of the Mosaic covenant extends from Exodus 30:1 to Deuteronomy 28:68 (Wansbrough, 2019). The key provision was the Law of Moses, containing six-hundred-thirteen commandments. The observance of the Saturday Sabbath was the seal of the covenant. This was the age of the Law (Ibid, pp. 17-30).

The Land covenant was made between God and Israel, like the Mosaic covenant (Deuteronomy 29:1-30:20) (Wansbrough, 2019), it promised land that was fulfilled during the Millennium period (Ibid, pp. 30-32). This will be the Millennium Age.

The Davidic covenant is the promise that the Messiah will come through the lineage of David. The covenant was confirmed in 2 Samuel 23:15; Psalm 89:1-52; Isaiah 9:24-25; Jeremiah 23:5-6; 30:8-9, 33:14-17, 19-26; Ezekiel 37:24-25; Hosea 3:4-5; Amos 9:11; Luke 1:30-35, 68-70; and Acts 15:14-17) (Wansbrough, 2019). This will be the everlasting age of eternity (Ibid, 32-34).

The final covenant is noted as the New Covenant but is more accurately stated as the renewed Covenant (Genesis 1:28-30; 2:15-17; Hosea 6:7) (Wansbrough, 2019). It promises the regeneration of the entire nation of Israel, forgiveness of sin, permanent indwelling of the Holy Spirit, the Sanctuary will be rebuilt, and the Law of the Messiah will supersede the Law of Moses. This ushers in the age of Grace leading to the Eternal State (Ibid, 34-40).

Looking at a broader and deeper message in the covenants, Klein and Spears group the covenants into four types, Blood, Salt, Sandal, and Betrothal, to unveil a profound interpretation of the covenants.

Types of the Covenants

These four phases represent a progressive pattern of a deepening relationship with God through Service, Friendship, Inheritance, and finally, Marriage. (Klein & Spears, 2016, p. 40).

Service Covenant (Blood)

The Adamic and Noahic covenants form the Blood Covenant group. When Adam and Eve were in paradise in the Garden of Eden, they disobeyed God by eating from the tree of the knowledge of good and evil. Before their fall, they were in the most intimate relationship of marriage with God. Their disobedience was a writ of divorce. The covenants God established thereafter were His redemption back to a state of marriage. God laid a path back to the most intimate relationship that Adam and Eve lost, the marriage covenant.

The first step in the pathway of restoration is to serve God in obedience by the sacrifice of blood. The Adamic and Noahic covenants are grouped together as this Blood Covenant. The covenant involves the shedding of blood. The blood of an animal was shed to make clothes for Adam and Eve. Likewise, Noah built an altar and took one of each kind of ritually clean animal and bird and burnt them whole as a blood sacrifice (Genesis 8:20-22) (Wansbrough, 2019) (Ibid, pp40-41).

Friendship Covenant (Salt)

The Salt Covenant, also called the covenant of hospitality and the covenant of friendship, is breaking salted bread. Abraham welcomed the Lord near the trees of Mamre when he went to greet three men standing nearby. Abraham bowed to them and welcomed them to his tent. He was told that Sarah, who was barren, would have a baby this time next year. Abraham was modeling the salt covenant and entered a friendship relationship with God. Now Abraham was a servant and friend of the Lord (Ibid, pp. 41-43).

Inheritance Covenant (Sandal)

The Sandal Covenant was also called the covenant of inheritance. In ancient times, Hebrews used old sandals to mark, weighted down with rocks placed at the boundaries of their property. Moving boundaries was forbidden by divine fiat (Deuteronomy 19:14). Eventually, sandals became a symbol of the concept of inheritance. The concept was illustrated in the book of Ruth. The guardian-redeemer, who had the inherited obligation to marry Ruth after her husband died, relinquished his obligation to marry Ruth by tossing his sandal to Boaz. Boaz accepted the inheritance and married Ruth (Ruth 4:8) (Wansbrough, 2019) (Ibid, pp. 43-44).

Marriage Covenant

The Betrothal or Marriage Covenant (Ibid, pp. 51-54) was the most intimate and sacred relationship with God. The development of servanthood, friendship, and inheritance culminates in marriage. The ultimate relationship with Jesus is to serve Him, to befriend Him, to be inherited in his family, and to marry Him. Humankind began in the Garden of Eden with the relationship of the marriage of Adam, Eve, and God. Adam and Eve tried to forfeit the relationship by sinning. Jesus restored the relationship through His redemptive sacrifice. Eternity begins with the betrothal of the marriage covenant with all believers. "Marriage is the ultimate fulfillment of all covenants" (Klein & Spears, 2016, p. 48).

Growth in a personal relationship with God begins with serving the Lord through the Blood Sacrifice of the declaration of faith and being obedient to His Word. Growing closer to the Lord is entering His invitation to the Salt covenant by making time to draw close to Him, Revering Him, listening to Him telling us what's on His heart, rejoicing at His counsel, trusting His corrections, celebrating, not competing with Him, having a pure heart, speaking with grace and loving Him unwaveringly, intimately, and sacrificially (Zhang, 2018).

Salvation is a personal inheritance. Scripture says, "Work out your salvation with fear and trembling" (Philippians 2:12) (Wansbrough, 2019). Growing in a personal inheritance relationship means earnestly and urgently working with the Holy Spirit to develop the fruit of the spirit (Galatians 5:22-23) (Wansbrough, 2019)and accepting Jesus's invitation to deeper intimacy (Revelation 3:20) (Wansbrough, 2019).

This covenant framework for biblical interpretation is Covenant Theology. It recognizes that the redemptive history revealed in Scripture is described in the covenants. This theology of the covenants was understood in ancient biblical times but not discussed often in Biblical literature. The eschatology of dispensationalism that arose almost nineteen hundred years later purported a different interpretation (Packer, 2012).

The Chronology of the Covenants

The chronological order in which God gave the covenants identifies His redemptive process for humankind. Judgments of the Tribulation are because of violations of the Noahic Covenant. The judgments come because humanity violated the everlasting covenant, which is the name given to the Noahic Covenant in Genesis 9:16. See Isaiah 24:5-6. The Davidic covenant establishes that the coming of the Messiah will usher in the period of grace. Thereafter the Land covenant assures land for Israel ruled with Christ. The land covenant is fulfilled in eternity. The Land covenant precedes the David covenant which is the eternal rule of Christ over all believers. Therefore, the order of the covenants shows the chronology of Christ's coming, the Tribulation, the Millennium period, and the Eternal rule of Christ. This identifies the chronology of the coming of Christ, followed by the Millennium, and ending with the Eternal state. The covenants do not describe the events of the Second Coming of Christ period, Armageddon, or the Great White Throne Judgment. However, the seven annual feasts of Israel shed additional light on the eschatological events.

Figure 39 identifies God's covenants. Figure 40 identifies the covenants chronologically.

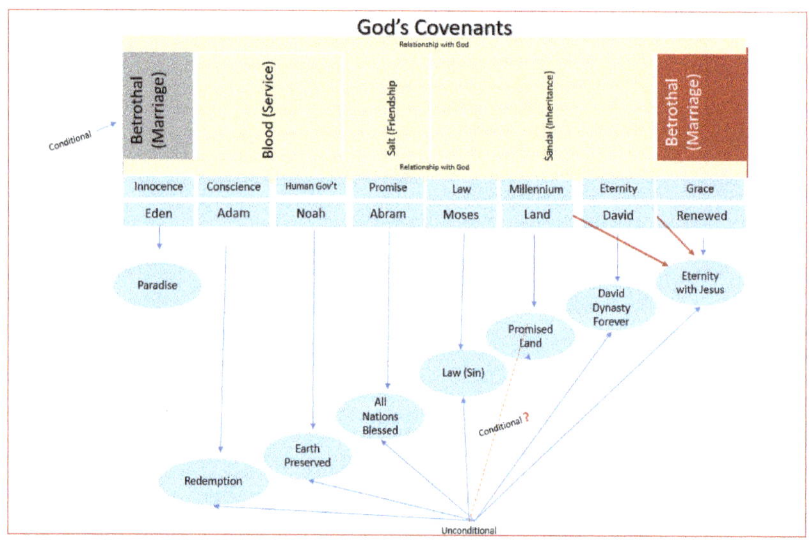

Figure 39: God's Covenants

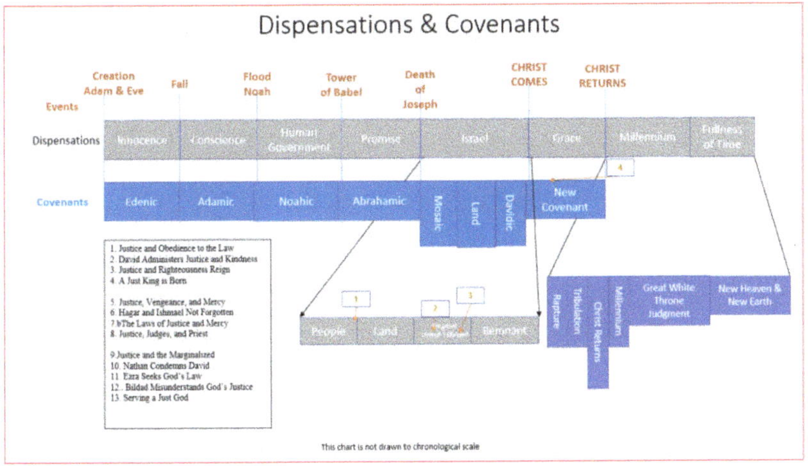

Figure 40: Chronology of Covenants and Dispensations

Evidence in the Passover Seder

The Passover Seder, meaning order, celebrates the Jewish holiday that commemorates the story of Exodus when Moses led the Israelites out of Egypt. It is a Jewish ritual dinner based on the *Haggadah,* a book of instructions, prayers, blessings, and stories that lays out the proper order for the ritual. The Seder sheds light on God's promise of redemption through the true Passover lamb, Jesus.

The order and procedures of the Seder are celebrated with four cups of wine that relate to the developing relationship with God in His Plan of Redemption. The Cup of Praise is relating the stage of serving Jesus in love. The Cup of Redemption relates the stage of loving friendship with Jesus. The Cup of Elijah relates the stage of family love, and inheritance with Jesus. In Jewish tradition Elijah is appointed to bring in the era of the Messiah of perfect happiness when all people are free. The Cup of Acceptance relates the intimacy of love in marriage to Jesus, the ultimate expression of love. Remember Figure repeated below. Notice that the Haggadah, column three, is the PTPM sequence in Revelation, column seven (Robinson, Passover Haggadah).

Evidence of PTPM

Marriage (Adam & Eve)	Covenants (Moses)	Passover Haggadah (Abraham)	Feasts (Priest)	Prophets & Early Church Fathers	NT Writers & Greek Scholars	Revelation (John)
Cup of (Sanctification)	Blood (Service)	Cup of (Praise)	[1]Passover (Crucifixion)	Rapture	Birth	Rapture
			Unleavened Bread (Burial)	Tribulation	Crucifixion	Tribulation
Cup of (Beginning)	Salt (Friendship)	Cup of (Elijah)	First Fruits (Resurrection)	Parousia	Resurrection	Parousia
			[2]Harvest (Pentecost)	Millennium	Pentecost (Paraclete)	Millennium
Cup of (Redemption)	Sandal (Inheritance)	Cup of (Redemption)	[3]Trumpets (Rapture)	Armageddon	Rapture	Armageddon
Cup of (Praise)	Betrothal (Acceptance)	Cup of (Acceptance)	Day of Atonement (Parousia)	Great White Throne Judgment	Parousia	Great White Throne Judgment
			Tabernacle (The Kingdom Age)	New Heaven & New Earth	New Heaven & New Earth	New Heaven & New Earth

*(4) Whole = all, entire
(7) Complete = end, finished

[1] First Coming
[2] Birth of the Church
[3] 2nd Coming

Evidence in the Seven Feasts of Israel

Levitt identifies the events of PTPM in the Seven Annual Feasts of Israel, summarized in Figures 43 and 44 (Levitt, The Seven Feasts of Israel, 1979). These figures provide information on the names of the feasts. Column one identifies the name of the English translation of the Hebrew name followed by the Hebrew spelling in block letters and its pronunciation. Sometimes, there will be more than one Hebrew spelling in block letters with the pronunciation. Column two provides the month, day, duration of the festival, the time of year, and sometimes a note about the season of the feast. The month is based on the two-hundred-eighty-day Hebrew calendar. Columns three through five prove the generic meaning and significance, the Jewish meaning, and the fulfillment in Christ. The final two columns provide notes on to Jewish ceremony and the related Christian ceremony when applicable. Christians do not observe the feasts and festivals.

Feast/Scripture	Month/Day (28-day Lunar)[8]	Meaning/Significance			Celebration	
		Generic	Jewish	Fulfillment	Jewish	Christian
1. Passover[1] פסח *Pesach* Lev 23:5	Nisan (1, 14 at even) (8 days) (Spring (Almond tree blooms at the end of winter)	Salvation Deliverance from Slavery (Exodus 12:5)	Delivery from the terrible night of the 10th plague (Matthew 25:27) (John 1:29)	Delivery from slavery to sin[7] *Crucifixion*	Haggadah Offering of the first fruits of the barley harvest	Communion
2. Unleavened Bread[2] מצה matsa Lev 23:6	Nisan (1,15 the next night) (7 days)	Thanksgiving for God's provisions	A holy walk with the Lord, the unleavened bread of life	*Burial*	Breaking, burying and resurrecting unleavened bread	N/A
3. First Fruits[3] הפירות הראשונים haperott harishonim הפרי הראשון haperi harishonn Lev 23:10-11	Nisan (Sunday following Unleavened Bread) (7 days)	Acknowledge the fertility of the land God gave them	Thanksgiving for spring harvest	*Resurrection*	A sheaf of the first fruits of the harvest is waved before the Lord.	N/A
4. Feast of the Harvest[4] Pentecost (paraclete) (Summer Harvest) חג הקציר khag haqatsir Feast of Weeks (Shavuot (weeks)) חג השבועות khag hashavu'ott Lev 23:15-16	Sivan (50 days after First Fruits)	Thanksgiving for harvest	Thanksgiving for summer harvest	*Paraclete* Recognize the gift of the Holy Spirit (paraclete) (First fruits gather by Jesus)	Offering of the fruits of the wheat harvest	N/A

Figure 41: Seven Annual Feast of Israel (1 of 2)

Feast/Scripture	Month/Day (28-day Lunar)[8]	Meaning/Fulfillment			Celebration	
		General	Jewish	Christ	Jewish	Christian
5. Trumpets[6] חצוצרות khatsotserott Lev 23:24 Rosh Hashanah (Year of Jubilee) Lev 24:8-10	Tishri (7,1)	Calling God's people to repentance	Ten days of repentance with the blowing of the shofar	*Rapture* 1 Thess. 4:16-17. 1 Cor. 15:51-52	Priest stood on the southwestern parapet of the Temple and blew the trumpet for the field workers to come into the Temple	N/A
6. Day of Atonement[6] יום כיפור yom qipur Lev 23:27 Yom Kippur	Tishri (7,10)	Day of confession	Confession for himself and the people	*2nd Coming (Parousia)*	Offering made by fire; Priest enter the Holy of Holies	N/A
7. Tabernacle[7] המשכן hamisheqann משכן mishqan Lev 23:34	Tishri (7,15)	Kingdom Worship (7 days)	The Lord's shelter in the Kingdom age	*Kingdom Age*	Build a shelter outside homes and worship in them, Offering of the fruits of the olive and grape harvest	N/A

[6] Day of Atonement, the most holy day
[7] Tabernacles
[8] Moon changes every day; Day begins at sundown = moonrise; (Gen.1:5 "And the evening and the morning were the first day.
[8] Christians do not celebrate these feasts, but they are prophetic typifying the 1st and 2nd coming of Christ. These feast show how Jesus fulfilled the meanings of the Jewish feasts.

Figure 42: Seven Annual Feast of Israel (2 of 2)

Arranging these feasts on a Jewish Calendar in Figure 41 shows that the first three feasts in the first year of Nisan represent the first coming of Christ. The birth of the Church occurs at Pentecost. The last three feasts represent the second coming of Christ. Column identifies the PTPM events of the Rapture, the Second Coming, and the Eternal State in chronological order.

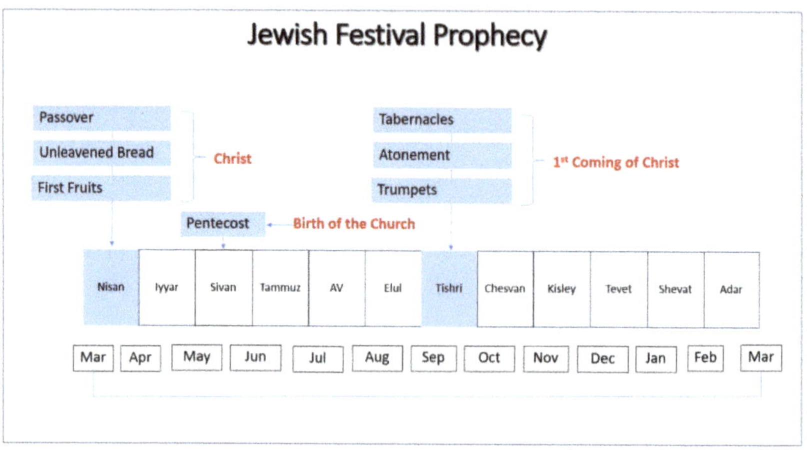

Figure 43: Prophecy in Jewish Festivals

PASSOVER

[5] On the fourteenth day of the first month, at event is the LORD's Passover.

FEAST OF THE UNLEAVEN BREAD

[6] And on the fifteenth day of the same month is the feast of unleavened bread unto the Lord: seven days ye must eat unleavened bread.

[7] In the first day ye shall have a holy convocation: ye shall do no servile work therein.

[8] But ye shall offer an offering made by fire unto the LORD seven days: in the seventh day is a holy convocation: ye shall do no servile work therein.

[9] And the LORD spake unto Moses, saying,

FIRST FRUITS

[10] Speak unto the children of Israel, and say unto them, When ye become into the land which I give unto you, and shall reap the harvest thereof, then ye shall bring a sheaf of the firstfruits of your harvest unto the priest:

[11] And he shall wave the sheaf before the Lord, to be accepted for you: on the morrow after the sabbath the priest shall wave it.

[12] And ye shall offer that day when ye wave the sheaf and the lamb without blemish of the first year for a burnt offering unto the LORD.

¹³ And the meat offering thereof shall be two-tenth deals of fine flour mingled with oil, an offering made by fire unto the LORD for a sweet savor: and the drink offering thereof shall be of wine, the fourth part of a Hin.

¹⁴ And ye shall eat neither bread, nor parched corn, nor green ears, until the selfsame day that ye have brought an offering unto your God: it shall be a statute forever throughout your generations in all your dwellings.

FEAST OF HARVEST (PENTECOST)

¹⁵ And ye shall count unto you from the morrow after the sabbath, from the day that ye brought the sheaf of the wave offering; seven sabbaths shall be complete:

¹⁶ Even unto the morrow after the seventh sabbath shall ye number fifty days; and ye shall offer a new meat offering unto the Lord.

¹⁷ Ye shall bring out of your habitations two wave loaves of two tenth deals; they shall be of fine flour; they shall be baken with leaven; they are the first fruits unto the Lord.

¹⁸ And ye shall offer with the bread seven lambs without blemish of the first year, and one young bullock, and two rams: they shall be for a burnt offering unto the LORD, with their meat offering, and their drink offerings, even an offering made by fire, of a sweet savor unto the LORD.

¹⁹ Then ye shall sacrifice one kid of the goats for a sin offering and two lambs of the first year for a sacrifice of peace offerings.

²⁰ And the priest shall wave them with the bread of the first fruits for a wave offering before the LORD, with the two lambs: they shall be holy to the LORD for the priest.

²¹ And ye shall proclaim on the selfsame day, that it may be a holy convocation unto you: ye shall do no servile work therein: it shall be a statute forever in all your dwellings throughout your generations.

And when ye reap the harvest of your land, thou shalt not make clean riddance of the corners of thy field when thou reapest, neither shalt thou gather any gleaning of thy harvest: thou shalt leave them unto the poor, and to the stranger: I am the Lord your God.

And the LORD spake unto Moses, saying,

TRUMPETS

Speak unto the children of Israel, saying, In the seventh month, in the first day of the month, shall ye have a sabbath, a memorial of blowing of trumpets, a holy convocation.

Ye shall do no servile work therein: but ye shall offer an offering made by fire unto the LORD.

And the LORD spake unto Moses, saying,

ATONEMENT

Also, on the tenth day of this seventh month, there shall be a day of atonement: it shall be a holy convocation unto you, and ye shall afflict your souls and offer an offering made by fire unto the Lord.

And ye shall do no work in that same day: for it is a day of atonement, to make an atonement for you before the Lord your God.

For whatsoever soul it be that shall not be afflicted in that same day, he shall be cut off from among his people.

And whatsoever soul it is that doeth any work in that same day, the same soul will I destroy from among his people.

[31] Ye shall do no manner of work: it shall be a statute forever throughout your generations in all your dwellings.

[32] It shall be unto you a sabbath of rest, and ye shall afflict your souls: in the ninth day of the month at even, from even unto even, shall ye celebrate your sabbath.

[33] And the LORD spake unto Moses, saying,

[34] Speak unto the children of Israel, saying, the fifteenth day of this seventh month shall be the feast of tabernacles for seven days unto the LORD.

[35] On the first day shall be a holy convocation: ye shall do no servile work therein.

[36] Seven days ye shall offer an offering made by fire unto the LORD: on the eighth day shall be a holy convocation unto you, and ye shall offer an offering made by fire unto the LORD: it is a solemn assembly, and ye shall do no servile work therein.

37 These are the feasts of the LORD, which ye shall proclaim to be holy convocations, to offer an offering made by fire unto the LORD, a burnt offering, and a meat offering, a sacrifice, and drink offerings, everything upon his day:

38 Beside the sabbaths of the LORD, and beside your gifts, and besides all your vows, and besides all your freewill offerings, which ye give unto the LORD.

39 Also in the fifteenth day of the seventh month, when ye have gathered in the fruit of the land, ye shall keep a feast unto the LORD seven days: on the first day shall be a sabbath, and on the eighth day shall be a sabbath.

40 And ye shall take you on the first day the boughs of goodly trees, branches of palm trees, and the boughs of thick trees, and willows of the brook; and ye shall rejoice before the LORD your God seven days.

41 And ye shall keep it a feast unto the LORD seven days in the year. It shall be a statute forever in your generations: ye shall celebrate it in the seventh month.

TABERNACLES (BOOTHS)

42 Ye shall dwell in booths seven days; all that are Israelites born shall dwell in booths:

43 That your generations may know that I made the children of Israel to dwell in booths, when I brought them out of the land of Egypt: I am the Lord your God.

44 And Moses declared unto the children of Israel the feasts of the LORD.

Evidence in the Bar and Bat Mitzvahs

The Bar and Bat Mitzvahs refer to a ceremony and a status for a child who reaches the age of thirteen for the boy or twelve for the girl. The terms "bar' and "bat' are defined as the children of the commandment. The ages used to be reversed. The ceremony is a culmination of the development of a child into adulthood. The stages of development begin with instruction from the mother. From ages birth to five years old, the child symbolically sits on the mother's lap and receives instruction in the Torah. The child then transitions to the father, from age five through to at least eight years old. The child learns things outside the house, like a trade. The next stage of development from age eight to twelve or thirteen is the separation from the parents. The emerging adult learns the Word of God from the Priest. The ceremony of adulthood is a Bar Mitzvah for the young man or a Bat Mitzvah for the young woman (Dies, 2017). Figure 44 summarizes the Mitzvah celebration.

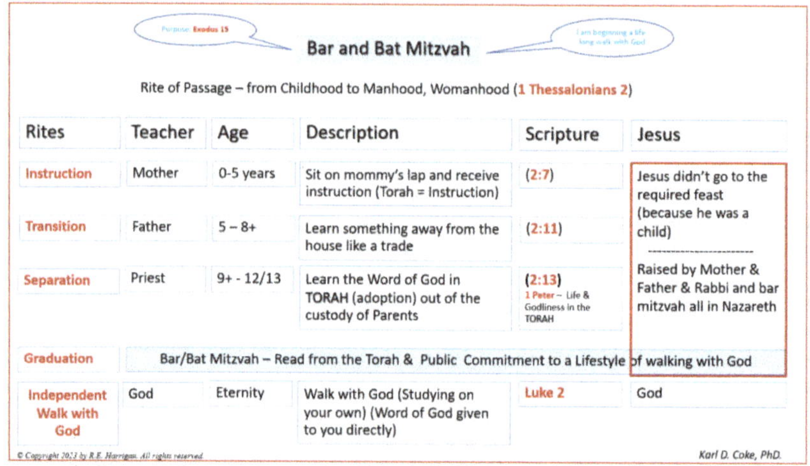

Rite of Passage – from Childhood to Manhood, Womanhood (1 Thessalonians 2)

Rites	Teacher	Age	Description	Scripture	Jesus
Instruction	Mother	0-5 years	Sit on mommy's lap and receive instruction (Torah = Instruction)	(2:7)	Jesus didn't go to the required feast (because he was a child)
Transition	Father	5 – 8+	Learn something away from the house like a trade	(2:11)	
Separation	Priest	9+ - 12/13	Learn the Word of God in TORAH (adoption) out of the custody of Parents	(2:13) 1 Peter – Life & Godliness in the TORAH	Raised by Mother & Father & Rabbi and bar mitzvah all in Nazareth
Graduation			Bar/Bat Mitzvah – Read from the Torah & Public Commitment to a Lifestyle of walking with God		
Independent Walk with God	God	Eternity	Walk with God (Studying on your own) (Word of God given to you directly)	Luke 2	God

    Karl D. Coke, PhD.

Figure 44: Bar and Bat Mitzvahs

Parallel of Redemption in the Birth of a Baby

God's Plan of Redemption is seen in the birth of a baby. Levitt collaborated with Margaret Matheson, an obstetrician who had delivered over ten thousand babies, to describe the birth of a baby from a biblical perspective. The Scriptures revealed that God's Plan of Redemption is seen in the physiological birth of a baby. Levitt asked Dr. Matheson to tell him in detail how a baby is made and how it grows. They discovered that the baby develops along the schedule of the seven feasts (Levitt, The Seven Feasts of Israel, 1979, pp. 21-28).

On the fourteenth day of the first month, the egg appears. On the fourteenth day of the first month was God's instruction for observing Passover (Leviticus 23:5) (Wansbrough, 2019).

Fertilization must occur within twenty-four hours, or the egg will pass on. Jews use the egg on the Passover table to symbolize new life. The egg represented was for Passover, and the idea of fertilization and planting the seed was for Unleavened Bread.

The fertilized egg travels down the tube at its own speed toward the uterus, taking two to six days before it implants. The Festival of First Fruits was the spring planting. The medical term for planting is implantation.

The embryo develops slowly until it becomes a fetus. It took fifty days for the baby to come to life. The baby was different from before (2 Corinthians 5:17) (Wansbrough, 2019). On the fiftieth day, the embryo becomes a human fetus. On the day of Pentecost, the unregenerated Israelites became new creatures.

At the beginning of the seventh month, the baby could discriminate sound. The baby's hearing was fully developed. The Feast of the Trumpet was the day of the awakening. The trump was sounded to announce the Lord descending from heaven.

Ten days into the seventh month, the fetal blood carries the mother's oxygen through the baby's system. The baby's blood changes in such a way that the baby can carry the oxygen it would obtain upon birth. The hemoglobin of the blood had to change from that of the fetus to that of a self-repirating and circulating human being. ("I have given you the blood for the remission of sin" (Leviticus 17:11) (Wansbrough, 2019). The Day of Atonement was the day of blood sacrifice.

On the fifteenth day of the seventh month, it is safe for delivery because the lungs are developed. The Feast of Tabernacles is the house of the Spirit. The Spirit is the air in the Bible. God blew breath into Adam to make him live. God breathed life into dry bones (Ezekiel 37:9) (Wansbrough, 2019). The believer will live once entering the kingdom.

The birth cycle is normally two hundred eighty days. Chanukah lies the right distance beyond the Feast of the Tabernacles to account for the actual birth of the baby in two hundred eighty days. Beyond the Kingdom is eternity with God. Chanukah took place in 165 BCE when the Temple was rededicated (Daniel 8:9-14) (Wansbrough, 2019). This shows that the Bible is not just poetry or mythology; it is the living Word of God (Levitt, The Seven Feasts of Israel, 1979, p. 29) Figures 47 and 48 summarize how the birth of a baby relates to God's Plan of Redemption.

Birth of the King

The cosmos shows the birth of the King. He was born on earth as the Lamb of God. Although His life was quickly snuffed out, His grand purpose was accomplished. He will still come as King when the Feast of Tabernacles arrives for all believers. Our Lord has progressed through Passover, Unleavened Bread, First Fruits, and Pentecost. He will be seen in the Feast of Trumpets, and He will return on the day of Atonement. The completion of His birth cycle will be seen when He is crowned as the rightful King of this Creation when the final Tabernacle is reached (Levitt, The Seven Feasts of Israel, 1979, pp. 28-30).

God's Plan of Redemption
Development of a Baby

Feasts (Priest)	Christian Fulfillment	Development Of a Baby	Revelation (John)
Passover (Crucifixion)	New Life (Egg)	Ovulation	Rapture
Unleavened Bread (Burial)	The Seed	Fertilization	Tribulation
First Fruits (Resurrection)	Resurrection	Implantation	Parousia
Harvest (Pentecost)	Harvest	New Creature (Fetus)	Millennium
Trumpets (Rapture)	Rapture	Hearing	Armageddon
Day of Atonement (Parousia)	Redemption	Blood (Hemoglobin A)	Great White Throne Judgment
Tabernacle (The Kingdom Age)	Kingdom	Lungs	New Heaven & New Earth
Chanukah)	Eternity	Eternal Life	

Zola Levitt, The Seven Feasts of Israel

Figure 45: Development of a Baby

280-Day Cycle	Physiological Birth Process	Comparison to the Seven Annual Feasts
14th Day of the 1st Month	The egg appears. *Ovulation*	PASSOVER: God's original instruction or the Passover celebration was on the 14th day of the first month. Leviticus 23:5. *Crucifixion, New Life*
15th Day of the 1st Month	Fertilization must occur within twenty-four hours, or the egg will pass on. *Fertilization*	UNLEAVENED BREAD: next day Leviticus 23:6 *Burial, New Life*
2 to 6 days in the 1st Month	The fertilized egg travels down the tube at its own speed toward the uterus, taking two to six days to implant. The implant is the moment when the fertilized egg arrives safely in the uterus and begins growth into a human being. *Implantation*	FIRST FRUITS: anytime in one to seven days Leviticus 23:10-11 *Resurrection*
50 days after implantation	A slowly developing embryo goes through stages until it becomes an actual fetus. It took 50 days. *New Creature (Fetus)*	FEAST OF THE HARVEST: Leviticus 23:15-16 *Paraclete, Harvest*
1st Day of the 7th Month	At the beginning of the seventh month the baby's hearing was fully developed. *Hearing*	TRUMPETS: Leviticus 23:24 *Rapture [PTPM Rapture]*
10th day of the 7th Month	Ten days into the seventh month important changes happened in the blood. The fetal blood changed in such a way to carry the mother's oxygen through the baby's system. *Blood (Hemoglobin A)*	DAY OF ATONEMENT: Leviticus 23:27 *2nd Coming*, **Redemption [PTP 2nd Coming]**
15th day of the 7th Month	The fifteenth day of development was the beginning of the safe delivery period because the two healthy lungs are formed, beginning of life available outside the womb. Lungs	TABERNACLE: Leviticus 23:34 *Kingdom Age, Kingdom [PTPM Millennium]*
Distance between Tabernacles to birth of the baby	Eternal Life	CHANUKAH, Festival of Dedication Daniel 8:9-14 (at the rededication of the Temple) *Eternity [PTPM Eternity]*

Figure 46: The Physiological Birth of a Child in Scriptures Adapted from Zola Levitt's The Seven Feasts of Israel.

Chapter 5: Evidence in Prophecies ראיות בנבואות (reayott banevuott) {השמים}

God charged the prophets who spoke of end times to present elements of the eschaton throughout the history of the Bible. Each of the selected prophets of the prophesied a part of the end-time story. Daniel prophesied the most comprehensive view of eschatology in the Old Testament. Daniel's prophecy parallels John's prophecy in Revelation in the New Testament. The eschatological prophecies are discussed in chronological order of when they prophets prophesied. Figure 47 shows the chronology of the prophets in the Old Testament.

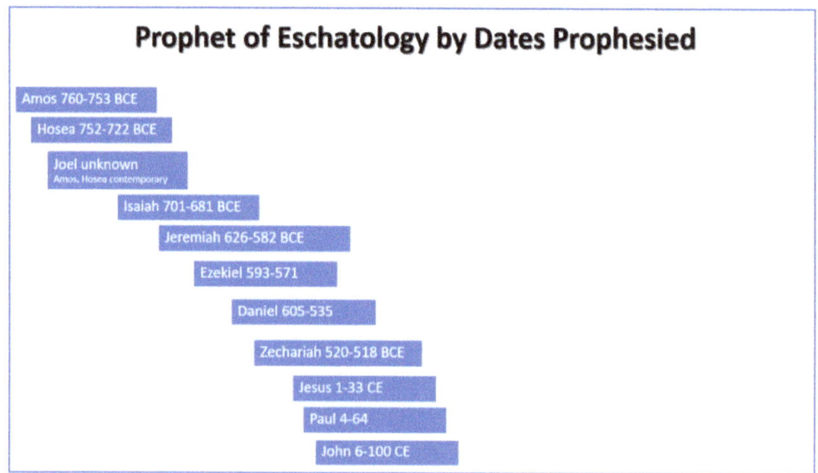

Figure 47: Prophets of Eschatology by Dates Prophesied

A definitive way to explore eschatological interpretation is to see what the Old Testament prophets prophesied in scripture. This is accomplished through comparing scripture against scripture throughout the whole counsel of God (Acts 20:27) (Wansbrough, 2019). It will verify the authenticity of the interpretation. Any perspective must be consistent with what is validated throughout the Bible. There are no contradictions in the Bible, so the scriptures will confirm each other. If they do not, the interpretations are faulty, or they are not based on Scripture. Looking at the parts of eschatology presented by the prophets will show consistency.

This chapter is the cornerstone of the proof of the thesis because Scripture is God's truth. The analysis will proceed with the order in which the apocalyptic books were written. The dates of the writing of other books are either unknown or difficult to state with certainty. However, Figures 51 and 52 show the chronology in the order they appear with standard translations and commonly accepted dates. Scripture from the books selected is highlighted in green (Life Amplified Bible, 1991).

Jewish eschatology began when God promised Abraham that through him, all nations would be blessed. His people will prosper, and God will be in their presence, watching over them. His descendants would receive a land flowing with milk and Honey (Exodus 3:8) (Wansbrough, 2019).

The chronology of the writings of the canon in figures 51 and 52 highlights in green the dates of the prophets who prophesied about end-time events. Not all dates are known, and not all prophets who testified about the end time are included. The books that contain Old and New Testament prophecies are highlighted in green.

Canonical Order of the OT Books of the Bible

Genesis: 1450-1410 B.C.	2 Chronicles: 430 B.C.	Daniel: 535 B.C.
Exodus: 1450-1410 B.C	Ezra: 450 B.C.	Hosea: 715 B.C.
Leviticus: 1450-1410 B.C	Nehemiah: 445-432 B.C.	Joel: 835-796 B.C.
Numbers: 1450-1410 B.C	Esther: 483-471 B.C.	Amos: 760-750 B.C.
Deuteronomy: 1450-1410 B.C	Job: 2000-1800 B.C.	Obadiah: 853-841 B.C./627-586 B.C.
Joshua: ?	Psalms: 1440-586 B.C.	Jonah: 785-760 B.C.
Judges: ?	Proverbs: 950 B.C.	Micah: 742-687 B.C.
Ruth: 1375-1050 B.C.	Ecclesiastes: 935 B.C.	Nahum: 663-612 B.C.
1 Samuel: ?	Song of Solomon: 950 B.C.	Habakkuk: 612-588 B.C.
2 Samuel: 930 B.C.	Isaiah: 700-680 B.C.	Zephaniah: 640-621 B.C.
1 Kings: ?	Jeremiah: 627-586 B.C.	Haggai: 520 B.C.
2 Kings: ?	Lamentations: 586 B.C.	Zechariah: 520-480 B.C.
1 Chronicles: 430 B.C.	Ezekiel: 570 B.C.	Malachi: 430 B.C.

(Source: Life Application Bible, 1991)

Figure 48: Canonical of OT Canonical Writings

Chronological Order of the NT Books of the Bible

Matthew: A.D. 60-65
Mark: A.D. 55-65
Luke: A.D. 60
John: A.D. 85-90
Acts: A.D. 63-70
Romans: A.D. 57
1 Corinthians: A.D. 55
2 Corinthians: A.D. 55-57
Galatians: A.D. 49
Ephesians: A.D. 60
Philippians: A.D. 61
Colossians: A.D. 60
1 Thessalonians: A.D. 51
2 Thessalonians: A.D. 51-52

1 Timothy: A.D. 64
2 Timothy: A.D. 66/67
Titus: A.D. 64
Philemon: A.D. 60
Hebrews: A.D. 70 (prior to Jerusalem's destruction in A.D. 70)
James: A.D. 49 (prior to the Jerusalem council of A.D. 50)
1 Peter: A.D. 62-64
2 Peter: A.D. 67
1 John: A.D. 85-90
2 John: A.D. 90
3 John: A.D. 90
Jude: A.D. 65
Revelation: A.D. 95

(Source: Life Application Bible, 1991)

Figure 49: Chronological Order of the NT Books of the Bible

Joel

As early as the eighth century BCE, the prophet Joel spoke of the "Day of the Lord." He said it was nearby. It would be a day of darkness and gloom, a day of clouds and blackness. (Joel 2:1-2) (Wansbrough, 2019). This figure of speech was used throughout the Old and New Testaments. In modern times this metaphor can loosely mean the Lord will have His day. He will intervene to fulfill his purpose. Joel said there would be wonders on Earth during that time. The sun will turn to darkness and the moon to blood. It will be a great and dreadful day. It refers to the time around the second coming of Christ, which Joel may not have understood.

Joel also prophesied the relative timing of the second coming of Christ. In Joel, the term describes two separate times of judgment. Joel 1 (Wansbrough, 2019) prophecy is the impending judgment of God's people. In Joel 2:31 and 3:14-16 (Wansbrough, 2019) he prophesied that the sun and moon would be blackened out before the Day of the Lord, the judgment in the eschaton.

Joel may not have known what he was prophesying in Joel 2 (Wansbrough, 2019). According to 1 Peter 1:10-12 (Wansbrough, 2019), the Old Testament did not always understand the meaning of their prophecies.

This look at Joel illustrates why it is important to interpret Scripture in the context of the whole Bible: the historical time and the culture gleamed from the original Hebrew language and literary style.

Amos

Amos also prophesied about the Day of the Lord. He said the Day of the Lord is darkness, not light. It will be very dark, and there will be no light in it. The Lord will despise people's feast days and solemn assemblies. He will not accept burn offerings nor listen to their songs. Judgment will run down as waters and righteous as a mighty stream (Amos 5:18-6:14) (Wansbrough, 2019).

Although Amos did not prophesy when the Day of the Lord was coming, the time refers to the Second Coming of Christ after the seven-year tribulation period, which is unknown (Revelation 10:11-15) (Wansbrough, 2019). This establishes the fact that the Lord will return to judgment.

Isaiah

Isaiah prophesied from 739-681 BCE to Judah, the Southern Kingdom of Israel. Judah turned from the Lord instead of serving God with humility and loving their neighbors. Judah offered meaningless sacrifices to God and treated their neighbors unjustly. Isaiah prophesied a message of condemnation (Isaiah 1-39) (Wansbrough, 2019) and salvation (Isaiah 40-66) (Wansbrough, 2019). He proclaimed the good news of forgiveness of sins and restoration through Jesus Christ (Isaiah 61:1) (Wansbrough, 2019). He prophesied Jesus' sacrificial death (Isaiah 52:13-53:12) (Wansbrough, 2019), and His return to claim His own (Isaiah 60:2-3) (Wansbrough, 2019) (Chuck Swindoll). Isaiah described the one-thousand-year Millennium period in more detail than other prophets.

20 There shall be no more thence an infant of days, nor an old man that hath not filled his days: for the child shall die a hundred years old; but the sinner being a hundred years old shall be accursed.

21 And they shall build houses, and inhabit them, and they shall plant vineyards, and eat the fruit of them.

²² They shall not build, and another inhabit; they shall not plant, and another eat: for as the days of a tree are the days of my people, and mine elect shall long enjoy the work of their hands.

²³ They shall not labour in vain, nor bring forth for trouble; for they are the seed of the blessed of the LORD, and their offspring with them.

²⁴ And it shall come to pass, that before they call, I will answer; and while they are yet speaking, I will hear.

*²⁵ The wolf and the lamb shall feed together, and the lion shall eat straw like the bullock: and dust shall be the serpent's meat. They shall not hurt nor destroy all my holy mountain, saith the LORD (**Isaiah 65:20-25**) (Wansbrough, 2019).*

Isaiah's description points to the Millennium period in Revelation.

⁴ And I saw thrones, and they sat upon them, and judgment was given unto them: and I saw the souls of them that were beheaded for the witness of Jesus, and for the word of God, and which had not worshipped the beast, neither his image, neither had received his mark upon their foreheads, or in their hands; and they lived and reigned with Christ a thousand years.

⁵ But the rest of the dead did not live again until the thousand years were finished. This is the first resurrection.

*⁶ Blessed and holy is he that hath part in the first resurrection: on such the second death hath no power, but they shall be priests of God and of Christ and shall reign with him a thousand years (**Revelation 20:4-6**) (Wansbrough, 2019).*

Almost seven-hundred-seventy-five years before John authored the book of revelation, Isaiah prophesied the Millennium period. This prophecy is a clear indication that there will be a Millennium period that will last one thousand years. Almost fifty years later, Daniel provided the most detailed prophecy of end times in the Old Testament in his seventh-week week vision,

Jeremiah

Jeremiah stated that the "day of days is coming" when the intentions God has for Israel and Judah will come to pass (Jeremiah 33:14) (Wansbrough, 2019). Jeremiah had a great eschatological vision. This prophecy will be realized when "a Branch of righteousness" reigns and ushers in "judgment and righteousness."

(Henebury, 2019). This is a reference to the second coming and the millennium period. Jeremiah alludes to divine covenants. The covenant with David is found in Jeremiah 33:17, 21-22 (Wansbrough, 2019) and 26. The Noahic covenant seems to be in Jeremiah 33:20 and 26 (Wansbrough, 2019). The Abrahamic covenant is in Jeremiah 33:22. (Wansbrough, 2019). The New Covenant, the Messiah, appears to be a merging of the separate covenants. Therefore, a single passage identifies five of God's unilateral covenants brought together in an eschatology setting (Henebury, 2019).

Verses 14 to 26 are the most sustained challenge to amillennial eschatology in the Bible (Henebury, 2019 [Routledge, 2012])

Ezekiel

Ezekiel presents his eschatological prophecies in his visions and predictions for the nation of Israel. Ezekiel was a priest who was exiled in Babylon. His vision of dry bones is about the restoration of Israel is familiar to most readers. Ezekiel had six visions in twenty-two years in captivity. They were grouped into three themes: judgment in Israel, Judgment on the nations, and future blessings for Israel. Eschatologically significant is his vision of God on His throne (Ezekiel 1) (Wansbrough, 2019). Ezekiel saw a divine throne chariot of the heavens. Just as human kings had chariots, deities were envisioned as chariots crossing the heavens, inspecting their domains, and exercising authority over them. Wheels supported the chariot thrones with four creatures identified as cherubim (Ezekiel 10:4) (Wansbrough, 2019). Each creature had four faces: a human, a lion, an eagle, and an ox (Ezekiel 1:10) (Wansbrough, 2019). A wheel was next to each cherub. Each wheel had a circle within it. The rim of each wheel had eyes. Daniel described the same blazing throne with wheels (Daniel 7:9) (Wansbrough, 2019).

English translations of Ezekiel's vision break down where the prophets describe "eyes" on the rims of the wheel. Ancient astronomical texts commonly describe shining stars as "eyes." Many translators fail to consider the astronomical context depicted by the four faces. This is another example of translations considering their culture and times instead of that of Hebrews.

Jewish captives might have believed that Yahweh had abandoned them forever. Babylonians could assume that their gods had defeated Yahweh and were ruling heaven and earth unopposed. Ezekiel was sending the message that God is still seated in his chariot throne at the center of his domain, which is the entire cosmos (Geuser, 2022). This vision of the four beasts and God on the throne is like Revelation 4: John was taken up to heaven. He was shown God on the throne, and four beasts were around the throne having similar descriptions.

Daniel

Daniel was exiled in the first wave of Babylonian deportation of Hebrews in 586 BCE. While in captivity in the year of Darius, son of Xerxes, Daniel was praying about the Scripture in Jeremiah that said captivity would last seventy years. He was pleading for God to forgive his people and bring them back to Jerusalem. While he was praying, the angel Gabriel came to Daniel to help him understand the prophecy. Gabriel explained the seventy weeks. The prophecy was divided into three parts: the first forty-nine years of restoration of Jerusalem, the next forty-four years before the Messiah would come, and the final seven years of tribulation at the eschaton. An end-time prophecy was described in his vision of the seventh week.

Certain terms should be understood when reading the Scripture in Daniel. The Day of the Lord is referring to the time when God will judge the world. It is mentioned several times in the Bible (Joel, Amos 5:15, First Colossians 1:8 &14, Second Colossians 1:14, Second Peter 3:12, and Revelation 16:14 (Wansbrough, 2019) to mention a few). God will intervene in history to complete His Plan of Redemption. It is painted as a time of destruction and darkness. Suffering and death. Scholars believe it will be during the time of Tribulation and will last for years. During the Tribulation, the Time of Jacob's Trouble will occur (Jeremiah 30:7) (Wansbrough, 2019). That time is when the Jews will be punished for rejecting Jesus as the Messiah. The Fulness of the Gentiles is when the full number will turn to Jesus, and God's blindness of the Jews will be removed. Only God knows that number (Romans 11:25-32) (Wansbrough, 2019). The Abomination of desolation is mentioned in Daniel and Matthew. Around 175 to 164

BC, King Antiochus IV Epiphanes erected an altar to the Greek god Zeus in the middle of the Israelite temple and sacrificed a pig. He wanted the Israelites to worship him. This caused the Maccabean Revolt (157-160 BCE) and resulted in a brief period of independence. A priest named Mattathias led the event. His followers became known as Maccabees. Abomination is a disgusting, despicable action. Dissolution means it results in destruction. Abomination of Desolation is the despicable act of placing an idol god on the sacred altar of the Jewish Temple and slaughtering a pig.

Daniel 12:11 (Wansbrough, 2019) in the Old Testament and Matthew 24:15 (Wansbrough, 2019), the abomination that maketh desolate, is an event that will happen again at the end of time. A future ruler will make a treaty with Israel. The treaty will be set up for seven years. Midway through that time, the ruler will put an end to the temple sacrifices and offerings and desecrate the Temple by placing an idol in the Holy of Holies. Desecration will continue until God's judgment.

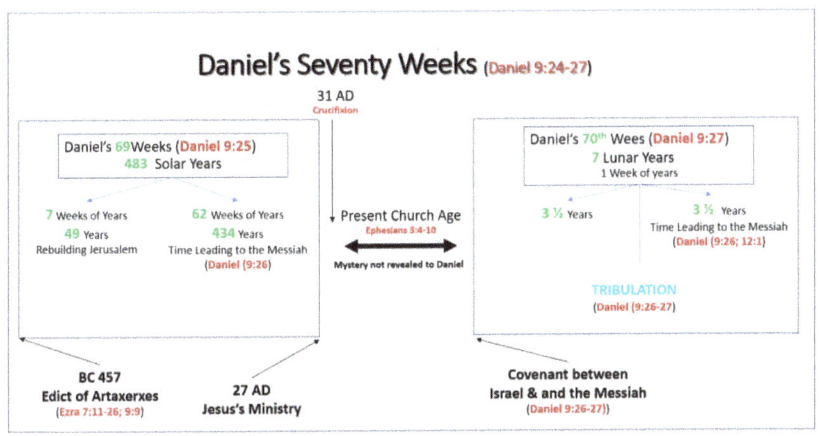

Figure 50: Daniel's Seventy Weeks

- The "seventy weeks" prophecy is one of the most significant and detailed Messianic prophecies of the Old Testament. It is found in **Daniel 9** (Wansbrough, 2019). The chapter begins with Daniel praying for Israel, acknowledging the nation's sins against God, and asking for God's mercy. As Daniel prayed, the angel Gabriel appeared to him and gave him a vision of Israel's future.

The Seventh week describes the Tribulation.

In Daniel's seventy weeks prophecy he described the PTPM chronological sequence of eschatological events. Daniel was a teenager when he was taken into captivity by the King Nebuchadnezzar of the Babylonian Empire. He was among the first to be deported and did not return to Judah. Being at least ninety years old when Cyrus, king of the Persian Empire, decreed the return. His vision of the seventy-week years described the eschatological sequence of the seven-year tribulation, the Parousia, and the one-thousand-year millennium rune (Daniel 9:24-27).

The vision was divided into three parts: first a one-week period, followed by sixty-two weeks, followed by a gap in time, concluding with a final week. The weeks were weeks-of-years totaled seventy weeks or four-hundred-ninety years. However, the gap between the six-ninety-year and the seventh-year is undetermined. That gap represents the time before Christ returns, which Scriptures say will not be known (reference).

The first seven years were the time to rebuild the temple. The next sixty-two weeks prophesied the success of the four world powers, from the Babylonians to the Medo-Persians to the Greeks led by Alexander the Great, concluding with the Roman Empire. The Western Roman Empire crumbled because of poor leadership, but the Eastern Empire, Byzantine, fell to the Ottoman Turks after one hundred years of fighting. (reference). After a prophetic gap of unknown years, the Tribulation will begin for a seven-year period; Christ will return at the end of the Tribulation to rule on earth in the Millennium period (see Figure 6).

Zechariah

In a series of visions, God told Zechariah that the Messiah would come and defeat the evil forces (5:11), the world would end (chapter 6), the temple would be restored, and the people would return to the temple. Chapters seven and eight are visions about the temple and the end of the world (8:10-14).

The Old Testament prophets foresaw elements of the plan of redemption, but they did not see the entire plan. In particular, they did not foresee the establishment of the Church and the Second Coming of Christ (Charles River Editors, 2020).

Old Testaments Chronological Prophecies of Eschatological Events

Date (BCE)	Prophet	Eschatological Even
835	**Joel**	Day of the Lord; Judgement of Israel (2nds half of the Tribulation) Judgement at the end of time (Great White Throne Judgment)
760-753	**Amos**	Da of the Lord (Tribulation) 2nd Coming
701-681	**Isaiah**	2nd coming Millennium
626-582	**Jeremiah**	Day of the Lord (Tribulation) God on the Throne Time of Jacob's trouble (2nd half of the Tribulation)
593-571	**Ezekiel**	Judgement on Judah (2nd half of the Tribulation) Four beast in heaven (God's throne)
605-535	**Daniel**	Abomination of Desolation The Great Tribulation / Day of the Lord (2nd half of the Tribulation) Time of Jacob's Trouble The prince that shall come & the two beasts. The number 666 2nd Coming Millennium
520-518	**Zachariah**	Eschaton Tribulation 2nd coming Millennium

Figure 51: OT Chronological Prophecies of Eschatological Events

Chapter 6: Evidence in Early Church Fathers עדויות של אבות הכנסייה הראשונים () {התנ"ך }

The evolution over the first seven centuries of early Christian eschatology from a pending eschaton to a systematic doctrine of "the last things" shows the beliefs of influential thinkers. Their thoughts cumulated in a common hope (Daley, 1991). That common hope illustrates that there was one unified understanding of eschatology. That mutual understanding persisted through the first two centuries. There is limited reflection on Christocentric and Pneumatic quality of Christian hope in the Patristic literature. However, the starting point is always the same. The Christian can look forward to the resurrection of the body, a merciful judgment, and a lasting, transforming, and fulfilling union with God. That is, until the influences of Plato, St. Augustine, Origen, Nietzsche, and Tertullian. Over the next fifteen centuries they confused the thought about eschatology based on God's Plan of Redemption. Figure 52 – 56 outlines the twelve periods of development of eschatological beliefs over the seven hundred years of the patristic age. Each figure identifies the eschatological period, the early Christian Fathers of the period, the underlining theme of their eschatological belief, and the contributions and insights made in that period (Daley, 1991, pp. 5-6).

The eschatology of Christianity in this period was focused on the imminent return of Christ in glory and the resurrection of the dead at the end of history by seven communities: the Jewish Christian sects, early biblical apocrypha, the apostolic father, the Odes of Solomon, the Shepherd of Hermas, and the Millenarian Christianity in Asia Minor. They recognized Jesus as the Messiah, but they continued to observe Jewish dietary and ritual practices. They cultivated good relations with their Jewish believers and promoted the adoption of Christology. Scholars were also influenced by the Gnostic conception of salvation and were interested in astrology and magic (Daley, 1991).

In the Jewish Christian sects, Eusebius attributed the doctrines of the imminent return of Christ and resurrection of the dead to the Jews converted by James. Epiphanius spoke of "Nazoreans" who followed the" Old Law" (Daley, 1991).

The first seven centuries of the early Christian church were known as the Patristic Age. Daley divides the history into nine periods, outlined in Figures 55-59. Each period is identified, followed by the list of the Early Christian Fathers, the theme of the person, and the eschatological implications. The history shows the development of eschatology in the seven centuries of the Patristic Age (Daley, 1991).

Patristic Age (1 of 5)

	Eschatological Period	Early Christian Fathers	Theme	Eschatology
1	Early Semitic Christianity and Christian apocalyptic	Clement Barnabas Ignatius of Antioch Polycarp	Visions of a new day	The history of Christian eschatology began in the apocalyptic hopes of salvation of the earliest Palestinian Christian communities. The Jewish Christian sects focused their hopes on the return of Christ in glory. The Ebionites, a Jewish Christian sect which viewed poverty as a blessing, maintained a materialistic view of the coming kingdom of glory (millennium) that will last a thousand years (According to Jerome best known for translating most of the Bible into Latin).
2	The Apologists	Aristides Justin Tatian Athenagoras Theophilus of Antioch	Making history intelligible	Central place to the Christian hope in a bodily resurrection. Often mingled eschatological expectations of apocalyptic Judaeo-Christianity with mythical and philosophical speculation on rewards and punishments.
3	Gnostic Crisis (150-200)	Irenaeus Hippolytus Epiphanius	Regaining the light	Gnosticism was a type of elitist religious thought present in Jewish and philosophical pagan circles and a wide range of Christian circles.

Figure 52: Patristic Age (1 of 5)

Patristic Age (2 of 5)

	Eschatological Period	Early Christian Fathers	Theme	Eschatology
4	In the West (200-250)	Tertullian Mimulus Felix Hippolytus Cyprian	Senectus Mundi	Apology gives way to controversial theology: replaced by bitter attacks on classical paganism, on Jewish and Judeo-Christian teachings, and on the occult speculations of the Gnostics. A spirit of cultural criticism and a strong moral tone dominate most of persecution. Christian writers concerned themselves to reflect ordinary people's beliefs about the afterlife, and used popular expectations of future reward and punishment.
5	Alexandrian and Critics (185-300)	Origen	A school for souls and its critics	Clement draws on the intellectualist, anthropocentric speculations of Platonic and Stoic cosmology, and on the esoteric mythically couched revelations of the New Testament apocrypha and Gnostic documents.
6	Latin in the age of Nicaea (303-313)	Victorinus of Pettau Lactantius	Dawn of the final conflict	Christian interest in apocalyptic speculation was revied in the Latin Church. The circumstances that led to such hopes were urgent and almost universal.
7	Eastern in the age of Nicaea (325-400)	4th - century Syriac writers Mid- 4th-century Greek writers	Facing death is freedom	Sixty years after the Council of Nicaea (325) were dominated by controversy over the Trinity conception of God.

Figure 53: Patristic Age (2 of 5)

Patristic Age (3 of 5)

	Eschatological Period	Early Christian Fathers	Theme	Eschatology
8	Latin 4th Century	Firmicus Maternus Hilary of Poitiers Zeno of Verona Ambrose Jerome	Redemptio Totius Corports	The second half of the 4th century saw the rise of Latin theological literature that met the central issues of Christian faith and controversy with a sophistication unknow in the West since Tertullian. The language and the rhetorical style of this literature were Roman, but the intellectual impetus still came form the East.
9	Greek 5th Century	John Chrysostom Cyril of Alexandria Theodore of Mopsuestia Theodoret of Cyrus Hesychius of Jerusalem Ascetical writers 4th and 5th century Greek apocalyptic	Grace present and future	4th century was dominated by bitter debates over the Nicene definition of Jesus' consubstantiality with the Father. The period followed the Council of Constantinople in 381 became a period of Christological controversy. The controversy was about the relationship of divinity and humanity in Jesus. It preoccupied the intellectual and political energies of Eastern Christianity until the end of the 7th century. The early decades of the 5th century Greek theological thought was dominated by the contrast between the methods of exegesis and the types of Christological formulation identified with the Church's two chief intellectual centers, at Antioch and Alexandria.

Figure 54: Patristic Ages (3 of 5)

Patristic Age (4 of 5)

	Eschatological Period	Early Christian Fathers	Theme	Eschatology
10	Latin 5th Century	Gaudentius of Brescia Maximus of Turin Sulpicius Severus Hilarianus Tyconius Augustine Liber de Promissionibus' Salvian Marseilles Pope Leo the Great Peter Chrysologus	Signs of Church triumphant	During the last decade of the 4th century the pressure on the roman Empire of barbarian invasions began to cast anxiety over Christian writers, particularly the Latin West. This dark mode continued through most of the 5th century. This was in sharp contrast to Eusebius and the political engagement of Ambrose. As roman civilization seemed to be on the verge of distinction, Christians became more convinced that the end of human history was at hand.
11	Eastern after Chalcedon	Non-Hellenic works Greek apocalyptic works Oecumenius, Pseudo-Dionysius, Severus of Antioch, John of Caesaraea; Leontius of Byzantium, 6th century Origenism, Zachary of Mytilene, John "Philoponus," Cosmas "Indicopleustes," Andrew of Caesaraea, Eustratius, Romanos "the melodist," Maximus the confessor, John of Damascus	Apokatastasis and apocalyptic	Two centuries after the council of Chalcedon (451) was occupied with Christology. There was controversy over the relationship of divinity to humanity in Christ that broke out with renewed force after the Council of Chalcedon. Last thing remained, a marginal theme touching on homiletic and ascetical works, couched in the tradition terms of the bible and the creeds.

Figure 55: Patristic Age (4 of 5)

Patristic Age (5 of 5)

	Eschatological Period	Early Christian Fathers	Theme	Eschatology
12	West 6th Century	Julianus Pomerius Caesarius of Arles Primasius; Apringius Gregory the Great	The end of all flesh	The final period of Latin Patristic theology can be identified with the 6th century. It was a time of violence, social turmoil, and political unrest. The Latin world was gradually brought under control of migrating Germanic peoples.

Compiled from The Hope of the Early Church, Daley.

Figure 56: Patristic Age (5 of 5)

Highlights of Jewish History

Prior to the Early Church period, the history of the Jews can be traced back to the ancient age when God called Abraham to become the father of nations. In their history in the Old Testament, the Jews' origin began as nomads wandering towards the land that God promised Abraham. They became known as Hebrews who were enslaved in Egypt for over two hundred years. After Moses led them to freedom from Egyptian bondage, they eventually became a nation and were called Israelites. The Israelites became a nation and eventually were conquered by four world powers in succession, the Babylonians, the Greeks, the Medo-Persian, and the Romans. There was a brief period between the Testaments that they gained their freedom from during the Maccabean Revolt (Daley, 1991).

History of the Christian Church (Schaff, Periods of Church History)

There is general agreement to divide the history of Christianity into three principal parts: ancient, medieval, and modern. However, there has been confusion and difficulty about the further details of the history of the Christian Church. Accounts vary by denominational differences, especially since the sixteenth century. For instance, the Reformation is more important to the Protestant church than to the Roman Church and of almost no importance to the Greek church.

The various stages of the life of the church can be called periods or ages. The beginning of a new period can be called an epoch or stopping and starting point. A reasonable division of history can be divided into nine periods which spread over the three principal parts of Church history. Ancient Christianity from the birth of Christ to Gregory the

Great, medieval Christianity from Gregory 1 to the Reformation, and Modern Christianity from the Reformation to the present.

The three periods of Ancient Christianity within the patristic era are called the periods of the Apostles, the Martyrs, and the Christian Emperors and Patriarchs. The three periods of Medieval Christianity are called Missionary, Papal, and Catholicism Reformatory. The three periods of Modern Christianity are called Reformation, Revolution, and Revival.

Apostolic Christianity began with the life of Christ and extended through the end of the Apostolic Church, approximately one hundred years. This was the time of the divine-human groundwork of the Church.

Medieval Christianity covers almost one thousand years. Gregory the Great represented a critical division in the Church. It was the last of the church fathers and the development of absolute papacy, as well as the conversion of the barbarian tribes. With the accession of Constantine, the Christian Church became the official Church of the Roman Empire. Christianity rose from persecution to the prevailing religion of the government. The first ecumenical council of Nicaea was held in the middle of Constantine's reign. The distinctive character of the church of Asia and Africa shifted to Western Europe. It transitioned from the Graeco-Roman nationality to the Germanic, Celtic, and Slavonic races. That accompanied a shift from the culture of the ancient classic world to modern civilization. The work of this era was performed by the Latin church, which implemented a firm hierarchical constitution. This work resulted in the bishop of Rome. Three popes stood out during this era. Gregory I (Gregory the Great (590)) marks the rise of the absolute papacy. Gregory VII (Hildebrand (1049), the summit of the absolute papacy, and Boniface VIII (1294) the decline.

The Modern Christianity era occurred among nations of Europe and started around the seventeenth century in North America. There was a split between those Christians regions into two hostile parts, those remaining on the old path and those striking out a new one. The Eastern church withdrew from the stage of history and became almost stagnated, except for modern Russia and Greece. Modern church history is the age of Protestantism in conflict with Romanism. It is the age of religious liberty and independence conflicting with the principle of authority. It was, and it is a time of conflict with teaching personal Christianity against an objective and traditional church system.

The sixteenth century saw the evangelical renovation of the church and the papal counter-reform. This was the most fruitful and interesting period of church history, except for the apostolic age. The seventeenth century was the period of adherence to and defense of the Reformed confessions of faith, polemic confessionalism (a system of government that mixes government and politics), and stagnation. The eighteenth century began the overturning of traditional ideas and institutions that resulted in a revolution in the state and infidelity in the church. There was deism in England, atheism in France, and rationalism in Germany, representing various modern apostasy from the orthodox confession of faith. The ninth century saw the further development of negative and destructive tendencies and the revival of Christian faith and church life. North America presented an asylum for all the nations, churches, and sects of the Old World. Peacefully separating the temporal and the spiritual power. The twentieth century was characterized by an acceleration of the secularization of Western society. Currently, Western worldviews are the opposite of Eastern worldviews. The twenty-first century is characterized by the pursuit of church unity and resistance to persecution and secularization. Figure 57 summarizes the period of Church history.

Period of Church History

Period	Dates (CE)	Age	Description
Ancient Christianity Church History The Patristic Era Church of the Fathers			
1st	1-100	Apostles	From incarnation to death of Apostle John Life of Christ and the Apostolic church
2nd	100-311	Martyrs	From death of Apostle John to Constantine, the first Christian emperor Christianity under persecution in the Roman Empire
3rd	101-590	Christian Emperors and Patriarchs	From Constantine the Great to Pope Gregory I Christianity in Union with the Graeco-Roman Empire, and amidst the storms of the great migration of nations
Medieval Church History Church of the Popes			
4th	590-1049	Missionary	From Gregory I to Hildebrand, or Gregory VII Christianity planted among the Teutonic, Celtic, and Slavonic nations.
5th	1049-1294	The Papal	From Gregory VII to Boniface VIII The Church under the papal hierarchy, and the scholastic theology.
6th	1294-1517	Catholicism Reformatory	From Boniface VIII to Luther The decay of mediaeval Catholicism, and the preparatory movements for the Reformation.
Modern Church – Church of the Reformers			
7th	1517-1648	Reformation	From Luther to the Treaty of Westphalia The evangelical Reformation, and the Roman Catholic Reaction.
8th	1648-1790	Revolution	From the Treaty of Westphalia to the French Revolution The age of polemic orthodoxy and exclusive confessionalism, with reaction and progressive movements.
9th	1790-1880	Revival	From the French Revolution to the present time The spread of infidelity, and the revival of Christianity in Europe and America, with missionary efforts encircling the globe.

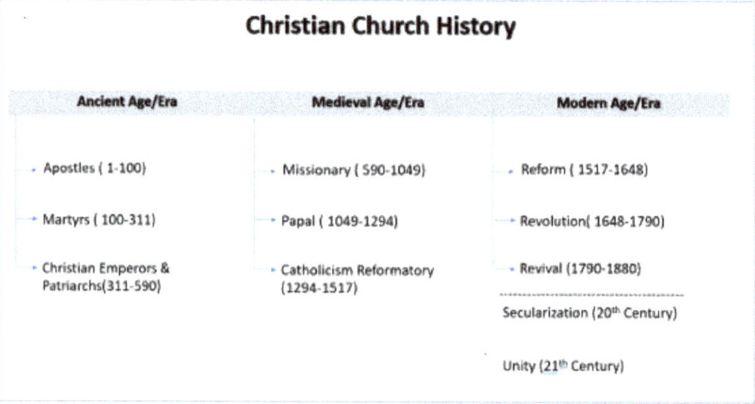

Christian Church History

Figure 57: Christian Church History

Noted Early Church Fathers

The key Early Church Fathers were Clement of Rome, Ignatius of Antioch, Papias, Polycarp, Tertullian, Origen, Eusebius, St. Jerome, and St. Augustine of Hippo.

Clement of Rome

Clement was a bishop holding office from 88-99 CE. He was the first apostolic Father of the Church and was one of the three chief Apostolic Father together with Polycarp and Ignatius of Antioch. He is known for his epistle to the church in Corinth.

Ignatius of Antioch

Ignatius of Antioch (c. 35- 108) was known from seven highly regarded letters that he wrote during a trip to Rome as a prisoner condemned to be executed for his beliefs. He wanted to counteract the teachings of the Judaizers, who did not accept the authority of the NT, and the *Docetists,* who held that Christ's sufferings and death were apparent but not real. His letters were cited as a source of knowledge of the Christian church at the beginning of the second century.

Ignatius represented the Christian religion in transition from its Jewish origins to its assimilation in the Greco-Roman world. He advocated a hierarchical structure of the church with emphasis on episcopal authority, insistence on the real humanity of Christ, and desire for martyrdom are subjects that have generated a discussion.

Papias (c. 60-130)

Papias (c. 60 – 130) Papias, bishop of Hierapolis in Phrygia (now in Turkey), and one of the Apostolic Fathers. His work Explanation of the Sayings of the Lord, although extant only in fragments, provides important apostolic oral source accounts of the history of primitive Christianity and of the origins of the Gospels. According to the 2nd-century theologian St. Irenaeus, Papias had known the Apostle John. The 4th-century church historian, Eusebius of Caesarea, critically records that Papias derived his material not only from St. John the Apostle but also from John the Presbyter, through whose influence he had infected early patristic theologians with a false Judeo-Greek millenarianism, the apocalyptic teaching that Christ would reappear to transform the world into a 1,000-year era of universal peace, and had implicated Christ in fantastic parables. Eusebius's antipathy to Papias consequently led him to severely edit the latter's text and preserve only short excerpts. Papias's interpretation of the Gospels was used by Eastern and Western Christian theologians down to the early 4th century.

Polycarp (c. 69-155)

Polycarp was martyred for his witness to Christ. According to the Martyrdom of Polycarp was bound and burned at the stake, then stabbed when the fire failed to consume his body. The sole surviving work attributed to him is the Epistle of Polycarp to the Philippians, a mosaic of references to the Greek Scriptures, which, along with an account of Martyrdom of Polycarp.

Tertullian (c. 155 or 160-220)

Tertullian lived around the time of Augustine. He named God as the Trinity the word is not in the Bible. Tertullian was a North African theologian polemicist who is a person engaged in controversial debate, and a moralist who, as the initiator of ecclesiastical Latin, was instrumental in shaping the vocabulary and thought of Western Christianity. He is one of the Latin apologists of the 2nd century. Knowledge of the life of Tertullian is based on documents written by men living more than a century after him and from obscure references in his own works.

Origen (c 185-254)

Origen is the father of Allegorical interpretation. He was the most important biblical scholar of the early Greek church. His Greatest work - *Hexapla*, was a synopsis of six versions of the Old Testament. His life's work was on the text of the Greek Old Testament and on the exposition of the whole Bible.

Eusebius (c. 260 – 339)

Eusebius (c. 260/265 - 339) wrote the *Ecclesiastical History,* a landmark in Christian historiography detailing church history that would have been lost. He was considered the father of Church History. He created extensive accounts of the first three centuries of Christianity. He preserved a wealth of early documentation that would have otherwise been lost. Eusebius' exhaustive research and painstaking concern for identifying original sources was unprecedented among ancient historians. Friends and associates in neighboring countries would visit him. He became the bishop Of Caesarea. Polemicists engaged in a controversial debate with him. He was an advisor to Constantine. Posterity suspected him of Arianism, an influential heresy denying the divinity of Christ, originating with the Alexandrian priest Arius c. 250-c.336). Arianism posited that the Father created the Son of God. Therefore, neither collateral with the Father nor of the same substance or essence used by the three persons of the Trinity in Christian theology. Eusebius made himself indispensable by his method of authorship, and careful excerpts from original sources saved his successors the painstaking labor of original research.

St. Jerome (c. 347-419/420)

St. Jerome was a far-reaching influence, particularly in the early Middle Ages. He was a Church Historian who gave us the word scholar, meaning from the skull. St Jerome translated the Septuagint into the Latin Vulgate. He was characteristically known as an anachronistic, old-fashioned, and belonged to a period other than that in which he existed. He was erudite, possessing vast knowledge and learning. St. Jerome studied the Classic, the ancient Greek and Latin literature and philosophy, the Bible, and Christian tradition. He was a humanist, which was a renaissance movement that turned from medieval scholars and returned to interest in ancient Greek and Roman thought. St. Jerome was a scholar rather than a deep thinker and a sound traditionalist rather than a speculative theologian. He had a turbulent career of scholarship and asceticism, participating in severe self-discipline and abstention from all forms of indulgence. Finally, he was known for his religious competence as an editor rather than as exegete.

St. Augustine of Hippo (c. 354-430)

Augustine of Hippo (c.354 -430) was the Latin father of the Church as the designation of the Roman Catholic Church. He was the most important figure in the development of Western Christianity, the bishop of Hippo (now Annaba, Algeria). As a renowned theologian and prolific writer, he was also a skilled preacher and rhetorician. St. Augustine's most important work was *The City of God*, a philosophical defense of Christianity that outlined a new way to understand human society. Augustine imagined the church as Confessions, a spiritual self-examination. He was recognized as a saint in the Catholic Church, the Eastern Orthodox Church, and the Anglican Communion, a preeminent Catholic doctor of the Church, and the patron of the Augustinians.

He was also recognized by Calvinists and Lutherans as one of the theological fathers of the Protestant Reformation. Figure 58 summarizes the names, dates, and contributions of the Early Church Fathers in chronological order of their years on earth.

Early Church Fathers
35-430 CE

Ancient	Medieval	Modern	Contemporary
3000 BCE (Invention of Writing)	476 CE (Fall of Western Roman Empire)	1402 CE (Columbus Discovered America)	1780 CE (French Revolution) - Present

Name	Dates	Noted for
Ignatius	35 – 108	Wrote Seven Epistles
Papias	60 – 1/30	False Millenarianism
Polycarp	69 – 155	Martyr
Tertullian	155 – 220	Defined the name Trinity which is not in the Bible
Origin	185 – 254	Allegorical interpretation
Eusebius	260/265 - 339	First three centuries of Church history would have been lost
Jerome	347 – 419/420	Translated bible to the Vulgate (Latin)
Augustine	354 - 430	Most important figure in the development of Western Christianity

Figure 58: Early Church Fathers (Daley, 1991, pp. 131-150)

Noted Greek Scholars of the Church Age

J.B. Lightfoot

J.B. Lightfoot (1828-1889) defended the authenticity of the *Epistles of Ignatius*. He was well known in England but not as well known in the United States of America. Lightfoot was a theologian and Bishop of Durham, enthroned at Durham Cathedral. He was chiefly concerned with the substance and the life of Christian truth ((*The Times*). He wrote commentaries on Galatians, Philippians, and Colossians. Lightfoot studied Apostolic Fathers.

Fifteen hundred pages of previously unpublished biblical commentaries and essays by Lightfoot were found in the Durham Cathedral. There were three volumes: Acts of the Apostles in volume one, the Gospel of John in volume two, and 2 Corinthians and 1 Peter in volume three.

Lightfoot was never married. He was the nephew of the Artists Joseph Vincent Barber and Charles Vincent Barber, grand of the artist and founding member of the Birmingham School of Art, Joseph Barber, and great-grandson of the founder of Newcastle's first library, Joseph Barber whose tomb is in Newcastle Cathedral.

A.T. Robertson

A.T. Robertson (1863-1934) focused on Greek words and definitions, preferring language study over theology. He did not incorporate culture in his writing. However, he was a voluminous writer. He wrote forty-four books, four grammars of the New Testament, fourteen commentaries and studies, six volumes in the series Word Pictures in the New Testament, eleven histories, and ten New Testament character studies. The capstone of his career was the 1914 book, "A Grammar of the Greek New Testament in the Light of Historical Research." Robertson receives accolades from all corners of the globe, including the Pope.

Marina Vincent

Marian Vincent (1834 – 1922) did word studies in the New Testament. He focused on grammatical aspects and not on culture. He was a Presbyterian minister at Columbia University, where he was a professor of the classics.

W.E. Vine

W.E. Vine (1873-1849) wrote the Expository Dictionary of the New Testament which was lauded for his detailed account. He Dedicated himself to his work with missionaries around the world, planting churches.

F.F. Bruce

F.F. Bruce (1910-1990) was a Scottish biblical scholar that shaped evangelicals. He supported the reliability of the New Testament. His first book, *"New Testament Documents: Are They Reliable"* (1943), was voted by the American evangelical periodical *Christianity Today* in 2006 as one of the top fifty books that shaped evangelism.

Periodical *Christianity Today* in 2006 was one of the top 50 books that shaped evangelicals.

Earl D. Radmacher

Earl Radmacher (1931-2014) focused on systematic theology. 2 Timothy 2:15 was life's mission. He was a Dutch scholar and President of Western Baptist Theological Seminary in Scottsdale, Arizona. He was quoted as saying, "Sitting in church Sunday after Sunday doesn't make one a Christian any more than sitting in a garage makes one a car."

Figure 59 summarizes the Christian Greek Scholars in the contemporary age.

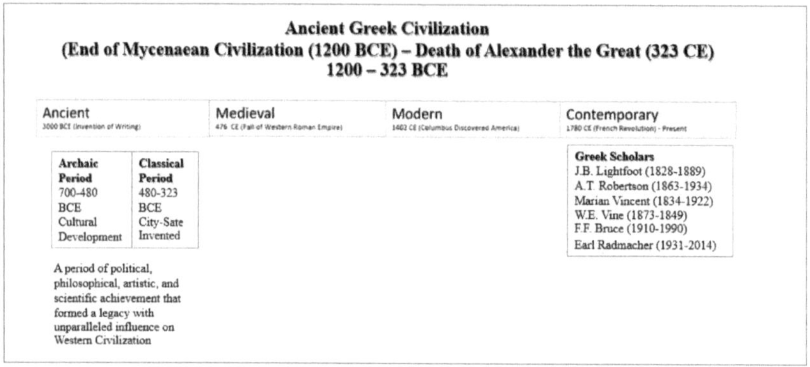

Figure 59: Ancient Greek Civilization

Chapter 7: Evidence in the Book of Revelation עדות בספר ההתגלות ('edutt basefer hahitegalutt) {הארץ.}

The book of Revelation describes end-time events consistent with the PTPM view. This can be seen by ordering the events as they appear in the chapters, as they appear in a chiastic structure, or as they appear in a menorah structure of the book. However, the sequence is obscured by reading challenges.

Communication Challenges

Understanding Revelation is a challenge for the 'unread,' those who have not read it, the 'read but did not understand,' and the 'unfit,' that is, the ones who read and understood but it does not fit into their message of peace and prosperity.

Unread

The 'unread' must depend on what others say about the eschatology unless they read about it in the Old Testament, particularly from Daniel, Ezekiel, and Zechariah. They listen to those who say the book is too hard to understand or it does not apply to them. J. Vernon McGee said it is easy, but familiarity with the whole Bible is required to understand it (Reference).

The Read

There are challenges for those who read Revelation and do not understand it. First, it is named Revelation, not Revelations, with an 's.' It does not reveal a multitude of revelations. Others call it the Book of Revelations, even ministers and pastors. There is only one revelation; the revelation from God was given to Jesus Christ. It is misleading to refer to the book as the Revelation of John. They did not read nor understand Jesus' Olivet, which was presented in three of the four Gospels: Matthew, Mark, and Luke.

One reason is that it sounds too scary. It talks about unparalleled death and destruction. It paints a picture of Jesus, the warrior, not Jesus, the peaceful servant. It sounds scary because they did not realize that the

Church would be raptured and will not experience the end times in Revelation, or they do not feel saved, or they do not believe. They may feel Revelation talks too much about judgment, forgetting it is the story of the end of God's Plan of Redemption and the beginning of eternal life of peace and righteousness. They did not pay attention to the prophecies throughout the Bible that refer to the events in Revelation. There is more detail in Revelation, but the events are all foretold throughout the Bible. They may not understand the book of Daniel, which is a parallel story of Revelation. They do not know God's plan of redemption that is told throughout the Old and New Testaments. Then, too, apocalyptic literature is unfamiliar to most readers. It is a genre that reveals hidden and future things. The subject matter is death and massive destruction. Apocalyptic literature is a lost art, not used or understood as a literary form. Literal forms like Star Trek, Game of Thrones, and Avatar are familiar. They know what to expect, and they understand the terminology. Others say Revelation has too many symbols that are not understood. Yet, all symbols are explained in the book or elsewhere in the entire canon. There are too many interpretations of eschatological events. And Revelation does not have an order to it, but it does.

Revelation Order of Events. There are at least three ways to identify the order of events in Revelation. One, distinguish between interludes, events on earth, and events in heaven. Two, arrange the events in a chiastic structure, figure 61. Three, rearrange the order of the chapters as reflected in God's Master Menorah.

Unfit

The 'unfit' are those who read and understand, but it does not fit into their message of peace and prosperity. They are those who did not want to understand Revelation. More than likely, they do not believe in the redemptive work of Jesus Christ. They may be paying attention to the disasters and judgment instead of the message of eternal fellowship with God.

Explaining and Teaching

Another challenge is that it is not preached or taught enough. Those who have read and understood Revelation may think It is challenging for one other reason. The person explaining it does not know how to explain or teach it. So consequently, confuses or misinterprets the Scripture.

Ministers and teachers seem to stay away from it because they focus on the wrong message. The message's emphasis in teaching may be on unparalleled death and destruction, not prosperity and power. They are concerned that there is no need to talk about Revelation because the Church will be taken up in the Rapture. There is significant knowledge contained in the book of Revelation. However, readers will be blessed for reading, hearing, and obeying the commands in Revelation (Revelation 1:3). They are confused about which interpretation is correct. The thesis of the paper is that PTPM is the only correct interpretation.

Revelation Theme, Organization, Timeline and Audience

The book of Revelation is the only book of the Bible that has no consensus about the general theme, organization, time frame, or target audience, leading to confusion and frustration (Lackey, A Revelation of Jesus, 2015, p. 14).

Lackey uses a chiastic structure that clarifies the timeline (lackey, 2015). A chiastic structure is a literary technique in which a sequence of ideas or concepts are presented and then repeated in reverse order. Lackey's chiastic structure divides the book of Revelation into ten sections that are divided into halves. The halves are the two themes in Revelation:" Satan's attacks on God and His people, and God's victory over Satan and his forces. The climax of the first half Satan's ultimate demonstration. The climate of the second half is God's ultimate demonstration of His Kingdom principles. Thus, the overall theme of the book of Revelation is the great controversy between God and Satan (Lackey, A Revelation of Jesus, 2015, pp. 35-37). Figure 60 summarizes the elements of Lackey's chiastic structure of Revelation.

Lackey uses this structure to clarify the timeline and shed light on other controversies. Preterist see prophecies as symbolic commentaries and predictions based on political, social, and religious issues of their time (Lackey, p/28), and the chronology of Revelation applies to the time it was written based on Revelation 1:1,3 - "… shortly come to pass." This preterist view does not harmonize with end-time themes such as the mark of the beast, the second coming of Christ, and the Millennium. (Lackey, p.58).

Futurists, reacting to the Protestant reformers who focused on the present, identified the pope as the antichrist and pushed the time of the antichrist into the future. More recently, dispensationalist writers have embraced the futurist view (Lackey, p.28). Elements of Lackey's chiastic structure of Revelation are in figure 60.

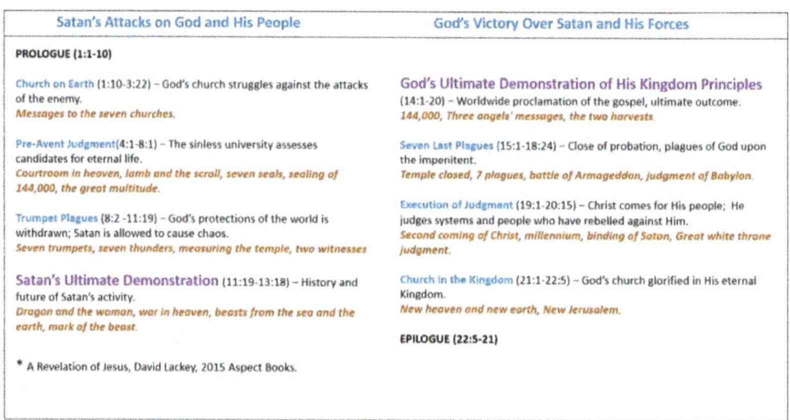

Figure 60: Elements of Lackey's Chiastic Structure of Revelation

Although Lackey's model seems to explain the timeline of Revelation, scholars challenge Lockey's chiastic structure. In 1942, Lund's seven laws of chiasmus laws governing chiastic structures did not help in applying the model to new examples (Lund, 1942, p. 40). In 1975, Clark, in his criteria types for establishing parallels in chiasms, concluded that no one type taken in isolation is adequate to establish chiastic parallelism (Clark, 1975, pp. 63-73). In 1980 Blomberg found that in parts of every book in Scripture, no criteria prevent using chiasmus where it was not intended (Blomberg, 1989). Criticism by scholars like Welsh, Boda, Dorsey, and Patrick continues (Rappleye, 2020).

Klein and Spears use the symbol of the Master Menorah to clarify issues in the book of Revelation. The Master Menorah is an inspiration that came to Klein and Spears.

The Master Menorah is composed of seven mini menorahs resting on the six branches and the central branch. It is a roadmap that groups related events together in chronological order (Klein & Spears, 2016).

The image of the Menorah plays a key role in understanding Scripture. In the book of Exodus God instructs Israel how to make it (Exodus 25).

In volume 3 of the Lost in Translation series, Klein and Spears use the Master Menorah to define the timeline in the book of Revelation, the Marriage Covenant, the Betrothal cups, and sin. (Klein et al., 2012, pp. 457-640). Criticism of the insights of the Master Menorah are currently not appearing.

The Revelation Story

Revelation begins with Jesus appearing to John on the Isle of Patmos with a message to seven Churches in Asia Minor. Jesus's messages to each church are He knows their works, His praises and rebukes for each church, His counsel, His warnings, and His promises to the overcomers, Figure 61.

Revelations Messages to the Seven Churches

	Ephesus	Smyrna	Pergamos	Thyatira	Sardis	Philadelphia	Laodicea
Description of Christ	holds 7 stars, walks among 7 candlesticks	first and last, was dead and is alive	has sharp sword with two-edges	son of God, eyes like flame of fire, feet like brass	has 7 Spirits of God, seven stars	holy, true, has key of David, opens and shuts	Amen, faithful and true witness, beginning of creation
Christ Knows Works	labour, patience	tribulation, poverty	dwelling-where Satan's seat is	charity, service, faith, patience	hypocrisy	none -specified	false claims, true condition
Praise	can't bear evil, tests teachers, hates Nicolaitanes	you are rich	hold fast my name, not denied my faith	last works better than the first	a few have not defiled their garments and are worthy	kept my word, not denied my name, kept the word of my patience	NONE
Rebuke	left first love	NONE	some that hold doctrines of Balaam and Nicolaitans	allowed Jezebel to seduce servants, repented not	works not perfect, seems alive but dead	NONE	lukewarm, wretched, miserable, poor, blind, naked,
Counsel	remember where fallen from, repent, do first works	don't fear, be faithful unto death	repent	repent, hold fast till I come	be watchful, strengthen what remains, repent, remember	hold fast	buy gold and white raiment, anoint eyes, repent, open door
Warning	I will come quickly and remove candlestick	NONE	I will fight against them	sickbed, great tribulation, death, reward according to works	I will come as a thief	NONE	I will spue you out of my mouth
Promises to overcomers	eat from the tree of life	crown of life, not hurt of the second death	hidden manna, white stone with a new name	power to rule nations, morning star	walk with me in white raiment, confess name, not blot name out	keep from hour of temptation, pillar in temple, name of God and city	sup with me, sit with me on throne

Figure 61: Revelations Messages to the Seven Churches

In the next event in Revelation, John sees a door in heaven, and he is told to see what will take place. What John sees is the action that begins the Tribulation period. PTPM begins with the Rapture, followed by the Tribulation. The Rapture event is not described in Revelation, but the presence of the twenty-four Elders implies the Rapture has happened. Revelation 2:25 and 3:10)

Rapture

Scripture through the Bible support the rapture event and it happening before the Tribulation begins (John 14:1-3; Romans 8:19; 1 Corinthians 1:7-8, 15:1-53, 16:22; Phil 3:20-21; Colossians 3:4; 1 Thessalonians 1:10, 2:19, 4:13-18, 5:9; 2 Thessalonians 2:1; 1 Timothy 6:14, 2 Timothy 4:1; Titus 2:13, Hebrews 9:28; James 5:7-9; 1 Peter 1:7, 13;1 John2:28-3:2; Jude 21, Revelation 2:25, 3:10) (Missler, The Book of Revelation: Commentary Handbook, 2020, p. 139).

When the Rapture comes, Christians will be resurrected. The restrainer, the Holy Spirit, will be removed, and the full power of the Antichrist will be revealed. Until then, the Holy Spirit restrains the secret power of the Antichrist (2 Thessalonians 2:7-8).

The events in Revelation align with the PTPM view, from Tribulation to the Eternal state.

Tribulation

Tribulation is the seven-year period of destruction and judgment. The first half of the Tribulation is the rise of the antichrist (Daniel 7:7) (Fruchtenbaum, The Footsteps of the Messiah, 2020). The second half of the Tribulation, called The Great Tribulation, was God's judgment. There were opposing views on the timing of the Great Tribulation.

Opposite Views of Tribulation.

Within conservative, evangelical Christian thought, two opposite viewpoints of the Great Tribulation have been expressed in a debate between theologians Kenneth L. Gentry and Thomas Ice (Gentry & Ice, 1999).

Tribulation as a past event (Dr. Gentry)

The Great Tribulation occurred during the 1st century. Those events marked the end of God's focus on exalting Israel. Jesus' prophecies marked the beginning of the Christianity in God's plan. The Tribulation is God's judgment in Israel for rejecting the Messiah. The Tribulation judgments will be centered on local events surrounding ancient [Jerusalem](), and also affecting other parts of the former [Roman Empire](). Jesus, as the Christ, governs the Tribulation judgments that reflect his judgment against Israel, showing that he is in heaven controlling those events.

Tribulation as a future event (Dr. Ice)

The Great Tribulation is still rapidly approaching. Those events marked the beginning of God's focus on and exaltation of Israel. The prophecy says the Christian era will be concluded just after the church is taken from the world. Rather than being God's judgment in Israel, it is the preparation of Israel to receive her Messiah. The judgments involve catastrophes that will affect the stellar universe and impact the entire planet. The coming of Christ in the Tribulation requires his public, visible, and physical presence to conclude those judgments (Gentry & Ice, 1999, p. 121).

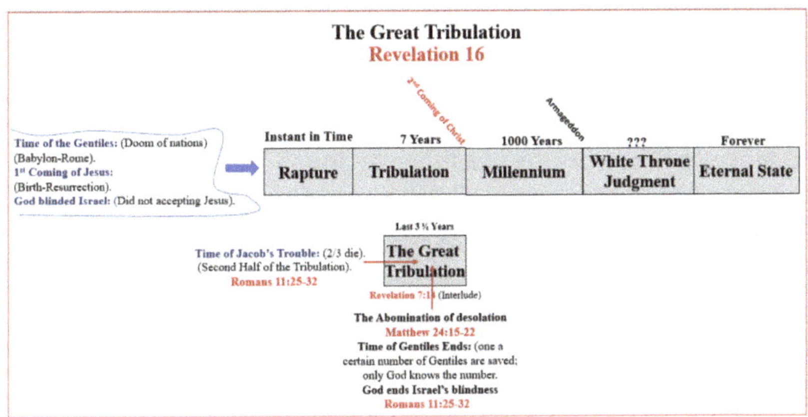

Figure 62: The Great Tribulation

Christ returns after the seven-year Tribulation and establishes His kingdom. The one-hundred-forty-four Jews from the twelve tribes of Israel and the Tribulation Saints ruled on earth with under Christ for one thousand years, called the Millennium.

Millennium

Millennium life is described in Isaiah 65 and Revelation 20. See Figure 63.

The Millennium Life

Isaiah 65:20-25	Revelation 20:4-6
20 There shall be no more thence an infant of days, nor an old man that hath not filled his days: for the child shall die an hundred years old; but the sinner being an hundred years old shall be accursed. 21 And they shall build houses, and inhabit them; and they shall plant vineyards, and eat the fruit of them. 22 They shall not build, and another inhabit; they shall not plant, and another eat: for as the days of a tree are the days of my people, and mine elect shall long enjoy the work of their hands. 23 They shall not labour in vain, nor bring forth for trouble; for they are the seed of the blessed of the LORD, and their offspring with them. 24 And it shall come to pass, that before they call, I will answer; and while they are yet speaking, I will hear. 25 The wolf and the lamb shall feed together, and the lion shall eat straw like the bullock: and dust shall be the serpent's meat. They shall not hurt nor destroy in all my holy mountain, saith the LORD.	4 And I saw thrones, and they sat upon them, and judgment was given unto them: and I saw the souls of them that were beheaded for the witness of Jesus, and for the word of God, and which had not worshipped the beast, neither his image, neither had received his mark upon their foreheads, or in their hands; and they lived and reigned with Christ a thousand years. 5 But the rest of the dead lived not again until the thousand years were finished. This is the first resurrection. 6 Blessed and holy is he that hath part in the first resurrection: on such the second death hath no power, but they shall be priests of God and of Christ, and shall reign with him a thousand years.

Figure 63: Millennium Life - Isaiah & Revelation

Armageddon

Armageddon' is **the symbolic name given to this event based on scripture references regarding divine obliteration of God's enemies.** The hermeneutical method supports this position by referencing Judges 4-5 where God miraculously destroys the enemy of Israel at Megiddo.

Great White Throne Judgment

The final judgment of the wicked is more of a sentence than a trial. The wicked are identified as the ones whose names do not appear in the Book of Life.

Eternal State

The New Heaven and New Earth represent all things renewed, all of God's creation. There is only God and His Creation.

SECTION III – Supporting Evidence

There is supporting evidence in the ology thinkers. Ologies are defined in this paper as thinkers whose subjects are stated with the suffix 'ology." Philosophy, psychology, sociology, psychology, psychology, and cosmology.

Chapter 8: Evidence in Greek Scholars עדויות של חוקרים יווניים () { כולו }

The Greek Scholars of the ninth through the twenty-first centuries had differing interpretations of eschatology. Noted among them were J.B. Lightfoot, A.T. Robertson, Marian Vincent, W.E. Vine, F.F. Bruce, and Earl Radmacher.

J.B. Lightfoot (1828-1889)

Lightfoot was well known in England more so than in North America. He was a theologian and Bishop of Durham, enthroned at Durham Cathedral. He was concerned with the substance and the life of Christian truth. He wrote commentaries on Galatians, Philippians, and Colossians, studied Apostolic Fathers, and defended the authenticity of the *Epistles of Ignatius*. Over one-thousand-five-hundred pages of previously unpublished biblical commentaries and essays by Lightfoot were found in Durham Cathedral and published. Three volumes set contained the Acts of the Apostles, Gospel of John, 2 Corinthians, 1 Peter. Lightfoot never married. Lightfoot was the nephew of the Artists Joseph Vincent Barber and Charles Vincent Barber, grand of the artist and founding member of the Birmingham School of Art, Joseph Barber, and great-grandson of the founder of Newcastle's first library, Joseph Barber, whose tomb is in Newcastle Cathedral.

A.T. Robertson 1863-1934

In Robertson's six-volume set of Greek words and definitions, he focused on language study over theology. As a Greek scholar, interlinear translations were focused on the gist and overview of the Greek language, not the details. He also did not deal with culture. He was not like Greek Scholars like Pythagoras (570-495 BCE), Socrates (469-399 BCE), Plato (427-347 BCE), and Aristotle (384-322 BCE), he focused on words and definitions. Robertson was accepted into Wake Forest College when he was sixteen years old. As a voluminous writer, he wrote forty-four books, four grammars of the New Testament, fourteen commentaries and studies, sixteen volumes in the series *Word Pictures in the New Testament*, eleven histories, and ten New Testament character studies.

In 1914 the capstone of his career was grammar of the Greek New Testament in the *Light of Historical Research*. He received accolades from all corners of the globe, including the Pope,

Marian Vincent 1834 – 1922

Vincent also focused on grammatical aspects of the Greek language and not culture. He was a Presbyterian minister, professor of the classics at Columbia University, best known for Word Studies in the New Testament.

W.E. Vine 873-1849

Vine was one of the greatest expositors of the Greek language. His Expository Dictionary of the New Testament provided detailed, extensive information on Greek words. He was an outstanding Greek scholar and dedicated himself to his work with missionaries around the world, planting churches. He is best known for *Vine's Expository Dictionary of New Testament Words*.

F.F. Bruce 1910-1990

Bruce was a Scottish biblical scholar. He supported the historical reliability of the New Testament. His first book, *"New Testament Documents: Are They Reliable?"* (1943), was voted by the American evangelical periodical *Christianity Today* in 2006 as one of the top 50 books that shaped evangelicals.

Earl Radmacher 1931-2014

Radmacher describes his mission as 2 Timothy 2:15, rightly dividing the Word of truth. He was a Dutch citizen and former President of Western Baptist Theological Seminary in Scottsdale, Arizona. The last of eight children, he is remembered as saying, "Sitting in church Sunday after Sunday doesn't make one a Christian any more than sitting in a garage makes one a car." Radmacher was a Systematic Theologian influenced by evangelist Billy Graham. Figures 60 and 61 summarize these influential Greek scholars by name and contributions in chronological order.

New Testament Greek Scholars (1 of 2)

Date	Name	Contribution
1828-1889	J.B. Lightfoot	Well known in England; Not as well known in the USA Theologian and Bishop of Durham, enthroned at Durham Cathedral He was chiefly concerned with the substance and the life of Christian truth ((*The Times*) Commentaries: Galatians, Philippians, Colossians Studied Apostolic Fathers Defended the authenticity of the *Epistles of Ignatius* His editions of *Epistles of Ignatius* and *Polycarp*. 2014 - InterVarsity Press published about 1500 pages of previously unpublished biblical commentaries and essays by Lightfoot found in Durham Cathedral. Three volumes – (1) Acts of the Apostles, (2) Gospel of John, (3) 2 Corinthians, 1 Peter. Never married. Nephew of the Artists Joseph Vincent Barber and Charles Vincent Barber and grand of the artist and founding member of the Birmingham School of Art, Joseph Barber and great grandson of the founder of Newcastle's first library, Joseph Barber whose tomb is in Newcastle Cathedral.
1834-1922	Marvin Vincent	Focus on grammatical aspects, not culture. Presbyterian minister Columbia University; Professor of classics Best known for Word Studies in the New Testament
1863-1934	A.T. Robertson	6-set volume; Interlinear; Greek Scholar Gives the gist, overview, not detailed. Does not deal with culture. Not like Greek Scholars – Socrates., Plato, Aristotle Gives Greek words and definitions.
1873-1949	W.E. Vine	More detail Outstanding Greek Scholar Dedicated himself to his work with missionaries around the world – planting of churches Best known for Vine's Expository dictionary of New Testament Words

Figure 64: New Testament Greek Scholars (1 of 2)

New Testament Greek Scholars (2 of 2)

Date	Name	Contribution
1910-1990	F.F. Bruce	England; Scottish biblical scholar Supported the historical reliability of the New Testament. His first book, New Testament documents: Are They Reliable? (1943), was voted by the American evangelical periodical Christianity today in 2006 as one of the top 50 books which shaped evangelicals.
1931-2014	Earl Radmaacher	Dutch Deceased 2014 Former President of Wester Baptist Theological Seminary Scottsdale AZ Systematic Theology Last of 8 children "sitting in church Sunday after Sunday doesn't make one a Christian any more than sitting in a garage makes one a car" Influenced by evangelist Billy Graham Life mission – 2 Timothy 2:15

Figure 65: New Testament Greek Scholars (2 of 2)

Greek Scholars from the early church period to the present are continuing to make significant contributions to the understanding of God's Word. However, they, like early church fathers and church leaders, are also misguiding and misinterpreting scripture in their zeal to uncover biblical truth. Carefully comparing their works with the truth of the Torah is critical to understanding eschatological Scripture, especially in the book of Revelation.

Chapter 9: Evidence in Early Church Leaders עדויות בכתבי הברית החדשה ('eduyott bekhitevey haberitt hakhadashah) {ואת}

Eschatology of Jesus in the Olivet Discourse

The Olivet Discourse is also known as the Little Apocalypse because it includes the use of apocalyptic language describing the eschaton. Jesus warned His followers that they would suffer tribulation and persecution before the ultimate triumph of the Kingdom of God.

The Olivet discourse is the last of the Five Discourses of Matthew and occurs just before the narrative of the Passion of Jesus. Beginning with the anointing of Jesus, according to the narrative of the synoptic Gospels, an anonymous disciple remarks on the greatness of Herod's Temple. Jesus responds that not one of those stones would remain intact in the building, and the whole thing would be reduced to rubble.

The disciples asked Jesus, "When will this happen, and what will be the sign of your coming and of the end of the age?" Jesus first warns them about things that would happen. O would claim to be the Christ, and there would be wars and rumors of wars. Nations will rise against nations. There will be earthquakes, famines, pestilence, and fearful events. There would be false prophets, apostasy, persecution of the followers of and the persecution of Jesus' followers. But Jesus identified them as "the beginnings of birth pains."

Jesus then warned the disciples about the abomination of desolation, "standing where it does not belong". After Jesus described the "abomination that causes desolation", he warned that the people of Judea should flee to the mountains as a matter of such urgency that they should not even return to get things from their homes. Jesus also warned that if it happened in winter or on the Sabbath, fleeing would be even more difficult. Jesus described this as a time of "Great Tribulation" worse than anything that had gone before.

Jesus then states that immediately after the time of tribulation, people would see a sign, "The sun will be darkened, and the moon will not give its light; the stars will fall from the sky, and the heavenly bodies will be shaken".

The statements about the sun and moon turning dark sound quite apocalyptic, as it appears to be a quote from the Book of Isaiah. The description of the sun, moon, and stars going dark is also used elsewhere in the Old Testament. Joel wrote that this would be a sign before the great and dreadful Day of the Lord. The Book of Revelation also mentions the sun and moon turning dark during the sixth seal of the seven seals, but the passage adds more detail than the previous verses mentioned.

Jesus states that after the time of tribulation and the sign of the Sun, Moon, and stars going dark, the Son of Man would be seen arriving in the clouds with power and great glory. The Son of Man would be accompanied by the angels, and at the trumpet call, the angels would "gather his elect from the four winds, from one end of heaven to the other".(Matthew 24:31)

Although most scholars, and almost all Christians, read this as meaning that the gathering would include people not only from Earth but also from heaven, a few Christians, mostly modern American Protestant Premillennialists, have interpreted it to mean that people would be gathered from Earth and taken *to* heaven—a concept known in their circles as the *rapture*. Most scholars see this as a quotation of a passage from the Book of Zechariah in which God (and the contents of heaven in general) are predicted to come to Earth and live among the elect, who by necessity are gathered together for this purpose.

Scholars widely believe the discourse to contain material delivered on a variety of occasions, in the Gospel of Matthew and the Gospel of Mark. Jesus spoke this discourse to his disciples privately on the Mount of Olives, opposite Herod's Temple. In the Gospel of Luke, Jesus taught over a period of time in the Temple and stayed at night on the Mount of Olives.

Jesus clearly identified the tribulation, the second coming, and the millennium in order.

Paul's Eschatology from Jesus in 1 Thessalonians

In 1 Thessalonians, Paul described rapture.

Chapter 10: Evidence in the Cosmology, Theology & Religion קוסמולוגיה, תאולוגיה ודת qosmologya te'ologya vedatt

Cosmology is the study of the origin and development of the universe, what it is, how it functions, what it can do, how it does what it does, and all things about it. There have been many theories about the universe. Historically, humankind has been content with the understanding that God created the universe. Only in the last one hundred years has that belief been questioned. A little knowledge is a dangerous thing.

Around 1930 it was discovered that the universe is in a state of expansion and started a finite time ago. This was the basis for the development of theories about cosmologies at the university like the Big Bang Theory, cyclic cosmology, multiverse cosmology, and finite and infinite cosmological theories.

The obscenity of these models of the universe abounds. These models have no first state for God to create in. They have no time that existed before the universe came into being – God created time. The story goes: Satan came to God and said he could create man. So, he scooped up a handful of dirt to make a man like God did. God told the devil, get your own dirt.

All scripture rests on Genesis 1:1: "In the beginning, God created the heaven and earth." The beginning refers to the beginning of creation, not the beginning of God. God has no beginning or end. God is. He said, "I am." No models or theories explain how the beginning of the universe is the basis for all things. The models do not explain spirituality.

The models do not explain time. Although time mathematically is the 4th dimension, God is dimensionless. God is infinitely dimensional and yet He is outside of dimensions, dimensionless. God is not time. He made time. In the beginning really means when God got ready, he cut out (*bara*) the earth from nothingness. God is neither "nothingness" nor "somethingness." God is.

A model is an imitation of what it is. God is not a model. A model is not God. An imitation of a think is not they think. A model of the universe is not the universe. Models describe the truths about nature. But we see darkly (scripture). God defined truth. Consequently, if models describe the truth, then models are God because God created truth. Models can only give a glimpse of reality, but only a glimpse. While models and theories are useful, they cannot rightly divide the Word of Truth. They are true until they are not. Einstein's first cosmological model described a static universe. That was believed to be true until it was not. Friedmann, Robertson, and Walker (FRW) discovered that the world is not static, it is expanding. The famous paradox about logic says that logic can be illogical. Russell's paradox says that the set of all sets that are not members of themselves is a paradox. It contradicts itself.

Humankind discovers truth sometimes through experiments and acceptance of results by peer review of findings. Peers are usually those individuals who have been taught to think like you. Isn't it interesting that thinking the same way that you think will lead to the same conclusions that you made?

The truth is what it is because God said it is. Truth is what God says it true, and time and everything except Himself. God did not need to create Himself. God is! God always existed. He said, "I am." He did not say "I was" or "I will be." He is not just "I am." He is not even "just" I am. He cannot be qualified with any adjectives.

The question of what happens to the universe at the eschaton, the eschatology of the cosmos, is answered by God. There will be a new heaven and a new earth, and all things will pass away (Revelation reference). Models and theories of the universe do not adequately address the eschaton. The big bang theory says in the decisive moments, the universe will be one large fireball with a temperature of infinity. There will be no more time or space. Where does it go? Physicists say matter is neither created nor destroyed; it only changes form. If that is true, then God is not telling the true about creation and re-creation. How can God create truth; how can God be truth and not be truthful. The starting point for all things is knowing that God is and then believing what he says, not allegorically or any other way.

Chapter 11: Evidence in Ologies ראיות בלוגיקה (reayott balogiqah) {נשען}

Bringing this thought to the study of eschatology is an attempt to incorporate a comprehensive approach to the study. Barton calls this an interdisciplinary approach (Barton, 2011). Thinkers throughout history have had positive and negative effects on scholarly understanding of Christianity. Figure 66 depicts the scope of this comprehensive approach to evidence against

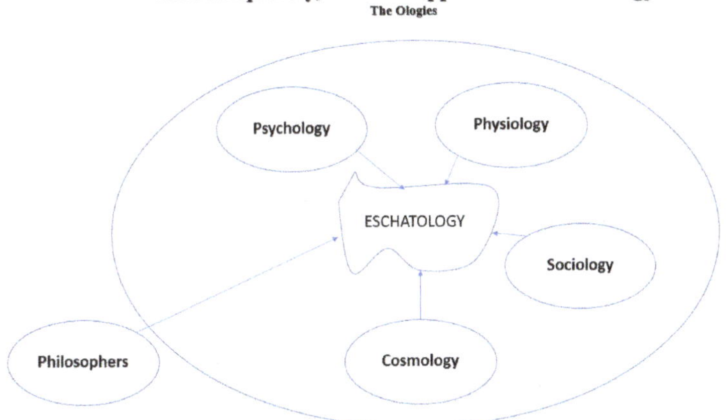

Figure 66: Scope of the Holistic Approach to Eschatology

Psychological Thinking

One of the questions Barton researched was whether the emotions of the first Christians conformed to the wider Greco-Roman society. He studied the eschatological subject of grief in the face of death using 1 Thessalonians 4:13-18, the Rapture passage (Barton, 2011, p. 586). The Thessalonians were dealing with the concerns of the Christians who died. Grief was compounded by ongoing social ostracism, separation from their traditional native religion, and harassment from their kinsfolk and friends (1 Thessalonians 2:14; 3:2-3). Death represented "a tear in the fabric of their eschatological faith" (Ibid, 587). Barton made four observations about Paul's response to the Thessalonians.

First, Paul clearly did what any father would do by offering consolation (1 Thessalonians 1:11). This was typical of the Greco-Roman emotions. Second, Paul gave feeling rules to control their grief and bolster their understanding (1 Thessalonians 4:13), which is also typical of society. However, Barton's third and fourth observations were atypical. Third, Paul's feelings on grief went beyond the Grego-Roman appearance to attain happiness in this life. Paul reconstructed the event to lift emotions by saying the dead are only "asleep" (4:13-15) (Ibid, 288). Fourth, Barton identified a sociological corollary to Paul's response. Thessalonian believers were not "those who had no hope." This focuses them on hope and heaven.

These observations emotions about eschatology are more intense and consoling than typical Grego-Roman response. More importantly, it illustrates that the Rapture was a deeply emotional event, not just an idea or an allegory but a multitude of psychological emotions with sociological implications.

Sociological Thinking

McConville discussed the idea of recognizing the prophets as a group, a 'social location,' when there is limited knowledge about the individuals. Observing how groups are recognized by societies, whether they fit in or out, and their support or disruption of the status quo. Studying prophets as a group by identifying different names they are called is one way to learn about prophets. They have been called "Seers" and "Men of God." Also, by identifying the ways they receive messages from God, particularly in speech and vision. For example, the prophets of the Northern Kingdom of Israel and the Mosaic covenant played a significant role in their thoughts. Southern prophets, in contrast, were influenced by "vision" relating to the temple and the Davidic covenant (McConville, 2002, pp. XIV-XV)

Thiessen defined the sociology of early Christianity as "the description and analysis of typical, interpersonal behavior displayed by members of early Christian groups. He points out that there are daunting obstacles to using sociological techniques in New Testament studies. There is a historical distance of nineteen hundred years. Early church writings are religious documents, and sociology has no satisfactory method for analyzing the divine or 'nonrational' elements that are important in religious practice. Also, the concepts and models of sociology are not given because conclusions are drawn from observations that are verified by scientific methods. They are based on the theory of evolution, not the truth of creation (Harrington, 1980 [Theissen, 1974, pp, 181-190]).

Gager and Thiessen applied the concepts of sociology to the development of the early church. Gager conceived Christianity as a social world in the making. He saw the group gathered around Jesus as a millenarian movement. They believed that the present reality would be overturned and the promise of heaven on earth would be fulfilled (Gager, 1975). This means the early church believed in the existence of the millennium as a future event, which is contrary to the preterist, millennial, and post-millennial views.

Thiessen bases his sociology on functional analysis. Religious movements were characterized by a conflict of social tensions and resolutions. For example, the poverty and social displacement of the Galilean fishers created a for against the secure and profitable trade of the average fishers (Ibid, 190). These social approaches help reinforce and even enhance the understanding of the early church beliefs and movements without more information about each prophet. On the other hand, there is much more understanding and misunderstanding that can be gleaned from the thinking of philosophers.

Philosophical Thinking

Christian philosophy started in the third century. A community of Christian named the Patristics emerged to deal with the lives, writing and doctrines of the early church theologians. Augustine was representative of the thinkers who believed that science and faith worked in harmony. Tertullian was representative of thinkers whose science and faith were in conflict. Others tried to differentiate them. The main purpose of the Patristics was to defend Christianity. This period of ideas lasted through the seventh century.

Following this period, the Scholastics, ninth to thirteenth centuries Pre-modern, fourteenth and fifteenth centuries Sixteenth century onward – coexist with independent scientific and philosophical theories.

The discipline of philosophy has been studied through several ways of thing. Aesthetics is thinking about beauty and taste. Axiology is thinking about the nature of value and valuation. Epistemology is thinking about the nature, origin, and limits of human knowledge. Ethical thinking is about what is right and wrong in human behavior. Logical thinking is about nature and types of logic. Metaphysical thinking is about understanding the fundamental nature of reality, and political philosophical thinking addresses the questions about the nature, scope, and legitimacy of public agents and institutions (citation). The Greek philosophers had a tremendous impact on the development of Western culture that drove how scripture was interpreted.

Pre-Socratic philosophers like Pythagoras, the mathematician, believed that humans originated from a single substance. Pythagoras prescribed a highly structured way of life supporting the doctrine of metempsychosis, the transmigration of the soul after death into a new body. He influenced a cult-based philosophy called Pythagoreanism. It was based on worshiping numbers, believing in reincarnation, and practicing vegetarianism (citation). Unfortunately, many of the philosophical thinkers led society astray.

The most influential ancient Greek Socratic philosophers were Socrates, Plato, and Aristotle. Socrates (470/469 – 399 BCE taught methods for asking thought-provoking questions, the Socratic Method, instead of lecturing his students. His student Plato (428/427 – 348/347 BCE) studied ideas about human behavior like ethics, virtue, and justice. His student, Aristotle (384-322 BCE studied physics, biology, and astronomy and was credited with the development of logic. Aristotle made pioneering contributions to philosophy and science. He identified the various scientific disciples and their relationship with each other. He was a teacher and founded his school in Athens, known as the Lyceum.

The thoughts of Plato (c. 428-348 BCE) were responsible for the development of Western culture. He was followed by Tertullian (155-220 CE), St. Augustine (354-430 CE), the scientific advances in the Age of Enlightenment (1715-1789/1804 CE), and Nietzsche (1884-1868). Western culture is different and even opposite from the original thinking in the Eastern culture of the early church. Western culture led to misinterpretations of scripture.

Plato said, "No man can be imagined to be of such an iron nature that he would stand fast in justice" if he was free to act without anyone's knowledge, Plato wrote, "No man would keep his hands off what was not his own when he could safely take what he liked out of the market." Plato was suggesting that ordinary humans do right only if others are watching. He argued that humans were capable of resisting temptation. He argued for an inner motivation for moral conduct. This thinking set the Greek world, and later the Western world, on a path leading to each person having an inner (individual) voice to distinguish and choose right from wrong (Richards & O'Brien, 2012, pp. 114-115 [Plato, Resp 2]).

Cosmology Thinkers

While scientists understanding of cosmology predicts that the universe will wind down and have no possibility for human life, Christian eschatology affirms that the entire physical cosmos will be renewed and re-created into a better eternal space.

The birth of Jesus as the rightful King is depicted in a cosmic way. Jesus was born on earth as the Lamb of God. He will return when the Feast of Tabernacles comes for all believers. Jesus progressed through Passover, Unleavened Bread, First Fruits, and Pentecost. He will be seen in the Feast of Trumpets. He will return on the day of Atonement. He will be crowned when the final Feast of the tubercles is reached (Collins, 1996, p. 346).

Theistic cosmologists are united in their ideas that there is one God who has created all that exists presently. While there are some similarities between the Biblical creation account and other ancient Near Eastern narratives, the Genesis account is significantly different from all other cosmogonies. In Genesis, there is no attempt to explain the origin of God. The is only one God acting alone. Many other ancient accounts describe creation as a violent struggle between rival gods. There are several examples of the uniqueness described in Genesis. The sun and the moon are not God's rivals; they are His handiwork. Creation by divine fiat in Genesis is unique in the ancient Near East. Other ancient accounts of new life require divine intervention and renewal through religious fertility rituals. The creation of light as the first act is only in Genesis. The power given to each species to replenish itself is given at creation and is not dependent on the rites of fertility cult (Ibid, p.361).

The centerpiece of classical Jewish eschatology and traditional Christian eschatological theory is the physical resurrection of the dead. Ancient Jews believed this was a future event. Some Christians believe that the resurrection has already begun (preterist and amillennialists). A Christian vision of the future, inconsistent with scientific predictions, is based on faith. The scientific predictions do not fit with the promise of a coming new creation (Ibid, 365).

Christian eschatology asserts that the new creation is neither a replacement for the present nor is it working out the natural evolutionary process of the world. Instead, the world will be transformed by a radically new act of God, which begins at the resurrection of Jesus (Ibid, p.366).

This cosmological view clearly refutes the preterist and millennium views. Figure 54 identifies the interdisciplinary group of thinkers. However, the group is not all-inclusive.

SECTION IV – Criticisms

Chapter 12: Evidence in Motivations and Fallacies ראיות במניעים ובטעויות (reayott bameni'im uvata'uyott) {על פסוק}

The most compelling evidence of PTPM is that premillennialism was the only view of eschatology for over two hundred years. No other view was given any consideration (Larkin, 1920, p. 4). Just because this doctrine was held in early church history does not mean it is correct. When coupled with its consistency with God's Plan of Redemption validates PTPM as the original view. Yet there are other compelling factors that PTPM is the only correct view.

God's Plan of Redemption is woven into the fiber of the Bible history and culture in marriage, the covenants, the Passover ceremony, the seven annual feasts, as well as the Bar and Bat Mitzvahs. The other views would change God's plan of redemption, creating a major contradiction in the Bible. The alternative view changes God's Plan of Redemption. Since the essence of the Bible is about the story of redemption, if that story changed, the Word of God would not be dependable. God does not change (Malachi 3:6).

Beyond these fundamental reasons for rejecting the alternative view of eschatology, there are specific reasons for rejecting each of the alternative views.

Preterist

Preterist view was developed by Jesuit Alcazar in 1614 CE to relieve the Pope from being called the Antichrist. Alcazar stated that the prophecy was fulfilled in the destruction of Jerusalem by Titus and the subsequent fall of the Roman Empire. That made the Emperor the Antichrist instead of the Pope (Larkin, 1920, p. 5). There are very few advocates of this view today. It was obviously politically motivated, not spiritually inspired.

Amillennialism

Contrary to the Amillennium view, the Destiny of Israel is in God's Covenants (Romans 9-11) (Wansbrough, 2019). Israel has a prophetic destiny. Mary was told by Gabriel that Jesus would sit on the throne of David, which did not exist at the time Luke 1:30-33 (Wansbrough, 2019) (Missler, The Book of Revelation: Commentary Handbook, 2020, p. 6)

Amillennialism led to an unbiblical view of the Church. After the Roman emperor Constantine issued the Edict of Milan in 313 CE that legitimated Christianity, there was a change in basic assumptions from the well-grounded premillennialism of the ancient church to fathers, amillennialism, and postmillennialism dominated eschatological thinking. The Church formed powerful alliances with the kings of Europe and lost interest in the literal prophecies about Christ's Second Coming (Grant Jeffrey) (Jeffrey, 2001, p. 129).

Postmillennialists

Post-Tribulation denies the New Testament teaching of His imminency. We are to expect Him at any moment (Philippians 3:20; Titus 2:3; Hebrews 9:28; 1 Thessalonians 1:10; 4:18; 5:6; Revelation 22:20), and He has not come yet. It also (Missler, The Book of Revelation: Commentary Handbook, 2020, pp. 184-185).

Requires the Church to be on earth during the Tribulation. Israel and the church are mutually exclusive (Daniel 9:26). The Church would experience God's Wrath. However, the promise is that the Church will not experience the Tribulation; it will be raptured and not experience it (1 Thessalonians 5:9; Revelation 3:10). How can the bride come with Him if He is coming to gather the bride? Also, who will populate the Millennium?

Dispensationalism

Dispensationalism believes in separate salvations for Jews. They are right in believing that God has a continuing role in His plan for Israel, the descendants of Abraham, Isaac, and Jacob. But, some believe that God has a separate path of salvation for the Jewish people. They forget that salvation is only in Jesus Christ. This is true for both Jews and Gentiles; Jesus will not rescue anyone who consciously rejects Him and His offer of salvation. Some dispensationalists are so focused on the divide between Israel and the Church that they think the teaching of

Jesus in the Gospels was only or mostly for Israel and not for the Church. Also, the Scriptures do not clearly identify the dispensations.

Posttribiulationism

Posttribulation expresses the view that one Christ will rapture the church after the tribulation period at His second coming. Believers will go through the Tribulation, but they will be protected (Revelation 3:10). Two, all believers will be resurrected at the end of the Tribulation (Revelation 20:4-6). However, only those who became believers during the Tribulation and then died will be resurrected at the end of the Tribulation period (1 Thessalonians 4:13-18). Three, saints are seen on earth during the Tribulation period, so the Rapture has not happened. There will be saints who live during the Tribulation period but, they became believers during the Tribulation period (Revelation 6:9-12). Four, in Matthew 24:37-40 "two men will be in the field; one will be taken up and the other left," meaning that not all saints will be raptured. However, this is not the Rapture (Luke 17:37).

Midtribulationsim

Midtribulationists view that one, Christ will rapture the church in the middle of the Tribulation period. The two witnesses caught up in heaven are representatives of the church (Revelation 11). However, there is no indication that these witnesses represent the church. Two, the church will be delivered from wrath which is the second half of the Tribulation (1 Thessalonians 5:9). However, the entire Tribulation period is wrath (Zephaniah 1:15, 18; 1 Thessalonians 1:10; Revelation 6:17; 14:7,10; 19:2). Three, the Rapture occurs at the last trumpet (1 Thessalonians 4:16-17) and the seventh trumpet sounds in the middle of tribulation. However, The seventh trumpet deals with judgment, not rapture. Failures like these in the descriptions of eschatology impact Christian faith and practice (Rowland, 2009, pp. 56-72).

There have been great thinkers and church leaders of the two thousand years which gave rise to several views about eschatology. Analysis of most of these perspectives has been based on logic, science, misunderstanding of Scripture, or political motivations. Very few of these eschatological views have been expressed as inspirations from God and were devised more than one thousand years after the establishment of the Church at Pentecost. Hence, they are questionable. Other century-long biblical debates have been dispelled when carefully reviewing the Scripture. For example, there is continuing debate over whether Daniel was written by two different authors, but Missler says Matthew 24:15 shows that Jesus acknowledged the author as Daniel (Missler, The Book of Daniel, 2004).

A general mistake in deeper interpreting the New Testament (הברית החדשה – habrit hakhadashah) is to look at the Greek translation. The mistake is that although most of the Old Testament (הברית הישנה habritt hayeshana) quotes from the Septuagint written in Greek. The Septuagint is a translation of the Torah written in Hebrew. The deeper meaning may be hidden in the Torah, not the Septuagint (Klein & Spears, 2016, p. 20).

Fallacies of the eschatological views can be explained by considering the timeline of their developments and the motivations of the authors. A four-thousand-year chronology analysis of these views, from the ancient age to the present, provides insight into the timing and motivations of these views.

Chronology of Eschatological Views

Figure 67 shows the eight eschatological views at the times they were developed in history. The premillennialism view was the view of the early church fathers over two hundred years. Although there was no emphasis on the rapture until the nineth century, historical premillennialism that included the rapture was understood. The amillennial view was adopted in the Church because of the articulation of St. Augustine of Hippo (356-430 CE). His attack on apocalypticism, that Christ will return to judge the world and create a new heaven and new earth, was the articulation of allegorical millennialism, arguing that there was no millennium period where Christ ruled (Zakai & Mali, 1993). The development of St. Augustine's allegorical eschatology was influenced by ancient Greek philosophers like Plato.

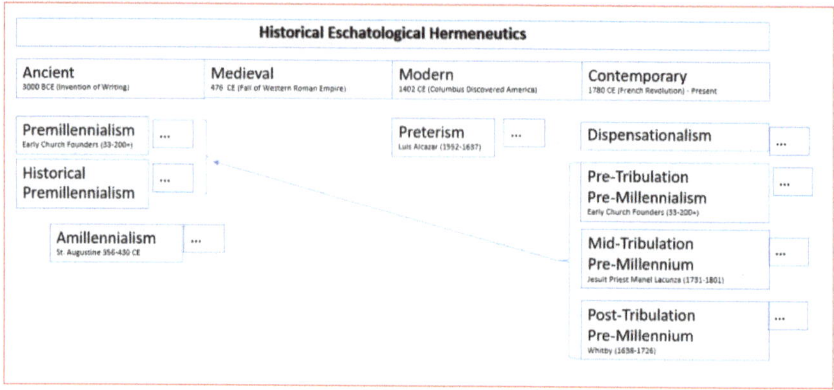

Figure 67: Eschatological Hermeneutics Timeline

Historical-criticism Analysis

The state of historical criticism approach to theological study is another source of fallacies in eschatological views. Historical criticism is an established approach to theological study and the harmony of the scriptures. It is literary judgment and commentation based on the context in which a work was written, including facts about the author's life and the historical and social circumstances of the time. The other type of criticism is textual and formal, which emphasizes examination of the text itself, disregarding outside influences on the text. Eta Linnemann challenges the validity of this view (Yarbrough, Trans., 1990/2001).

Chapter 13 Evidence in Historical Criticism:

Modern Bible scholarship has drifted far from the truth. The assumptions are so influential and inherently dangerous. Her general thesis is that theological and biblical research is most often pursued under atheistic influences. She analyzed the ideas that have shaped Western thought through four centuries, explaining how secular humanism, the Enlightenment, and German idealism have influenced Western universities in general and biblical scholarship. She argued that historical criticism constitutes an ideological system rather than the objective scientific method scholars say they observe. She exposed the presuppositions and dangers of the historical-critical system.

> *"Every leader and participant in our educational system owes it to themselves and to the public to face the issues starkly laid out in this volume. Intellect is in severe trouble today, and Eta Linnemann shows clearly why. Her analysis sets the agenda for responsible Christian intellectuals and ministers in our day." —Dallas Willard, University of Southern California. "*

> *She offers important insights and challenges to all who, within the academic enterprise, seek to be faithful interpreters of the Scriptures as the Word of God." —E. Earle Ellis, Southwestern Baptist Theological Seminary*

Eta Linnemann and the Historical-Critical Methodology

Impact on Western Culture (Yarbrough, Trans., 1990/2001, pp. 23-43)

Universities had their foundations in pagan institutions. In 529 BCE, the university in Athens was closed because of its pagan character. In the Middle Ages late twelfth century, the university was re-established in conjunction with renewed interest in aspects of pagan culture. The body of civil law contained laws from pre-Christian times. Aristotle was a pagan philosopher whose writings were the foundation of the first university in Paris (Yarbrough, Trans., 1990/2001).

Scholasticism embarked on bringing the new rational knowledge into agreement with the articles of faith. This effort set the tone for theological exertions in the late Middle Ages. It was assumed that man required the worldly wisdom of paganism alongside God's Word to make intellectual progress. The Bible became the authority only in areas of redemption and the Christian life. In contrast, Aristotle became the source of all valid knowledge of the world, such as natural science, social analysis, and the like (Ibid. p.26).

At the beginning of modern thought, humanism made the decision to reject God and make man the measure of all things. What was said about God was revealed by the human spirit, not God's Word. God's word was judged by the standard of humanistic culture (Ibid, p.27)

The Enlightenment period did not produce anything new. It only established the conditions for the humanist agenda. Francis Bacon said that every thought was found by inductive reasoning. He separated reason and science from faith and religion. Hobbes radically separated faith and thought by saying that faith belonged in the realm of absurdities and contradictions. He said, "There is no concept in the human understanding which did not first of all spring, entirely or partially, from the sense organs" (Ibid. p.29).

By the classical period, humanism matured in German idealism. The educational system became rooted more deeply in the image of man. Kant's philosophy impacted literature. Lessing, Schiller, and Goethe impacted poetic inspiration. Their characters took on lively and convincing features, becoming prototypes of the modern individual. Hegel's philosophy impacted the teaching of history.

In the Age of Technology, the intellectual starting point of technology was based on enlightenment and the humanistic concept of education. God was methodologically excluded. Researchers were respected and revered without question. The effect of atheistic intellectualism resulted in its ultimate confirmation. It was difficult to oppose thinking that produced the machines used daily. They organized the transportation systems. They furnished central heat and electricity that have become essential to modern life.

Parallel of Ancient Israel and the Modern West

What has happened to Western culture has a parallel in the history of Israel. Israel had split into two kingdoms, Israel in the north and Judah in the south. It was God's response to King Solomon's sin. Solomon provoked God by marrying foreign women for political reasons and allowing temples to be erected for their false gods. When Jeroboam became king of Israel in the North, he did evil continually despite being warned. He appointed priests for the high places from all sorts of people (1 Kings 13:33). He institutionalized the sin of apostasy by installing golden calves. He imposed strange gods on Israel by lying. He said the false gods brought them out of Egypt. Sinful and 'pious' flesh was encouraged to develop unhindered.

The pattern that crept in for Israel and for the West was similar, if not the same. First, only a few, one person, consciously made the decision not to regard God's Word any longer. That person was the instigator of a trend. Second, the flesh and sin were strengthened and given legitimacy by the leadership it followed. Life seemed right to fleshly tendencies instead of life in the spirit. Third, the fleshly life became normal, and a seductive undertone was set in motion. The question of what god had in mind was no longer relevant. Man decided his life goals without consulting God. Fourth, the tendency was guided by those in power. Everything is based on a humanistic worldview and a tolerance that permits everyone to be blessed however he sees fit. Fifth, the trend becomes a monopoly and a conditioning factor. Sixth, the one who commits himself to this way no longer sees it from God's point of view. However, God views it as a sin.

Eta Linnemann proclaims that Bible scholarship has drifted far from the truth. Historical-critical Theology is taught in universities all over the world. (Yarbrough, Trans., 1990/2001)

Historical criticism of biblical literature is a method of study and criticism that emphasizes the interpretation of biblical literature (exegesis, hermeneutics, history, archaeology, and Classical scholarship) (Yarbrough, Trans., 1990/2001).

In *Historical Criticism of the Bible*, Eta Linnemann tells how modern Bible scholarship has drifted far from the truth and why its assumptions are nonetheless so influential and, thereby, inherently dangerous. In part 1, she analyzes the ideas that have shaped Western thought through four centuries, explaining how secular humanism, the Enlightenment, and German idealism have influenced Western universities in general and biblical scholarship. In part 2, she argues that historical criticism constitutes an ideological system rather than the objective scientific method scholars say they observe—exposing the presuppositions and dangers of the historical-critical system.

"Every leader and participant in our educational system owes it to themselves and to the public to face the issues starkly laid out in this volume. Intellect is in severe trouble today, and Eta Linnemann shows clearly why. Her analysis sets the agenda for responsible Christian intellectuals and ministers in our day." —Dallas Willard, University of Southern California. "

She offers important insights and challenges to all who, within the academic enterprise, seek to be faithful interpreters of the Scriptures as the Word of God." —E. Earle Ellis, Southwestern Baptist Theological Seminary

Chapter 14: Historical Criticism הביקורת ההיסטורית habiqorett hahissetoritt ‏{ לך מזרחה. }

Historical criticism is the study of biblical literature that emphasizes the interpretation of biblical documents in the light of their contemporary environment. In her criticism of the university system in Germany, Christian scholarship in general, and particularly in the Western interpretation of Scripture, Eta Linneman argued against the methodology of historical criticism. See figure 68 for a historiography of the anti-Christian roots of atheism.

Historiography of Anti-Christian Roots of Atheism

Historical Period or Person	Impact
Middle Ages	Resorted to pagan philosophy as the means of gaining intellectual orientation
Humanism	Declared man to be the measure of all things
Enlightenment	Decided to acknowledge as truth only that which had been derived at inductively
Descartes	Starting premise had gained acceptance, according to which the only possibility of verification was through conferring validity to doubt
Lessing and Reimarus	Proclaimed the "ugly ditch" between "contingent facts of history" and "eternal truths of reason" and made popular through Nathan the Wise the idea that no one can say what the true faith is
Kant	His critique of pure reason and his conception of "Religion within the Bounds of Rason" began to gain acceptance
Goethe's Faust	Drew the consequences from Kant's criticisms of reason and attempted to ground faith in human religious experience rather than divine revelation
Schleiermacher	His point of departure in criticism of the Bible, a result of Enlightenment philosophy, began to gain acceptance in biblical exegesis
Semler	

Adaptation of Historical Criticism of the Bible, p.31

Figure 68: Historiography of Anti-Christian Roots of Atheism

SECTION V – Revelation Revisited

Chapter 15: Revelation from a Hebrew Perspective

Revelation from a Hebrew Perspective *התגלות מנקודת מבט עברית* (hitegalutt minequdatt mabatt'iveritt) {*שלום* }

God has chosen to make His presence known through the Father, the Son, and the Holy Spirit. As a tripod has three legs, there are things that are anchored on threes. Mankind, in God's image, is body, spirit, and soul. The soul of man is intellect, emotions, and will. S successful marriage of a male and female is anchored in the relationship of husband, wife, and God. The process of salvation is regeneration, sanctification, and glorification. Believers are married to Jesus through the entire story of the Bible. The books of the Law or Torah are the marriage contract, Joshua to Jude is the marriage preparation, and Revelation is the betrothal.

The book of Revelation, from a Hebrew perspective, rests on three solid supports: its Hebraicness, the menorah framework, and the four types of covenants, see figure 64.

Fundamental Truth Triads

Triads	1	2	3
Trinity	The Father	The Son	The Holy Ghost
Man in God's image	Body	Spirit	Soul
The Soul of Man	Intellect	Emotions	Will
Male-Female Marriage	Husband	Wife	God
Salvation	Regeneration	Sanctification	Glorification
The entire Bible is believers' marriage to Jesus	Torah is the marriage contract	Joshua to Jude is the marriage preparation	Revelation is the betrothal
Revelation	Hebraicness	Menorah	4 Covenant Types

Figure 69: Fundamental Truth Triads

With the understanding of this three-legged anchor, the study of Revelation can be enlightening, comprehensible, and instructive instead of confusing and difficult. After all, the Bible begins with instructions about how to live in the Torah, and it ends with instructions on how to be ready for the eschaton in Revelation (Klein & Spears, 2009, p. 24).

Hebraicness is the condition and fact that everything in Revelation is Hebrew. John the Apostle was Hebrew. He wrote Revelation in Hebrew. Revelation was written for Hebrews and believers grafted into a Hebrew people and culture. God originally spoke to Abraham in Hebrew, for him to communication in Hebrew to Hebrews. All communication was originally Hebrew. Moses wrote the Torah in Hebrew. Paul said he heard a voice speak to him in Hebrew on the Damascus Road (Acts 26:14). Jesus was Hebrew. Unless the original ancient Hebrew is used as the source for interpretation, there are bound to be significant errors and misunderstandings of the Book of Revelation.

The second leg of the Revelation triad is a structure or framework. The menorah provides that framework. God ordained the golden menorah. He poured His Spirit in Bezalel for him to make the original menorah for worship (Exodus 35:30-33) (Ibid, pp.112-113). The menorah had seven stems called branches that held the candles. The center branch was used to light the other candles on the six branches. There were three branches on each side of the center branch. The center lamp was the "eternal light" (Leviticus 24:2), also called the shemesh, or plumb line (Zechariah 4:1-14). There is a lamp with nine branches called the chanukiah. It is used in the celebration of Hanukkah in recognition of the rededication of the Second Temple in Jerusalem.

God's Master Menorah

The Master Menorah is composed of seven mini menorahs resting on the six branches and the central branch. It is a roadmap that groups related events together in chronological order (Klein & Spears, 2016).

Led by the Holy Spirit, Klein & Spears discovered the usefulness of the expert menorah. They applied it to how it identified to order of the chapters in Revelation, removing the confusion and perception that Revelation was a list of organized, disjoint events. They also applied the Master Menorah to the Satanic counter-covenants.

The third and final leg of the Revelation triad is interpreting Revelation in the light of four types of covenants.

Hebraic Understanding of Revelation

"Many people who attempt to interpret the book of Revelation do so according to their own sets of preconceptions and presumptions. Many of these preconceptions, in turn, are based on other misunderstandings that overlay each other and somehow "coalesce together" into a mishmash of faulty deductions – entire cathedrals resting on a few quivering bricks, standing on the edge" (Klein & Spears, 2016, p. 22).

On the other hand, the Hebrew hermeneutic used a rigorous system of logic where the scriptures operated on four levels simultaneously: direct and simple (*p'shat*), hinting (*remez*), commentary and comparison (*darash*), and deep and hidden (*sod*). The Greek translators used "translator's Greek," which was not spoken Greek. Scholars call it "sloppy Greek" (Klein & Spears, 2009, pp. 16-19).

The ancient Hebrews were immersed in a multilanguage culture because the major trade routes of that era went through Israel. To facilitate their trade, they had to be fluent in the languages of their buyers and merchants. They spoke at least four languages: Hebrew, Greek, Aramaic, and Latin. John the Revelator was Hebrew. Revelation was written in Hebrew. The Scripture was written for a Hebrew audience. At least ninety-two percent of the Scriptures in the entire Bible were originally written in Hebrew (Klein & Spears, 2016, p. 9).

Using the original Hebrew in the context of the Hebrew culture and language provides a deeper and correct understanding and interpretation. Revelation, in terms of simple English is the betrothal of the redeemed to Jesus. "The primary conceptual metaphor on which Revelation rests is the ancient Hebrew marriage covenant" (Klein & Spears, 2009, p. 26).

Figures 70-72 show Klien & Spears' selected interpretation of symbols and names in the book of Revelation (Klein & Spears, 2016).

Revelation Interpretations - Modern vs. Hebrew (1 of 3)

	MODERN INTERPRETATION	HEBREW INTERPRETATION
Organization	Revelation is an unorganized event	Structure based on Menorah
Plot	Story of the end of time	Story of the marriage betrothal of Jesus
24 Elders	The raptured church or Angelic beings	24 elders are the 12 apostles and the leaders of the 12 tribes of Israel
Living Creature (4:6)	Michael – Warrior (Prince) of God Gabriel – Messenger of God	Michael – Warrior (Prince) of God Gabriel – Redeemer of God Raphael – Healer of God Uriel – Light of God

Figure 70: Revelation Interpretations -Modernvs. Hebrew (1 of 3)

Revelation Interpretations - Modern vs. Hebrew (2 of 3)

	MODERN INTERPRETATION	HEBREW INTERPRETATION
Events on Earth		
1st Rider on the White Horse *Deception)	Rapture The word Crown is a loose translation.	Rider is not the Messiah. Hebrew word is *atarah*, a part of the tallit (prayer shawl) neckband or collar.
2nd Rider on Red Horse (War)	Will bring about the Battle of Armageddon	This is not Armageddon yet, there are four separate wars that have not happened yet
3rd Rider on the Black Horse (Famine)		
4t Rider on the Pale Horse (Death)		

Figure 71: Revelation Interpretations - Modern vs. Hebrew

Revelation Interpretations - Modern vs. Hebrew (3 of 3)

	MODERN INTERPRETATION	HEBREW INTERPRETATION
Events in Heaven		
144,000	Gentiles (Jehovah Witnesses)	Come from the 12 tribes of Israel. (12x12) means perfected righteous government, this will not change
144,000	End time Jews	Groomsmen – blood descendants of Abraham, Isaac, and Jacob (L.2799)
Four Angels standing at the four corners of the earth	Have authority over all the earth, holding back the winds	From a broader perspective God has maintained a wall of protection around humankind to bless and keep safe and do better and greater things 1.2609 'Holding back the winds' an idiom meaning Tod is holding back His blessing on the harvest (Deuteronomy 28-29) …
Main Storyline	End time disasters, plagues, ward, and judgments of God on earth (curses)	Two Brides, Two Destinies – events leading to the Wedding of the Lamb (blessings)

Figure 72: Revelation Interpretations - Modern vs. Hebrew (3 of 3)

The role of Israel (fallacy of replacement theory) (Fruchtenbaum, Jurik, et al., 1994).

[Ending] God's Plan of Redemption revealed the plan through the Bible. His plan was complete in the story of Revelation. The story has often been misunderstood by scholars, clergy, and laypeople. However, it is unfolded through the original Hebrew language that existed in the East. Knowing the true story with all its splendor, instruction, and blessings, GO EAST! PEACE!

לך מזרחה. שלום. lekhe mizerakhah. shalom.

Appendix - Coda קודה (kudah)

Conclusions (Coda)

This research led me to insights that are helping my personal journey in life and my walk with Christ. Those insights revolve around the meaning of end times, the study of theology, and the pedagogy of communicating the Hebrew Eastern perspective to Western Greek thinkers.

End-time revelation is not just revelation about the end of time. It is a revelation about Jesus Christ throughout time, from beginning to end, from Genesis to Revelation. The Bible helps us know something about Jesus through the finite lens of time. One day, we will know Him through the infinite time of eternity.

As a theologian, I have come to realize the value of the various views of eschatology is not necessarily to discover the right path to the eschaton or identify errors or motivation in eschatological thoughts. The value is in recognizing the thoughts of scholars and Church leaders in the context of time and the impact of their thoughts on humanity. Thinking and understanding change over time. Growth, decline, and detours are part of the Christian journey of disciples, leaders, and scholars. Theology is a journey, not a destination. It seeks to learn more about God and develop a closer relationship with Him. The study of theology must be undertaken as an evolving story of how the Bible and God are understood.

Teaching and learning are two sides of a cion. We must learn in order to teach, but we learn when we teach. Teaching Scripture properly requires knowing the context of history, culture, language, literature, and politics. We also need to know what we can about the personalities and perspectives of the writers, the audiences at the time of the writing, and the audience currently being taught. Teaching is a corporate process. We are not meant to study alone and not even pray alone. Early Christians did not go off to their secret closet; they just walked a foot away from the crowd, and others could hear them pray. That is what Jesus did when he was in the garden of Gethsemane. Teaching is learning. Teaching is listening. Teaching and learning are awareness. When we are in a state of awareness, we see beauty and experiencing peace and love, no matter what is going on around us, or to us, or in us.

Praying is awareness of God and His Creation, nature, animals, and, of course, humankind. Awareness is communication. That is the way we can pray without ceasing. Pray is mostly listening to God, the Trinity, and to each other.

I will use the Hebrew way of studying scripture in four ways. Studying engages our body, mind, and soul. To know thyself is a holistic experience, awareness of us and others. Preparation for studying is making sure our body, mind, and spirit are fresh, meaning that studying is eating right, exercising, thinking the right thoughts, and being in a Spiritual state.

He told us that He is going to return and live in heavenly fellowship with our Lord in a new heaven and a new earth. He said, in a twinkling of the eye, with the last trump. In the meantime, we must do all we can individually and collectively to go back to living Christianity.

The only way we can do this is to get on our knees. "Questions are solved on one's knees, not through ransacking commentaries" (Yarbrough, Trans., 1990/2001, p. 112), and then Go back to His Hebrew Scriptures and learn and live what He says. Translate His Scripture as to what they say, not interpret which scriptures as to what we think they mean. Apply them, yes, that's interpretation, but first, know what He meant, not what we mean or what they mean. We can only look back at the Eastern context (history, culture, language, and motivations) and go forward by contrasting the Western and Eastern worlds to see where and how to correct our interpretations.

The rapture, tribulation, 2nd coming of Christ, the 1,000-year millennium, Armageddon(s), the great white throne judgment, and the final, eternal, new heaven and new earth are the end time events; there are no other correct interpretations.

Thank God for God. In the name of Yeshua, I pray. Shalom!

The proper interpretation of God's plan of redemption is found throughout the Scripture in the Torah, Tanakh, and ancient Greek manuscripts.

Appendix – Becoming Me

Becoming Me:

Snippets of how I was, how I am, and how I hope to be!

(The good, some of the bad, and just a little of the ugly.)

Preface

This appendix is not an autobiography. It is a random set of reflective statements about some things that have happened are happening, and I hope they will happen in my life. My purpose for writing this is threefold. (1) I promised my children that I would write something about myself for them and for a father's legacy for generations to come. (2) I want to share my ongoing journey of becoming the me that each person experiences uniquely personally. My writings are a continuing evolution of becoming in the spirit of Gordon Allport's psychology of personality, which he says can be discovered by looking within ourselves (Allport, 1955, 1983, p. 23), and Becoming Michelle Obama (Obama, 2018). I want to share with my generation so they will know something about me, my perceptions, and my thoughts. (3) I want to share how God continues to bless me in spite of me and what a wonderful life I am living.

Sometimes, the stories are in chronological order but are mostly categorically ordered. For example, when I talk about the couples who inspired me the most, they are in chronological order of the eight cities in the seven states we lived in as a family. As the Bible has books written about major and minor prophets where the distinction is the length of each book, not the importance of the prophet, so too, the importance of each topic is not measured by the amount of space I give to the person or situation. No distinction is made in my writings based on the number of words I used to write about an individual or event. Remember that prophets like Elijah, Elisha, and Nathan do not have books about them in the canon, but they are just as important as Isaiah, Jeremiah, Ezekiel, and Daniel.

I mentioned a lot of relatives, but certainly not all, and not all with the same amount of detail. If I left anyone out or offended anyone, please let me know. I will correct it in the next book that I am writing that will be available next year, 2025. These are the relatives and people who came to my mind as having an impact on me and were in my spirit when I drafted these stories.

These snippets reflect primarily on the positive aspects of my life. That is not to say that my life, family, and relationships were without issue. We are all normal in the since that we have challenges, problems, and issues. Hopefully, my reflections will provide encouragement and hope for who you are becoming on your uniquely personal journey of life. Glory to God.

This appendix is divided into fourteen short chapters in somewhat random order and ends with my concluding remarks.

Chapter 1: Marriage

Chapter 2: Immediate Relatives

Chapter 3: Our Children

Chapter 4: Best Friends

Chapter 5: Best Couples Friends

Chapter 6: Inspiring People & Events

Chapter 7: Inspiring Clergy

Chapter 8: Religious Experiences

Chapter 9: Memorable Moments

Chapter 10: Education

Chapter 11: Work & Careers

Chapter 12: Trama Revisited

Chapter 13: Regrets

Chapter 14: My Life's Goals

Chapters can be read randomly. However, there is something to be gained by reading sequentially by page number order because it is the order I that the subjects came to my spirit. Once I wrote down the order and labeled them chapters, I did some minor sorting to make them reflect somewhat of a timeline. As I thought and wrote about each subject I jumped back and forth among the chapters based on what I was thinking about at the time.

Appendix – Becoming Me

Chapter 1: MARRIAGE

Genesis 2:18

> *"It is not good that the man should be alone;*
> *I will make him a help meet for him."*

God established marriage as a covenant. It is a means of serving and glorifying God. If the Lord wills, next year, December 30, 2025, will mark our sixtieth wedding anniversary. Our marriage is truly being blessed every day. It took years of spiritual growth to realize that marriage is between husband, wife, and God. When I came to that realization, marriage became more wonderful than it was when we started, and I did not think that was possible.

I met Elaine through my best friend in college, Henry McCain, at the end of the Fall semester of my junior year. Henry lived about 25 miles south of the college, but he stayed in the dorm (the 'residence hall' in today's vernacular). I stayed there, too, since I was living in New York City at the time. Henry invited me to his house over the weekend for some home-cooked meals. While we were there, Henry took me to his high school reunion, where I met Elaine briefly. I was standing outside the football field at night in the lightly drizzling rain. Henry and I walked over to Elaine and one of her female classmates. While Henry and Elaine reminisced for at least 10 minutes, my heart watched Elaine. I was fascinated by her beauty but more captive by how she expressed herself and her obvious intelligence. I fell in love immediately.

This feeling of love was a total shock because I was in a mental state for the past few months in school where I was tired of dating and focused on studying to become a professor of mathematics. Overwhelmed by Elaine's presence I interrupted Henry and whispered in his ear to ask the girls out for drinks. Elaine declined and told Henry she wanted to get back to her grandparents' house before it got too late. She and her siblings lived with her grandparents while her mother, who was divorced at the time, worked in New York City to earn money for her family. The result of that encounter was that Elaine and I said no more than hello and goodbye, nice to meet you. She showed no interest in me.

Henry and I returned to campus after that weekend in October 1965. I was more determined to focus on my studies and "give up girls" after being ignored by Elaine, but I could not get her out of my mind. I felt that I did not make a good impression on her because I was too reserved and dressed down. I had a reputation on campus for being a smooth dresser from New York.

A few weeks later Henry suggested that we go with the basketball team for a scrimmage game at South Carolina State College. Neither one of us played on the team. We traveled with the team so we could meet girls from other colleges. I declined because I was "tired of dating." When Henry told me Elaine was a student there, I immediately changed my mind. During the scrimmage game Henry found Elaine in the campus library studying with a group. He asked her to join us to talk and catch up. I had an agreement with Henry that he would not monopolize the conversation this time. He would re-introduce me and step back. As the three of us walked to Elaine's dorm I started the conversation of my life. We talked for a few hours until the game was over, and we had to get on the bus with the basketball team to return to the campus. Elaine had a boyfriend on her campus who was visiting his parents in Florida. The most poignant thing about that conversation was that Elaine told me, "I don't like jive talk, I am a serious person." After I got over the hurtle of trying to smooth-talk to her, we had a serious conversation about life.

We continued the conversation in letters to each other during the next few weeks. I went home with Henry for Thanksgiving, but this time, it was to spend time with Elaine. Henry arranged a few foursome dates where Elaine and I were able to talk more. Well, after the Thanksgiving break, Elaine and I continued writing to each other. Christmas came, and I went home with Henry again. At this point, Elaine and I were getting serious about each other. So, after meeting Elaine briefly in October, spending Thanksgiving and Christmas together. Shortly after Christmas, before it was time to go back to our respective schools, I invited Elaine to a club in Augusta, GA, where I played the drums in a jazz trio. During one of the breaks, I asked Elaine to marry me. The rest is history. She said yes, we eloped on December 30, 1965, and were married in the courthouse in Augusta, GA, by judge Iree Pope, witnessed by Elaine's grandparents. Not even my brother who was attending college with me knew. It had to be love, we are still happily married 58 years later.

When we married in our junior year Elaine was attending South Carolina State University in Orangeburg, SC., and I was attending Paine College in Augusta, GA, about 75 miles away. I was not driving then so Jimmy and I caught the bus to Orangeburg and a cab to the Pinkney house. Jimmy and I registered for separate rooms. Mrs. Pinkney checked us in. Elaine stayed with me, and Jimmy had a young lady from the campus stay with him. We asked if there was a store nearby to get a few items. We were told there was a store downstairs in the hotel. When we went downstairs, we saw the store gated and locked. Mr. Pinkney came, opened the door, got behind the counter and said, "How can I help you." After we bought our items, we went back to our room and ordered dinner. Mr. Pinkney delivered the food that his wife cooked.

We stayed for a few days. On April 1st, April Fools' Day, I invited Jimmy to my room. Elaine and I were in bed. I said, "Jimmy, I would like you to meet my wife." Jimmy, who was never without words, just stood in silence long enough to realize I was not kidding. He turned and left without a word. He returned about an hour later and said congratulations, and we talked. I kept the secret for three months, December 30 – April 1, because when I confided in him about my desire to get married, he thought he talked me out of it. Over the months and years Jimmy became like a protective big brother to Elaine. That was the only time in my life and for the rest of my life that I did not confide in my brother.

The next day we noticed that construction was going on in the back of the hotel. When we asked Mrs. Pinkey about it, you guessed it, she said her Mr. Pinkney was doing the construction. The experience of seeing Mr. Pinkney do everything was funny and amazing. Finally, when it was time to go, we asked for a cab. When we when downstairs to catch the cab, Mr. Pinkney was waiting in his car to take us to the bus stop.

Chapter 2: IMMEDIATE FAMILY

Genesis 1:28

"And God blessed them, and God said unto the,
Be fruitful and multiply ...

We were a family of five, my mother, father, sister, brother, and me. I am the youngest sibling, and my sister is the oldest. We are the only two survivors as I am writing this story. I am living in Greensboro, N.C., and my sister is living in Orlando, FL. Start with my father first, whose love for his family showed in his dedication and commitment to work several jobs to care for his family and always took what little time he had to talk with us individually and collectively.

POP (Alpheus James Harrigan, Sr.). My father was born in St. Thomas, VI. He was raised by my grandmother. He left home at 16 to work in New York City and sent money back to his mother. As we were growing up, Pop worked two jobs to make ends meet at home. He asked Mommy to stay home and care for the children, me, my brother, and my sister). I do not remember if mommy ever worked outside the home. After odds-and-end jobs like painting houses, he eventually worked Monday-Friday from 3 -11 PM at the New York Transit Authority as an assistant dispatcher. Two years before he retired, he because a full dispatcher, which he tried for years to pass the test for the promotion.

During the day, he worked at ITT, a telegraph company, from 8 AM to noon and all day Saturday. As a teenager, I worked part-time with ITT after school and on Saturdays. On Saturdays, Pop and I left the house together. We rode the subway to ITT headquarters on Canal Street to pick up mail to take to our respective office locations. I enjoyed going to work with my father.

Pop often told us to be careful where he walked. He joked that we might step in a puddle of something that would take the souls off our shoes. Ironically, one day, he stepped on a banana peel while at work and broke his arm so much for watching where we walked.

Pop grew up speaking English and Patios French, a local dialect of French in St. Thomas. He taught himself Spanish and Italian and loved to meet people in the streets and converse with them in their languages. He wanted to be a medical doctor but had not had the opportunity.

He was a prolific reader. On Sundays, the only day he did not have to work, he loved to read the New York Times cover-to-cover and the Reader's Digest Magazine. The magazine always featured a 20-word vocabulary test. He got upset when he missed two words. I was pleased when I got two words right. I did not like to read. As pop read, I sat on the floor by him and shined all the shoes I gathered from the family.

Every Sunday morning, I went to the local newsstand to buy the New York Times for Pop. Gradually, neighbors in other apartments in our building and in other buildings in the block started asking me to buy their Sunday papers. Before I knew it, I had a lucrative paper delivery business at 12 years old. Oddly enough, I never got robbed carrying my pockets bulging with quarters.

In Booker T. Washington junior high school, I remember copying book reports from book summaries instead of reading the assigned book and drafting my own report. The teacher would call me to her desk every time, point out a word in the report, and ask me the meaning, to which I always reply, "I don't know." She would send me back to rewrite the report. Bless her heart, she always gave me another chance, so I did not fail the class.

Pop loved family. He looked forward to family gatherings in the apartment, whether it was his side, my mother's side, or both. In those days, we never had family reunions, but when we gathered in small groups, he always loved to dance to calypso music.

He was a talker and a wealth of information. When I came home from college during the summers, he would ask me what I had learned. He would always say, "Is that all?" When I asked him a question, he would flood me with information. I once told Pop, joking about his overwhelming information, "I asked you for a drink of water, and you gave it to me from a "firehose."

Pop and I had memorable, personal times together on Sundays for about two years when he and I went to Sunday School and church. My mother and siblings did not come. However, the whole family attended a Baptist church on special occasions, especially for Easter.

Pop's mother came from St. Thomas to New York City and lived here about two years and lived with Pop's youngest brother, Uncle Holger. I never asked or thought about why she came and returned to St. Thomas. Still, I enjoyed visiting her and eating my favorite West Indian dish – fungi. Fungi, or cou-cou, is a **Caribbean** dish made with cornmeal, okra, and butter.

I love my relatives on my father's and mother's side. I have so many fond memories of the good times at family gatherings and personal one-on-one times with many of them. I learned things because they were all talkers. For example, my Uncle Holger taught me to make toasted tuna fish sandwiches. He was a supply officer on a Navy ship and often was on voyages for six months.

After my mother died, my father and brother came to live with me and my family in Greensboro, NC. Later, my father and brother moved to a nearby home. My father bought the house.

Although Pop never smoked, he died of throat cancer a few days before his 82nd birthday on July 23, which was my birthday. He contracted cancer from a lengthy career in the system, where he was constantly exposed to fumes from the trains and the filth of the underground, where he worked in a small office with three people. He could see the trains through the six-foot-long, dirt-covered, wall-to-wall window in the office. Observing the trains was part of the job of dispatching.

MOMMY (Emily Peterson Harrigan). My father met my mother in night school where they were studying for their GED diploma. They were happily married and distinguished role models of marriage all their lives. When she passed, my father did not date or remarry, although the 'older ladies' loved him. He liked to go to dinner at their houses and talk non-stop to their husbands.

Mommy was the youngest of four sisters. Two of her sisters lived in New York. The place they met daily was at my mother's house. Pop was usually working. Mommy was quiet, kind, and very loving. She enjoyed being with family, particularly her older sisters, Aunty Hattie and Aunty Ruby. Although Aunty Hattie would make it challenging for mommy sometimes because, when my sister Patsy wanted something that mommy could not give Patsy, Aunty Hattie would. Her other sister, Aunty Annie, lived in August, GA, and so did Uncle Sambo and Uncle Enoch with their wives and families.

Mommy loved music. She played classical music in the living room of our apartment. I do not know when they bought the piano. To my knowledge, she never played outside the home. She may have played in the church as a little girl when she lived in Augusta. I only remember the piano always being there. My parents paid for my piano lessons while I was in junior high school. I kept the piano until I passed it on to my granddaughter, Sophia, who plays better than I ever did. I am so proud of her.

My mother was also learning to play the guitar. I do not know when she bought it. Mr. Smith, who lived in a building next to ours came over sometimes to teach her. Our family was close to the Smiths.

I got my love of music from my mother. I learned to play the piano to the level of Moonlight Sonata, but I loved to play the drums. In my junior year of high school my parents bought a set of drums for me. They were top-of-the-line, black, Ludwig, 5-piece drum set with Zildjian symbols with all the accessories, including a cow bell with a rolling case to house the snare drum and accessories. My parents paid a lot of money that they sacrificed for me. The other 4 drums had individual cloth covers. I loved that set, but I sold it to Frank Abel's brother when I left for college, thinking that when I needed them again, I could buy a new set. Frank Abel was my high school classmate who was an accomplished musician somewhere in Europe, I think France. That sale became a mistake in retrospect because, in my junior year in college, I started playing the drums in nightclubs. My brother and I scraped up enough money to buy a cheap, white pearl, 3-piece set and symbols, no other accessories, and no cases.

Mommy had her sad moments. I caught her many times in the kitchen alone, weeping because she missed her mother. I remember Mommy being upset with my Aunty Annie when she came to pick us up from the summer in Augusta. I was about 5 years old and a highly active, playful, mischievous child. Our teenage first cousin Godfrey rode his bicycle over to Tutt's restaurant, across from the "home-house," where we were playing with our friends. He agreed to take us back to Aunty Annie's funeral home, about 3 blocks away. Patsy, Jimmy, and I hopped on the back of the bicycle. I was in the back. Godfrey told me to hold my feet out so they will not get caught in the spokes of the wheel. We did not get 6 feet on our journey before I put my foot in the spokes, and we all tumbled down. I had a hole in my angle area that was bleeding. We finally got to Aunty Annie's funeral home, where she saw what happened to my ankle. She was so frustrated with little incidents I had been having all summer she says, "Oh boy, go and sit down somewhere."

A few days later, when my mother arrived, she had the doctor look at my foot. The doctor told her the wound should have been dressed right away because gangrene was about to set in. Needless to say, she had a few words for her big sister. Mommy was absolutely right to chastise her sister. However, in partial defense of Aunty Annie, my aunt had enough of my reckless acts. A couple of weeks earlier, Aunty Annie had to have one of her workers drive me to the hospital in the funeral home ambulance. My head was wrapped in a towel that was turning red from blood. I had been playing on the swing screen door of the home-house by opening the screen door as far as I could and jumping on the door to catapult myself into the living room. The spring of the door broke, hit my head, and drew dripping blood. As it turned out, it was a minor cut requiring no stitches. That was the most traumatic incident of many false alarms that I had throughout the summer.

I remember taking mommy to the doctor because pop was at work, Patsy was married, and Jimmy was in college. The doctor said she was going through a change of life. That night, while I was sleeping, my father took her to emergency. I did not know until he returned the next morning. He told me she had a bleeding ulster and was hours from dying.

Mommy and I had fun together often. I stayed in the kitchen and helped whenever she made pound cake from scratch. Patsy and Jimmy did not hang around the kitchen much, although they always suddenly appeared to help me eat the remaining cake batter. The three of us put our spoons in the bowl at the same time. It was fun. When mommy made cornbread, she would always have a personal pan for me. I loved cornbread and greens. When I came home from the hospital recovered from pneumonia, she said she would fix me anything I wanted to eat. I was about 5 years old. I told her I wanted collard greens and cornbread. I contracted pneumonia because my mother was gone for the day, and my father was taking care of me. He went to sleep, and I played with toys, putting them in a tub of water for hours on end. The apartment was cold and drafty, and my shirt was damp all day.

As children, we had Caster Oil, Three-sixes (666), and other bad-tasting medicines to cure any cold. At that time, the drug stores even sold over-the-counter penicillin. But I hated castor oil. Whenever my mother tried to give me Castor Oil at 5 years old, she and her sisters who were visiting had to catch me, sit me in a chair, hold me down while they wrapped me in a towel like a strait jacket, and pry my mouth open. My mother said I was an obedient child in general, but not when it came to Caster Oil. Today, I still will not touch the stuff or give it to my worst enemy.

I enjoyed my mother's family too. My uncle Pete was an MP in the Army, and he taught me how to iron shirts and how to dress. Years later, when their only daughter got married. Elaine and I travelled to the wedding. I had not talked to my uncle in at least a year. When I saw him, it confirmed that he taught me to dress. We independently selected the same style tuxedo, a striking gray jacket with black and gray pin-striped pants. The accessories were the same also, and we did not rent them from the same shop. He was an unbelievable cook, although that was not his profession. I am not sure what his profession was. I know he was a star athlete in basketball and football in high school in Augusta, GA. He worked in a men's garment factory in New York.

Aunty Reena, his second wife, was a secondary school vice principal in New York City. She and Uncle Pete taught us how to entertain. They often gave dinner parties at their upscale condominium in upper Manhattan. Jimmy and I hosted at their parties to take coats, brought drinks, and took care of their guest. Uncle Pete and Aunty Reena were the first in the family to buy a color TV for their living room and a buy portable color TV for their only daughter, Lisa, who I baby sat many times.

Aunty Hattie reinforced the work ethic for my brother and me. She had us come to her house on the weekends, where she would assign chores. It usually took an hour or so. She paid us 25 cents each. That was enough to go to the RKO movie around the corner and buy lots of snacks. The movie ticket costs 5 or 10 cents for about 3 hours of entertainment: a news reel of current events, 5-10 cartoons, and a featured movie. One time, we found a peanut bag between the seats we chose to sit in. It was brimming with pennies, nickels, dimes, and quarters. Jimmy and I stayed in the movie all day and got sick buying and eating snacks.

PATSY (Patricia Ann Harrigan): Is the oldest sibling, six years older than me and four years older than my brother, Jimmy. We called her the Red Cross because we went to her to supply our wants, usually money. Patsy is outgoing and friendly, always surrounded by friends. Being the oldest grandchild in the family on my mother's side, "they" spoiled her. But she was the one her friends gravitated to.

For years since Patsy was about 16 years old she gave an annual New Years Eve party in our apartment. At least 100 people crammed into the small apartment every year from all five boroughs of Manhattan. She did not have to invite anyone to the party; they always knew when and where it was. In fact, when she married, Jimmy took over the tradition for a year. After he left for college, they still kept coming but it eventually stopped when I turned everyone away each year for the next three years. After the parties, Patsy usually had sleepovers for five or six of her friends. I only remember Dale, who I had a crush on and Faith. Imagin, I was 10 years old when she had her sixteen-year-old girlfriends at her sleepovers. I was so little, and they felt I was so "cute" that they let me stay up and listen to a girl talk about the party, boys, and life. That is how I developed a crush on Dale.

When we were growing up, we had a dog named Trixy. One day, we heard Patsy say ouch, and then the dog hollered. When Patsy was asked what happened, she said, "the dog bit me, and I bit him back."

Patsy was president of a Manhattan Chapter of the Xinos(fillin) Sorority when she was in high school. She attended a high school named the Fashion Institute of Technology in New York City. She is a creative designer and artist of women's clothing but never had the opportunity to pursue her passion. She loves to travel and has had the opportunity to go to Paris, France.

When I was a newborn baby, she held me out of the four-story window of our apartment to show me to her friends, which almost frightened mommy to death.

Patsy loved to clean. On Christmas mornings, Jimmy and I woke up at our usual time, around 4 AM, to see what Santa brought us. We often played until 7 AM, when everyone was starting to get up. When Patsy woke up, she chased us out of the room to straighten up before relatives started visiting in the afternoon. Our house was the meeting place for the family.

Patsy and I always got along, but there was a period of time when we could not talk to each other about religion or politics because of the significant differences in beliefs and practices. The difference was resolved when we began to study the Hebrew language and scriptures together. It was the common denominator of our differences. We can talk about anything now.

Patsy married Louie Villa, a neighbor living in the same block. When they lived in the Bronx, I used to visit them and would go to a local bakery factory a few blocks away to get donuts fresh out of the oven. Louie introduced me to putting ice in my milk to drink with the donuts, ice-cold milk. I still drink mike like that today.

Patsy and Louie have three wonderful children, Tonya, Dana, and Gia, who are successfully navigating life in the face of life's challenges. They live in separate states. Tonya is the Christian warrior of the family and the keeper of the family heritage. Dana was a blossoming engineer when she had a car accident that left her mentally challenged, but she seems content in a warm and caring living facility. She has two grown daughters, Melissa and Stephanie. Gia is a successful attorney and has two wonderful, successful children, Rob and Tia. My prayer for them is they migrate, somehow, to the same city and continue navigating life together.

Louie will always be like a big brother to me. I stayed in touch with him and visited him in Orlando, FL, a few years before his death. Although I stayed for less than an hour, it was a joyous reunion. Louie used to take Jimmy and me for rides in his car. He taught me how to play a variety of card games, most notably Bid Whist, which carried me through college dorm competitions with excellence. I have to confess; a few times, Louie took us ice skating in New York. The problem was we played hooky to go. Fortunately, we never got in trouble.

When I think of my sister I think of a resilient, caring, loving person who is angered by the Lord and accepting her lot in life even though she only had fleeting moments of realizing her dreams. I admired his intellect, sociability, gregariousness, trendy clothing style yes, and his way with the ladies. Jimmy and Susan Taylor were soulmates who never realized their potential together.

JIMMY (Alpheus James Harrigan, Jr. aka Papa Razi). I was closer to him than anyone in the family. He was my friend and role model. We could talk about anything. Jimmy was a bookworm in his early years. At the age of 12, he read the entire 20-volume encyclopedia that was in our house. He did not spend time in the street like me. Although he was 2 years older, I felt the need to protect him, although I never had to, because he did not know the street like me.

When Jimmy was in elementary school, his teachers recognized his intelligence, and they knew he was not applying it. One semester, the teacher met with our parents to address Jimmy's failing and low grades. At home, my parents asked Jimmy why he was not trying his best, encouraging him to do better. His response was, "The more I do, the more they want me to do." The next grading period, he decided to do his best; he earned all A's. He even entered a contest on the radio and won an authentic full-feathered Indian bonnet about 4 or 5 feet long. He was clearly a quiet, reserved, stay-at-home intellect in his early years.

One Christmas, Jimmy and I got bows and arrows for Christmas. The bows were sold by strength based on age. Since Jimmy was two years older, he had a much stronger bow. I had a weaker bow, but I could not bend the string to shoot my arrow. He tried to help me and pulled too hard, breaking my bow. That was the only thing I toy I had for Christmas, so I had nothing new. That was a long, sad day. I was not angry with Jimmy. I was just sad that I could not shoot my bow and arrow.

Growing up, we had several dogs in the apartment, one at a time, but all named Trixy. Unfortunately, one time, Jimmy and I traumatized our Trixy. We repeatedly took Trixy to the top of our double-decker bed and tossed him off until he yelled out, limped away, and hid. When Pop came home, he said we broke Trixy's leg. Pop put a splint on Trixy's leg and doctored him until he was well; we could not afford professional treatment. Trixy must have forgiven us because we did not play that game anymore, and he continued to love us like he always did.

I loved the dogs and cats we had over the years, but I learned a valuable lesson about cuddling animals too much. I must have been about 6 or 7 years old when I chased Trixy around the apartment. Trixy ran under a bed that was against the wall in a way that he could not escape. I cornered him where he could not move and began snuggling my face up to his. It was hot in the apartment. The apartment was usually extremely hot or very cold, rarely exactly right. Suddenly, Trixy grabbed my nose and wiggled it back and forth until I managed to escape. Needless to say, I ended up getting a few tiny stitches. It was an ordeal getting me to the clinic because only Patsy, Jimmy, and I were home at the time. Fortunately, my neighbor helped up; she was a registered nurse and the mother of one of my closest friends, Chucky. My mother met Mrs. Gaetan at the clinic, and we were in-and-out in about an hour.

The incident happened close to Christmas. When my mother brought me home that same afternoon Patsy and Jimmy were so angry with me. They were considering that the cost of the clinic would mean there was no money for Christmas. They told me I ruined their Christmas. I was devastated because I looked up to both siblings. Thank God that Christmas was one of the best we had up to that point.

Jimmy liked exotic animals, but he never got the pets that he wanted. I remember him asking for a bald eagle, which he said he could keep in the bathroom in the tub. He also asked for a black panther.

Jimmy changed overnight. It was when he fell in love when he met Valery in the summer of his eighth grade in school. Suddenly, he stopped reading books and began hanging in the street. He learned karate to defend himself. Incidentally, Jimmy started taking care of me in the streets.

We were working in the summer of 1964 during school break for HARYOU (Harlem Youth Opportunities Unlimited), an American social activism organization founded by psychologists Kenneth Clark and Mamie Phipps Clark in 1962. The group worked to increase opportunities in education and employment for young blacks in Harlem. They received a federal grant for Project Uplift intended to prevent riots from happening again. Jimmy came to my rescue one day at lunchtime. I just finished eating at Woolworth's on 125th Street. I was approached from two different directions by men who pretended to not know each other. One man asked me for directions and wanted me to show him to the Teresa Hotel a few blocks away. The other man coming from the opposite direction happened to hear the conversation and offered to help. After the first man said he would pay us $10 each to take him to the hotel, I was making about $20 a day at HARYOU, we started out towards 7th avenue. As I was about to cross the street Jimmy yelled out my name from the adjacent corner across the street. I yelled that I would be right back. He yelled again, and the men ran.

Befuddled when Jimmy walked over to me, he explained that those men had been running that game all day. They were going to take me to the hotel and rob me. My brother taught me what I did not know about the streets and saved me from danger many times.

Jimmy was outgoing and popular wherever he lived. Jimmy loved to dance. His favorite club was the Palladium in New York. He danced so well with all the ladies that he never had to pay the steep cover charge to enter the club. He was a good advertisement for the club.

Jimmy had an enterprising spirit. With a BS in mathematics and an MS in business administration he never worked a "real job" in his life. He worked now and then in ground-floor level jobs but did not stay long. Jimmy almost did not get his BS degree. When it came time for graduation, the registrar told him he was missing a lower-level math course. He produced a letter, written and signed by the registrar, that wavered the requirement. The registrar did not honor the letter; he simply said that he should not have written it. We were all furious, especially since he was told days before graduation and our parents were coming from New York. He marched, but he did not receive his degree until the end of the summer.

Unethically, I did more than I should to help him and his math major friends to graduate. You see, every student had to pass a comprehensive exam in their major subject area. I was a junior and considered a scholar at that time, and I finished all the requirements for a degree in mathematics in my junior year, but I was not allowed to take the exam until my senior year. Somehow, Jimmy and his friends found a discarded carbon paper copy of the comprehensive exam. They brought it to me, and I solved the problems for them. It turned out to be the actual exam. They all passed. Shame on me! It got worse. I was so furious with the school for denying Jimmy's degree that I took matters into my own hands. I went back to New York for the summer, enrolled in the class as Jimmy, passed as Jimmy, and he graduated that summer. Shame on me again!

His passion from childhood and throughout life was photography, not mathematics. Jimmy had professional cameras since he was in the 5th or 6th grade. When he was in his late teens, he was a freelance photographer for Pop's cousin, who published a local newspaper in Harlem. He took pictures of people and events around the city, particularly of "good-looking" women. He was known for walking up to a beautiful woman and saying, "You look good enough to know me."

After graduating from college, he moved to Atlanta, GA, to attend Atlanta University. When he completed his MBA, he opened a photography shop on Peachtree Street in Atlanta. He was there for several years before moving back to New York City.

Jimmy married twice. First, in Atlanta, GA, to Janet, a Muslim lady with three children, when he became a Muslim. He treated those children like they were his own. They divorced, but I do not remember why.

Until his death, he was married to Kitty Maddox. They were married for ??? Fill years, definitely were soul mates. They loved to hang out in Greensboro, dance Latin dances, have fun, and tend to a small garden and a grapevine behind their house.

Jimmy died seven days after his 73rd birthday. He passed eight weeks after being diagnosed with pancreatic cancer. He had no idea that he was sick. Jimmy went to emergency because he was feeling weak and lost 15 pounds in about two weeks. The doctor showed no social grace or patient sympathy. The doctor came to Jimmy's bed in the hospital and said, "do you want the bad news or the bad news." He proceeded to tell Jimmy that he had cancer and he had six weeks to live.

RODNEY (That is me): I experienced growing up in the ghetto of Harlem in New York City in the 1950s and 60s in a loving family of father, mother, sister, and brother, despite living in an apartment building infested with mice and roaches in an environment of gangs, numbers, prostitution, and teenage pregnancy. Unaware of what God was doing in my life, I was born into a God-fearing, loving family. I survived the ghetto when so many friends did not live to reach the age of 20. Yet, I experienced "success" in Corporate America, academia, the religious arena, and even music. To God be the glory for the things He has done in the lives of my family and me.

I am the youngest sibling, six years younger than my sister and two years younger than my brother. Patsy and Jimmy liked to send me to my parents or relatives to plead for what they wanted because I was the "baby." Unbelievably, I enjoyed it. I was doing something for my big sister and big brother. My mother said I was an obedient child, but if I was, it was because I saw the whippings Patsy and Jimmy got and knew not to do those things. Besides, I beat myself up enough with the mischiefs I mentioned earlier.

My early aspiration in life was to be a father. I loved and admired my father and mother so much. By the time I was in junior high school, I wanted to be a jazz drummer, and I did become one for a brief time in college. In college I wanted to be a professor of mathematics. When I started working with computers in corporate America, I wanted to be a senior systems engineer. That developed into a desire to become a Chief Information Officer (CIO), which I did as Vice Chancellor of Information Technology. But now, I am devoted to the intense study of God's Word, getting a closer relationship with Him.

Chapter 3: ELAINE'S FAMILY

Psalm 68:8

"God setteh the solitary in families …

Elaine's family is a huge part of my life's experience and is a tremendous blessing. I feel like I have always been a member of the family. Compared to my family, Elaine's family stayed in contact with each other much more than mine. Twenty years into our marriage I was still meeting relatives and spent a lot of time during family gatherings and visits. To me, her mother, Inez, was the most special by far. She was like a second mother and told me so when my mother died. From the first day she saw me, she greeted me like I was her birth son. Other than my mother, Inez was one of the kindest people I knew, second only to her mother, Big Mama. Big Mama was so kind and giving. She cooked the best meals.

I used to catch the bus from Augusta to Edgefield during the Spring semester of my senior year at Paine College. Elaine was 75 miles away, attending South Carolina State University. I would go to Mr. John Henry Lloyd's barbershop, Elaine's grandfather, and wait for him to end his day and drive me to the grandparents' house. I would call Elaine and say: "Guess where I am? I am at Big Mama and Papa's house eating grits with red eye gravy and ham." Needless to say, Elaine was happy to come to visit her grandparents, but she has some punitive words about being there when she could not, in love, of course. I did not have a car or drive, so I could not pick her up. I did not learn to drive until two years later.

Elaine has two brothers. Donald became a fiery minister. It seemed like he was converted overnight, instantly quoting an enormous number of Scriptures. My role model is Johnny, a caring, compassionate person who raised himself up from living in the streets of Harlem to becoming a community-based barber in Jacksonville, FL, where he sponsored programs for school supplies for kids. I am always inspired by how he lifted himself out of the mirey clay and is living the Christian life.

Elaine has four sisters: Beverly and Mary, from her first marriage to Eddie Mims; Linda, a stepsister; and Vonnie, a half-sister from her second marriage to Harold Ross. Beverly is the "village reporter." She spreads the news on everything she can find out. Over the years, when

Elaine and I moved, several times Beverly usually ended up living near us and sometimes with us. She is very giving, but I have to say I was disappointed when she stayed away from Elaine since Elaine has Alzheimer's and is blind from Glaucoma. She said she could not stand to see Elaine in that condition. Beverly called or came sparingly but not like a sister should especially since Elaine constantly called out her name for years, now not so much. In Elaine's sickness, she really yearned for Beverly. Beverly was married three times and has two sons, Stuart and Ryan. Mary is a free-spirited sister who loves an enjoyable time and staying engaged with family. She is studying and teaching the Word. The Lord will call her to ministry; only He knows. She checks on Elaine regularly and is always sending her something or visiting her from Maryland. Mary was married to Sidney Smith. They have one child, Arielle. Linda lives in upstate New York. She is a devoted wife to Peter Roberts, and they have one child, Cory. They keep the lines of communication open with Elaine, especially during holidays and birthdays. Vonnie lives in Alabama; she was married to Tony and had tw0 children, Jazman and Jusrin. Vonnie can really pray moving prayers. Vonnie has been sick over the years, but she hangs in there so well.

Elaine has a lot of friends. She was always loving and a natural leader. In high school she established the "Sevenettes," a group of seven young ladies who carried themselves with respect and dignity in all the activities they did in and out of school. She also has a friend named Alva Lewis, who was one year ahead of her in school. Alva's parents were schoolteachers and extremely strict on Alva. As a testimony of the integrity and reputation of Elaine and her grandparents who Elaine lived with, Alva's parents would only let Alva have sleepovers at Elaine's grandparents' house. Alva grew up to be a beloved and powerful principal in Edgefield, SC.

Chapter 3: OUR CHILDREN

Psalm 127:3-5

"3 Lo, children are a heritage of the LORD: and the fruit of the womb is his reward.4 As arrows are in the hand of a mighty man, so are children of the youth. 5 Happy is the man that hath his quiver full of them: they shall not be ashamed, but they shall speak with the enemies in the gate.

Pamela and Sherrice were born three years apart at Columbia Presbyterian Medical Center in New York City, the same hospital in which I was born. During that time there were not a lot of black nurses. When Pamela was born, hospitals did not allow fathers in the delivery room, but we did go through classes on what to do when we brought our wives in and stayed with them until they took her to the delivery room, like how to keep her calm. In one of the classes, a nervous father listened to step-by-step instructions on which door to enter the hospital, what elevator to take, what floor to go to, and more. When the instructor finished, the nervous father said, "What do I do after I open the door to enter the hospital?" He obviously was too nervous to hear any of the steps. When it was time to bring Elaine home from the hospital, I was petrified at the thought of holding Pamela. I did not want to hurt our delicate baby. The nurse sensed my reluctance, and no one else was with me to help bring Elaine and Pamela home. So, the nurse just took Pamela out of Elaine's arms and put Pamela in my hands, saying, "Take care of your baby." I have been holding Pamela ever since.

When Sherrice was born three years later, in the same hospital, the procedure was the same. When we got to the point where the nurse greeted us, it was the same black nurse. The changes that were happening in such a large hospital were unbelievable. She smiled and greeted up by saying affectionately, "Are you back again?" One important addition to the hospital procedure was that fathers could go into the delivery room. When it was time, I was taken to the delivery room, where I sat by Elaine and held her hand. When Sherrice came out, there was no sound of a baby crying. Sherrice was silent. I could see the doctor and a score of nurses leave Elaine's bedside and rush Sherrice over to another side of the delivery room. I was so glad they seated me in a chair by Elaine; otherwise, I would have blanked out in fear. Elaine sensed something was wrong and asked me what was happening. I tried to assure her that everything was okay, but I gave my fear away. Elaine says, "Then why are you squeezing my hand so tight." At that point, Sherrice yelled out a loud newborn baby sound; a relief engulfed the room, the doctor, and all the attendants.

Our children are our very lives and mean more to us than life itself. I know that Elaine and I would give our lives for them. Our priorities are God, spouse, and children: Pamel and her husband Isaac, Sherrice and her husband Bryan, and their daughter Sophia, our only grandchild. They are amazing. I can author books about all of them.

Pamela: I see the essence of Pamela in her spirit of retention, kindness, independence, positivity, determination, her heart for God, and a prayer warrior like Sherrice.

Retention: Pamela has a great memory. We sometimes call her a human recorder because she remembers everything. I am amazed at how she retains so much information that she needs for her three businesses, accounting, law, and insurance.

Kindness: Pamela always had a spirit of kindness. No matter what the situation is, she treats people with kindness and respect.

Independence: When she was 5 years old, she wanted to ride her tricycle to school by herself. The school was around the corner; she did not have to cross any streets; a school crossing guard was at the corner, so we let her. Of course, I followed her in my car, slowing up traffic as I was moving about 5 mph. When Pamela was little, she wanted to do everything herself. Her favorite saying was, "I do it."

Positive: Pamela is always positive about life and people. Even when she was diagnosed with Breast Cancer, instead of being gloomy and depressed, in spite of being afraid, she began studying all she could about the disease and gradually changed to a healthier lifestyle for the whole family. Pamela has been in remission for over fifteen years.

Determination & Perseverance: I remember when she was in law school. She returned to school after working as a CPA in Corporate America for 15 years. She wanted to know more about the legal side of accounting so she could do the best for her clients. Law School was tough, but she saw it through and is now a licensed attorney. One night when she was preparing for class, she called Elaine. Pamela told Elaine that she was talking on the phone, doing her homework, crying, and eating dinner all at the same time because she did not have time to do them separately.

Heart for God: Pamela's faith in Jesus Christ and understanding of the Bible are strong. On a light note, when Pamela was in college Elaine, and I had a cook-out for our daughters and their dates. Pamela was in the house quite a while before she joined us. When she came outside, she had obviously been reading the Bible, which she had in her hand.

Prayer Warrior: Pamela's prayers are filled with sincerity more than emotion. She knows what to say and covers all aspects of the situation. Sherrice is the same way.

I gave Pamela the label "Mother Hen" because she nurtures the family and constantly sacrifices for all of us.

Pamela was married to Gregory Young for several years, but they just were not compatible. They parted as friends, and we still speak to him occasionally. We still call Gregory our son.

Gregory: Gregory is a brilliant song and technical writer, producer, mechanical engineer, and a decent artist who is reserved to the point of appearing indifferent. While he could have a brilliant career as a researcher his first love is music. That is where he spends most of his time in Georgia, writing and performing on the guitar. When he completed his MS degree in Mechanical Engineering, his advisors practically begged him to work on his PhD, but Gregory would have no part of it.

I gave Gregory the label the sleeping giant, and I hope that giant will be awakened through a phenomenally successful music career. Everyone deserves to live their dreams, in the service of the Lord, of course.

Thankfully, Pamela married her childhood sweetheart, Isaac McCorkle, and they are unbelievably compatible. Pamela & Isaac are meant to be together.

Isaac: Isaac is sociable, sensitive, and an exceptionally caring person. He has an uncanny ability to focus on the minutest thing while taking in everything that is going on around him. That is why you can see him deeply engrossed in a football game and simultaneously comment in a conversation that he was not part of. Sometimes, when I am riding with him, although he is driving, he points out things to me like, "Did you see those two birds perched on the telephone wires way up there? Or even, did you see that large insect on the sidewalk, while having a conversation with me about a Bible class we are taking together. He reads all the time, and he talks all the time (smile). Who can do both.

I gave Isaac the label disciplinarian and counselor because in spite of his ability to focus and be what is going on all around him, he loves to take over situations and instruct, even discipline people on what they should be doing. He has even "gotten on me" about what I should or should not be eating. He is a great son. His profession happens to be counseling, and he definitely knows the Lord.

Sherrice: Sherrice's essence is her intellect, leadership, the strength of conviction, balance, and sense of adventure.

Intellect: Sherrice is quick-witted, analytical, creative, and disciplined. When you discuss a subject with her, you better be ready because she will bombard you with questions, analyze the logic of what you said, pointing out inconsistencies if they exist, and synthesize a solution or take a position, leaving you with questions yourself why you didn't think of that. She could easily be a lawyer.

Thorough: Sherrice quickly evaluates every aspect of a situation before she acts.

Leadership: Elaine was the matriarch of our family until her sickness. Sherrice assumed the position not by consensus or agreement or even by choice. It just happened, naturally. She is the leader of our household, her parents' household, and any other household that would dare to invite her in. I see signs that Sophia will assume the leadership position one day before Sherrice is ready.

Strength of Conviction: When Sherrice was 3 years old, she made up her mind that she wanted to attend Howard University. Her decision came from her experience Elaine and I graduating from Howard. Elaine completed her BS in Psychology, and I completed my MS in Computer Science. We gave a grand party inviting family and friends from New York to a celebration in a first-class hotel in Washington D.C. Everyone reserved rooms for the night. Our children and their cousins stayed in the suite for the night. They particularly like the black marble bathroom in the suite.

Sherrice never wavered, even when she was offered a full scholarship and a stipend   to attend North Carolina A&T State University. Howard University had not offered her anything but admission to the university. It worked out though, she received a scholarship from Howard that we fought for, and Sherrice graduated with honors.

When Sherrice was about 10 years old, she came to the top of the stairs to politely ask Elaine to come there. We were in the basement of our home, entertaining friends. Elaine told Sherrice to wait a minute, and she would be right there. Sherrice continued to calmly ask, "could you please come now?" So Elaine did. When Elaine got to the top of the steps, Sherrice burst out in tears, saying, "I have a stable in my finger." Sherrice was obviously in pain, but she kept her emotions at bay while she tried to do the right thing. That certainly took a lot of strength and conviction.

Balance: Very few people find or even look for balance in life. Sherrice has always been conscience of life being more than work but always business savvy; that is why she resigned from Wachovia when she was a Vice President with a promising future. She did not want to devote her life to a company. Her business acumen surfaced at an early age. She always saved money in heriggy bank. One day, when we had no cash to buy some treats, we asked Sherrice for a "loan." She lent us the money; however, she charged us interest.

Engineering Skill: Sherrice could have been an engineer, but she married one. She is always promoting and examining processes, finding out how things work, and fixing them.

Adventurous: When Sherrice was in high school, a few days after we bought a car for her, she and her best friend Trina drove 25 miles to explore the territory. Her driver's license was only a few days old. When she graduated from college, we had a tough time convincing her not to accept a job offer in New York City. She was perfectly comfortable living by herself in an apartment, even though we had relatives there.

Sherrice is such a strong leader and quick-witted that she can express impatience and intolerance when communicating with others. I gave Sherrice the label "Task Master" because she usually takes charge of any situation, determines what needs to be done, and checks to make sure it has been done correctly.

Bryan: Bryan, Sherrice's husband, is brilliant, heavily credentialed, and has a sharp sense of biting humor.

Heavily credentialed: Bryan has BS and MS degrees in civil engineering. A professional civil engineer, PA licensed, and has had two international tours of duty and several commands, leading construction projects, retiring as a Lt Colonel. He also graduated from the coveted War College. He worked as a civil engineer in city government and federal governments overseeing construction projects. With all of that, he is a successful entrepreneur.

Biting humor: Bryan has a way of telling you what he thinks with biting humor. He comes out of nowhere with unexpected zingers you have to think twice to get the message. For example, I recently bought furnishings for their in-law suite where we are currently living. I asked what he thought? Bryan responded, "It looks nice." Then came the zinger. As he walked out of the room, he said, "I wouldn't buy it."

Family person: Married since 1998, Bryan takes care of his family not only with provisions but with thoughtful gifts, vacations, as well as excursions, and visits with his family. Yet he takes time to get with the guys, too.

I labeled Bryan the overseer and commander because he is particular about things and has an eye for detail. He enjoys visiting engineering sites and inspecting the work. He has a keen eye and definite opinions about how things should be, which he expresses.

Sherrice & Bryan have done amazing things together and clearly love each other. But can you imagine the challenge of the commander and the taskmaster being able to raise their sweet daughter, Sophia, born in 2013?

Sophia, our only grandbaby: They are raising Sophia to be well-rounded and know the Lord. Sophia loves school; at 10 years old, she has been playing the piano for about six years. She recently began playing the flute in the band at school. She attends a gymnastics class weekly as well as regular Girl Scout meetings. She is polite and respectful all the time (smile).

We love Sophia. Before Elaine got sick, she gave Sophia love with discipline that only special grandmothers can do at the same time. I am different; grandparents have a duty to spoil their grandchild (smile). That's

Official and Unofficial God Children: Elaine was always reaching out to help others, espically family. When we went to Cleveland, OH so I could attend graduate school at Case Institute of Technology, we where just 22 years old and had no money. My fellowship paid for tuition, books and a living allowance. We convenced Elaine's aunt and uncle to let their two oldest girls, Barbara and Yvonne, who had just finished high school, to come stay with us, so they could have a chance to explore

Erika Mann, goddaughter: I can remember one moment that solidified the depth of your love for Erika. When she was a college, Elaine & I made a surprise visit to her when she was in college. I cannot remember why we made the trip but I know we felt compelled to go. I know we care for her deeply. I will never forget the moment Eliane and Erika saw each other. The love just flowed from heart to heart and engulfed my with so much love and joy. To this day, we still think about and feel that moment.

Stuart Jones, godson: Beverly and Troy are Stuart's parents. Stuart has always been close to us and at times he lived with us. Pamela and Sherrice see him as a real brother. He is super intelligent and super funny. He is always a bright light in the family.

Ivan McClean, godson: Ivan is the son of Kenneth and Louise McLean. Over the years we have seen him grow from a tiny baby to a strong, committed, family loving man. He has always been special to us. We never spent a lot of time with him, sometimes at Kenneth & Louise's family picknicks to which we were privledged to be invited, but we always talked about Ivan everytime we were with Kenneth & Louise so it feels like we have been with him throughout his live's journed.

Cheice Tearte, goddaughter: Curtis and Gloria are Cheirce's daughter. Curtis is one our my best friend. Cherice's wedding was one of my memoberable moments that I talk about later. We hear about her from Curtis and Gloria and occasionally make contract but

Bryson Evans, godson: Bryson is the son of Stanley and Princilla Evans. We were very close when they were in graduate school at Howard University. We lived in the same apartment build, The

Deauville Appartments in Tokoma Park, MD. Pamel was in kindergarten and Sherrice was in day care when we met. They moved into the apartment building a few days after we did. We were anxious to meet them so when we saw them moving in I went to them and offered to help. I introduced myself and told them we had just moved from New York City. They were very friendly but I noticed that either Stanley or Princilla was with me every step I made. I found out after we became good friends that they were watching me because I was from "New York." Inspite of the way we met. We became great friends. They both graduate with PhD's and moved to Tennessee. When they had their first of 3 children they asked us to be Bryson's grandparents. We exchanged visited from time to time and sent their children gifts for special occasions. Somehow we lost touch after Stanley died early in their lives.

Kim Waller: Kim is like our godchild. Eline was her advisor when Kim pledge Delta Sigma Thetha Socority, Inc. Elaine and Kim developed such a close relationship that extends to this day. I fortunately was caught up the love that they shared so, I them Kim too.

Tabier Shine, Tabier also pledge Delta Sigma Theha Sorocity, Inc also, and just like Kim, Elaine bounded with Tabier. They are like daughters to use and they always visit when they come to Greensboro.

Chapter 4: BEST FRIENDS

Proverbs 27:9 TPT

> *"Sweet friendships refresh the soul and awaken our*
> *hearts with joy,*
> *for good friends are like the anointing oil that yields*
> *the fragrant incense of God's presence."*

All my friends feel like best friends. A best friend is the one or ones I am with at the time. I have been blessed with many deep, enduring friendships throughout my life. I have fond memories of friendships with my best friends who have gone on, Jimmy, William, Henry, and Kenneth linger more than others. At one point, three of them were my best friends at the same time, Jimmy, Henry, and Kenneth. I do not know how to explain that, but I know what I feel in my heart and soul. Unfortunately for me and glory for them, three are deceased. I cannot find William. I miss them so much.

I have already written about my brother, Alpheus James Harrigan, Jr., Jimmy, who was my best blood brother friend. He was the best of the best.

William Silver was my *childhood best friend*. Growing up in Harlem, we had a unique compatibility that I do not think is duplicated anywhere. And for the record, it was not sexual. In fact, during those days, both of us hated and were scared of "gays." The images we had of gay people were old, muscular men who took in groups on "stoops" in Harlem and taunted men and boys as they walked by, whistling at them and inviting them to spend time with them. Also, there was an Annual Gay Parade originating in a show at the famous Apollo Theatre on 125th street, where gay people put on heavy makeup, long hair, and fancy dresses and pranced around Harlem. It was not only disgusting to us but definitely frightening.

William and I liked so many of the same things that you did not find other people our age doing: We liked waking up early in the morning just before the sun came out to go on our respective fire escapes that attached to the outside of each apartment and was accessible through a window. We did that to watch the morning glories we grew in Flower Point open up to the rising sun. We loved spending all day Saturdays on Theatre Row on 42nd Street, going to see one movie after another until it was almost dark. We loved lifting weights together, usually in one of our apartments or sometimes on the roof of our building. We loved playing board games, especially Monopoly, until midnight. We were both fascinated with mathematics, and each earned undergraduate degrees in mathematics. William earned a B.A. degree in mathematics from Williams College, and I earned a B.S. in mathematics from Paine College. We both loved jazz drumming and attended a mid-day drumming convention in the 48th Street area in New York, where the stores along the street all sold drums.

The only thing we did not have in common was girlfriends. I had a girlfriend, but William was not interested, that is, until one summer. Christina was spending the summer with her grandmother, whose apartment was next door to William. They met, fell in love and the rest is history. I did not see much of William for the rest of that summer because he was madly in love.

I do not know what happened to William. We lost contact after we graduated from undergraduate school, except for one summer. I bumped into William downtown on Madison Avenue in NYC during lunch break. We asked each other where we were working. Ironically, both of us became computer programmers in different companies. We still liked doing the same things, even in our choices of careers.

I pray William is still here, and I will run into him. If not on earth, then in heaven.

Henry McCain – Henry was *my best college friend*. I met Henry McCain at Paine College in Augusta, GA. We started out as just acquaintances. There was no instant friendship. Sometime in our first year, were started to grow close. We found ourselves going out with the guys to meet girls, teaming up in gym class, doing gymnastics together, playing ping pong, and doing a lot of things together. The friendship deepened when we were selected to be the two physics lab assistants. We had keys to the building and the lab, so we could go in at night and work on math and physics problems on the long, large board in the lab. After some time, we had become so close that Henry, who lived on campus, often invited me to his home for his mother's good cooking. Our friendship continued to grow during and after college.

During the early years of our friendship, Henry looked up to me and followed me. I used to beat him in every game we played. In later years, it was reversed. We played chess in college dormitory competitions. I always beat Henry. We loved math but I was the better student. I always won at ping pong and any other game we played.

Henry followed whatever I did. In my junior year of college, I announced that Elaine and I eloped. He turned to Dot, his high school girlfriend who was a first-year student at the college, and he said, "Dottie, let's get married" that summer, they did. In my senior year when I was awarded a fellowship to attend Case Institute of Technology in Cleveland, OH, Henry immediately applied and was accepted at Temple University in Philly. The couple took a trip to NYC in our senior year. Henry drove his Volkswagen. I had not learned to drive yet, even though Henry tried to teach me. We drove to New York on a tank of gas and $35 amongst us. We hoped that when we got there, Elaine, my parents, and Henry's older siblings would finance our return. They did, thank God. One time, we visited Henry & Dot in Philly and announced that Elaine was pregnant. Henry turned to Dot and said, "Dottie, let's have a baby," and they did. Over the years, we have had two daughters (Pamela and Sherrice). Henry & Dot had five (Jimmy, Marcus, Yolanda, Jonathan, and Joshua).

One time Elaine and I went to Philly to help Henry give a surprise birthday party for Dot. Henry managed to keep Dot out of the house while Elaine and I helped prepare for the party. Henry was in and out getting things for the party while Elaine cleaned, mopped floors, decorated, arranged chairs and all the things you do for a party. When it was time to sing Happy Birthday and cut the cake, Henry brought the cake out. The inscription on the cake was Happy Birthday, Dottie and Rodney. I was really surprised because our birthdays were not in the same month. I was also a little perturbed because Henry and Elaine conspired to have me work like a slave for my own party (smile).

The tables really turned during one of the trips we made to Philly. Henry & Dot drove us to the train station after we spent several days with them. It was late afternoon. There was a bowling alley across from the train station, so Henry and I decided to bowl since we had an hour before the train left. Elaine and Dot watched as Herny beat me game after game. I was determined to win so I kept saying let us play one more game. We did until we missed the train. We returned to their house and spent another night. We did not have children then. That incident happened time after time when we visited them regularly in Philly.

When we moved to W. Hartford, CT., Henry & Dot visited us for a few days. Henry and I sat down for a game of chess. Henry had never won a single game against me over the years. He told me that night he had really learned chess. Of course, I chuckled. It was about 10 PM when we started playing; our wives had gone to bed. Henry won the first game and every game that night. I kept Henry up until 3 AM, playing another game. Henry got so sleepy that I had to wake him after each move, saying in the discussion, "Wake up, Henry, it's your move." He would wake up, move one peace, and say, "Checkmate." I do not think I won or outperformed Henry ever again. But Henry remained closer than close until his sudden death.

Willaim Harris. William (Bill, Goofy) and I became friends at Paine College sometime after Henry. He was a year ahead so we didn't connect immediately. The time I remember becoming close friends was when we were roommate in the Honors Dorm. The Honors Dorm was the first dorm that Paine College provided for student scholars. It was unique because there was no supervision. All other dorms on campus had live-in dormitory directors. We were the odd couple. I was always organized and neat, Bill was the opposite. He played the Center position on the college basketball team, I was terrible in scrimmage games in gym class. He was from the south and I was from the north. I was known on campus for being a smooth dresser. In fact, one year I won't the contest as the best male dresser in the Collete among students, faculty and staff. Bill just didn't have it when it came to dressing. Yet, we connected to the point where Bill invited me to go home with him some weekends to get a home cooked meal, just like Henry did. I sort of taught him how to dress. But Bill taught me and inspired me to run for chairman of the student government. He was chair in his senior year and I followed as chair the next year, my senior year.

Through the years we stayed in contact but rarely saw each. Our careers when in opposite directions. While I spent years climbing the Corporte ladder. Bill earned his PhD and became a Dean at Indiana University. I remember Bill calling me to ask my opinion about becoming president at our alma mater, Paine College. He was concerned that if he accepted the position he could not continue is academic research as an historial. I told Bill he didn't have a choice, it was is obligation. I didn't know enough to say it was his calling. After his tenure as President of Paine College, he went on to serve at several institutions including Alabama State University,, Texas Southern University, Fort Valley State, and Texas College.

Kenneth McLean. Kenneth was my spiritual best friend. I met Kenneth when we moved to Greensboro, NC after Elaine took Pamela and Sherrice to Sunday School at White Oak Grove Baptist Church. She was looking for a church home and I stayed home. When Elaine dropped the children off, Kenneth stopped her and as her to stay for his adult class Sunday School. The next Sunday Elaine insisted that the whole family sould attend. The rest is history.

We did many things together, most often initiated by Kenneth, who was a friendship leader. He always initiates things for groups, couples, and one-on-one things to do. Most of all, I am grateful for him, who inspired me as my Sunday School teacher to become one myself, which has become a major part of my life's work over the past 40 years. Kenneth was a role model as a man's man; he took a position on issues, expressed his concerns and suggestions, and did not try to go along to get along. Kenneth & Louise Elaine and I planted a one-acre garden together on his land. As a city boy, I had no idea what I was getting. After the garden was planted, Kenneth said we needed to get a tiller to keep the weeds out. My response was what is a tiller, and what weeds are you talking about. We worked so hard that summer that I never had a garden again. I never went fishing in New York, but Kenneth took me fishing a few times in a rowboat on a private pond owned by one of his friends. We talked about God and life. Sometimes just the four of us would go out to dinner, trying different restaurants and different foods, Kenneth's suggested the restaurant most of the time. For years, Kenneth initiated and planned one-week annual vacations for five couples every second week in July. He would rent a van, and we travel to Tennessee and go from there to places like Arkansas and Mississippi. We saw shows, visited the Bill Clinton Presidential Library, and went to greyhound dog races and casinos.

I spoke at their funerals, and each time, I thought I was going to die first, not because I felt better, but rather because I felt physically weaker, morally less convicted, and least of all, unworthy to be blessed with long life.

At Jimmy's funeral I talked about how close we are but quite different. Jimmy was tall and slender; I was shorter and bordering fat. Jimmy was very smart, and I struggled in school. Jimmy was a bookworm, and I hated to read. Jimmy was outgoing and outspoken; I was shy. Jimmy was a lady's man; I am not. But I always knew that Jimmy and I were woven together into a tapestry of many colors, inseparable and one.

When Henry's son Jonathan died, I attended his funeral with a message to Henry. I felt how broken Dot and their children were. I told Henry that it was Jonathan's choice not his. Henry's sisters told me after the funeral, that Henry needed to hear those words from his best friend.

When I spoke at Henry's funeral, we were asked to limit our comments to 10 minutes. I kept recalling the many facets of our friendship until I was asked to stop after 20 minutes or so. I tried to stay within the allotted time, but I could not stop the outpouring of love I had for Henry.

Pat and Jerry, and Elaine and I were close as a couple. When Jerry Posey passed, I had a little more time to talk at His funeral. So, I reminisced about our times together as a couple, how he and I called Pat and Elaine, AM and FM radio because they talked non-stop to each other. How I, 5'10", challenged Jerry, 6'4", to a basketball game only when his leg was in a cast. The couples went to many restaurants together, and Jerry always ordered salmon.

Recently, my last best spiritual friend, Kenneth McLean, died. I have known Kenneth McLean since 1982, shortly after we moved to Greensboro, NC. I thank him for inviting me to attend Sunday School and inspiring me with his teaching. He is the reason I have been teaching Sunday School for almost forty years. Kenneth had a way of making everyone his friend. He is the epitome of a friend that is closer than a brother. Elaine and I did so much with Kenneth and Louise. We went to dinner regularly; we planted a 1-acre garden together. As a city boy who did not know anything about gardening, I will never do that again. He and Johnny Williams planned and arranged the annual one-week couples trips every second week in July. Five couples traveled together in a van and stayed in a cabin large enough for every couple to have a separate room. We used the van to tour the surrounding city and state activities. He invites us to his family cookout, and the list goes on and on. Kenneth and I had many one-on-one talks and even when to buy suits at local men's clothing stores. His life taught me how to live a Christian life.

There were three best friends and their families that we meet over a period of several years. Trey McCarther moved the the house across the street from where we lived in Greensboro, NC. We lived on Bancroft Rd. which deadended into a penpenduclar street name Luewood. We moved there because of my job with IBM. Trey, Melba, & Kisha, their daughter, moved to be LtC commander of the Army ROTC program at NCA&T State University & Elon College. They were their for about two years and moved to Morehead, NC. Trey bought the house before he left and moved to ___. LtC Walter Watson, Joice, and Zannie rented the house because he became the next commander of the Army ROTC program. They moved to Columbia SC when they left. Elaine and I moved to Columbia for a few years because of you job with IBM. We got to know the Watsons parents very well. When the Watsons left Greensboro, LtC Johnny Williams rented the house because Johonny became the commander for the Airforce ROTC program at NCA&T State University. Johnny, Coralee and Kimberly moved back to Sm

With each family we shared so many good times through diners at each others houses, and at restaurants, games nights, moves and many other occasions. We still stay in touch with each other. Johnny and Coralee were part of an annual week-long trip that we took every second week in July with with two other couples. Trey eventually, joined us after his wife passed and he eventually married Gloria. We continued those trips for years until Trey passed.

My best friends were special in many different ways, but together, they enriched many dimensions of my soul and spirit. I will always be bless for the special ways and times together with my best friend.

Chapter 5: BEST COUPLES FRIENDS

Ephesian 4:1-3

¹ I, therefore, the prisoner of the Lord, beseech you that ye
walk worthy of the vocation wherewith ye are called,
² With all lowliness and meekness, with longsuffering,
forbearing one another in love;
³ Endeavouring to keep the unity of the Spirit
in the bond of peace.

I already talked about Kenneth & Louise and LTC Johnny & Coralee Williams.

Myrtis & Jesse. Elaine's cousin Myrtis and her classmate Jesse were much younger than Elaine and me, but we began establishing a special friendship when they were in school at Talladega College. After they graduated and married the friendship deepened rapidly. We felt like they were our equals and watched with awe the way they worked together. Jesses was killed on Highway 25 when a truck slammed into him as he was getting on the highway in his car. He was listening to the Word of God when it happened. Their baby, Stephanie, was only Fillin ? years old. We watched Myrtis as a single parent raise Stephanie. We watched Myrtis continue in church, sorority, and educational activities. We watched her go against the odds and complete her EdD. We watched her as she raised her daughter, who earned her EdD. We watch her advance through her career in educational leadership. We watched her successfully establish a charter school against all odds. All the time, she has maintained a home of joy, laughter, and family gatherings. I cannot tell you how many times Myrtis received us in her home, provided delicious meals, and made us feel like we were home. I named her "Mighty Myrtis," and recently, she was labeled in a local newspaper article as "the legend."

Jackie & Ernest became our best friends in Maryland. Jackie was Pamela's first-grade teacher. I took Pamela to a local grocery store to buy candy. Pamela introduced me to Jackie. Jackie looked so young I thought she was Pamela's classmate. Shortly after that encounter, Jackie asked Pamela if she knew whether her father was a member of a fraternity called Omega Psi Phi. She did not think Pamela would know. Pamela responded matter-of-factly to Jackie, "Yes, my daddy is a Que." Jackie's husband Earnest was a "Que." We met, became friends, and did everything together. Pamela and Sherrice are so attached to them that they call them Aunt Mommy and Uncle Daddy. When Jackie and Ernest were living in the Atlanta, GA area, they invited us to various celebrations, but this time, they invited us to their 40th anniversary. To our surprise it was a catered dinner just for the four of us, served by the chef they hired. It was fabulous.

Pat & Jerry Posey. Like we met Jackie & Ernest through Pamela, we met Pat & Jerry through Sherrice. Sherrice and Trina attended Northeast Middle School in Greensboro and remain best friends even today. Trina has fillin two children. Pat and Elaine loved to talk. I named them AM and FM radio. We did a lot of things together. Jerry talked and was outspoken too; I was a listener, so we got along great. Jerry loved basketball and was toweringly tall. I called him Kareem. Once, Jerry injured his leg, and I took the opportunity to challenge him to a basketball game; of course, he laughed but did not take me up on it.

Elaine and I did a lot of things with couples and in groups. There was a group of couples that always included Pat and Jerry that we when to the movies with. After the movie, we gathered at our house for a potluck meal, fellowship, and lively discussion of the movie. As many times as we enjoyed meals together at various restaurants, Jerry always ordered salmon. When Jerry died a few years ago, I was honored to say words at his funeral. I pointed out that he would always order salmon.

Chapter 6: INSPIRING PEOPLE & EVENTS

1 Thessalonians 5:11

> ***Wherefore comfort yourselves together,***
> ***and edify one another,***
> ***even as also ye do.***

Augusta, GA and Edgefield SC

Musical Exposures: My parents provided many opportunities for me to find and develop my talents. I had private piano lessons for a few years when I was in junior high school. I had lessons in tap-dancing and singing also. They bought a professional "trap-drum " set for me in high school. I was best at playing the drums. To this day, I cannot sing or tap-dance, but I am learning to play the keyboard because I always liked the piano.

During my years at Paine College, Henry and I formed a band called the "Pain Relievers." We recruited Grady Cunningham. It was odd because Henry was on the trumpet, Grady Cunningham on the trombone and I was on the drums. I do not think there has ever been or will ever be a trio of trumpets, trombones, and drums again. There was no college band, so the students, starving for live secular entertainment in a Methodist school in the 60's, enjoyed the noise.

I played professionally in a different trio. This nightclub jazz/blues trio was different, with a piano player, a trumpet player, and me on the drums. We usually played in Augusta, GA, but one time, we played in Aiken, SC, and were surprised when Franky Lymen joined in to sing with us. Franky was stationed at Fort Gordon in Augusta, GA, at the time. He was frequently in the news and was with his group "Franky Lymen and the Teenagers." Franky was the Stevie Wonder of the 60s. His brother also had a group called Louie Lymen and the Teenchords.

Big Mama & Papa: During the last semester of our junior year, Elaine and I attended separate colleges, 75 miles apart. Since Elaine & I were married, we got together at Big Mama and Papa's house. They were parents and spiritual guides to us. We enjoyed many moments with them, from eating watermelon on their back porch to reading the Sunday school lesson before going to church, visiting relatives, having unbelievably tasty meals, and so many other things.

Once I was visiting Elaine before we were married, and we fell asleep on the couch. It was cold, so we were heated by an old kerosene stove. When we woke up, we were filled with soot, and so were the living room curtains, walls, ceiling, and floor. Needless to say, we cleaned and painted the living room that week.

One summer, Papa asked me to help him paint the tin roof of their house. He laid a rickety ladder made of tree logs against the side of the house and climbed to the roof without hesitation. I was scared, but hoping not to expose my fear, I climbed up. He showed me how to stroke the brush to get the grain right, gave me a bucket of silver paint, and left me there while he attended other maintenance tasks. I soon became comfortable painting the roof in the hot sun for hours. I felt useful and proud as a city boy gone country. Getting down off the roof by the rickety letter was no fun and quite a spectacle; fortunately, nobody saw me, and I miraculously did not get hurt.

After we had finished college some time ago and although we lived in Maryland, we bought a trailer on their property and set up a vacation home. We all felt that we would live in it for an extended period of time, years, but we never did. The presence of the trail and the hope of living next to them brought joy to all of us. All of Big Mama's and Papa's children had moved to New York and only visited home usually for Christmas.

Elaine and I occasionally socialized with Mattie, Elaine's cousin, and her husband, Isaac. For some reason, I remember an expression on Isaac's face. We were at a nightclub, I believe, in Augusta. I took a picture of Isaac with his mouth wide open and steering into the camera like Muhammad Ali did when he won the fight against Sonny Liston to become the heavy weight champion of the world. Although we did not get together often, we had fun when we did.

Every time we visited Touge and her daughter, Stacey, on those South Carolina visits, we had a laughing, enjoyable time.

Aunt Ruth was Touge's mother. She was a strong and funny woman. I loved her stories that showed how independent she was. She kept a loaded rifle in her house and was not afraid to use it. I am glad that during the time that I knew her, which was several years, she never did.

Shaws Creek Baptist Church is our spiritual refuge. I always feel that I come to the well to renew our souls. I was baptized there a few years after I married Elaine. Elaine was baptized there at 12 years old. Pamela and Sherrice were baptized there when they were young fillin. Elaine and I have plots for our graves in the front of the church next to Big Mama and Papa's graves.

The pastor of Shaws Creek, Paster RC Holloway, was our spiritual leader. Not only did he baptize me, but he also ordained me and Elaine as deacon and deaconess. I had been asked to be a deacon at Faith Baptist Church by Pastor Albert E. Graves less than a year earlier, where we attended church in Gibsonville, NC. I declined because I did not feel ready. Pastor Holloway came to me and said, "I am going to ask you a question, and your answer is yes." He asked/told me to be a deacon, and I said yes. Pastor Grave, who pastored the church we attended when we lived in Greensboro, NC, and his wife came to the ordination in South Carolina. We were so moved by their presence because Pastor Graves did not preach that Sunday in his church. That was the first time in his lengthy career in ministry that he did not conduct services at his home church. When we moved back to Greensboro, Pastor Graves asked me again, and I accepted.

Pastor Holloway was always leading us somewhere. He appointed me as Minister of Education and had Elaine and I conduct many church seminars. He also appointed us to lead annual overnight retreats which we conducted for about 10 years. He was part of the officiating team that married Pamela and Sherrice that married in a double-wedding ceremony in 1998. I am forever grateful for his leadership in our lives.

There were two couples in the church that taught us what it meant to work in the church, besides Big Mama & Papa. They were Aunt Ann & Uncle Burnell and Thomasina & Andrew Bouknight. They labored physically and spiritually for the church. When they were in their mid-80s, they laid tile panels on their knees in the fellowship hall, and they were prayer warriors.

Elaine and I stayed overnight at Aunt Ann and Uncle Bernell's house several times. We woke up in the mornings to delicious home meals. I remember we started every breakfast with a prayer followed by everyone reciting a Bible verse. They helped us with all of our retreats.

Fillin The Bouknights …(Zanni & Son)

Over the years, when we visited South Carolina, we occasionally stayed overnight with Cousin Willie Mae. She and Elaine's mother were best friends growing up. She retired from her catering business. Every morning when the noisy rooster woke us up, she was in the kitchen fixing breakfasts to remember. She cooked all kinds of meals for us; my favor was turkey wings. I do not know if they were baked in the oven, fried on the stove, and smothered in gravy, probably all three. They were simply good. She and Elaine talked for hours about family, and I listened, sometimes falling into a relaxing, peaceful sleep. Sometimes, she would pack us in her car with fishing rods and take us to a private pond owned by someone she knew. She taught us how to fish, although I did not learn too well.

In the last semester of my senior year at Paine College, Elaine left her senior semester at South Carolina State University in Orangeburg, SC, to join me in Augusta, GA, because she was not allowed to live in the campus dorm as a married woman, which would be a "bad influence" on the girls. My how things have changed. Elaine was the working person in the house, and I was a full-time student, and I cooked all the meals. What a reversal. We had several friends at Georgia Pacific, where Elaine worked full-time. One name I remember is Archie. He brought our first Christmas tree to the house. One of her friends was a white lady married to a white police officer. Although this was during the time of the 1960's Civil Rights movement, we became good friends. Years later, after we were living in New York, the couple came to visit us.

I was so ashamed of an incident that happened to them while they were visiting us. They drove to our co-op apartment, parked their car, and came up to the 14th floor where we lived. I asked to police officer where he parked his car. I found out that he parked it on a side street just outside the complex and he did not lock it. We hurried down to lock his car. Only 15 minutes had passed from the time he parked until we returned to his car. It was too late; his CD Player was gone. I was embarrassed because when he immediately flagged a fellow police car down, the policemen were white, and he flashed his Georgia badge to identify himself; they stopped, asked him a few questions, told him to report it to the nearest police station, and drove off.

Cleveland, OH

We were not in Cleveland long enough to establish close friendships. But we had inspiring and memorable moments. I was in graduate school, and Elaine was finishing her degree at Cleveland State. The most inspiring time he had there was to be in the midst of the election of Carl Stokes, the first Black mayor of a major city in America.

The sad moment came after Ottis Redding performed at Cleveland's iconic Leo's Casino in December 1967. Elaine and I decided not to attend because we were short on money, and we knew the rapidly rising star, who was considered one of the greatest singers in American music history, would have many more performances that we could attend. Flying on his way to his next performance in Wisconsin, Ottis's plane crashed in the icy lake Monona just four miles from the airport. He died with seven of the members of his band, the Bar-Kays.

Josephine and Kenneth were Uncle Sambo's and Josephine's children at least once a year if not more, to hunt. He was a jolly yet sincere and serious man. He clearly loved Big Mana and Papa. He came for the fellowship more than for hunting. Uncle Thomas sold me our second car, a Ford station wagon when we lived in a co-op, Masaryk Towers, near Delancy Street in Manhattan, NYC. I do not remember the year. I was not even driving then. Elaine did all the driving. I did not learn to drive until we moved to Takoma Park, Maryland. I was about 27 years old. Growing up in New York, I did not need a card and neither my father nor mother knew how to drive, nor my siblings either.

I remember Elaine used the park the car overnight behind the Masaryk Towers in an area that did not have parking meters. Every time we went to the car it had been burglarized, the doors were opened, but nothing was stolen. We did not have a CD Player or anything in there worth stealing, and they did not want the tires, but it was a nuisance to have them break the locks open and move blankets and things around. So, Elaine and I decided to keep the door unlocked after so many break-ins. We never had another incident. They were practicing how to break into cars, and it was no 'fun' when it was unlocked and there was nothing to steal.

Uncle Willie & Aunt Marie Jefferson: Uncle Willie was the pall bearer for Big Mama and Papa's wedding. He still lived in the house where they were born in Edgefield, SC. I met Uncle Willie and Aunt Marie the first year we were married. I was fascinated with Aunt Marie's quick wit and rapid speech. I joke that President John F. Kennedy, who was said to read 2,000 words per minute, could not read as fast as Aunt Marie could talk. Uncle Willie had a memory better than any elephant and he maintained it until his death, short of 100 years old. I used to sit and marvel (fillin) that Elaine would ask him about family history, and he would expound on the who, what, where, when, and how when he was in his 80s and 90s. I learned from their dedication to each other and especially their children. I learned how diligently and steadfastly Uncle Willie took care of Aunt Marie during the time of her sickness. I learned the importance of family history. In his later years, I would reach to shake his hand and slip him $20 every time we visited, not that he needed anything; he had plenty of land, resources, and the support of his 10 children who and successful careers and good people.

Aunt Jean and Uncle Al lived about a football field away from Uncle Willie on the same dirt road. I loved visiting them with Elaine. Once, I visited them without Elaine who when on a trip with her cousins. When Uncle Al was 102 years old, he complained to us that the doctors would not give him legs. Both his legs had been amputated to his knees, but he wanted to walk.

On Elaine's father's side (Eddie Mims) Elaine's grandmother, known as Margie Brown, was, in my words, a pistol. She was a commanding, dominating woman who marched to her own drums. She has six sons, gave them money and guns, and made them feel they could do anything they wanted. Her son Eddie married Elaine's mother. Eddie was a charming, likable man when he was sober but abusive when he got drunk, which was often. He was known to come home drunk, late at night, wake her up, and demand they she cook a meal for him. Elaine's mother finally divorced after he hit her on her head with the butt of a rifle. That caused her to suffer periodic severe epilepsy for the rest of her life. He went to jail for a few years. At the end of his life, I mellowed and reached out to his children, but Eddie and Inez never got back together.

Elaine had an uncle named Thomas who was related to that side of the family. He lived in New York and loved to come back to Edgefield to hunt deer. He always stayed with Big Mama & Papa when he came. Uncle Thomas was a positive and kind person. He sold us his old Ford station wagon when we lived in New York, the car that the gangs broke into regularly for practice.

Elaine's stepfather's side (Harold Ross): Harold Ross's parents were Burnice & Gus Clark, better known as Mother & Pamp. They owned cleaners in Ossining, NY. We thought of them as the Jeffersons on TV. They participated in all the family gatherings. They visited Inez often. I cannot help but think that they came just for dinner and to be pampered. Inez was a great cook. Speaking of Mama, I never called her by her name. I always called her Mama. The most memorable thing I have about them is Pampa, Harold, and I, and occasionally others, played poker at the dining room table. We played for high stakes, a penny-ante, and no more than a nickel raise. It was intense and funny. Whenever I lose a hand. I would pretend to bang my hand on the table in discussion. They got a kick out of my antics. After a while, they looked to me, acting up.

I do not have too much to say about Harold. I did not hate him, but I did not admire him either. We had fun piling up together as a big family going on trips in the Penn Meat company vehicle that Harold's boss, Stanley, let him have for his personal use when he was not delivering meat in it. I am still dealing with forgiveness with Harold. Trivial things billed up about his habits over the years, but the final straw was when Mama died. He went to her funeral in Jacksonville, FL where they were living, but when they had her second funeral in Queens, NY, he did not go. He was in and out of the hospital all his life, having had polio. He said did not feel up to travel. That could have been understandable, but within a week or so, he drove by himself to New York to visit Mama's brothers, sisters, and his New York. I am really trying to forgive him. Everybody has faults.

New York City, NY

Much of our five years in New York, we lived in a condominium in lower Manhattan. Our two girls were born there, in the same hospital where I was born, Columbia Presbyterian Hospital.

On my mother's side (Peterson), there was Aunty Annie & Uncle Herbert, Uncle Enoch & Aunt Louise, and Uncle Sambo & Aunt Josephine, who all lived in Augusta, GA, where they were born and died; they never moved. Aunty Hattie & Uncle Locke, Aunty Ruby & Uncle Mack, and Uncle Pete/Eggy & Aunty Rena lived in NY. After moving to New, they never moved again.

Aunty Ruby & Uncle Mack. Uncle Mack's brother, who lived in North Carolina, asked them to take care of his three children, Doris, Laura, and Herman, in New York when they were young. Herman was my age, about 9 or 10, and his sisters were teenagers. Herman and I are like brothers to this day. We had so many adventures together.

Uncle Pete & Aunty Rena have one child, Lisa, who I used to babysit regularly. Uncle Pete and Aunt Rena were the "classy" couple of the family. They were always putting on high society parties. When we were teenagers, they always asked Jimmy and me to take coats and sometimes fix drinks. In the early 60s, they bought a color TV that cost around $1,000 and a portable color TV for Lisa in her room.

Aunty Rena always gave thoughtful, extraordinary gifts for Christmas. One Christmas, she gave me a set of plastic soldiers because she knew I loved to play with plastic figures. That gift was incredibly special because the box of plastic soldiers was not sold in stores. It had to be ordered and mailed, which took at least a month to deliver. Aunty Rena obviously thought about my gift at least one month before Christmas.

In NY Mommy and her sisters and brother were close to their cousin Naomi Manning. Naomi and her husband had five children: Waymon, Oliver, Allen, Naomi, and Kenneth. I knew Naomi and her children because she lived in New York. She visited my mother often and attended family gatherings, especially the annual Thanksgiving dinner at Aunty Hattie's house.

Father's side (Harrigan)

Pop had two brothers, Uncle Eric, and Uncle Holger, living in New York and one sister, Aunty Ruby Rhymer. He had another brother, Henry, and a sister, Ina, living in their hometown of St. Thomas, VI. He had one other brother, Uncle Herbert who relocated several times, so he lived in St. Thomas, Florida, and New York and other places.

Uncle Eric was married to Aunt Pearl and had two sons, Eric & Freddy. My brother and I loved to go to Aunt Pearl's house. One day at Aunt Pearl's house, Jimmy and I were visiting our cousin Junie, who was there also. Junie was reaching his hand into their fishtank, trying to squeeze the goldfish, which would have killed the fish. Eric and Fredy asked him to stop several times, but Junie refused. So, Eric and Freddy said, "Let's go downstairs and play." We sat on a park bench, and Eric told Junie that he needed to learn to stop when his cousins said stop. Then Eric whistled a strange whistling sound. Suddenly, about 20 guys came from every direction and asked Eric what was wrong. They were members of Eric & Freddie's gang. After they were told what Junie was doing, they crowded around Junie and started to threaten and taunt him. Eric called them off before they hurt Junie.

From that point on, whenever Junie visited, he was the most obedient and polite person you ever saw.

After Uncle Eric & Aunt Pearl divorced, Uncle Eric married Aunt Sara. Uncle Eric & Aunt Sara often visited Elaine and Me because Uncle Eric and Aunt Sara lived in the same complex as Elaine and me, Masaryk Towers, near the Williamsburg Bridge off Delancy Street, to shop in the stores owned by Orthodox Jews. The area was known for shopping for quality merchandise at very low prices.

Uncle Holger & Aunt Laura had one son, Louie. Mommy, Pop, and the children visited them regularly, especially when our grandmother Zaphyra, Pop's mother, lived with Uncle Holger and his family for about a year before returning to St. Thomas, VI. I thought that Aunt Laura was so beautiful.

Aunty Ruby Rhymer and Uncle Wally had three children, Ricky, Ruel, and Doreen. Our family visited them as well. When I returned to New York after finishing college I gave my set of drums that I used while I was in school to Ruel. He was a budding drummer.

Uncle Henry and Aunt Lula-Bell had two children, Geraldine and Henry Jr., who we called Junie. When Elaine and I visited St. Thomas in 1976, we stayed with Junie. He taught at the University of St. Thomas. We knew Junie and Uncle Herbert's two children, Wayne and Dale well because they lived in New York for a few years. Years later I literally bumped into Junie at the Omega Psi Phi Conclave in Charlotte, NC. It was so good to see him and learn that we were members of the same fraternity.

Uncle Herbert was married twice, first to Miriam, who I never met, and later to Irma, a German lady. They had no children. I never knew why Junie, Wayne, and Dale were together like three brothers since Junie's father was Uncle Henry, and Wayne and Dale were Uncle Herbert's children. Elaine and I enjoyed good times with them when we were living in Masaryk Towers. Uncle Herbert worked in the Masaryk Towers and eventually became a self-employed cap driver. It was extremely expensive to buy a license for a medallion to own a cab in New York back then cost upwards of $100,000.

Aunt Ina & Uncle Steel lived in St. Thomas, VI. They lived on a hill in what we called a mansion that cost $75,000 in the 1950's, I think. We were attending an employee recognition event in Puerto Rico at a celebration event called the IBM Golden Circle. I was one of the top 1,000 Systems Engineering Managers recognized in IBM's Data Processing Division of 100,000 employees. I will always remember how one-morning Aunt Ina and Uncle Lionel took Elaine and me to breakfast, the one and only time we visited in St. Thomas. I ordered orange juice. Aunt Ina told the waiter, "No, bring him a rum and coke." It was carnival time. We stayed for a week and partied night and day. I do not think I was sober that whole week.

One day, while we were visiting our Uncle Henry and Aunt Lula-Bell in St. Thomas, we heard a lot of noise, followed by a lot of sirens in the streets and a sense of panic throughout the city. We when to a hill near Uncle Henry's house and witnessed the devastation from fairly far off. American Airlines Flight 625 Boeing 727-100 crashed, killing 37 of the 88 passengers on board. A year or so later, we learned that the runway was built to extend out into the ocean because, approaching St. Thomas, planes had extraordinarily little room to land. The runway led straight into a mountain, so there was no room for error.

Elaine's Mother's side (Lloyd). Uncle Bubber and Aunt Belle Lloyd lived around the corner from Elaine's parents. The two houses shared a common fence, show they two families often visited each other by climbing over the fence instead of walking around the street. Uncle Bubber owned a barber shop and was known by his friends as the mayor of St. Albans. Both families often had parties at each other's houses and went to dances sponsored by organizations they were members of. Uncle Bubber and his brother, Uncle Ronald, bought new cars every two years. Uncle Bobber usually bought Cadillacs and BMWs, and Uncle Ronald bought a Bonneville. After five years, one of the reasons Elaine and I moved to the Washington DC area, actually Tokoma Park, MD, was a job promotion, but we were happy to move to cut down on the parties and dances. We bought new outfits for every dance they invited us to, at least two or three times a year.

Uncle Bubber and Aunt Belle had two children, Johnny and Kim. They lived in St. Albans, Queens. We were remarkably close to them also. We even took a 3-day vacation together, although they were our seniors by at least 25 years. Uncle Bubber & Aunt Belle lived in a house that was adjacent to Elaine's mother's house. They shared a common fence that everyone climbed over to get to each house instead of walking around the street. Elaine's mother's house was the family meeting place for food and fellowship. Uncle Bubber and Aunt Belle's house was the place for parties and fun. However, each household was known for good home cooked food, fellowship, and parties.

Uncle Ronald and Aunt Honey had three children, Marvin, Jackie, and Kenneth. They lived in the Bronx. We stayed in touch with them also. The children were much younger than Elaine and me, but we enjoyed them when we visited our uncles and aunts.

Aunt Ruby and Uncle Bill Hogan had four children who were also younger than Elaine and me, Stevie, Romana, Jackie, and Shawn. We stayed in touch with all the children and loved them all dearly.

Thinking about my aunts and uncles, I am not sure why we call some aunts and some aunty. We tended to call relatives on my mother's side, aunty and aunt on my father's side, and Elaine's relatives, but not consistently.

Takoma Park, MD

Stanley & Princilla Evans. We met Stanley & Princilla in Takoma, MD. We lived in our Deauville Apartment complex in Tokoma Park until we bought a home a few years later. Stanley & "Prin" moved into the Deauville apartments a few weeks after we did. By that time we were a family of four, Elaine & I, Pamela and Sherrice, our daughters. Stanley & Prin were both Ph.D. students at Howard University majoring in chemistry. By the way, they both graduated and became professors, Prin was at Fisk University, and Stanley was at Meharry Medical College in Nashville, TN.

I saw them in the elevator the day they were moving in, and we exchanged introductions, after which I offered to help them carry their belongings to their department. They accepted the offer. We could have been more efficient in the move the three of us took turns going to their car and getting a load to carry. Instead, one of them was always with me as I went back and forth. How odd! Later, as we became good friends, they told me that when I introduced myself and said I was from NYC, Harlem even, they said they did not want to leave me alone because I might steal something, so they took turns watching me throughout the move. Needless to say, I did not, and we became great friends. When they had their first child years later, they asked us to be Bryson's godparents. Although we never lived in the same city or state after they moved to Tennessee, we maintained contact, and we visited them in Tennessee.

I remember how down-to-earth and jolly Stanley was. You would never guess from his conversations that he would become a researcher in the field of chemistry. He loved to talk about everyday things and his fishing trips; one former co-worker called it 'idle chit-chat." Stanley came with us when we were looking for a house. I introduced him to the elderly couple who were selling their house. After chatting with Stanley for a few minutes the man asked what Stanley did for a living. When Stanley told him he was a doctor, immediately the man sat down in a nearby chair, took off his shoe, and said, "My foot is really hurting me. Can you look at it?"

I have a memory about Stanley that I recall more often than I would like to. I got a call from Prin saying Stanley died when he was in his seat attending a funeral. That image stays with me and when reinforced when I witnessed a similar incident in my home church, Shaws Creek Baptist Church, in Trenton, S.C., a few years later.

Jackie & Ernest. We connected with Jackie & Ernest through Pamela. Pamela and I were in a neighborhood grocery store buying candy when Pamela was 6 years old. She spotted Jackie in the store and introduced me to her. I thought Jackie was one of Pamela's classmates since she looked so young, although she was by herself in the store. But quickly, Pamela said, "This is Jackie, my first-grade teacher." A few days later, Jackie asked Pamela if her father was a member of the Omega Psi Phi fraternity. Jackie thought Pamela may not know about the fraternity. Pamela quickly and proudly replied, "Yes, my father is a "Q." Jackie and her husband, Ernest, and Elaine and I got together shortly after that. The friendship grew rapidly and deeply. Jackie and Ernest came to be known to Pamela and Sherrice as Aunt Mommy and Uncle Daddy.

Ethel & Charles Briggs. When we were living in Maryland, I pledged the Omega Psi Phi fraternity, and sometime later, Elaine pledged to the Delta Sigma Theta sorority; we became close when Charles pledged to me, and Ethel pledged to Elaine. When they had their only child, Cory, we became his Godparents. Our families, especially Pamela and Sherrice, are close to Cory and his wife today.

Fraternity/Sorority Gatherings. I pledged the Omega Psi Phi Fraternity with four other men: John Mercer, in law school; Sonny Smith, who was working on an accounting degree; Doug Person, working on an M.S. in sociology; and Curtis Tearte, working on an M.S. degree in history. I was working on an M.S. degree in Computer Science. We called ourselves the Fraternizing Five. Our theme song was "Dancing Machine" by the Jackson Five; although I cannot say we were a machine, we did pretty well. The Omega colors are purple and gold. The brothers gave me a tough time during our pledge period because I had the nerve to drive all five of us to every pledge meeting in my yellow-gold Oldsmobile Omega.

Elaine pledged to the Delta Sigma Theta Sorority. Twenty-five women were in her circle. They were named "The Esoteric 25." There is no room in this paper to write about all the things we did together, but one highlight was many of the members of each chapter met regularly to bowl with our custom-made monogram bowling balls.

West Hartford, Connecticut

Carol & Victor Gellineau. When IBM moved us to Connecticut, we lived in West Hartford. Carol and Victor have three children, Victor, Carmen, and Maria. They lived in a gated community. The children could walk to each house via a closed-to-traffic street about 100 yards long that ran from the side of our house to the back of the gated community. When the children played at each house, they never wanted to leave. I do not know if the children spent more time at Gellineau's or at our house. I know that they never wanted to leave either place, and they were always asking their parents for permission to stay a little longer.

Carol & Victor hosted many poker parties at their house for close couples. There were four couples that came regularly. Elaine did not come because she did not like to play poker. I do not think Gwin came regularly with Doug, but it was truly a lasting friendship and lots of fun. The stakes were simi-high. I usually lost or won up to $200. That was a lot of nickels and quarters and sometimes one dollar that we bet. Victor, the father, liked our house too. He thought nothing of showing up unannounced, having dinner, and heading home after he finished without Carole.

Carol was a former model who modeled at the time my sister also modeled, but they did not know each other. Victor was in marketing with Heublein. I was a manager with IBM at the time. Elaine and I agreed that she would stay at home and raise the Children. Before we left Connecticut, Elaine when back to work for Aetna Insurance Co. and later as Vice Principal at King Phillips Elementary School. She also finished her coursework for a M.S. degree in Education Administration at the University of Harford. She took the final comprehensive exam in Greensboro, arranged by her advisor, and was awarded the master's degree.

Bernetta & Thurman Evans. Therman is an inspiring speaker who sometimes substitutes for Jesse Jackson. Therman is an M.D. who practices natural medicine. He and Bernetta have two sons, Thermon and Clayton. We worked with Therman and Bernetta in their Operation PUSH community program. I taught a small class in computer literacy on Saturdays that was open to all ages through Operations PUSH. I used a Radio Shack TRS-80 (Tandy Radio Shack) personal/desktop computer I purchased from a community service grant that I received from IBM. The TRS-80 (1977) was the most readily available personal computer except for the Apple 1 (1976), which was not well known or readily available, and the Commodore PET (Personal Electronic Translator), superior for its two processor chips that allowed you to run the Commodore and Apple 1 native mode, To this day no other personal computer uses native mode in for two computers. The personal computer today uses one native-mode computer and simulates another computer using "virtual" processing.

The external hard drive was not developed yet, so the TRS-80 attached a cassette tape player external an external storage device. IBM had not introduce their personal computer until 1981. When they did, it became the gold standard, and major companies started ordering them by the thousands, replacing the monitors attached to the main-frame computers with personal/desktop computers. When IBM entered the marketplace with the personal computer, the TRS-80 became nicknamed Trash-80. It was funny to me because I worked with very sophisticated, for the time, multimillion-dollar main-frame computers introduced as the System/360 (a.k.a. IBM/360) in 1964. I started working for IBM as a computer/systems engineer in the era that main-frame computers ushered in the essential machine for all major operations through the use of major multimillion-dollar "applications." The IBM/360's ushered in second-generation computers.

I learned an odd but valuable lesson about value and money from my TRS-80 computer class. The classes were sparsely attended, and the students were not always attentive, except for the youngest ones, who were really thirsty. The classes were free because I purchased the minimal supplies needed to run the program with the grant money. When the grant ran out, I started a nominal fee of $5.00 for a 6-month program for anyone who did not have a steady source of income; everyone else was free. All of a sudden, the adults became more attentive and did not miss a class because "they wanted their money's worth." What they did not appreciate for free they wanted when it cost them a nominal $5.00 for six months of instruction. Go figure! Starbucks (1971) had already started their drive toward $5.00/cup of coffee. Message: people have to see value and be personally invested, in whatever form that takes, to be committed to their involvement with an endeavor.

LouBertha & Richard Wharton – I cannot remember how we met LouBertha& Richard Wharton. I know it was through Elaine, in her connection with the school system, where LouBertha was an administrator. They are both retired educators with doctorate degrees. They exposed us to some of the finer things in life through their elaborate dinner parties and the stories of their families. For example, Richard's father was featured on a US Postal stamp and their appreciation of the opera. They still invite us to their home for rest and relaxation in Florida, in a gated community with a guard to allow entrance. Their sons, Jonathan and ???) are handsome, intelligent successful people. Jonathan is a doctor and professor at Fillin ???. He is a published author.

Nancy & Lloyd King – Nancy and Lloyd lived with their two children, Godfrey and Lance, within walking distance from our house. I used to play tennis against their young sons. They were just learning but I knew just enough to play both of them simultaneously, me against them. I was taking tennis lessons too, so I was a little better than they were. My tennis teacher used to instruct me to "go through to the ball." Nancy worked at Aetna Insurance company in a significant, analytical position; I cannot remember where she met Elaine. I think Elaine was working at Aetna at that time. We had long talks about life, living in white neighborhoods, and raising children.

Hal's Restaurant was the meeting place every Sunday after church for the Black professional community. We always enjoyed talking and joking and having a great time while bonding more every Sunday.

Leslie & Isaac Clarke were also friends that we visited. I was so impressed with Isaac's wine seller in his basement. Sadly, Isaac was stabbed to death in his office by one of his patients. It was such a devastating loss for everyone. I remember him for his kindness and down-to-earth spirit.

Janet & Jim Jackson have two daughters _______ . Jim was a Vice President for Connecticut General. They lived in a mansion-like older home that had a separate staircase office the kitchen that had been used for the maids' quarters before they bought the property. Jim told me that the old-fashioned home with soaring ceilings cost $2,000 per month to heat when they lived there in the mid-1970s.

Doug & Gwen were our community activity friends who we worked at the Artist Collective and Operations PUSH. They had one fillin daughter, Meg. Doug held a leadership position in a church, but it was not pastoring. I never asked what denomination, but it was probably methodist. He traveled a lot for his church. When he was in Greensboro he visited us where we moved when we left Connecticut.

The Artist Collective was founded in 1970 and led by Dolly, a Broadway dancer & her husband, world-renowned alto-saxophonist, composer, and educator Jackie McLean. The Artist Collective is an interdisciplinary arts and cultural institution emphasizing the cultural and artistic contributions of the African Diaspora. Pamela and Sherrice attended the school and participated in the African Rite of Passage Yaboo Celebration of Coming of Age. I have fond memories of my time with the Artist Collective. I served as Chair of the Board for a few years. I remember one time I was practicing the drums in the basement of the Collective when Jackie walked in with his sax and joined me. We played for quite a while, and he encouraged me to start playing publicly in the Hartford area.

Greensboro, NC

We met LTC Trey & Melba McCarther and their daughter Kisha when we moved to Greensboro, NC, in 1982. Trey & Melba moved across the street from us for two years while Tray was stationed at North Carolina Agricultural and Technical State University to lead the ROTC program. We often went from house to house to visit each other. Trey was a member of the Men's Choir at White Oak Baptist Church, were we also attended. I played the drums for the church so Trey would always insist that I go to rehearsals in his pickup truck named Big Red. The colder the weather got and the worse weather conditions of ice and snow, the more Trey would insist on pressing on to the Church. After Trey retired and they moved to Mt Airy, NC, we stayed in touch. When Trey had business in Greensboro, he would always call ahead so Elaine could make a strawberry pie for him. After Melba passed, he eventually married Gloria. He and Gloria went on the annual couples trips that Kenneth organized.

Shortly after meeting Trey we met Pat & Jerry Posey who have two children, Tony, and Trina. We met them through Sherrice because she and Trina became best friends. The four of us and other couples got together periodically to go to a movie together. Everyone would come back to our house for fellowship and a potluck supper to talk about the movie and life. We had dinner with Pat and Jerry many times. We went to a variety of restaurants, and Jerry would always order salmon. We were so close that when I bought my next car, we gave my old Omega Oldsmobile to Tony. I do not know who was the happiest, Tony, Trina, Jerry, Pat or Elaine and me.

Shortly after settling into our home in Greensboro, Elaine took Pamela and Sherrice to Sunday School at White Oak Grobe Baptist Church. I did not go; I decided to relax after a tiring week. That is when we met Kenneth. He was an Adult Sunday School Teacher. He saw Elaine leaving after dropping the children off and told her to stay for his class and told her to bring her husband next time. That was the beginning of a best friend, best-couple-friendship with Kenneth and Louise. When they adopted Ivan, we were asked to be god parents, and we joyfully accepted.

Walter & Joice Watson move across the street, renting Trey's house after they left. Walter replaced Trey as the commander of the

NCA&TSU ROTC. They had one daughter, Zanny. Sherrice and Zanny became remarkably close friends.

After LTC Walter Watson and their family finished his command. LTC Johnny & Coralee Williams rented Trey's house. LTC Williams replaced LTC Watson as commander of the ROTC. They had one daughter, Kimberly. Sherrice and Kimberly became particularly good friends. By the time the Williams left to retire in Smyrna, TN, we were best friends. It was Kenneth and Johnny who planned the five couples' vacations. Trey and Glory drove early in the morning to Kenneth's house in Greensboro. Elaine and I and Thomas and Liddy Slade joined them at Kenneth's house, and all got in the rented van, and we headed on vacation. The first stop was to pick up Johnny and Coralee in Smyrna.

On one of our vacation trips, we went to a Greyhound racetrack. I was bragging about how I was going to win all this money by picking the fastest dog. I knew nothing about racetrack betting, not horses or greyhounds. I picked dog number 2. Toward the end of the race, I did not see my horse through the window where we were watching. It turned out that the dog never made it past the view we had from the window. The last dog to cross the finish line was my dog, and a trainer was carrying him. The couple teased me about my pick. For years, every time we went on those vacations, the greyhound incident came up in outbursts of stomach-hurting laughter, even when we did not go to the track. We went to the greyhound trace a few times over the years. I never won anything, but I did not stop boasting.

William Harris

Curtis Tearte

Kenneth McLean. Recently, my last best friend passed. I have known Kenneth McLean since 1982, shortly after we moved to Greensboro, NC. I thank him for inviting me to attend Sunday School and inspiring me with his teaching. He is the reason I have been teaching Sunday School for almost forty years. Kenneth had a way of making everyone his friend. He is the epitome of a friend that is closer than a brother. Elaine and I did so much with Kenneth and Louise. We went to dinner regularly; we planted a 1-acre garden together. As a city boy who did not know anything about gardening, I will never do that again. He and

Johnny Williams planned and arranged the annual one-week couples trips every second week in July.

Five couples travelled together in a van and stayed in a cabin large enough for every couple to have a separate room and bath. Usually, we all met in a common area in the cabin for breakfast prepared by the ladies. After breakfast, we got in the van and explored the area. After breakfast, we used the van to tour the surrounding cities and states. Normally, we had lunch and dinner while we explored, but sometimes, we had dinner in the cabin.

Kenneth and I had many one-on-one talks and even went to buy suits at local men's clothing stores. He would strike up a conversation at any time with anyone. He would always start his conversations with "Hey, young man" or "Hey, young lady." His life taught me how to live a Christian life.

Deacon and Sister Cole. Deacon and Sister Cole mentored Elaine and me. We met them at White Oak Grove Baptist Church, the first church we joined when we moved to Greensboro. Every Sunday Deacon Cole gave me a handwritten list of Scripture he wanted me to know. Then, the next Sunday asked me something about the Scripture that he gave me the previous Sunday to see if I read the Scriptures, he gave me. The last time I saw him, he was in his 80s, and he was scheduled for major surgery, which he never recovered from. Elaine and I were visiting Deacon and Sister Cole at their home. As physically weak as he was, he pulled out a handwritten list of Scriptures for me to learn.

Over time they exposed us to church activities on a regional and national level. On the regional, they brought us to the Guilford Education and Missionary Baptist Association of 21 churches. We not only got involved in visiting churches in the association, but we also helped positions in the association. I was a member of the Pastors & Deacons Union and the First Vice President of Sunday School. Elaine was President of BTU (Baptist Training Union). When we told the Association that we were moving, they surprised us about a month before with a plaque commending us for our service.

On the national level of church activities, Elaine and I went on a bus trip with the Coles to a Lock Cary Foreign Mission Convention in Pittsburgh, PA. I will never forget the powerful preaching we heard throughout the few days of the convention. Many years later, I still remember a minister preaching in 1 Corinthians 16:9, "For a great door and effectual is opened unto me, and there are many adversaries." I am still getting revelation from the meaning of that Scripture.

Our close and incredibly special friends in our Christian journey are Drs. Robert & Sandra Howard. We met them first at NCA&T. Pamela was in Dr. Robert Howard's finance class during the same semester their daughter, Robin, was in my computer science class. Eventually, the Howards invited Elaine and me to speak to their Young Adult group at Providence Baptist Church in Greensboro. Not long after we spoke and having attended several services at Providence Baptist Church, our family of six, Elaine and I, and our daughters and their husbands joined Providence Baptist Church together. We began working with the Howards in their Black History Quiz Bowl class, then became Sunday School teachers for the Young Adult class. Our friendship continues to grow.

When I retired from Corporate America and became Vice Chancellor at NCA&T State University, I hired my former student, Robin, who was working in Corporate America, and I eventually promoted her to a director-level position.

Robin, Leslie & Pamela. Leslie Fort, daughter of the Chancellor at NCA&T, Robin and Pamela became best friends. They periodically went to dinner and stayed until the wee hours of the morning. Dr. Fort and I were always the restless, worried fathers who would call our daughters while they were dining to make sure they were safe. They got in the habit of not telling us where they were going in fear that we might come to find them. We probably would.

I met Robin when she was a student at NCA&T. That semester, Robin was in my computer science class, while Pamela was in Dr. Howard's finance class, Robin's father. It was years later that Elaine and I became close friends of the Howards. Several years after Robin graduated and worked in Corporate America, she came to my office at NCA&T. She asked if she could volunteer as a web developer and work in a college environment. I accepted her as a volunteer, but I worked towards getting a position authorized so I could hire her. I was finally able to hire her and make the appointment retroactive, so Robin received a substantial back payment check.

I eventually promoted Robin to a director-level position and often called on her for advice. One time, I asked her to explain a concept in object-oriented programming to me. In her explanation, she used the illustration of a red fire truck. When I thanked her and compliment her on her explanation, Robin said to me, "Mr. Harrigan, you taught me that when I was in your class."

Robin passed last year. We are all devastated by her loss. She did so much to help many, including us. One thing I will remember her for is how she organized and coordinated the rehearsals and performances of the Providence Band consisting of high school students and the band director from Dudley High School, college students, and a few grownups like me.

Maurice Tyler. Maurice was also one of my outstanding students who still stays in touch with me. I had almost the same experience with Maurice that I had with Robin. Maurice came to me for a job during his successful Corporate Career. I immediately hired him because I had a director's position open. He was the most technically savvy student I had in all my years of teaching, and he became my top employee. I asked him to explain a concept to me, and he did an exquisite job. When I thanked him, he responded the same way as Robin, saying the exact same words, "Mr. Harrigan, you taught me that when I was in your class."

We reconnected with Dr. Rodell & Cedar Lawrence and established an extraordinarily strong friendship while we lived in Greensboro. Rodell and Elaine dated in college before Elaine and I met and married. That is a long, delightful story that I may go into in future "becoming" statements. Rodell invited us to serve on the Board of Engineering Education at South Carolina State University in Orangeburg, SC, where he served as the Board's chair. We drove to Orangeburg, SC, for two-day monthly meetings for almost two years. This reunion solidified our long-lasting best friend friendship. In later years, I recommended him, and he served on the Board of Trustees of Paine College, my alma mater, with me. Rodell has two children, Barham and Regina, who are doing quite well.

Columbia SC

I moved to Columbia, SC for a little more than a year, I was on assignment managing IBM's International Insurance Program. Elaine joined me after six months. We stayed there until I retired from IBM and returned to Greensboro. Her sister Beverly stayed in our Greensboro home with her sons and my father during our absence.

Columbia was 50 miles from Elaine's home church, Shaws Creek Baptist Church in Trenton, SC. Being that close, we attended church regularly. Elaine grew up there and had many friends and family in the church and in the area. She grew up playing in the churchyard with George Brightharp, who became a renowned paster in the area. His father was the Pastor of Shaws Creek when they were growing up. I have the highest respect and admiration for Pastor George Brightharp. He is one of the best preachers I have ever heard or known.

During the time we lived so close to Shaws Creek, Elaine and I were ordained as deaconesses and deacons. I was honored that Pastor and Mrs. Graves attended our ordination. Pastor Graves was our pastor during the time that we lived in Greensboro. He asked me several times if I wanted to be a deacon. I declined each time because I did not feel worthy. I became a deacon at Shaws Creek because Pastor RC Holloway took a different approach to getting me to serve as a deacon. He came to me one day and said, "I am going to ask you a question, and your answer is yes." He asked me to be a deacon, and I said yes. In a few years, Pastor Holloway appointed me as Minister of Education and, for 10 years, had Elaine and I leading annual overnight retreats for Shaws Creek Baptist Church members and invited guests.

When Pastor and Mrs. Graves attended our Sunday ordination, Pastor Graves had never missed a Sunday in either of his churches, White Oak Grove and Faith Baptist Church in all his years of preaching, until he missed the Sunday of our ordination. I have always felt incredibly special and spiritually connected to Pastor Graves. I wish like he told me he also wished, that we could spend more time together in the Lord. He is going on ahead of me, but one day we will.

Chapter 7: INSPIRING CLERGY

Romans 10:14

*How then shall they call on him in whom they have
not believed?
And how shall they believe in him of whom they
have not heard?
And how shall they hear without a preacher?*

George Brightharp, Edgefield, SC – Pastor Brightharp grew up with
Elaine. His father was the Pastor of Shaws Creek Baptist Church for
many years. George and Elaine used to play around the churchyard
together. I am inspired every time I think about him because he is such
a great preacher and "real" Christian. He is a writer, philanthropist,
politician, and phenomenally successful entrepreneur running two
funeral homes. Most of all, he is a friend and a man of not only his
word but the word of God.

Pastor Edward Lloyd. Elaine's grandfather's nephew became a
minister after his wife abandoned him and went to fillin live "the high
life" in New York City. She left him with their three teenage daughters
who he continued raising. He became a committed, caring, loved
pastor in South Carolina and never married again. He prayed for our
family many times when he called just because he was thinking about
us. His brother, Floyd Lloyd is just as kind and loving person as his
brother, Edward. Floyd serves his church as a deacon. When there is
any kind of family gathering Floyd will be there, quiet and unimposing
but always greeting everyone. They are about ten years older than
Elaine, and I see them as our big brothers.

Pastor RC Holloway was the Pastor of Shaws Creek Baptist Church in
Trenton, SC, until he retired a few years ago. Not only did he demand
I serve in his church as a deacon, but he had complete trust in Elaine
and me to do church seminars and lead church retreats. Deacon. After
moving back to Greensboro, we could not attend Shaws Creek
regularly. Out of respect for us, every time we came back, he
acknowledged us from the pulpit and asked us if we had any comments
for the church.

Pastor Albert E. Graves pastored two churches and preached on
alternate Sundays at White Oak Grove in Greensboro, NC, and Faith
Baptist Church in Gibsonville, NC. He convinced me to be on the

Trustee Board at White Oak Gove and eventually to serve on the deacon board at Faith Baptist Church. Pastor Graves lived a model Christian life. It was not until his death that I learned about all the untiring efforts he made to serve his surrounding communities. He truly had wisdom from God. If I found out after his death that he wanted me to be the executor of his will. I was so honored, but I did not choose to be in a position to override or have our family's desires.

Bishop Brooks retired a few years ago from Mt Zion Baptist Church, Greensboro, NC, but he still preaches as a guest minister and appears on Christian talk shows frequently. We never joined his church because we were committed to working with Pastor Graves, but we attended Bishop Brooks's overnight retreats and other church activities.

Bishop Brooks was always there for us. He officiated the double wedding of Pamela & Gregory and Sherrice & Bryan. He officiated the marriage ceremonies of Elaine's sister, Mary, in our backyard. He officiated our 50th Wedding anniversary when we renewed our vows, and he officiated the marriage of Pamela & Isaac, also in our backyard. We also worked with Bishop Brooks in the Guilford Missionary Baptist Association.

Once, I was charged with a crime that took three years to be dismissed with prejudice, meaning that I could not be charged again for that crime. During that ordeal, several of the ministers with that Elaine and I conducted workshops and seminars abandoned me and declined to stand up for my character. Bishop Brooks was so highly sought after during that time that there was a two-week wait to see him in his study. Yet, Bishop Brooks contacted me, gave me his personal cell phone number, and told me to call him any time. I will never forget him for his loving support.

Pastor Dr. Howard Chubbs pastored Providence Baptist Church, Greensboro, NC. He advised me not to plea bargain if I did not commit the crime. Others, even a prominent judge advised by my attorney to settle with a plea bargain. The case was a nightmare. When the case was dismissed, I was nominated by church members to serve on the deacon board. I was selected, ordained, and eventually served as the board secretary for many years.

Pastor Dr. Clarence Johnston pastored Elm Grove Baptist Church. I met him through the Association, where he served as the Moderator.

We became friends, and he invited me to speak to the Men's group at his church. We used to jest about who was mentoring who; of course, he was mentoring me, but he liked to say I was his mentor.

Pastor Annette and Deacon Dickens are good friends that we met at Faith Baptist Church. We developed a warm friendship through the many religious and social occasions we spent together. One such occasion was when we treated them to dinner at the restaurant located at the top of the Jefferson Pilot Building. We ate alligator soup together, the first time for all of us. We went on overnight marriage retreats together. Deacon Dickens and I served on the Deacon Board together. Elaine and I even conducted a seminary for Pastor Annette's church that she founded years after we left Faith Baptist Church. Pastor Dicken's church was small, but she was powerful and had the strongest faith I have ever known. When she passed a few weeks ago, I learned from her eulogy preached by her son that she had passed all over the world and never had to pay for any of her trips because she had faith that the Lord would supply her needs.

Chapter 8: RELIGIOUS EXPERIENCES

1 Corinthians 15:58

Therefore, my beloved brethren, be ye steadfast, unmoveable, always abounding in the work of the Lord, forasmuch as ye know that
your labour is not in vain in the Lord.

During my childhood years, from adolescence to about 18, when I went to college, I had varying exposures to religion. My father took me regularly to the Church of Illumination in Manhattan, a Presbyterian Church. I enjoyed the Children's Sunday School in the basement of the church and was taken upstairs to the sanctuary at the end of Sunday School. Sunday School was great, but I did not understand anything that went on in the main service. For example, my father sang in the men's choir. The choir was seated in the back of the church, and they stood up in place to sing. The sermons made no sense to me. The children sat together in the front right side of the church, so unfortunately, I was as far away from my father as I could be. My mother, sister, and brother stayed home. My mother, the youngest of her sisters, was convinced by her sister, Aunty Hattie, that ministers were no good because she caught her minister husband in her bed with another woman. Pop and I only attended regularly for about 2 years when I was not a teenager yet. I do not know why we stopped attending. I do not remember ever asking why.

For years, I went with my friends to various Bible studies and religious events held in meeting places, churches, and homes. I just enjoyed those kinds of events even though I can't articulate why I enjoyed them or what I heard or learned. Maybe it was being in the presence of people who loved the Lord. I had exposure to various church doctrines, not realizing what doctrines were.

I attended Bible study with my elementary school buddy and fellow drummer, John Pate. His family had a 'Bible study recital' of some sort where I sang with the other students, 'Jesus wants me for a sunbeam, to shine on Him each day.' I don't remember the rest. I do not remember if I invited my parents; they may have been there. I am sure they would have come if I invited them. Anyway, that is when I felt the Holy Spirit. I cried either during or after the song. At the time I thought the feeling was embarrassment singing in front of an audience.

It wasn't until I finished college and was married with children that I understood what that was.

One time, Mrs. Silver, my best friend's mother, took Willaim, his sister Naomi, and me to a church meeting at a hotel. The experience was interesting but frightening. The preacher was Daddy Grace. He was seated in a Roman-type chariot carried by four men. Everyone was standing because there were intentionally no chairs in the room, perhaps because they could get more people in the room if there were no chairs. When he was seated, he was presented with an oversized doll-type house made of money in large domination bills. When he spoke, people started shouting all around me. Frightened and confused, I tried to cling to Mrs. Silver. Suddenly, Mrs. Silver broke into an uncontrollable shout. Willaim and Naomi seemed to be as shocked as I was. I will never forget how lonely, afraid, and abandoned I felt. I couldn't wait for the service to be over. We also attended Eastern Star Meetings with Mrs. Silver. That may have influenced me to become a 32nd-degree Mason when I moved to Greensboro, NC, almost 30 years later.

When I was a teenager, I attended Catholic services sometimes with my girlfriend and witnessed communion. It seemed unsanitary to me for the congregation to come up to the priest, sip out of the same cup, and watch the priest drink any wine left over in the cup after everyone was served. Then he wiped the cup with a white cloth. Part of the Catholic sermons were spoken in Latin, and I only knew the English spoken at home, spoken in the streets, and studied in college.

My brother was a Muslem and often went to 125th Street in Harlem to hear MalcolmX speak. When my brother graduated from college and moved to Atlanta, GA, he married a Muslem lady who had three children. I didn't have a problem with his religion. I perceived that my brother wanted to be in the midst and here the dynamic speaker. At that point in my life, I had been exposed to Baptists, Methodists, Catholics, Bahai and who knows what other kinds of faiths.

In Booker T. Washington Junior High School, in Manhattan, I was exposed the Jewish faith. The school population was mostly Hispanic and Jewish. I remember hearing the Jewish students talk about Bar and Bat Mitzvahs and how they had to attend Jewish classes after school.

At Paine College, a methodist school, I majored in mathematics and minored in philosophy and religion. I began to get serious about understanding religion, but I did more thinking and becoming aware of doctrine, but I didn't "study" it like I now wished I had. The professors were excellent, but I didn't focus. In my second year of College, I enrolled in a class about the survey of the Old Testament. The professor was Dr. Delamont. He was an excellent teacher and had ghost-authored a book named The Stained-Glass Window." I was awed over having a teacher who actually wrote a "book." By this time in my matriculation, I had transitioned from a disinterested student who expected to "flunk out," to being perceived as a budding scholar. I was perceived by my classmates as one of the top students in the college because at the Honors' Convocation" at the end of my freshmen year I received the two top honors in the of the College, the achievement in mathematics award and the achievement in physics award. No freshmen had ever received both awards in the same year. However, I was not doing well in Dr. Delamont's Old Testament class. Since the Paine College community of 500 students, in addition to teachers and staff, all knew each other there was a lot of open communication.

As a warning to me, Dr. Delamont announced to the class, "Mr. Harrigan, unless you get an 'A' on the final exam, you will fail this class." There went my reputation as a scholar, especially since Mrs. Hill announced the same thing an hour ago in her English class. Well, I was blessed; I got 'A's' on each exam and made final grades of 'C's. Those were the only two C's I had on my transcript when I graduated as the number one student with the highest grade point average. But look at the opportunity I missed, the opportunity to learn the Old Testament from Dr. Delamont's perspective.

I didn't get any better at studying Christianity until long after I graduated because, in my senior year, I enrolled in a special seminar. I did well but I didn't study like I should or read the assignments carefully. The seminar was taught at Dr. Shephard's house, which was on campus. She and Dr. Delamont taught jointly. There were only six students in the class. We were given reading assignments on various religious topics and had open discussions. I didn't always read, and I faked some of the discussions, another missed opportunity, shame on me. I wish I could relive that seminar. I wish I could tell them that I have become a Doctor of Theology. I wish I had the knowledge, enthusiasm, and relationship with God then that I have now. What wonderful conversations we would have.

I dated a girl in college who practiced the Baha'i faith. We didn't talk about her faith very much, but she had different views on some topics that germinated from her faith. The Baha'i faith believes that all major religions come from the same divine source, including Buddha, and Muhammad, and the search for knowledge is based on reason and evidence. These tenets are contrary to Christianity.

When I married Elaine since we moved so much for career opportunities, we attended and became members of several Baptist churches; Shaws Creek Baptist, White Oak Grove Baptist, Faith Baptist, and Providence Baptist. We were also involved with the Guilford Educational & Missionary Baptist Association. Elaine became the BTU (Baptist Training Union) Director of the 21-church membership of the Association. I became the 1st Vice President of the Sunday School. In succession planning, the 1st Vice President was always the successor of the current president. We left Greensboro before I had the opportunity to serve. I cannot tell you what I really learned and really believed through all of this.

In spite of the various religious experiences I had, I can only honestly say I started developing a relationship with God. That came long after I met my wife and graduated from college.

Chapter 9: MEMORABLE MOMENTS

Philippians 4:8

Finally, brethren,
whatsoever things are true, whatsoever things are honest,
whatsoever things are just, whatsoever things are pure,
whatsoever things are lovely, whatsoever things are
of good report;
if there be any virtue, and if there be any praise,
think about these things.

Marriage & Parenting: There is nothing like the experiences of marriage and parenting. I talked about my marriage to Elaine. She made me who I am by showing me how to know and worship the triune God. I am crying when I admit that when I met Elaine and had all these religious experiences and education, I was uncomfortable saying the name "Jesus." I knew Jesus academically, but I did not know Him and how to call on Him. Forgive me, Lord.

Witnessing and living the blessed privilege of marriage to Elaine, parenting our daughters Pamela and Sherrice, and grandparenting our granddaughter, Sophia, is the source of my joy and my reason for living, only second to knowing my Lord and Savior, Jesus Christ.

Macy's Day Thanksgiving Parade: For several years, Pop took Patsy, Jimmy, and me to the Macy's Day Thanksgiving Parade while Mommy prepared the turkey meal at home. We rode the subway to 34th Street but we walked home, about 4 miles. After standing for hours while we watched the parade, I did not feel like walking. During the walk home, I always got sleepy, so Pop picked me up and carried me the rest of the way home, which was at least half the trip. I do not know if Patsy and Jimmy were angry about that but when we came home, I jumped out of Pop's arm, full of energy. Mommy was finishing the dinner and Patsy started to tidy up for the relatives to come throughout the day. Jimmy and I went off to play with our friends.

Visit by Professor Gabriel: Professor Gabriel was a relative somehow, I think, on my mother's side. He came to stay with us for a few days. Patsy was in a Catholic school in Augusta, GA, staying with Aunty Annie so Professor Gabriel stayed in her room. I did not say much to him. I did not know what to say anyway, but I was in awe of his presence, a real professor in our midst who stayed in his room with the door closed.

Acceptance in the High School of Music & Art: When I was in the 9th grade, I applied for admission to Music & Art. At the time, there were two magnet schools that specialized in the arts. The other school was the School of Performing Arts. If you are familiar with the movie Fame. It was based on the School of Performing Arts. Sometimes I refer to them as rival schools but there was never a perceivable revival. They were separate islands that never competed against each other. The students in each school focused on their craft not school competition. There were other magnet schools that specialized in a variety of disciplines, like Bedford-Stuyvesant, which focused on academic excellence, and the School of Math and Science. The magnet schools were open to students from all five boroughs in NYC. Entrance to the schools was based on student GPAs and standardized tests. I took a written test in the auditorium at Music & Art. They asked all kinds of questions about music that I did not know.

A few months later, the principal of my junior high school was making his morning announcements over the loudspeaker. This time, he was announcing students by name who had been accepted in the various magnet schools. When he said my name and announced that I was accepted to attend Music & Art, it was one of the happiest days of my life as a teenager; instantly, I felt special and called home to tell my mother as soon as it was time to change to the next class period. But by the grace of God, I do not know why I was accepted because I did not do well on the written music test, and there was no audition like I had when I was accepted in Juilliard (which I could not afford to attend) after graduating from high school.

I was not a strong student academically. The magnet schools emphasized rigorous academic excellence with their specialization, like music. The only thing is could figure was that I was considered the best drummer in my school orchestra and dance/jazz band. Now I know it was God. Unbelievably, I actually had a small fan club of girls who would sometimes show up at my front door on Saturdays.

NYC Borough Wide Orchestra: I was selected as the First Percussionist in the NYC Borough Wide Orchestra conducted by Lenard Bernstein (famed American conductor, composer, pianist, music educator, author, and humanitarian). The members of the orchestra were required to attend rehearsals throughout the semester in preparation for the final concert in May. The last 2 or 3 rehearsals of the 100-piece orchestra were joined by a 100-piece choir that had been rehearsing separately. The performance was recorded. I can still see and feel that experience. Unfortunately, living in New York, there was a downside. At the final rehearsal and the night of the concert there were rumors of a gang fight after the concert that added to the anxiety of performing.

1963 Final Concert of the Senior Orchestra at the High School of Music & Art. I was a graduating senior at the final rehearsal of the Senior Orchestra. The Senior Orchestra was the premier performing group at the school. Only the best musicians were selected to play in this orchestra. The students had backgrounds of studying music as children. The orchestra was known for being "perfect," that is, they did not make mistakes. There could be a question of interpretation of a piece but never a question of execution. I was the first percussionist in the orchestra, lead drummer in the jazz band conducted by Donald Bird, renowned jazz trumpeter, and the first percussionist in the NYC Borough-wide Orchestra conducted by Lenord Bernstein. I certainly was a skilled performer, even slightly well-known. The concert was to be performed that same evening for family and friends throughout the city. We were going to perform all movements of Igor Stravinsky's Firebird Suite. I was the first percussionist responsible for the timpani parts which required making a series of bold, pounding, often solo drum rolls. The conductor, Mr. Richter, queued me in. My left hand hit the first timpani, my right hand missed the second timpani, and my mallet fell to the floor. I had done the unthinkable; I made a mistake. Mr. Richter stopped the entire orchestra and just stared at me for what felt like an hour. He would have removed me from my position and the orchestra, except the concert was to take place in a few hours, and no one else knew the part. That night, thank God, I made no mistakes at the concert. That experience taught me humility like I never felt before. That humility sits on my shoulder and stays with me at all times.

1967 Graduation from Paine College: I never thought I would graduate from college. I barely made it through high school. My grades were average, but every student had to pass a state-wide Regents Exam in every major subject to earn a diploma. Each exam was 3 hours long. I thought I was not graduating because I failed the Physics Regents Exam. In retrospect, I am not sure why I even took physics. I was not a good student, except in math. Even in math I stopped after algebra in the 11th grade. I had struggled through geometry and was not about to take the next course in solid geometry. Ironically, I majored in math at Paine College and completed all the math courses in my junior year; go figure. I also received the award for the best student in physics go figure. The Regents Board announced that the Physic exam was too hard, so they lowered the passing grade by 10 points, so I passed. However, I received a general diploma, not an academic diploma, because I did not take all the academic courses. I attended the High School of Music & Art and focused on music courses. I was a drummer, a "percussionist," and expected to be a jazz musician.

My graduation was like a dream to me because I did not think I would finish college, and I had no interest. The subjects seemed too hard to me. When my brother would come home from college during school breaks, I perused his books, particularly analytical geometry, and was convinced that I was not made for college. I attended Paine College for two reasons. First, my parents wanted all the children to get an education. I went to college to please them, figuring that I would flunk out in a year or two. That would show that I tried, and I could return to New York to be a jazz drummer. Secondly, I had a UNCF scholarship. I received that scholarship by the grace of God.

The scholarship was based on my score on an exam. I remember I was nonchalant when I took the exam. I was so tired of taking regent exams that I played with the test. I went back and forth, answering 4 or 5 questions and randomly marking down answers for the next 4 or 5 questions. I had no idea of my score, and I did not care.

As I prepared to leave for college my mother had a long talk with me. She beseeched me to stay out of trouble in college. You see, my brother was expelled from Paine College at the end of his sophomore year for having a gun in his room. By the way, he returned to school the next year, and we were in college together for two years until he graduated. It was the time of the civil rights movement, and everybody had guns. He got caught because the college officials kept a close eye on "northerners" in their southern town. My mother did not want me to do anything but concentrate on my studies. Well, I arrived at the college in August, but by November I was in trouble, not because of involvement in the civil rights movement. I am embarrassed to admit that I was in the lobby of the girl's dorm after curfew, and I had the smell of alcohol on my breath, according to the Dean of Students. I was put on a restriction that could not be imposed today.

In a formal letter from the Dean of Students, Dr. Stenhouse, my restrictions were as follows: (1) I could not walk on the side of the campus near the girls' dorms. (2) I could only go off campus to attend church on Sunday or take my close to the nearby Chinese laundry. If I attended church, I had to tell the Dean about the sermon I heard. Dean Stenhouse was an ordained minister, so I could not make up anything. (3) I could only go to class and the library. I could not go to basketball games or attend any sports events. I could not watch TV with the guys in the dorm where I was staying. There was no such thing as portable TV in individual rooms, so I could not watch TV. No one could afford one. (4) I could use the public phone in the lobby for emergencies only. So, I stayed in my room. Those restrictions were the best thing that could have happened to me. I kept the letter of restrictions for many years. I wish I could find it now. Those restrictions were illegal and definitely not enforceable today.

In my room, out of boredom, I studied and did my homework, particularly during the times I could hear the excitement of the basketball games in the gym from my window. I started to do well in my classes. By the end of the school year, I had A's and B's in every subject. I was on restrictions from the middle of November until classes resumed in mid-January because I did not go home during the break and stayed on campus. The rest is history. Not only did I not funk out, but I also graduated with the top honors. I graduated first in my class of 1967 and received the only two cash awards presented at graduation for outstanding academic achievement and student government leadership.

My memorable moment of pride and humility was when, as the school's tradition, as the top graduate, I followed last in the processional of the graduating class into the ceremony and led the graduates in the procession ending the ceremony, while my parents, relative and friends watch.

Fiftieth Wedding Celebration: Fifty years later, our children gave us a big 50th Wedding Anniversary and we renewed our vowels. As of this writing we are two years from our 60th Wedding Anniversary. I tried to talk our children out of a big celebration. They refused. Reluctantly, we accepted it. It was such a wonderful, blessed occasion. It is up there with our most memorable treasures.

Our Children's Double Wedding Ceremony: In 1998, Pamela and Sherrice got married in a double wedding ceremony. Walking down the aisle with a daughter on each side to join them at their husbands was more than a memorable moment. It was like a fairy tale for me, beginning with the rehearsal and dinner the evening before the wedding. When I walked into the newly million-dollar renovated chapel at Bennett College, I saw over 100 people standing around. I asked what they were doing in the chapel. I was told that they all had parts in the wedding, including the three directors and the four photographers and videographers and the three officiating pastors.

The girls and Elaine got seated in the limousine. I was planning to drive my car to the hotel where the ceremony would take place. The driver walked up to me and told me that he brought a second driver to drive my car so that I could get in the limousine. I couldn't thank the driver enough for those special moments the four of us had in the limousine. I gave him a one-hundred-dollar tip.

I have to admit that leading up to the wedding, I was not very understanding. I had a different vision which was similar to Steve Martin in the movie, "Father of the Bride." Elaine and the girls envisioned a grand celebration, and I envisioned a cook-out gathering. Elaine and I eloped. I was suspiciously eyeing their future husbands every time they were in my midst. I had already changed the vow to say, "Who blessed these unions," and the parents would all stand up and say, "We do." instead of "Who gives these bridges away." I made it clear that we were not giving them away. I wanted hot dogs, hamburgers, and ribs for the cookout. They served steak and salmon on every plate. I was looking for light Hors d'oeuvres. They served jumbo shrimp and had a beautiful ice sculpture in the middle of the buffet table, leaning in the dining room. To top it off, every time an RSVP came in that said they would not be able to attend, I almost yelled out a hardy "Yes!" I had calculated that every confirmation of attendance was $50 per guest, and that was just for the food. We had invited 200 to the wedding and 400 of our closest friends to the reception. It took me a while to come to my senses. I finally acquiesced, realizing what a special occasion this was going to be. If I had to do it over, I would never object to anything they wanted to do.

There were many highlights during the wedding ceremony. Probably the best highlight was just before the presiding pastor, Bishop Brooks, completed the vows; on his signal, the husbands took a few steps from their brides and sang a duet to them that brought astonishment and tears of joy to everyone. Who knew they could sing.

Cherice Tearte's Wedding. Cherice was named after our Sherrice. As Cherice's godparents, Curtis & Gloria, invited us to her wedding. At the time, Curtis was a senior executive in IBM. In fact, in his final years at IBM, he was a member of the IBM Corporate Management Committee, composed of the 60 top executives in IBM. We were honored to be seated in the first row with Curtis and Gloria. It was a beautiful wedding and reception. Elaine and I were moved by the memorable moments and the special attention the family gave to us.

Chapter 10: EDUCATION

2 Timothy2:15

Study to shew thyself approved unto God,
a workman that needeth not to be ashamed,
rightly dividing the word of truth.

I pursued doctorate degrees in several disciplines but never finished until I completed the doctorate degree in theology (ThD). After graduating from Paine College, first in my class, I attended Case Institute of Technology (now Case-Western Reserve) in Cleveland, OH, on a fellowship that paid for tuition, books, and a stipend for living expenses. I started school in the summer and stayed in the graduate student housing. I was enrolled in their PhD program in mathematics. I was the only Black person in the program. There was only one Black in the undergraduate program. While I was there, I attempted to finally get my driver's license.

That summer I paid for private driving lessons from a Cleveland police officer. He was a good instructor and we bonded. He even sold me one of his cars. When I went to the DMV to take the driver's test, I was nervous, and it was raining. The examining officer accompanied me to my car. At first, I could not find the windshield wipers, so I fumbled a little getting started. The situation went downhill from there. The officer told me to drive out of the parking lot and <u>turn right</u> onto the street. Surely, I could follow instructions, I graduated first in my class with a B.S. degree in mathematics and I was enrolled in a Ph.D. program in mathematics. I proceeded out of the parking lot to the street, put on my signal, and <u>turned left</u>. The officer yelled at me, saying, "Stop the car; you are going to kill me in here."

Before the next semester (Fall 1968) started, I traveled back to South Carolina, leaving my car parked in the graduate student parking lot. I went to get Elaine, my wife of only six months, who had stayed to work on her undergraduate degree at South Carolina State University. We returned to Cleveland and brought two of her cousins who had just graduated from High School. We wanted to help them get a good start in life.

On our trip back to Cleveland, we, I should say, Elaine, drove through the mountains. It was a cold, snowy night, and the car heater stopped working. The four of us bundled up in blankets, Elaine and I in the front, Elaine's cousins, Barbara and Yvonne in the back. It was not long before it began to be unbearable. So, we found our way to a restaurant. It was Denny's. We stayed there for the night with other stranded drivers. In the morning, we made it to a garage where the mechanic diagnosed the problem. He fixed it in less than a minute. The fuse had blown. We did not have a lot of money among us, so I was hesitant to ask what it would cost, but I did. He said, "15 cents." All I could think about was how we could have frozen to death for lack of a 15-cent repair.

When we finally arrived in Cleveland, we went to the apartment that we had arranged to rent earlier that month. The lady that greeted us said plainly that she did not know we were Black and that she would not rent to us. There was not much we could do, so I went to a phone booth and started calling places; cell phones were not introduced to the public for another 15 years. I found an apartment, but the renting agent, hearing my name "Harrigan," assumed I was white. She cautioned me over the phone that Black people were living there also. I chucked to myself and told her that it would be no problem. When she rented the apartment to us, she acted as if she never said that.

I left Case Institute of Technology in the middle of the Fall semester. Elaine was pregnant, but that was the excuse I gave to the family for returning to New York City where Elaine and I had a lot of relatives. The real reason for leaving was quite different. I was in an extremely competitive environment with students that I was unable to bond with, remember that I was the only Black. The other students were graduates of Cal Tech and MIT, so I felt intimidated. I studied so hard and so long that I began to act like what I call "a nutty professor." I would sleep at night and dream that I was solving a problem on one of the boards in the graduate math room, where other students who were working on their doctorates each had assigned desks. There were no women in the doctoral program at that time. As I dreamed of working on a problem, I was conscious that I was dreaming. I solved the problem and began to talk to myself in the dream. I kept repeating, "Please don't wake up until I can memorize the solution." I studied the solution and suddenly woke up and wrote the solution on paper. I knew I was either going crazy or turning into my image of a bumbling, stumbling, babbling professor who didn't know whether he was awake or dreaming. I had said I wanted to earn a Ph.D. in mathematics so I could be a professor. That was it; right there, I decided it was time to escape from the world I was entering. In retrospect, that was a bad move. I was not in tune with the Holy Spirit at the time, so I did not realize that I was being blessed with a special ability that needed to be acknowledged, to thank God, and to develop it.

I went to see my advisor that next day. It was Friday. I made an excuse that I needed to leave school because I was too much in debt and my wife was pregnant. When he asked me about it, I told him my debt was $10,000. I figured that was a pretty high number considering that the $2,500 stipend I was receiving was sufficient to live well. Remember I was the only Black person in graduate school majoring in mathematics. He told me that he did not have access to that kind of money. Before I could finish saying that I understood, he continued, "but it is the weekend. I cannot get it to you until Monday." I said thank you. I went back to the apartment and explained to Elaine that we had to leave to go to New York right away because the school was going to "keep me." Elaine's stepfather, Harold, took the train from New York to Cleveland and drove us back to New York a few days later. I never contacted my advisor or the school; how foolish of me.

That experience began my downward spiral of taking the GRE several times, enrolling, and being accepted into doctoral programs in a variety of disciplines while being employed by IBM. I would withdraw from school over and again in favor of moving to advance my career in IBM. Next, I enrolled in a doctoral program in operations research at New York University after being selected and having attended IBM's prestigious internal school called the Systems Research Institute.

Early in the operations research program, I was promoted to a position in Washington, D.C. I enrolled in a program in computer science and earned an M.S. degree from Howard University in Washington, D.C. I enrolled in a Ph.D. program in computer science at George Washington University. I completed one semester, and I felt the Ph.D. program was not as difficult as the M.S. program I completed. But I withdrew from the program when I was promoted to my second management position in Hartford CT. I was frustrated with my GWU advisor anyway. He required me to take a class in Computer Data Structures. I explained that I had taken the course already. It was an intensive programing class that took a lot of time. Since he insisted that I take it anyway I enrolled and computer the course in a summer semester at GWU. It was an intensive programming class. I think I wrote ten complex programs in two months. When I sat with my advisor the next semester, he asked me why I took the data structure class. I told him because he told me to. He said, "I'm sorry I told you that. You already had it."

I began concentrating on my management career and did not enroll in any schools in Hartford. I held several positions during that time. I was the Systems Engineering Manager in the largest Branch Office in IBM measured by sales and revenue. There were about 300 branches throughout the United States run by Branch Managers. The Branch Manager position was a "field general" position and the main contact for multi-million-dollar computer sales. We won the "President's Award" for being the first branch to have 1-billion dollars in sales in a single year. In fact, the trophy that had previously been moved each year to the best branch was retired in our branch in recognition of the milestone achievement. The branch had 6 sales managers, 3 were senior level account executives. There was one administrative manager, and I was the only Systems Engineering Manager.

I supported all the sales managers. My team of systems engineers provided technical advice and support to IBM sales representatives and large insurance companies. While in the Hartford area, I was also promoted to a position commuting to Boston, MA. I was an Equal Opportunity Programs (EOP) officer. My duties included auditing branch offices from Maine to Upstate NY for compliance with the federal OFCCP equal opportunity office and addressing personal issues and compliance. Since IBM had a reputation for hiring the best people and paying more than the industry average, instances of performance issues were rare. However, a branch manager could lose his or her job for violating internal personal practice. It was such as powerful position that ever branch is visited to audit always welcomed me by name on their fillin marques. This made my position very powerful. I left that assignment after a year when I appointed to lead the IBM effort of a 70-million joint project between IBM and Aetna Insurance Company to implement Aetna Agency Management Systems in 1400 locations throughout the USA using IBM Series 1 minicomputers. The project was announced in the Wall Street Journal and monitored by IBM branches around the world because of being one of a few pioneering efforts of joint development and deployment between IBM and their customers.

After the Harford/Boston experience, IBM honored a request from NCA&T, in Greensboro, NC, for me to be a loaned executive through the IBM Faculty Loan Program for the purpose of assisting them with the implementation of junior and senior-level courses in their new B.S. program in computer science. NCA&T requested me by name. IBM appointed me, and I taught all the junior and senior-level classes for two years. The professors in the department were mathematicians who were working on computer science degrees and were not ready to teach higher-level courses. I had the honor of helping to graduate the first class of computer science students. At the completion of that assignment, I returned to the IBM local branch office and worked as a systems engineer supporting large-mainframe, multi-million-dollar computers. That led to an opportunity for me to develop the consulting business in the Carolinas and Virginia and become a Branch Manager. During those years, I enrolled in several doctoral programs that I did not complete: Ph.D. in Computer Science at UNC in Chapel Hill, NC; Ed.D. in Educational Administration at UNCG, Greensboro, and NC; Ed.D. in Psychometrics at UNCG.

I was promoted to an international position to manage the consulting program for IBM's Insurance Industry Sector Services based in Columbia, S.C. During that time, I started looking into Seminary Schools. I was never called to the ministry; I was interested in studying God's word more deeply and getting closer to Him. I retired from IBM while I was in Columbia, SC, and moved back to Greensboro, NC.

When Elaine and I returned to Greensboro I worked as an independent consultant. I decided that I was finished with chasing a doctorate degree. For several years, I had no urge to go back to school. Then, my son-in-law Isaac (my son) told me about an affordable and scholarly school that offers a doctoral degree in theology and counseling that he was attending. It was the Guildford School of Theology (GST) located in Greensboro, NC. GST offered on-site and hybrid remote access courses. I enrolled and graduated with a doctorate in theology degree (Th.D.). Finally, I earned a doctorate degree. Because of my technical, management, and leadership experiences in Corporate America, Government, and Academe, I was honored to be appointed Dean of Academic Affairs at GST. Now, when I am asked how long it took me to earn my Th.D. degree. My answer is based on my long journey to earn a doctoral degree and my age, which will be 80 in 2025, God willing. I like to respond, "over 56 years." I like to blame my career moves on the reason for taking so long, but that is only an excuse; I just did not persevere, and my passion weaned at times. By the way, by the time this book is published sometime this year (2024), I will have earned a second doctorate, an Ed.D. in Counseling Psychology, and I will reopen my consultant business based on my years of experience as an executive coach. The emphasis will be on pastoral counseling, which means biblical-based counseling.

Those academic pursuits afforded me the opportunity to teach. I taught computer science, mathematics and business in colleges and universities in some of the states where we were living. I taught at Post College in Connecticut, at Federal City College (now University of the District of Columbia in Washington, DC), at NCA&T State University in Greensboro, NC, at Winston Salem State University in Winston Salem, NC, and at Bennett College in Greensboro. I was offered a position to teach management classes in IBM's management school in Terrytown, NY but I declined because it was not a good career move at the time.

I held many positions. In corporate American, I was a systems engineer, a systems engineering manager, a professional services manager, and the senior project manager for a US-wide $70 million joint project between Aetna Insurance company and IBM that was announced in the Wall Street Journal in the 1970's, a business development manager, a branch manager, and, an international project manager for the IBM Insurance industry.

In academe, I was an instructor, assistant professor, associate professor, associate chair of the computer science department, associate dean of undergraduate programs for the College of Engineering, associate dean of administration for the College of Engineering, associate vice chancellor for information technology and vice chancellor for information technology.

In Christian ministry, I was a Sunday school teacher in several churches, minister of education, trustee, vice president of Sunday School for the Guilford Education and Missionary Baptist Association, deacon in three churches in North and South Carolina, and secretary of the deacon board, all positions I tried to avoid.

Chapter 11: WORK & CAREERS

John 9:4

I must work the works of him that sent me,
while it is day: the night cometh,
when no man can work.

I had my first paying job at 12 years old. I was a self-employed paper carrier. My father always sent me to the newsstand early Sunday morning to buy the Daily News. First, neighbors in the building would listen out for me and ask me to bring the Daily News to them. The thick newspaper cost 25 cents. They would give me 50 cents to buy the paper and keep the change. After a while neighbors in other buildings would call me from their windows as I walked down the street and made the same arrangement.

I had two paying jobs in my high school years. One was delivering telegrams after school and on Saturdays for ITT (International Telephone and Telegraph Company), which I talked about earlier. The other paying job was tutoring. A Jewish family paid me to tutor their son in math. I went to his house several times a week to prepare him for the Regent exam in mathematics. The State of New York required students to pass 3-hour subject-based exams in addition to passing the class. The math exams were difficult and required learning the nuances of the questions and problems. Although I was not a good academic student in High School, I was good in Algebra. When my teacher assigned homework to solve 10 problems, I would always do at least 20. She told me that no matter what grade I received on the regent exam, I earned a 99 in her class. Booklets of previous Regent exams were available for practice. The first time I took an Algebra practice exam I failed miserably. After taking the 3-hour practice exams about six times, I scored in the 90s. When I took the actual regent exam, I scored 92. My student almost passed the exam. He scored 64, which was heartbreaking because 65 was passing. I expected him to score in the high 70s or low 80s based on how he solved problems during our tutoring sessions.

He and his parents thanked me and explained that they saw significant improvement in his understanding of Algebra and believed he would pass it the next year. I graduated that year and went off to college. We never stayed in touch, but I heard he passed the next year.

During the summer after completing my sophomore year in college, I worked in New York City as a student counselor for HARYOU (Harlem Youth Opportunities Unlimited). HARYOU was a social activism organization founded by psychologists Kenneth Clark and Mamie Phipps Clark in 1962.

In my senior year of college, I was the physics lab assistant along with Henry McCain. We were paid $50/month, which, by the way, paid for my campus apartment, where Elaine and I stayed during our first six months of marriage.

When I graduated from college, I began my professional career in information technology. First, as a COBOL programmer with Royal Globe Ins. Co., in NYC. After one year, I was accepted by IBM after passing an entrance exam. During my time with IBM, I held many positions: systems engineer in NYC, Consultant Services ... in Bethesda, MD, Project Manager in Bethesda, Systems Engineering Manager in Hartford, CT., EOP Personnel Manager in Boston, MA, National Project Gemini Manager in Hartford, CT, Faculty Loan Executive, Greensboro, NC, Business Development Manager in Greensboro, NC, Consulting Services Branch Manager in Greensboro, and finally IBM Insurance Industry International Sector Manager stationed in Columbia, SC. Each time I relocated to a different city, I taught in local colleges and universities.

I also held positions in Greensboro as Vice President of Training for Discovery Learning Inc., and Director of Information Technology and Instructor for the Center for Creative Leadership.

Chapter 12: TRAMA REMEMBERED

Philippians 4:6

Be careful for nothing;
but in everything by prayer and supplication with thanksgiving
let your requests be made known unto God.

Funeral Home in Augusta, GA. Growing up in Harlem and spending summers in Augusta, GA, with my aunt, who owned a funeral home, death was no stranger to me, but I am still traumatized by what I witnessed at the funeral home to the extent that I still shutter when images come to mind. I remember playing at my aunt's funeral home when I was five years old. I saw the ambulance bring bodies that were covered in bloody sheets. Sometimes the bodies were of small children my size and even babies. Sometimes, there was more than one dismembered body in the ambulance. I could tell by the shape of the bodies covered in bloody sheets.

Big Brother Sonny Key. Twenty-year-old Sonny Key was my big brother and guardian against everything evil I was exposed to in Harlem. He died in a car accident when I was around 12 years old. He and his friends were driving south to visit relatives. The car slid under a truck, killing everyone instantly. I still see the image of my big brother in the casket and remember how his mother said he died from a broken neck.

Gang Threats. I remember a gang threat at P.S. 113 Elementary School when I was in the fourth grade. It may be hard to believe but I was with my brother and Andrew at a dance at night, at our elementary school, at nine years old. Our lives were threatened at gunpoint with zip guns, chains, and knives. They said they were going to kill us when we got outside. Although we lived three blocks away and attended school there, we were from a different gang territory. The school was in the territory of the Englishmen, and we were from the territory of the Imperial Knights. My brother, who was always the brave one amongst us, managed to sneak out of the dance while Andrew and I pretended to enjoy ourselves. Jimmy came back in about 15 minutes with the Imperial Knights and rescued us.

Brutal Fights. I remember during recess in the schoolyard, which was gated, by the way, a few boys slammed a student against the wall and repeatedly punched him in the face until they decided to stop. There was no teacher on duty to stop the attack.

Classmate's Truck Tragedy. I remember Alfred in junior high school. He was the class clown entertainer and friendly with everyone. One Monday, Alfred did not come to school, and he had never missed a class. Our school used to give awards for perfect attendance, and Alfred always got one. The teacher reported that he was killed when he rushed off the bus stopped on the side of a highway that was carrying Alfred and other children on a weekend excursion. He was not supposed to get out of the bus, but as soon as the door opened, he rushed out and tried to run across the highway. The teacher reported that he was holding onto the truck while being dragged a few hundred feet until his leg came off. He let go, and the back wheels of the truck ran over his face. The teacher told the gory details because there were students in the class who were on the bus and they would have told their own version of the story, which they did anyway. I felt like I was there, and I still see it happening.

The Jackson Tragedy. I remember the Jackson family. They seemed like a model family. The mother and father seemed happy; they had two daughters who became popular models appearing at times in Jet Magazine in pictures of them visiting princes and other royalty in foreign countries. They also had a son my age. They moved from our street in Harlem to a beautiful home in the suburbs of Queens. We were pretty close to the family before and after they moved. They often invited us to dinner at their home in Queens. My brother and I played with their son in their basement, where there was a model train set on a large table that could seat 25 or 30 people if chairs were placed around them, which there weren't. The table was set up in scenic countryside where we used a remote control to direct the trains. Controls that we held. I especially like Mrs. Jackson's chicken made with a special red, sweet sauce that I never knew or cared to know how she made it.

One day, the New York Newspaper reported that Mrs. Jackson was stabbed to death by her husband. As traumatic as those incidents had on my psyche, it did not affect me as much as it probably should. I had become used to hearing about and witnessing tragedy.

Mommy was hospitalized because she had a stroke. Her condition was serious but stable. A complete recovery was expected. I took a week off from work to be by her bedside. When I arrived, she was conscious but in a state of delirium. Although she could see, when I leaned over to kiss her ,I told her, "This is Rodney." She recognized by voice and said, "my son, Rodney?" I stayed by her side every evening for a week. I had the night shift and Aunty Hattie had the day shift. During the day I cleaned and painted the co-op apartment where she and Pop lived and slept until it was time for him to go the hospital on the night shift. Aunty Hattie ordered a new carpet, and the apartment was ready for mommy's return.

As I stayed by her bedside, I witnessed her remarkable recovery. She recovered from a state of delirium to the vibrant, energetic but graceful lady she was. During the first few days of the week, I was there, the doctor asked her to repeat a few numbers to evaluate her awareness and cognition. She could not and looked at him like he was crazy. But the end of the week when the doctor acted her to repeat numbers, she repeated them rapidly, repeated them backwards and look at him again like he was crazy for asking her. This morning, I was about to catch a plane back home and I said goodbye. She was going to be released the next day. I kissed her and she said goodbye. She had an odd expression on her face that I had never seen. I assumed she was expressing that she knew I had to and did not want me to leave. We were close. That night, Tonya, my sister's oldest daughter called me in tears. She said Nana is dying. I helped Tonya calm down and asked her to let me speak with the doctor on duty who was in the room. I asked him what was happening. He told me that there was nothing that could be done for her, a blood clot had travelled to her heart, and she was dying. I asked him how long she had to live, and he said, "maybe a few hours." In shock, I caught another plane that same night and was at the hospital about 2 hours from the time I talked to the doctor. My cousin Herman picked me up at the airport and drove me to the hospital. As we were the elevator doors opened for us to go mommy's ward my father, sister, brother, and Aunty Hattie were about to come out. They were all crying and told me that mommy was gone. I was told later that my father fainted when mommy was pronounced dead, and they had to administer to him briefly in the hospital. They loved each other so much.

I remember when my father died, on my birthday no less. Although I was the youngest child, I felt like he was handing his legacy of hard work and family dedication to me. I felt honored and respected, but I must admit, I did not feel settled that he achieved all he wanted. I missed him so much that I dreamed had this strange recurring dream off and on, even sometimes now. I kept dreaming that Pop kept getting out of his casket and started going somewhere. I when to him and said each time, "Pop, get back in the casket, you are dead." Then I woke up.

My mother's death was the hardest for me to accept. The years I spent with my mother when Pop was usually at his day job, Patsy was away in Catholic school in August, GA and later married, and Jimmy was away in College in Augusta, GA after Patsy came home, where so special. I felt like I had a special bound and commitment to take care of her, even though most of that period she was not sick.

Nevertheless, Jimmy's death left me empty. We could and did talk about every honestly, sincerely, and trustingly. No one else have I had this openness with, except God.

Andrew Clark. Andrew was like a brother. He was in the middle of Jimmy and me in age. Andrew often came with me to practice for a Sunday School play. As we walked 2 miles together to the church, Andrew found a twenty-dollar bill on the ground. He eventually gave me about one dollar but that was all. I did not mind too much because he was my company at those play rehearsals. As a teenager, Andrew eventually drifted away from us and got involved with a shady group of guys. He was with them when they were arrested for pickpocketing. That was the beginning of his slide into drugs. He did not go to jail, and sadly, that arrest was on his record. Although he was not actually involved, his crime was that he was hanging with the wrong crowd.

That incident kept Andrew from his dream of enlisting in the US Air Force like his brother. He started using drugs and eventually overdosed. Someone told us that he was in the hospital. When Jimmy and I went to see him and to get him to turn around he said, "You know me, I will try anything once." Andrew vowed to get off drugs. About a year later, when Jimmy and I were in college, our mother told us that Andrew died from an overdose. I felt like I lost another brother.

Atlanta Attack. I remember when Jimmy was living in Atlanta. He had finished his M.S. in Business Administration at Atlanta University and had a successful business on downtown Peachtree Street. I was living in Takoma Park, Maryland. One night I received a call from a hospital in Atlanta about my brother. I had not talked to Jimmy in over a year which was not unusual, sometimes we did not stay in touch, but when we connected, it was like only a day had passed. The hospital spokesperson said Jimmy asked me to come to his bedside. Jimmy had never called me for help. The spokesman said he had a broken leg and a long spike in his ear that could cause death, and they were going to be removed immediately. Needless to say, I booked a fight that night and made it to the hospital. By the time I got there, the pin had been successfully removed, and Jimmy was okay. He had been in a karate fight when someone broke into his business location. I brought him home where Elaine and I kept him until he fully recovered. After that incident, Jimmy returned to New York City.

Chapter 13: REGRETS

John 14:27

> *Let not your heart be troubled, neither let it be afraid.*
> *Peace I leave with you, my peace I give unto you:*
> *not as the world giveth, give I unto you.*

I am blessed so much in my life that I really cannot fret over regrets, but there are some things I would have liked to have done differently. Yet, I know that I would not do them differently because I would have to be a different person from what I was at the time. These regrets are for anyone who cares to consider changing themselves along their life'

Chapter 14: MY LIFE'S GOALS

journey as I continue to do in my life.

I wish I had realized the presence of God and His will for my journey, not just me but my family, too. I wish that I had spent more time enjoying family and friends and less time chasing dreams of so-called "success." I wish I had stayed connected with my Harlem friends. I wish I had more vacations with my wife and children. I wish that I had taken Sherrice to Disney World; she always wanted to and didn't get a chance until she and her husband took their daughter twice so far.

I regret that Elaine and I are spending our twilight years together without Elaine being herself. Her condition is preventing her from realizing the joy of being together, but I am thankful and blessed that I am taking care of her rather than Elaine taking care of me.

I wish I had more perseverance to complete things I started, like the five doctoral programs I started in five different disciplines. Then again, I believe my regrets were part of the preparation for what I am doing now and what God is preparing me for next, whether life on earth or in heaven.

As a developing Christian theologian and pastoral psychologist, I am trying to understand and strengthen my faith in Jesus Christ, my Lord and Savior.

Chapter 15: APOLOGIES

I apologize for leaving out some people who have impacted my life. For example, as I was finishing this document I reconnected with several people from my teaching years. For example, Dr. Alton Thompson, and Professors Tammy McNeil, Dr. Martha Haigler, and Professor Sharron Brown. In future publications I will write about the impact they and others had on my life. For now, to all those who helped me on my journey of becoming I say THANK YOU S0 MUCH!!!

Habakkuk 2:2-4

> *[2] And the LORD answered me, and said, Write the vision,*
> *and make it plain upon tables, that he may run that readeth it*
> *.[3] For the vision is yet for an appointed time,*
> *but at the end it shall speak, and not lie:*
> *though it tarry, wait for it; because it will surely come,*
> *it will not tarry.[4] Behold, his soul which is lifted up is not*
> *upright in him:*
> *but the just shall live by his faith.*

There were three things I wanted to be throughout my life: (1) a husband and father, (2) a jazz drummer, (3) a professor of mathematics., in that order. My wife changed my life for the better, much, better. We will be married 60 years on December 30, 2025, God willing. We have two wonderful Christian daughters who are married to wonderful men whom I call my sons. I never became the great jazz drummer that I thought I would be, but I still enjoy sitting with blues and jazz bands when I can.

I thought I was supposed to be a jazz drummer. Throughout my teen years in Harlem, I was exposed to so much live great music and famous artists of soul, jazz, and classical genres, at the Apolo Theatre on 125th Street in Harlem. I was in the lines to see great singers like Fats Domino, James Brown, Little Richard, Glady Knight and the Pips, Smokey Robinson and the Miracles, Frankie Lymon and the Teenagers and his brother Louie Limon and the Teen chords. Frankie Lymon was the Stevie Wonder of the 1950s-60's, with many big hits like "Why Do Fools Fall in Love." I had a chance to play behind him in my senior year in college when he was stationed at the Ft. Gordon Army base in

August, GA. I was playing in the Ponderosa nightclub in Aiken, SC, when he joined us to sing a few songs.

I was exposed to jazz particularly the greats like John Coltrane and Thelonious Monk and others at Birdland, the jazz capital of the world, through Donald Byrd when he was our high school jazz teacher at Music & Arts High School. He arranged for us to get into Birdland even though we were under the age required to enter. He encouraged me to play like Elvin Jones. I used to tell him, "Nobody plays like Elvin Jones." Donal Byrd brought upcoming stars to our rehearsals, like Herbie Hancock, who became famous in the 1970s.

Donald Byrd allowed our jazz band to play Elijah, the title song of his album, before it was recorded. I played a drum solo at our performance of Elijah for the high school students. Years later, he repeated a similar experience at Howard University but took it to another level. He formed a jazz group with students he taught. They were called "Donald Byrd and the Blackbirds. They recorded several albums and became a popular, very successful group.

I was exposed to classical music in high school and became the first percussionist of the Senior Performing Orchestra at Music & Art. I was also chosen as the first percussionist in the borrow-wide high school orchestra in 1962 and again in 1963. One of the years, Lenard Berstein conducted orchestra.

After high school, I was accepted after auditioning to attend the Manhattan School of Music, one of the two most prestigious music schools in the United States at the time. The word was that the Manhattan School of Music was harder to get in and Juilliard was harder to stay in. I was accepted in the Manhattan School of Music, so I did not apply to Julliard. I knew I didn't have the money to attend either school, I just wanted to see if I could get in.

I was the leader of the dance band in Junior High School and actually had a fan club. In high school of was considered the air-apparent to Billy Cobham who what one year ahead of me at Music and Art. He is considered the definitive fusion drummer of the 1970's. I played a short, private session with Jackie McLean, the renowned sax player when just the two of us played in the basement of at the Artist Collective, Inc. in Hartford, CT, an interdisciplinary arts and cultural institution serving the Harford region in the 1980's. who encouraged me to start playing publicly when I was a systems engineering manager working for IBM.

I had a humbling music experience in High School that resonated throughout all my experiences in life. The final performance of the Senior Orchestra at the High School of Music & Arts would take place in just 3 hours, and graduation was just a few weeks away. We were in our final rehearsal. Understand, the musicians were the senior performers in this 100-piece orchestra. Many of them had been playing their instruments and taking private lessons since they were young children in elementary school. They just finished 3 years of studying music, practicing their instruments, and performing many times. We were all "experts," or at least quite accomplished. At that level of accomplishment, no one made a mistake; at least, any error was a misinterpretation of the music, not a wrong note. We were rehearsing Firebird Suite by Igor Stravinsky. I was the first percussionist, and my tympani parts were large throughout the suite, but this part was huge in the last movement of the finale.

Dr. Richter, the conductor, queued me in to lead the closing with a drum roll that crescendos to practically drown out the orchestra. Remember, I was quite accomplished, having been playing since my first year in junior high school; I had taken private lessons outside of school and had been taught at Music & Art. I was the first percussionist in the jazz band orchestra, and even the first percussionist in the borrow-wide orchestra of the best high school musicians in all of New York City. I was at the top of the heap, ready to graduate and become a professional jazz drummer. You guessed it. I missed the right drum (I am right-handed) and dropped the mallet on the floor. All you heard was the left hand trying to roll by itself. Needless to say, I was embarrassed. The conductor was so stunned he dropped his lowered his baton to his side, and the orchestra stopped. He just stared at me and had no words. There went my stellar reputation. He would have dismissed me from the orchestra, not just taken me out of the coveted first percussionist position if he could not. The person was only 3 hours away, no one else knew the part, it was tricky, and there was no time to rehearse the whole one-hour performance. So, after his long pause, he just lifted his baton back into the air and instructed the orchestra to begin a few bars before the incident. Thank God I played the piece flawlessly, as I had done so many times before. Everyone was relieved and happy, especially me, but I do not remember ever talking to the conductor again.

I am professor of Theology (Th.D.), and I am a Counseling Psychology (Ed.D.) and a practicing Pastoral Counselor.

CONCLUSION: CONTINUING BLESSINGS!!!

I encourage and challenge you to recall things in your life that come to mind as I am doing. There are many reasons for this, not the least of them is because you owe it to your family, your generations, and your friends to know you for who you are.

There is no question in my mind that God is with us continuing to bless us on our journeys of becoming, even when we don't see it, even when we don't believe it.

God is good, all the time!!!

References

Allport. (1955, 1983). *Becoming: Basic Considerations for a Psychology of Personality.* Yale University Press.

Ashley. (2023, February 15). Convenant Theology Vs. Dispensationalism. *Biblereasons.com.* Blog6.

Baker & Andrews. (2020). *Timeline of World History.* Thunder Bay Press.

Barton. (2011). Eschatology and the Emotions in Early Christianity. *JBL,* 571-591.

Bennett. (2011). The Manufacture of Hope: Religion, Eschatology and the Culture of Optimism. *International Journal of Cultural Policy.*

Blomberg. (1989). Structure of 2 Corinthians 1-7. *Criswell Theological Review 4.1,* 3-20.

Bradford & Korman. (Accessed: 2023). *Lesson 6 - Genesis 6.* Retrieved from Torah Class: Seed of Abraham Ministries: https://torahclass.com/

Charles River Editors. (2020). *Christian Eschatology: The History and Legacy of Christianity's Beliefs about the End of the World.* Charles River Editors.

Charles River Editors. (2020). *Christian Eschatology: The History and Legacy of Christianity's Beliefs about the End of the World.* charles River Editors.

Clark. (1975). Criteria for Identifying Chiasm. *LB 35,* Linguistica Biblica 5.

Collins. (1996). *Cosmology and Eschatology in Jewish and Christian Apocalypticism.* E.J. Brill.

Daley. (1991). *The hope of the Early Church: A handbook of Patristic Eschatology.* Baker Academic.

Davis. (1990). *The First Seven Ecumenical Councils (325-787): Their History and Theology.* The Liturgical Press.

Dies. (2017). *Bar/Bat Mitzvah: The Complet Planning Guide.* A Newbiz Playbook Publication.

Dimock. (2018). Editor's Column: Historicism, Presentism, Futurism. *PMLA.*

Encyclopedia Britannica Editors. (2020). *Council | Christianity.* Encyclopedia Britannica.

Encyclopedia, E. o. (2022, February 22). *Hope*. Retrieved from Encyclopedia Britannica: https://www.britannica.com/topic/hope-Christianity

Erickson. (2015). *Introducing Christian Doctrine, Third Edition*. Baker Academic.

Fruchtenbaum. (2005). Israel and the Messianic Kingdom. *A Messanic Bible Study from Ariel Ministries*. ariel Ministries.

Fruchtenbaum. (2020). *The Footsteps of the Messiah*. Dispensational Publishing House.

Fruchtenbaum, Jurik, et al. (1994). *Israelology: The Missing Link in Sysmatic Theology*. Ariel ministries Inc.

Gager. (1975). *Kingdom and Community: The Social world of Early christanity*. Prentice-Hall.

Gentry & Ice. (1999). *The Great Tribulation--Past or Future?: Two Evangelicals Debate the Question Paperback*. Kregel Academic.

Gentry & Wellum. (2018). *Kingdom through Covenant: A Biblical-Theological Understanding of the Covenants*. Crossway.

Geuser. (2022, November). *What Does the Vision in Ezekiel 1 Mean?* Retrieved from Logos: https://www.logos.com/grow/vision-ezekiel-1-mean/#:~:text=Comparing%20his%20vision%20to%20Babylonian%20iconography%20reveals%20that,inspecting%20his%20domain%20and%20exercising%20authority%20over%20it.

Gill. (2019, June 29). The Jewish Calendar's Months and Years.

Grenoble. (2005). *Saving Languages: An Introduction to Language Revitalization*. Cambridge University Press.

Heiser. (2022, April 29). *Biblical Studies*.

Henebury. (2019, October 08). Jeremiah's Great Eschatological Vision (Part 4).

Hoekema. (1979). *The Bible and The Future*. William B. Eerdmans Publishing Company.

Hoeksema. (1951). *Amillennialism*. Reformed Free Publishing Association.

Hughes. (1989). *The True Image: The Orgin and Destiny of Man in Christ*. Inter-Varsity Press.

Ice & Gentry. (2009, May/June). The Trouble with Preterism. *Israel My Glory*.

Jeffrey. (2001). *Triumphant Return: The Coming Kingdom of God.* Frontier Research Publications.

Keller. (2020). 5 Peatures that Made the Early Church Unique.

Klein & Spears. (2009). *Lost in Translation Volume 2: The Book of Revelation Through Hebrew Eyes.* Covenant Research Institute.

Klein & Spears. (2016). *Lost in Translation: Rediscovering the Hebrew Roots of Our Faith.* Selah Publishing Group, LLC.

Klein et al. (2012). *Lost in Translation Series Volume 3: The book of Revelation: Two Brides, Two Destinies.* Covenant Research Institute.

lackey. (2015). *A Revelation of Jesus.* Aspect Books.

Lackey. (2015). *A Revelation of Jesus.* Aspect Books.

Lackey. (2015). *A Revelation of Jesus.* aspect Books.

Larkin. (1920). *Dispensational Truth or God's Plan & Purpose in the Ages.* EPBM *Echo Point Books & Media).

Levitt. (1979). *The Seven Feasts of Israel.* Zola Levitt.

Levitt. (1979). *The Seven Feasts of Israel.* Great Impressions Printing & Graphics.

Life Amplified Bible. (1991). Zondervan & The Lockman Foundation.

Lund. (1942). *Chiasmus in the New Testament.* University of North Carolina PRess.

McConville. (2002). *Exploring the Old Testament: A Guide to the Prophets.* IVP Academic.

McGraft. (2007). *Christian Theology: An Introduction* . Oxford.

Missler & Missler. (2009). *The kingdom, Power & Glory: The Over.* Koinonia House.

Missler. (2004). The Book of Daniel. *The Book of Daniel Read by Dr. Chuck Missler.* Koinonia House.

Missler. (2020). *The Book of Revelation: Commentary Handbook.* Koinonia House.

Moltmann. (1993). *Theology of Hope: On ground and the Implications of a Christian Eschatology.* Harper & Row.

Natalij. (n.d.). *Time, metaphysics of.* Routledge Encyclopedia of Philosophy.

Nation. (2022, December 22). Jesus in every Book of the Bible. *LifeWay Research.*

Newport. (2000). *Apocalypse and Millennium Studies in Biblical Eisegesis.* Cambridge University Press.

Noe. (2006, December). An Exegetical Basis for A Preterist-Idealist Understanding of the Book of Revelation. *JETS*, 767-796.

Obama. (2018). *Becoming*. Croown.

Olson. (1999). *The Story of Christian Theology: Twenty Centuries of Tadition Reform*. InterVarsity Press.

Packer. (2012). *An Introduction to Covenant Theology*. The Fig Classic Series.

Rappleye. (2020). Chiasmus Criteria in Review. *Biblical Studies Quarterly 59, Supplement*, 289.

Richards & O'Brien. (2012). *Misreading Scripture with Western Eyes*. IVP.

Robinson. (2006). *Essential Torah: A Complete Guide to the Five Books of Moses*. Schocken Books.

Robinson. (n.d.). *Passover Haggadah*. Mark Robinson.

Rowland. (2009). *Eschatology of the New Testament Church* (Vol. The Oxford Handbook of Eschatology). Oxford Academic Press.

Russell. (1878). *The Parousia: A Critical Inquiry into the New Testament Doctrine of Our Lord's Second Coming*. T. Fisher Unwin.

Schaff. (Periods of Church History). *Periods of Church History*. Retrieved from Bible Hub: https://biblehub.com/library/schaff/history_of_the_christian_church_volume_i/section_4_periods_of_church.htm

Schwertley. (1999). Is the Pretribulation Rapture Biblical? . *Grace Online Library*.

Seekins. (1999). *Hebrew Word Pictures: How does the Hebrew Alphabet Reveal Prophetic Truths?* Hebrew World.

Simon. (1999). *Torah: The Five Books of Moses*. Jewish Publication Society.

Stern. (2001). Calendar and Community: A History of the Jewish Calendar, 2nd Century BCE to 10th Century CE. *Oxford Academic*.

Tanakh Jewish Bible: Jewish Publication Society 1917 Translation. (1919). Jewish Publication Society.

Wansbrough. (2019). *Revised New Jerusalem Bible (RNJB)*. Darton, Longman & Todd.

Westminister Divines. (2021, May 12). The westminster Confession of Faith. *Ligonier Ministeries*.

Wilcox, e. a. (1991, Sept.). Reluctant Warriors: Premillennialism and Politics in the Moral Majority. *Journal for the Scientific Study of*

Religion, 30(3), 245-258. Retrieved from
https://www.jstor.org/stable/1386971

Wright IV & Martin. (2019). *Encountering the Living God in Scripture: Theological and Philosophical Principles for Interpretation.* Baker Academy.

Yarbrough, Trans. (1990/2001). *Historical Criticism of the Bible: Methodology or Ideology? Reflections of a Bultmannian Turned Evangelical.* Kregel.

Zakai & Mali. (1993, December). Time, History and Eschatology: Ecclesiastical History from Eusebius to Augustine. *The Journal of Religious History, 17*(4), 393-417.

Zhang. (2018, April 12). 8 Ways to Build a Friendship witih God.

Figures

הפירוש הנכון של תוכנית הגאולה של אלוהים נמצא בכל התורה, התנ"ך וכתבי
היד היווניים העתיקים שלך

Meaning of the Hebrew phrase above: "The correct interpretation of God's plan of redemption is found throughout the Bible and in the ancient Greek manuscripts". Use the Reverso app to translate the other Hebrew words and phrases in this document.

Glossary

A

Abomination of Desolation: The Abomination of Desolation is a term used in the Bible, particularly in the books of Daniel and Matthew, to describe a sacrilegious act or object that desecrates a holy place, typically the Temple in Jerusalem.

The phrase first appears in the Book of Daniel (Daniel 9:27, 11:31, and 12:11). It is often interpreted as referring to events during the 2nd century BCE, specifically the actions of Antiochus IV Epiphanes, who erected an altar to Zeus in the Jewish Temple and sacrificed pigs on it.

Jesus refers to the Abomination of Desolation in Matthew 24:15 and Mark 13:14, predicting a future event where a similar act of desecration will occur. This prophecy is often associated with the end times.

The term is not specifically mentioned in the Book of Revelation. The term has been subject to various interpretations over time. Some see it as a historical reference to the actions of Antiochus IV, while others view it as a future event linked to the Antichrist and the end of the world.

Allegorical: A method of interpretation in which biblical texts are understood as metaphorical or symbolic, truths rather than literal historical events.

Amillennium: A belief in Christian eschatology that the "millennium" mentioned in Revelation 20 does not represent a literal thousand-year reign of Christ on Earth. Instead, it symbolizes the current church age, during which Christ reigns spiritually from heaven.

Amos: One of the twelve minor prophets in the Old Testament. His book focuses on themes of social justice, divine judgment, and repentance. Amos emphasized the need for genuine worship and ethical behavior.

Apocrypha A collection of ancient writings included in some versions of the Bible but not considered canonical by all Christian traditions. These texts are often viewed as valuable historical and religious literature.

Apocrypha	Theme
1 Esdras (3 Esdras)	Restoration of Jerusalem, religious reforms, faithfulness to God's law.
2 Esdras (4 Esdras)	Apocalyptic visions, divine judgment, hope for restoration, the problem of evil and suffering.
Tobit	Divine providence, faith and piety, marriage, healing, almsgiving, and angelic intervention.
Tobit	Divine providence, faith and piety, marriage, healing, almsgiving, and angelic intervention.
Judith	Courage and faith, divine deliverance, the role of women in God's plan, warfare, and deception.
Additions to Esther	God's providence, Jewish identity, deliverance from enemies, prayer and fasting.
Wisdom of Solomon	Wisdom, righteousness, immortality of the soul, justice, divine retribution, and idolatry.
Ecclesiasticus (Sirach or Ben Sira)	Practical wisdom, moral conduct, praise of wisdom, family life, and social justice.
Baruch	Repentance, confession of sins, hope for restoration, wisdom, and Jerusalem's future glory.
Letter of Jeremiah	Critique of idolatry, faithfulness to the one true God, and the futility of worshipping idols.

Prayer of Azariah and Song of the Three Holy Children	Faithfulness under persecution, divine deliverance, praise and worship in the fiery furnace.
Susanna	Justice, innocence, divine intervention, the vindication of the righteous, and the role of women.
Bel and the Dragon	Critique of idolatry, divine deliverance, faithfulness, and the power of the true God.
Prayer of Manasseh	Repentance, confession of sins, and God's mercy and forgiveness. (2 Chronicles 33:12-13)
1 Maccabees	Jewish resistance, faithfulness to the covenant, warfare, heroism, and religious freedom.
2 Maccabees	Martyrdom, divine intervention, the resurrection of the dead, and the sanctity of the temple.
3 Maccabees	Written in Koine Greek, likely in the 1st century BCE, tells the story of the persecution of Jews under Pharaoh Ptolemy IV Philopator in Ptolemaic Egypt. Despite its title, it does not relate to the Maccabean Revolt but rather describes events that occurred earlier. The book is included in the Biblical Anagignoskomena (Deuterocanon) in the Eastern Orthodox Church.
4 Maccabees	A philosophical treatise that explores the theme of reason's supremacy over passion, using examples from Jewish history, including the martyrdom of Eleazar and the seven brothers. It is also included in the Biblical Anagignoskomena in the Eastern Orthodox Church

These themes can offer rich insights into the historical, religious, and ethical contexts of the period.

Apocalyptic Literature A genre of biblical and extra-biblical writings that reveal divine mysteries about the end times and the ultimate triumph of good over evil. These texts often contain vivid imagery and symbolic language, such as the Book of Daniel and the Book of Revelation.

Apocalypse Derived from the Greek word "apokalypsis," meaning "revelation" or "unveiling." It refers to the disclosure of hidden things, particularly relating to the end times and the final judgment. The term is often associated with catastrophic events leading to the ultimate renewal of creation.

Apologetics: A field of Christian theology that defends the faith, often through reasoned arguments that support the biblical perspective of end times. It is a branch of theology that involves the systematic defense and rational justification of the Christian faith. The term comes from the Greek word "apologia," which means "a reasoned defense" or "a speech in defense."

Apologetics: Provides reasons for the truth claims of Christianity and to respond to objections, criticisms, and questions about the faith. It defends the faith.

Arianism: Arianism is a theological doctrine that originated in the early 4th century, attributed to Arius, a Christian presbyter from Alexandria. The central tenet of Arianism is the belief that Jesus Christ, the Son of God, is not co-eternal or of the same essence (*homoousios*) as God the Father. Instead, Arius argued that the Son was a created being, brought into existence by the Father, and thus subordinate to Him.

This doctrine sparked a significant controversy within early Christianity, leading to intense debates about the nature of the Trinity.

The First Council of Nicaea in 325 AD was convened in part to address this dispute, ultimately condemning Arianism as heretical and affirming the consubstantiality (*homoousios*) of the Father and the Son in the Nicene Creed.

Despite its condemnation, Arianism persisted for centuries in various forms and influenced many groups, including some Gothic and Germanic tribes. It remains a pivotal chapter in the history of Christian theology, particularly in discussions about Christology and the doctrine of the Trinity.

Armageddon (Revelation 16:12-16): Armageddon is the prophesied location of a final battle between the forces of good and evil, often interpreted as the culmination of end-times events. The name "Armageddon" is derived from the Hebrew "Har Megiddo," which means "Mount of Megiddo." Historically, Megiddo was a site of many ancient battles.

> **Armageddon (Revelation 16:16)** takes place during the sixth bowl of God's wrath, part of a series of judgments poured out upon the earth. Armageddon is seen as the location for a climactic battle involving the forces of good and evil before the return of Christ.

> **Gog and Magog (Revelation 20:1-8)** appear after Armageddon. This battle happens after the thousand-year reign of Christ (the Millennium). Satan is released from his prison and deceives the nations (Gog and Magog) to gather them for a final rebellion against God.

Ascension: Christian belief where Jesus Christ ascended to heaven forty days after His resurrection. It is celebrated as the Ascension of Jesus and signifies His exaltation and the promise of His return.

B

Bar and Bat Mitzvahs: Bar Mitzvah (for boys) and Bat Mitzvah (for girls) are important Jewish coming-of-age ceremonies. "Bar Mitzvah" means "son of the commandment," and "Bat Mitzvah" means "daughter of the commandment." These ceremonies mark the transition from childhood to adulthood in the Jewish community. When a Jewish boy turns 13 and a girl turns 12, they become responsible for observing Jewish commandments and laws.

Bar Mitzvah:
- Occurs when a boy turns 13.
- The boy is called to read from the Torah (the central reference of the religious Judaic tradition) in a synagogue.
- It signifies his obligation to follow Jewish laws and traditions.
- Often celebrated with a festive meal and sometimes a party.

Bat Mitzvah:
- Occurs when a girl turns 12.
- Similar to a Bar Mitzvah, the girl may also read from the Torah or lead a service, depending on the denomination of Judaism.
- It represents her commitment to Jewish responsibilities and adulthood.
- Also celebrated with family and friends, usually with a special meal and sometimes a party.

Both ceremonies are milestones in a young Jewish person's life, celebrating their new roles and responsibilities within the community.

BCE (Before Common Era): CE (Common Era) / AD (Anno Domini): The shift from using "AD" (Anno Domini) to "CE" (Common Era) and (Before Christ) to "BC" and "BCE" (Before Common Era) was driven by a desire for more inclusive and religiously neutral terminology. Here are the key points:

- Historical Context
  - Origins of AD and BC: The AD/BC system was introduced by the Christian monk Dionysius Exiguus in the 6th century to calculate the dates of Easter. "Anno Domini" means "in the year of our Lord," referring to the birth of Jesus Christ2.
  - Introduction of CE and BCE: The terms "Common Era" (CE) and "Before Common Era" (BCE) were first used in the 17th century. Johannes Kepler, a German astronomer, used the Latin term "annus aerae nostrae vulgaris" (year of our common era) in 1615.

- Reasons for the Change
  - Inclusivity: CE and BCE are considered more inclusive and sensitive to non-Christians, as they do not explicitly reference Jesus Christ3.
  - Academic and Scientific Use: Since the late 20th century, CE and BCE have become popular in academic and scientific publications to provide a neutral way of referring to historical dates.
  - Adoption
  - Gradual Transition: The transition from AD/BC to CE/BCE has been gradual and varies by region and context. It is more commonly used in academic, scientific, and interfaith contexts.

This change reflects a broader effort to use language that is respectful and inclusive of diverse religious and cultural perspectives

Becoming Me: can be found in the appendix of this paper. It describes people, places and situations that happened in my life, Rodney E. Harrigan. Becoming me focusing on many people who influence me and how God is good through my journey of becoming who I am. It is not a biography, just some excerpts to see the kind of person I am. There are two reasons for this section. First is that my children want me write about my life so I can leave a written legacy. The second is so other readers can know something about me, the author, so they can see deeper into my writings. Mu plans are two write a "Becoming me" section in the other two books I plan to write. The second book is being published, the third book is in the final writing stage.

C

Cannon: The official list of books that are considered inspired and authoritative scripture. For Christians, the canon includes the Old and New Testaments. Different branches of Christianity (e.g., Protestant, Catholic, Orthodox) may have slight variations in their canons.

CE (Common Era) / AD (Anno Domini): The shift from using "AD" (Anno Domini) to "CE" (Common Era) and (Before Christ) to "BC" and "BCE" (Before Common Era) was driven by a desire for more inclusive and religiously neutral terminology. Here are the key points:

- Historical Context
    - Origins of AD and BC: The AD/BC system was introduced by the Christian monk Dionysius Exiguus in the 6th century to calculate the dates of Easter. "Anno Domini" means "in the year of our Lord," referring to the birth of Jesus Christ2.
    - Introduction of CE and BCE: The terms "Common Era" (CE) and "Before Common Era" (BCE) were first used in the 17th century. Johannes Kepler, a German astronomer, used the Latin term "annus aerae nostrae vulgaris" (year of our common era) in 1615.
- Reasons for the Change
    - Inclusivity: CE and BCE are considered more inclusive and sensitive to non-Christians, as they do not explicitly reference Jesus Christ3.
    - Academic and Scientific Use: Since the late 20th century, CE and BCE have become popular in academic and scientific publications to provide a neutral way of referring to historical dates.
    - Adoption
    - Gradual Transition: The transition from AD/BC to CE/BCE has been gradual and varies by region and

context. It is more commonly used in academic, scientific, and interfaith contexts.

This change reflects a broader effort to use language that is respectful and inclusive of diverse religious and cultural perspectives

Chronos Time: A concept of linear, measurable time, often associated with historical events in the Bible. In Greek mythology Chronos (Kronos) is often personified as the god of time. The concept of "Chronos time" refers to linear, sequential time, the kind of time that we measure with clocks and calendars. It is quantitative and continuous, moving forward at a constant, unchanging rate from past to present to future.

Covenantism

Covenants (with God): A **covenant** with God is a solemn agreement between God and His people involving promises, stipulations, and mutual commitments. Covenants may be conditional or unconditional. These are the covenants in chronological order:

- **Adamic Covenant (Conditional)**: God made a covenant with Adam in the Garden of Eden, requiring perfect obedience for eternal life. Adam was required to obey God's command not to eat from the tree of the knowledge of good and evil. Adam's failure led to the Fall. Genesis 3:15 (KJV): "And I will put enmity between thee and the woman, and between thy seed and her seed; it shall bruise thy head, and thou shalt bruise his heel. "Genesis 2:16-17 (KJV): "And the Lord God commanded the man, saying, Of every tree of the garden thou mayest freely eat: But of the tree of the knowledge of good and evil, thou shalt not eat of it: for in the day that thou eatest thereof thou shalt surely die."

- **Noahic Covenant (Unconditional)**: After the Flood, God made a covenant with Noah, promising never to destroy the earth by flood again. Genesis 9:11 (KJV): "And I will establish my covenant with you; neither shall all flesh be cut off any more by the waters of a flood; neither shall there any more be a flood to destroy the earth."

- **Abrahamic Covenant (Unconditional)**: God promised Abraham that he would be the father of many nations, and that all peoples would be blessed through him. This includes the Land Promise. Genesis 12:1-3 (KJV): "Now the Lord had said unto Abram, Get thee out of thy country, and from thy kindred, and from thy father's house, unto a land that I will shew thee: And I will make of thee a great nation, and I will bless thee, and make thy name great; and thou shalt be a blessing: And I will bless them that bless thee, and curse him that curseth thee: and in thee shall all families of the earth be blessed."

- **Land Promise (Unconditional)**: Genesis 12:7 (KJV): "And the Lord appeared unto Abram, and said, Unto thy seed will I give this land: and there builded he an altar unto the Lord, who appeared unto him. "Genesis 15:18-21 (KJV): "In the same day the Lord made a covenant with Abram, saying, Unto thy seed have I given this land, from the river of Egypt unto the great river, the river Euphrates: The Kenites, and the Kenizzites, and the Kadmonites, And the Hittites, and the Perizzites, and the Rephaims, And the Amorites, and the Canaanites, and the Girgashites, and the Jebusites."

- **Mosaic Covenant (Conditional)**: At Mount Sinai, God gave the Law to Moses, establishing the terms of the relationship between God and Israel. Exodus 19:5-6 (KJV): "Now therefore, if ye will obey my voice indeed, and keep my covenant, then ye shall be a peculiar treasure unto me above all people: for all the earth is mine: And ye shall be unto me a kingdom of priests, and an holy nation. These are the words which thou shalt speak unto the children of Israel."

> Exodus 24:7-8 (KJV): "And he took the book of the covenant, and read in the audience of the people: and they said, All that the Lord hath said will we do, and be obedient. And Moses took the blood, and sprinkled it on the people, and said, Behold the blood of the covenant, which the Lord hath made with you concerning all these words."

- **Davidic Covenant (Unconditional)**: God promised David that his lineage would produce an everlasting kingdom. 2 Samuel 7:12-16 (KJV): "And when thy days be fulfilled, and thou shalt sleep with thy fathers, I will set up thy seed after thee, which shall proceed out of thy bowels, and I will establish his kingdom. He shall build an house for my name, and I will stablish the throne of his kingdom for ever. I will be his father, and he shall be my son. If he commit iniquity, I will chasten him with the rod of men, and with the stripes of the children of men: But my mercy shall not depart away from him, as I took it from Saul, whom I put away before thee. And thine house and thy kingdom shall be established for ever before thee: thy throne shall be established for ever."

- **New Covenant (Unconditional)**:

  With Humanity through Christ: God promised a new, eternal covenant through Jesus Christ, offering salvation to all who believe.

  Jeremiah 31:31-34 (KJV): "Behold, the days come, saith the Lord, that I will make a new covenant with the house of Israel, and with the house of Judah: Not according to the covenant that I made with their fathers in the day that I took them by the hand to bring them out of the land of Egypt; which my covenant they brake, although I was an husband unto them, saith the Lord: But this shall be the covenant that I will make with the house of Israel; After those days, saith the Lord, I will put my law in their inward parts, and write it in their hearts; and will be their God, and they shall be my people. And they shall teach no more every man his neighbour, and every man his brother, saying, Know the Lord: for they shall all know me, from the least of them unto the greatest of them, saith the Lord: for I will forgive their iniquity, and I will remember their sin no more."

  Hebrews 8:6-13 (KJV): The author of Hebrews expounds upon the New Covenant, showing its fulfillment in Christ.

Summary

- Covenant of Works (Adam): Genesis 2:16-17
- Noahic Covenant: Genesis 9:11
- Abrahamic Covenant: Genesis 12:1-3, Genesis 15:18-21
- Land Covenant: Part of the Abrahamic Covenant
- Mosaic Covenant: Exodus 19:5-6, Exodus 24:7-8
- Davidic Covenant: 2 Samuel 7:12-16
- New Covenant: Jeremiah 31:31-34, Hebrews 8:6-13

These covenants collectively form the backbone of the biblical narrative, demonstrating God's unfolding plan of redemption and relationship with humanity.

Covenant Theology: Covenant Theology is a system of biblical interpretation found within Reformed and Presbyterian traditions. It views God's relationship with humanity as established through a series of covenants, which are solemn agreements between God and humans that outline mutual commitments and promises.

Cosmology: Cosmology in the biblical sense refers to the understanding and description of the universe and its origin, structure, and purpose as presented in the Bible. It encompasses the creation, organization, and ultimate fate of the world, as well as humanity's place within it.

Crucifixion: Crucifixion is a method of execution used in ancient times, particularly by the Romans, in which a person was nailed or bound to a cross and left to die. This form of capital punishment was typically reserved for slaves, criminals, and enemies of the state. Crucifixion is most famously associated with the execution of Jesus Christ, a central event in Christian theology.

Culture: Biblical culture refers to the customs, traditions, social norms, beliefs, and practices of the people and societies depicted in the Bible. It encompasses the historical and cultural contexts in which the biblical narratives took place, providing insight into the daily lives, religious practices, and societal structures of ancient peoples in the biblical world.

D

Daniel: One of the major prophets of the 6th century BCE Daniell was a Noble Jewish youth taken into Babylonian captivity by King Nebuchadnezzar II. Daniel is revered in Judaism, Christianity, and Islam for his wisdom, faith, and prophetic insights. His story is detailed in the Book of Daniel, which is considered one of the most important prophetic books in the Old Testament.

- **Key Events in the Book of Daniel**
  - **Captivity and Training**: Daniel, along with his friends Hananiah, Mishael, and Azariah (later known as Shadrach, Meshach, and Abednego), was taken to Babylon and trained in Babylonian culture and language.
  - **Interpretation of Dreams**: Daniel gained prominence by interpreting King Nebuchadnezzar's dreams, including the famous dream of a statue made of various metals.
  - **Fiery Furnace**: His friends, Shadrach, Meshach, and Abednego, were thrown into a fiery furnace for refusing to worship a golden statue but were miraculously unharmed.
  - **Lion's Den**: Daniel was thrown into a lion's den for praying to God despite a royal decree but was saved by divine intervention.
- **Prophetic Visions**
  - Four Beasts: Daniel had a vision of four beasts representing different kingdoms.
  - Ram and Goat: Another vision involved a ram and a goat, symbolizing future empires.
  - Handwriting on the Wall: Daniel interpreted the mysterious handwriting on the wall during King Belshazzar's feast, predicting the fall of Babylon.
  - Legacy

Daniel's Seventy Weeks Prophecy: Found in the Book of Daniel, this prophecy outlines the timeline for significant events in Israel's future, including the coming of the Messiah and the events of the Tribulation.

Day of the Lord: A biblical phrase referring to the time when God will intervene in human history to execute final judgment and bring redemption to His people.

Dispensationalism: Dispensationalism is a theological framework within Christian eschatology that interprets the Bible as divided into distinct periods or "dispensations," each reflecting a specific way God interacts with humanity.

- Dispensationalists identify seven dispensations:

    o Innocence (before the Fall)
    o Conscience (Adam to Noah)
    o Human Government (Noah to Abraham)
    o Promise (Abraham to Moses)
    o Law (Moses to Christ)
    o Grace (Church Age)
    o Kingdom (Millennium)

- Literal Interpretation: Dispensationalism emphasizes a literal interpretation of the Bible, particularly prophetic texts. This means understanding scripture in its plain, ordinary sense, unless context dictates otherwise.

- Israel and the Church: A central tenet of dispensationalism is the distinction between Israel and the Church. It posits that God's promises to Israel (Abrahamic, Mosaic, and Davidic covenants) will be literally fulfilled in the future millennial kingdom, distinct from the Church Age.

- Eschatological Focus: Dispensationalism often involves a premillennial, pretribulation rapture view, where Christ will return before a literal 1,000-year reign (millennium) on Earth, preceded by a period of tribulation.

- Historical Development
    o John Nelson Darby: Often considered the father of modern dispensationalism, Darby (1800-1882) was an

Irish theologian who systematically developed these ideas.

- o Schofield Reference Bible: Published by Cyrus I. Schofield in 1909, this study Bible popularized dispensationalist ideas in the United States and globally.
- Influences and Criticisms
    - o Influences: Dispensationalism has profoundly influenced evangelical Christianity, particularly in the United States. Its emphasis on prophecy has impacted both religious thought and broader cultural perspectives on end times.
    - o Criticisms: Some critique dispensationalism for its rigid compartmentalization of biblical history and for what they see as an overemphasis on eschatological speculation.

Doctrine & Theology Doctrine is a statement of fundamental beliefs about God, His creatures, and their relationship to Him. Theology is the study of God through systematic analysis and Coherent statements of Christian doctrine. It is biblical and studied in the context of human culture (Erickson, 2015, p. 19).

E

Early Church Fathers: The term "Early Church Fathers" refers to influential theologians and leaders in the early centuries of Christianity who contributed significantly to the development of Christian doctrine and practice. While the Bible itself does not explicitly mention the "Church Fathers," these individuals played a critical role in interpreting and preserving the teachings of the apostles and the early church.

They were early Christian writers who are believed to have had direct contact with the apostles or their immediate disciples. Their writings are among the earliest Christian documents outside of the New Testament.

Apologists: There were early Christian writers who defended the faith against external criticisms and misconceptions were called apologists. Examples include:
- Justin Martyr: Known for his "Apologies," which defended Christianity to the Roman authorities.
- Tertullian: Coined the term "Trinity" and wrote extensively to defend Christian doctrine.

Patristic Theology: The study of the writings and teachings of the Church Fathers is known as patristics or patrology. This body of work includes theological treatises, biblical commentaries, and letters addressing various aspects of Christian life and doctrine.

Contributions
- Doctrine Development: The Church Fathers were instrumental in the formulation of key Christian doctrines, such as the nature of the Trinity, Christology (the study of Christ's nature and work), and soteriology (the study of salvation).
- Scriptural Interpretation: Their writings provided early interpretations of biblical texts, helping to shape the canon of Scripture and guiding the church's understanding of biblical theology.

- Church Practices: They influenced the development of liturgical practices, ecclesiastical structures, and Christian ethics.

Historical Context

- The Church Fathers lived during a time of significant challenges and transitions for the early church, including persecution, theological controversies, and the spread of Christianity throughout the Roman Empire and beyond. Their writings reflect their efforts to address these challenges and articulate a coherent and unified Christian faith.

By preserving and elaborating on the teachings of the apostles, the Early Church Fathers laid the foundation for the development of Christian theology and practice

Ecumenical Councils: Ecumenical councils are formal assemblies of bishops and other church leaders convened to discuss and settle matters of doctrine, practice, and church administration within the Christian faith. The purposes of the councils were to address and resolve theological disputes and heresies, to define and articulate Christian doctrine and orthodoxy, and to establish or amend church practices and disciplinary measures.

The attendees were primarily bishops and other high-ranking ecclesiastical officials from various regions. Lay representatives and theologians may also be present, depending on the council. The decisions made by ecumenical councils are considered authoritative and binding for the Christian Church. These decisions often shape the core beliefs and practices of the Church.

The term "ecumenical" means "universal" or "worldwide," indicating the councils' significance for the entire Christian community. The early ecumenical councils were primarily convened by Roman emperors or other political leaders to address pressing theological issues.

Table of the First Seven Ecumenical Councils

Council	Date	Convoked by	Reason	Decisions Made
First Council of Nicaea	325 AD	Emperor Constantine I	Address Arianism and establish uniformity in Christian doctrine	Condemned Arianism, formulated the Nicene Creed, established the date of Easter
First Council of Constantinople	381 AD	Emperor Theodosius I	Reaffirm Nicene Creed, address Macedonianism	Expanded the Nicene Creed, condemned Macedonianism, affirmed the divinity of the Holy Spirit
Council of Ephesus	431 AD	Emperor Theodosius II	Address Nestorianism and the title of Theotokos for Mary	Condemned Nestorianism, affirmed Mary as Theotokos (God-bearer)
Council of Chalcedon	451 AD	Emperor Marcian	Address Eutychianism and Christological controversies	Defined the two natures of Christ (divine and human) in the Chalcedonian Creed
Second Council of Constantinople	553 AD	Emperor Justinian I	Address the Three Chapters controversy	Condemned the Three Chapters, reaffirmed the decisions of previous councils

Council	Date	Convoked by	Reason	Decisions Made
Third Council of Constantinople	680-681 AD	Emperor Constantine IV	Address Monothelitism	Condemned Monothelitism, affirmed the doctrine of two wills (divine and human) in Christ
Second Council of Nicaea	787 AD	Empress Irene	Address Iconoclasm	Restored the veneration of icons, condemned Iconoclasm

These councils played a crucial role in shaping Christian doctrine and addressing various theological controversies.

Eschatology: The study of end times and final events in history, particularly in relation to the Second Coming of Christ, the Tribulation, and the establishment of God's Kingdom on Earth.

Eschaton: The term eschaton refers to the final events in the history of the world, often associated with the end times or the ultimate destiny of humanity. It comes from the Greek word "ἔσχατον" (eschaton), meaning "last" or "end." In theological contexts, especially within Christian eschatology, the eschaton encompasses a range of concepts and events, including:

- **Second Coming of Christ**: The anticipated return of Jesus Christ to Earth, as prophesied in the New Testament. This event is expected to bring about the final judgment and the fulfillment of God's kingdom.
- **Resurrection of the Dead**: The belief that all the dead will be resurrected at the end of time, some to eternal life and others to eternal judgment.

- **Final Judgment**: The ultimate judgment of all humanity by God, determining their eternal destiny based on their deeds and faith.
- **New Heaven and New Earth**: The creation of a renewed and perfected world where God will dwell with His people, as described in the Book of Revelation.

ESM (Eastern Synergetic Methodology): ESM is the acremen for the Eastern Synergetic Methodology method conceived in this book. "Eastern" means Hebrew Bibles and Hebrew Hermeneutics are used to further understand contemporary Bible translations. "Synergetic" means understanding and interpreting Scripture in the context of history, culture, language, linguistics and ologies (philosophy, psychology, sociology, and cosmology). The is an innovative approach to faith-based, pastoral counseling.

Exegetes: An exegete is a scholar or interpreter who performs exegesis, which is the critical analysis and interpretation of texts, particularly religious scriptures. The term "exegesis" comes from the Greek word "ἐξήγησις" (exēgēsis), meaning "explanation" or "interpretation."

- **Role**:
    - Exegetes are individuals who analyze and interpret texts to uncover their meaning, context, and implications.
    - They often focus on religious texts, such as the Bible, Quran, or other sacred writings.
- **Methods**:
    - **Historical-Critical Method**: Examines the historical context, authorship, and original audience of the text.
    - **Literary Analysis**: Analyzes the literary forms, structures, and rhetorical devices used in the text.
    - **Theological Interpretation**: Explores the theological themes and doctrinal implications of the text.
    - **Linguistic Analysis**: Studies the original language of the text to understand its nuances and meanings.

- **Purpose**:
  - To provide a deeper understanding of the text's meaning and significance.
  - To clarify difficult or ambiguous passages.
  - To apply the text's teachings to contemporary life and practice.
- Examples of Notable Exegetes
  - Origen: An early Christian theologian known for his extensive biblical exegesis and theological works.
  - John Calvin: A Protestant Reformer who produced influential commentaries on various books of the Bible.
    - Rashi: A medieval Jewish scholar renowned for his commentaries on the Hebrew Bible and the Talmud.

Exegetes play a crucial role in helping believers and scholars understand and apply the teachings of sacred texts

Ezekiel: **Ezekiel** was a prophet-priest of ancient Israel who lived during the 6th century BCE. He was among the Jewish exiles taken to Babylon after the fall of Jerusalem. Ezekiel is known for his vivid visions and symbolic acts, which conveyed God's messages to the Israelites during their captivity.

- Ezekiel
  - Name: Ezekiel (Hebrew: יְחֶזְקֵאל, "God is strong" or "God strengthens")
  - Era: Flourished in the 6th century BCE
  - Role: Prophet and priest
  - Location: Exiled in Babylon, near the Kebar Canal
  - Notable Events:
    1. Vision of the Four Living Creatures: Ezekiel's inaugural vision of God's glory, depicted as a chariot with four living creatures.
    2. Prophecies of Judgment and Restoration: Ezekiel delivered messages of both impending judgment and future restoration for Israel.

- **The Book of Ezekiel**
  - The Book of Ezekiel is one of the major prophetic books in the Old Testament. It records Ezekiel's visions and prophecies over a period of approximately 22 years, from 593 to 571 BCE. The book is structured around three main themes:
  - Judgment on Israel (Chapters 1-24):
  - Ezekiel's initial visions and his call to be a prophet.
  - Prophecies of the impending destruction of Jerusalem due to the people's idolatry and sin.
  - Judgment on the Nations (Chapters 25-32):
  - Pronouncements of judgment against various nations, including Ammon, Moab, Edom, Philistia, Tyre, Sidon, and Egypt.
  - Future Blessings for Israel (Chapters 33-48):
  - Messages of hope and restoration for Israel.
  - The famous vision of the valley of dry bones symbolizing the resurrection and renewal of the nation.
  - Prophecies about the future temple and the establishment of God's kingdom.
  - The Book of Ezekiel is known for its rich symbolism, apocalyptic imagery, and profound theological themes, including the presence of God, purity, and individual responsibility.

F

Feasts of Israel: The feasts are deeply rooted in Israel's history and religious practices, each carrying significant spiritual and communal meanings. God commanded the feasts in the Old Testament, primarily in the books of Exodus, Leviticus, and Deuteronomy. God commanded the feast for remembrance and commemoration (Passover, Unleavened Bread), Thanksgiving and Worship (First Fruits and Pentecost), Reflection and Repentance (Trumpets and Day of Atonement), Community and Unity (Tabernacles).

Feasts of Israel: Feasts of Israel mapped to the events of Revelation

Feasts Mapped to Revelation Events

Feast	Month (Hebrew)	Purpose	Description
Passover (Pesach)	Nisan (March–April)	Commemorate the Israelites' deliverance from Egypt	Celebrated with a Seder meal, remembering the Exodus and the passing over of the angel of death.
Unleavened Bread (Chag HaMotzi)	Nisan (March–April)	Symbolize purity and the haste of the Exodus	Seven-day feast where only unleavened bread is eaten, symbolizing the removal of sin.
First Fruits (Yom HaBikkurim)	Nisan (March–April)	Offer the first fruits of the harvest to God	Offering the first sheaf of the barley harvest at the Temple, acknowledging God's provision.
Pentecost (Shavu'ot)	Sivan (May–June)	Celebrate the giving of the	Marked by the reading of the

		Torah and the wheat harvest	Book of Ruth, offering of first fruits, and all-night study of the Torah.
Trumpets (Yom Teru'ah/Rosh Hashanah)	Tishri (September-October)	Begin the civil new year and call to repentance	Blowing of the shofar (ram's horn) to signal the start of the ten Days of Awe leading to Yom Kippur.
Day of Atonement (Yom Kippur)	Tishri (September-October)	Seek atonement and reconciliation with God	A solemn day of fasting, prayer, and repentance, seeking forgiveness for sins.
Tabernacles (Sukkot)	Tishri (September-October)	Commemorate the Israelites' wilderness journey and God's provision	Seven-day festival where people dwell in temporary shelters (sukkot) to remember the Israelites' journey in the desert.

Feasts Mapped to Events in the Book Revelation

Feast	Month (Hebrew)	Purpose	Event in Revelation	Description
Passover (Pesach)	Nisan (March-April)	Commemorate deliverance from Egypt	**Rapture**	Symbolizes deliverance and salvation through Christ's sacrifice
Unleavened Bread (Chag HaMotzi)	Nisan (March-April)	Symbolize purity and haste of Exodus	**Tribulation**	Represents purification and testing of the believers
First Fruits (Yom HaBikkurim)	Nisan (March-April)	Offer the first fruits of the harvest	**Second Coming**	Symbolizes Christ as the first fruits of resurrection
Pentecost (Shavu'ot)	Sivan (May-June)	Celebrate giving of the Torah and harvest	**Holy Spirit's Empowerment**	Represents the outpouring of the Holy Spirit and the spread of the Gospel

Feast	Month (Hebrew)	Purpose	Event in Revelation	Description
Trumpets (Yom Teru'ah/Rosh Hashanah)	Tishri (September-October)	Begin the civil new year and call to repentance	**Armageddon**	Represents the call to repentance and preparation for final judgment
Day of Atonement (Yom Kippur)	Tishri (September-October)	Seek atonement and reconciliation	**Great White Throne Judgment**	Represents the ultimate judgment and atonement of all humanity
Tabernacles (Sukkot)	Tishri (September-October)	Commemorate wilderness journey	**New Heaven and New Earth**	Symbolizes God's provision and the eternal dwelling with God

Explanation

- **Passover (Pesach)**: Passover's focus on deliverance and salvation parallels the concept of the Rapture, where believers are delivered from the coming wrath.

- **Unleavened Bread (Chag HaMotzi)**: The Feast of Unleavened Bread's emphasis on purity and removal of sin relates to the Tribulation period, a time of testing and purification.

- **First Fruits (Yom HaBikkurim)**: The offering of first fruits symbolizes Christ as the first to be resurrected, aligning with the Second Coming when believers are resurrected.

- **Pentecost (Shavu'ot)**: Pentecost's celebration of the harvest and giving of the Holy Spirit can be seen as a symbol of the Holy Spirit's empowerment during the end times.

- **Trumpets (Yom Teru'ah/Rosh Hashanah)**: The sounding of trumpets for repentance mirrors the call to repentance and preparation for the final battle at Armageddon.

- **Day of Atonement (Yom Kippur)**: The Day of Atonement's focus on reconciliation and judgment aligns with the Great White Throne Judgment, where final atonement is made.

- **Tabernacles (Sukkot)**: The Feast of Tabernacles' theme of dwelling with God correlates with the New Heaven and New Earth, where God's people will dwell with Him eternally.

Figures of Speech: Figures of speech are rhetorical devices that use language in a non-literal or imaginative way to create a particular effect or meaning. They enhance the expressiveness and depth of writing. Here are a few common figures of speech:

Examples from the Book of Revelation

- Metaphor: An implied comparison between two unlike things, suggesting they are alike in a certain way.
  - Lamb: Revelation 5:6 - "Then I saw a Lamb, looking as if it had been slain, standing in the center of the throne..." The Lamb represents Jesus Christ as the sacrificial Redeemer.
  - Sword: Revelation 1:16 - "In his right hand he held seven stars, and out of his mouth came a sharp

double-edged sword." The sword symbolizes the power and authority of Christ's words.

- Simile: A direct comparison between two unlike things using "like" or "as."
    - o White as Snow: Revelation 1:14 - "His head and hair were white like wool, as white as snow..." This describes Christ's appearance, emphasizing purity and holiness.
    - o Voice Like Many Waters: Revelation 1:15 - "His voice was like the sound of rushing waters." This simile conveys the power and majesty of Christ's voice.
- Symbolism: The use of symbols to represent ideas or qualities.
    - o Seven Lampstands: Revelation 1:12-13 - "I saw seven golden lampstands, and among the lampstands was someone 'like a son of man'..." The seven lampstands symbolize the seven churches.
    - o Beast with Seven Heads and Ten Horns: Revelation 13:1 - "And I saw a beast coming out of the sea. He had ten horns and seven heads..." The beast represents a powerful and malevolent entity opposed to God.
- Hyperbole: Hyperbole: Exaggerated statements not meant to be taken literally.
    - o Mountains Fleeing: Revelation 16:20 - "Every island fled away and the mountains could not be found." This exaggerated imagery emphasizes the cataclysmic nature of God's judgment.
- Allusion: Allusion: An indirect reference to another text or historical event.
    - o Tree of Life: Revelation 22:2 - "On each side of the river stood the tree of life, bearing twelve crops of fruit, yielding its fruit every month." This alludes to the Tree of Life in the Garden of Eden, symbolizing eternal life and healing.

Fulness of the Gentiles: A term referring to the period when a complete number of non-Jewish believers have come to faith, signaling the end of the "time of the Gentiles" and the start of God's judgment on Israel.

G

God's Plan of Redemption: God's Plan of Redemption is a central theme in Christian theology, outlining how God provides salvation and restoration to humanity through Jesus Christ. Here's a structured overview:

Key Elements of God's Plan of Redemption

- Creation:
    - Genesis 1-2: God created the world and humanity in His image, establishing a perfect relationship with them.
- The Fall:
    - Genesis 3: Humanity's disobedience (Adam and Eve's sin) led to the fall, bringing sin and separation from God into the world.
- Promise of Redemption:
    - Genesis 3:15: God's promise of a Redeemer who would crush the serpent's head, foreshadowing Jesus Christ.
- Covenants:
    - Noahic Covenant: God's promise to never again destroy the earth with a flood (Genesis 9).
    - Abrahamic Covenant: God's promise to Abraham to make him a great nation and bless all nations through his descendants (Genesis 12:1-3).
    - Mosaic Covenant: God gave the Law through Moses, highlighting the need for holiness and revealing the seriousness of sin (Exodus 19-24).
    - Davidic Covenant: God's promise to David that his lineage would produce an eternal king, ultimately fulfilled in Jesus (2 Samuel 7).
- Prophecies of the Messiah:
    - Throughout the Old Testament, prophets like Isaiah and Micah foretold the coming of a Savior who would redeem God's people (Isaiah 53, Micah 5:2).

- Incarnation and Ministry of Jesus:
    - Birth of Jesus: Fulfillment of the prophecies with the virgin birth (Matthew 1:18-25, Luke 1:26-38).
    - Ministry: Jesus' teachings, miracles, and demonstration of God's kingdom (Gospels).
    - Atonement: Jesus' sacrificial death on the cross to atone for humanity's sins (John 19:16-30, Romans 3:25).
- Resurrection and Ascension:
    - Resurrection: Jesus' victory over sin and death through His resurrection (Matthew 28, 1 Corinthians 15).
    - Ascension: Jesus' ascension to heaven, promising to send the Holy Spirit and return again (Acts 1:6-11).
- The Church:
    - Pentecost: The outpouring of the Holy Spirit, empowering the believers to spread the Gospel (Acts 2).
    - Mission: The Church's role in proclaiming the message of redemption and making disciples (Matthew 28:18-20).
- Second Coming and Final Restoration:
    - Second Coming: Jesus' promised return to judge the world and establish God's eternal kingdom (Revelation 19:11-16).
    - New Heaven and New Earth: The ultimate fulfillment of redemption with the creation of a new heaven and new earth, where God dwells with His people forever (Revelation 21-22).

- Purpose and Significance

- Reconciliation: Restoring the broken relationship between God and humanity.
- Salvation: Providing a way for humanity to be saved from sin and its consequences.
- Eternal Life: Offering believers eternal life with God through faith in Jesus Christ.

- God's Plan of Redemption reveals His love, mercy, and justice, demonstrating His desire to restore and renew all of creation.

Gog and Magog: Gog and Magog are names that appear in the Bible and other religious texts, often associated with apocalyptic prophecies and end-times scenarios. Here's a structured overview:

- **Biblical References**
    - Ezekiel 38-39:
        1. Gog: Described as a prince or leader from the land of Magog.
        2. Magog: A land or nation from which Gog originates.
        3. Prophecy: Ezekiel prophesies that Gog and his allies will invade Israel in the "latter days," but God will intervene and destroy them.
    - Revelation 20:7-10:
        1. Gog and Magog: Symbolic names representing the nations that will rise against God and His people at the end of the millennium.
        2. Final Battle: After Satan is released from his prison, he will deceive the nations (Gog and Magog) to gather for battle against the saints, but they will be defeated by divine intervention.
- **Historical and Geographical Interpretations**
    - Ancient Identifications: In ancient times, Gog and Magog were often associated with various tribes or nations, such as the Scythians, Huns, or other nomadic groups.
    - Medieval Legends: During the Middle Ages, Gog and Magog were sometimes linked to the Vikings, Mongols, or other invaders.
    - Modern Interpretations: Some contemporary interpretations view Gog and Magog as symbolic representations of future geopolitical alliances or conflicts.

- **Cultural and Religious Significance**
    - Jewish Tradition: In Jewish eschatology, Gog and Magog are seen as enemies to be defeated by the Messiah, ushering in the Messianic age.
    - Christian Tradition: In Christian eschatology, Gog and Magog are often viewed as apocalyptic forces that will be defeated by Christ at the end of the millennium.
    - Islamic Tradition: In Islamic eschatology, Gog and Magog (Yajuj and Majuj) are depicted as corrupt and destructive tribes that will be released before the Day of Judgment.

Summary: Gog and Magog are significant figures in apocalyptic literature, symbolizing the ultimate battle between good and evil. Their exact historical and geographical identities remain a subject of interpretation and debate

Great White Throne Judgment: The final judgment, where all the dead are resurrected and judged according to their deeds, as described in the Book of Revelation. I call it the "Sentencing," because anyone going before the Throne does not have his/her name in the Book of Life. They are all being sentenced to eternal burning in Hell. The Church and the believers who turned to God in the Tribulation, after the Church is Raptured will be judged (for Rewards) on the Bema Seat of Christ (2 Corinthians 5:10; Romans 12:10-12; 1 Corinthians 2:12-15).

Greek Scholars: Notable Greek scholars of the 19th and 20th centuries;

19th and 20th Century Greek Scholars

Name	Lifespan	Contributions to Christianity
J.B. Lightfoot	1828-1889	Renowned for his commentaries on the Epistles of Paul, his work on the Apostolic Fathers, and his role in the revision of the King James Version of the Bible2.
A.T. Robertson	1863-1934	Renowned for his work on New Testament Greek, including "Word Pictures in the New Testament" and "A Grammar of the Greek New Testament in Light of Historical Research".
Marvin Vincent	1834-1922	Known for "Vincent's Word Studies in the New Testament," providing detailed exegesis and lexical analysis of New Testament Greek.
W.E. Vine	1873-1949	Best known for "Vine's Expository Dictionary of New Testament Words," which traces the meanings of Greek words in the New Testament.
F.F. Bruce	1910-1990	Influential evangelical scholar, author of numerous commentaries and books, including "The New Testament Documents: Are They Reliable?" and "Paul: Apostle of the Heart Set Free".
Earl Radmacher	1931-2014	Prominent theologian and educator, known for his work on systematic theology and his advocacy for free grace theology.

H

Haggadah & Seder:
- **Haggadah**
  - Definition: The *Haggadah* (Hebrew for "telling") is the text or book that serves as a guide for the Seder.
  - Purpose: It contains the narrative of the Exodus, along with instructions for the Seder rituals, prayers, blessings, songs, and commentary.
  - Content:
    - Scriptural passages and rabbinic interpretations recounting the Exodus.
    - Instructions for performing each step of the Seder.
    - Songs and prayers such as *Dayenu* and *Chad Gadya*.
  - Role: The Haggadah is the script that shapes the flow and content of the Seder.

  - The Seder and the Haggadah are both central to the celebration of Passover in Jewish tradition, but they refer to distinct elements of the observance:

- **Seder:**

  - **Definition: The word *Seder* means "order" in Hebrew, and it refers to the ceremonial meal that takes place on the first night (or first two nights in some traditions) of Passover.**
  - **Purpose: The Seder is structured to retell the story of the Israelites' liberation from Egypt, as commanded in Exodus 13:8: "And you shall tell your son on that day..."**
  - **Components: The Seder includes specific rituals, prayers, and symbolic foods like:**
    - **Matzah (unleavened bread)**
    - **Maror (bitter herbs)**
    - Charoset (a mixture symbolizing the mortar used by enslaved Israelites)
    - Four Cups of Wine (symbolizing redemption)

- o Experience: It's an interactive event with storytelling, singing, and participation by attendees, including children asking the "Four Questions" (*Mah Nishtanah*).

- **Key Difference:** The Seder is the event or ritual meal, while the Haggadah is the text used to guide and structure the Seder. Think of the Seder as the experience and the Haggadah as the blueprint for that experience.

Hebrew Culture: Hebrew culture refers to the traditions, practices, values, and way of life of the ancient Hebrews, who were the ancestors of the Jewish people. This culture is rooted in the Hebrew Bible (Tanakh) and is shaped by its historical context in the Ancient Near East.

Key aspects include:

- **Religion and Monotheism**: The Hebrews were pioneers of monotheism, worshiping Yahweh as the one true God. Their faith and covenant with God deeply influenced their social and moral systems.

- **Language and Literature**: Hebrew, a Semitic language, was central to their culture. It was not only their spoken language but also the medium for sacred texts like the Torah, which recorded their laws, history, and poetry.

- **Social Structures**: Society was organized around family and tribal units. The concept of the "covenant community" emphasized unity and shared responsibilities.

- **Ethical and Moral Laws**: The Torah set out laws governing justice, community living, worship, and morality, influencing their way of life.

- **Festivals and Rituals**: Feasts like Passover and rituals such as circumcision held deep religious and cultural significance.

  The legacy of Hebrew culture continues to influence Jewish practices and has had a profound impact on Western thought and religion. Hebrew culture profoundly shaped biblical texts and influenced neighboring civilizations in several ways.

- **Influence on Biblical Texts**
- **Covenant Theology**: The Hebrew concept of a covenant with God is central to the Bible. It frames the narrative of divine promises, laws, and expectations, which guide much of the Old Testament, especially in books like Genesis, Exodus, and Deuteronomy.

- **Legal and Ethical Codes**: The Torah, particularly Leviticus and Deuteronomy, reflects the Hebrews' detailed moral and legal systems. These laws not only regulated societal behavior but also emphasized justice, mercy, and holiness.
- **Historical Records and Poetry**: Hebrew culture valued oral traditions and later written records. Psalms, Proverbs, and historical books like Kings and Chronicles reveal their deep respect for both divine worship and historical documentation.
- **Prophetic Literature**: The prophets, rooted in Hebrew culture, addressed societal issues while calling for repentance and faithfulness. Their writings showcase a strong sense of justice, hope, and the covenantal relationship with God.
- **Broader Influence on Civilizations**

  - Monotheism in a Polytheistic World: Hebrew monotheism stood out in the ancient Near East, influencing later religious traditions, including Christianity and Islam. The emphasis on a single, all-powerful God had a lasting impact on Western thought.
  - Language and Script: The Hebrew alphabet and language laid the foundation for other Semitic languages and influenced the development of written traditions in neighboring cultures.
  - Ethical Principles: The moral teachings of Hebrew culture, such as the Ten Commandments, spread through Judeo-Christian traditions and contributed to the ethical frameworks of Western societies.
  - Integration and Preservation: While the Hebrews interacted with dominant empires like Egypt, Babylon, and Rome, their cultural identity endured. This ability to integrate certain external influences

while preserving their heritage helped transmit their ideas globally.

- **Eschatological Prophetic Literature in the Bible**

Eschatological texts (those dealing with the "end times") are deeply woven into Hebrew culture. These passages often emerged during periods of crisis or oppression, offering hope of divine intervention and ultimate justice. Key examples include:

  - Isaiah: In Isaiah 2:2–4, there is a vision of the "latter days" when nations will gather in peace to the mountain of the Lord. This reflects the Hebrew hope for a future era of divine rulership and harmony.
  - Ezekiel: His "dry bones" vision (Ezekiel 37) symbolizes Israel's restoration. Chapter 38 introduces Gog and Magog, representing cosmic battles, themes echoed in later apocalyptic texts like Revelation.
  - Daniel: Particularly chapters 7–12, Daniel's prophecies detail visions of successive empires, the rise of a final evil ruler, and God's ultimate kingdom. These writings heavily influenced Jewish apocalyptic literature and early Christian eschatology.
  - Zechariah: With imagery like the Mount of Olives splitting (Zechariah 14:4) and the nations worshiping the Lord, Zechariah combines judgment and restoration themes.

The vivid imagery in these texts—cosmic upheavals, divine judgment, and renewal—reflected both cultural resilience and theological anticipation, deeply embedded in Hebrew religious thought.

Hebrew Hermeneutics: An ancient method of biblical interpretation that includes four levels: **P'shat** (literal), **Remez** (hint), **D'rash** (allegorical), and **Sod** (hidden/mystical). This method is critical for understanding prophecies within their cultural and historical contexts.

Hebrew Perspective: The Hebrew perspective refers to the worldview, values, and beliefs rooted in ancient Hebrew culture, religion, and traditions, primarily as expressed through the Hebrew Bible (Tanakh) and subsequent Jewish thought.

- **Worldview**
    - Monotheism: Central to the Hebrew worldview is the belief in a single, sovereign God (Yahweh) who is the Creator and sustainer of the universe. This contrasts sharply with the polytheism of surrounding cultures (Genesis 1:1; Deuteronomy 6:4).
    - Covenantal Framework: Life is seen through the lens of the covenant—a binding relationship between God and His people. This concept underlies the narratives of Abraham, Moses, and David (Genesis 12:1-3; Exodus 19:5-6).
    - Linear History: Unlike cyclical views of history common in the ancient Near East, the Hebrew worldview embraces a linear progression of time, with a definite beginning (creation) and an anticipated culmination (Messianic era).

- **Values**
    - Holiness and Obedience: The call to be "holy as God is holy" permeates the Torah (Leviticus 19:2). Obedience to divine law (Torah) is central to the Hebrew ethos.
    - Justice and Righteousness: Prophetic literature underscores the importance of justice (mishpat) and righteousness (tzedakah). These values emphasize fairness, compassion for the vulnerable, and ethical living (Micah 6:8; Isaiah 1:17).
    - Community and Solidarity: Hebrew culture values the collective identity of the people, stressing unity and care for one another, particularly the marginalized (widows, orphans, and strangers) (Deuteronomy 10:18-19).

- **Beliefs**
    - God's Sovereignty and Providence: The Tanakh portrays God as actively involved in human history,

guiding and redeeming His people (Psalm 103:19; Exodus 3).

- o Human Dignity: Rooted in the belief that humans are created in the image of God (imago Dei), the Tanakh affirms the inherent worth and moral responsibility of every person (Genesis 1:26-27).
- o Hope and Restoration: Prophetic visions of eschatological restoration reflect the belief in God's ultimate justice and renewal of creation (Isaiah 65:17-25; Amos 9:11-15).

Hermeneutics: The theory and methodology of interpreting Scripture, especially concerning biblical texts related to prophecy. This book emphasizes that correct interpretation requires historical, cultural, language, and linguistic context.

Hebrew Marriage: God's marriage covenant holds deep theological and symbolic significance in biblical thought. It is a metaphor used in Scripture to describe the intimate, covenantal relationship between God and His people, often likened to the union between a husband and wife. This imagery emphasizes themes of love, commitment, faithfulness, and redemption.

- Here are some key aspects of its significance:
  - o **Covenantal Relationship:** The marriage metaphor highlights the idea of a binding covenant. Just as marriage involves mutual commitment, the relationship between God and His people is based on promises:
    - ▪ **God's Faithfulness:** God vows to be faithful, providing love, protection, and provision (Hosea 2:19-20; Isaiah 54:5).
    - ▪ **Human Response**: His people are called to respond in faithfulness, love, and obedience (Deuteronomy 6:5).
  - o **Symbol of Intimacy**: The marriage covenant reflects the deep, personal relationship God desires with His

people. It transcends formality, symbolizing intimacy, trust, and mutual delight (Song of Solomon is often interpreted in this light on a spiritual level).

- o **Theme of Faithfulness and Betrayal**: The marriage imagery underscores the pain of unfaithfulness (spiritual adultery) when God's people turn to idolatry or other forms of disobedience. Books like **Hosea** vividly portray Israel's unfaithfulness as an adulterous spouse and God's relentless love as a faithful husband seeking to restore the relationship.

- o **Redemption and Restoration**: In prophetic literature, the marriage covenant often carries eschatological hope. God promises to restore the broken covenant and bring His people back to Himself. For example:
    - **Isaiah 62:4-5 depicts God rejoicing over His people as a bridegroom over a bride.**
    - **Hosea 2:14-23 speaks of God's plan to renew the relationship with His unfaithful "bride."**

- o **The New Testament Fulfillment**: In the New Testament, the marriage covenant is expanded and fulfilled in Christ.
    - Jesus is depicted as the Bridegroom, and the Church is His Bride (Ephesians 5:25-27; Revelation 19:7-9).
    - The ultimate marriage banquet (Revelation 19:6-9) symbolizes the consummation of God's covenant with His people at the end of time, reflecting themes of unity, joy, and eternal love.

- o **Practical Implications**

The marriage metaphor also offers a model for human relationships, particularly the institution of marriage, which is intended to reflect God's covenantal love, faithfulness, and selflessness (Ephesians 5:22-33). This covenant not only illustrates God's deep love and commitment to His people but also serves as a framework for understanding the larger biblical narrative of creation, fall, redemption, and restoration. Here is how these themes developed in Revelation, and how it ties to Hebrew cultural practices

- **The Marriage Theme in Revelation**
    - **The Bride and the Lamb**: Revelation portrays the Church as the Bride and Jesus Christ as the Lamb/Bridegroom. This imagery is most vividly captured in:
    - **Revelation 19:7-9: The "Marriage Supper of the Lamb" symbolizes the final, joyous union between Christ and His redeemed people. The bride (the Church) is described as clothed in fine linen, representing the righteous acts of the saints.**
    - **Revelation 21:2, 9-10: The New Jerusalem is described as a Bride adorned for her husband, symbolizing the ultimate fulfillment of God's covenant with His people.**
- **The Betrothal Stage**: In Hebrew marriage customs, betrothal was a legally binding period where the bride and groom were committed to each other, though the marriage was not yet consummated. Similarly, the Church is in a betrothal-like phase, awaiting the return of Christ (the Bridegroom) to complete the covenant.
- **The Bride's Preparation**: Revelation emphasizes the bride's readiness, linking it to the cultural practice where the bride would prepare herself for the groom's arrival. This preparation mirrors the Church's call to holiness and faithfulness (Revelation 19:8).
- **The Final Consummation**: The eschatological marriage in Revelation reflects the ultimate fulfillment of God's promises—complete union with His people. This corresponds to the marriage ceremony in Hebrew culture, where the groom would take the bride to his home, marking the covenant's consummation.
    - **Connections to Hebrew Cultural Practices**
    - Revelation draws directly from Hebrew marriage customs to communicate profound theological truths:

- **The Bridegroom's Preparation**: In Hebrew tradition, the groom would leave to prepare a place for his bride, often at his father's house. This is echoed in Jesus' promise in John 14:2-3, which Revelation fulfills when Christ returns to dwell with His people forever (Revelation 21:3).
- **The Processional Arrival**: The arrival of the groom to claim his bride was a celebratory event. Revelation mirrors this with Christ's triumphant return at the Second Coming (Revelation 19:11-16), leading to the marriage supper.
- **The Marriage Feast**: Hebrew weddings culminated in a festive banquet, a symbol of joy and union. The "Marriage Supper of the Lamb" in Revelation 19 draws from this practice, representing the eternal celebration of God's covenant with His people.
- **Theological Significance:** The marriage covenant theme in Revelation underscores key elements of God's relationship with His people:
  - **Faithfulness**: Despite humanity's unfaithfulness, God remains committed to His covenant.
  - **Hope and Restoration**: The eschatological marriage assures believers of ultimate redemption and eternal communion with God.
  - **Holiness**: The Bride's preparation reflects the call to righteousness and readiness for Christ's return.

Here's a table summarizing the steps and stages of ancient Hebrew marriage, along with their approximate time frames and durations:

Stages of the covenantal and communal nature of marriage in Hebrew culture, emphasizing commitment, preparation, and celebration

Stage	Time Frame/Duration	
Shiddukhim (Matchmaking)	The families arranged the marriage, often involving negotiations and agreements.	Could occur during the early years of the individuals, as marriages were often prearranged.
Eirusin (Betrothal)	A formal engagement marked by the signing of the ketubah (marriage contract). The groom paid the mohar (bride price) and gave gifts (mattan). The bride prepared for the wedding.	Typically lasted 6 months to 1 year.
Nisu'in (Wedding Ceremony)	The groom arrived to take the bride to his home, followed by a celebratory procession and feast.	The ceremony and feast could last 7 days or more, depending on the family's resources.
Yichud (Consummation)	The couple entered the bridal chamber to consummate the marriage, symbolizing the covenant's completion.	Occurred on the wedding day or night.

Hebrews, Israelites, Jews: The terms Hebrews, Israelites, and Jews are related but not entirely interchangeable, as they reflect different historical and cultural contexts. Here's a breakdown:

- Hebrews
    - The term "Hebrews" is the earliest designation, first used in the Bible to describe Abraham (Genesis 14:13). It likely derives from the word 'Ivri, meaning "one who crosses over," possibly referring to Abraham's journey across the Euphrates River.
    - It was used to describe the descendants of Abraham, Isaac, and Jacob, particularly in the context of their nomadic lifestyle and interactions with other nations (e.g., Egyptians referred to them as Hebrews during their enslavement).
    - Hebrews: Used from Abraham's time (~2000 BCE) through the patriarchal period and early interactions with other nations.

- Israelites
    - The term "Israelites" originates from Jacob, whose name was changed to Israel after wrestling with an angel (Genesis 32:28). His descendants, the twelve tribes, became the nation of Israel.
    - This term was used during the period of the Exodus, the conquest of Canaan, and the united monarchy under Saul, David, and Solomon.
    - After the division of the kingdom (circa 930 BCE), the northern kingdom retained the name Israel, while the southern kingdom became Judah.
    - Israelites: Predominantly used from Jacob's time (~1800 BCE) through the united monarchy and the divided kingdoms.

- Jews
    - "Jews" comes from "Judah," the name of the southern kingdom and one of Jacob's sons. After the Babylonian exile (6th century BCE), the term began to encompass all Israelites, as most of the returning exiles were from Judah.

- o By the time of the Second Temple period, "Jews" became the common term for the descendants of the Israelites, especially in the context of their religious and cultural identity.
- o Jews: Emerged after the Babylonian exile (~6th century BCE) and became the primary term during the Second Temple period and beyond.

Each term reflects a specific phase in the history of the same people, emphasizing different aspects of their identity.

Historical Criticism: Historical criticism, often referred to as the historical-critical method, is a scholarly approach to studying and interpreting texts, particularly biblical and ancient writings, by analyzing their historical context. This method seeks to uncover the origins of a text, its authorship, the historical and cultural environment in which it was written, and its intended audience. By doing so, it aims to understand the text's original meaning and purpose.

- Key aspects of historical criticism include:

  - o **Authorship Analysis**: Determining who wrote the text, including whether it was a single author or multiple contributors.

  - o **Source Criticism**: Examining the sources or materials that the author(s) may have used to compose the text.

  - o **Contextual Analysis**: Investigating the social, political, and cultural conditions of the period to see how they shaped the text.

  - o **Dating the Text**: Establishing when the text was written to situate it within its historical timeline.

  - o **Textual Development**: Exploring how the text may have evolved or been edited over time.

This method is especially significant in biblical studies, as it helps scholars understand the historical realities behind sacred texts, the influences of surrounding cultures, and the intent of the authors. Historical criticism often contrasts with purely theological or literal interpretations, as it emphasizes historical and literary evidence over doctrinal presuppositions.

Homiletics: Homiletics is the art and science of preparing and delivering sermons or religious discourses. It is rooted in theology and communication and aims to effectively convey spiritual truths, moral teachings, and scriptural interpretation to a congregation or audience.

Key elements of homiletics include:

- o **Biblical Exegesis:** Analyzing scripture to ensure the sermon is deeply rooted in the text's meaning.

- o **Structure and Organization:** Crafting a clear, logical flow for the sermon, often including an introduction, main points, and conclusion.

- o **Thematic Focus:** Centering the message around a specific theme or idea to provide clarity and unity.

- o **Audience Engagement:** Adapting the sermon to the needs, culture, and understanding of the audience to ensure relevance and impact.

- o **Delivery Techniques**: Employing tone, body language, and rhetorical skills to make the message compelling and memorable.

Homiletics bridges theology and pastoral care, as it involves not just the dissemination of knowledge but the spiritual nurturing of a community. It's a fascinating blend of scholarly preparation and heartfelt communication.

I

- **Idealist, Futurism, and Historicism**: each represents a different interpretive framework, particularly in the study of eschatology and biblical prophecy:
- **Idealism**
    - This perspective interprets biblical prophecies symbolically or allegorically, rather than literally.
    - Prophecies are seen as timeless spiritual truths or moral lessons that are not tied to specific historical events or future occurrences.
    - For example, in the Book of Revelation, Idealists might view the battle between good and evil as an ongoing, universal struggle rather than a literal future event.
    - Strength: Highlights the ethical and theological messages of the text.
    - Limitation: Lacks historical specificity, which can frustrate those seeking concrete connections to history or the future.
- **Futurism**
    - Futurists interpret prophecy (especially in apocalyptic literature) as predictions of events that will happen at the end of human history or in the "end times."
    - This approach is common in many evangelical and dispensationalist traditions. For example, the "Antichrist" and "Great Tribulation" are seen as events to come.
    - Strength: Provides a clear framework for eschatological expectations.
    - Limitation: Can lead to speculation about the timing and nature of future events, sometimes at the expense of current ethical or spiritual applications.

- **Historicism**
  - Historicists see biblical prophecies as unfolding throughout human history, corresponding to specific events, eras, or figures.
  - For example, this view often aligns aspects of Revelation with historical events like the fall of the Roman Empire or the Reformation.
  - Strength: Seeks to connect prophecy with tangible historical developments, creating a narrative of divine action in history.
  - Limitation: Interpretations can vary widely, and they often risk being influenced by the interpreter's cultural or political context.

Each framework reflects a different way of grappling with the text's meaning and purpose. Since you're exploring theological contexts and eschatology,

- **Incarnation**: The term **Incarnation** refers to the theological belief that God became human in the person of Jesus Christ. It is central to Christian doctrine and encapsulates the idea that Jesus is both fully divine and fully human. This concept is derived from the Latin word *incarnatio*, meaning "to become flesh."
- **Isaiah**: Isaiah is renowned in eschatology for his profound visions of divine judgment, restoration, and the ultimate fulfillment of God's kingdom. His prophecies, particularly in the latter chapters of the Book of Isaiah, have significantly shaped both Jewish and Christian eschatological thought.
  - **Key Eschatological Themes in Isaiah:**
    - **The Messianic King**: Isaiah prophesies the coming of a righteous ruler from the line of David, often interpreted as the Messiah (Isaiah 9:6-7; 11:1-10). This figure is depicted as bringing justice, peace, and the restoration of God's people.

- **New Jerusalem**: Isaiah envisions a future where Jerusalem becomes a center of divine glory, peace, and prosperity (Isaiah 60-62). This vision has influenced Christian concepts of the "Heavenly Jerusalem" in Revelation.
- **Universal Salvation**: Isaiah extends the scope of salvation to all nations, emphasizing that God's kingdom will include people from every corner of the earth (Isaiah 2:2-4; 56:6-8).
- **The Day of the Lord**: Like Joel, Isaiah speaks of the "Day of the Lord" as a time of divine judgment and ultimate redemption (Isaiah 13:6-13). This theme underscores the dual aspects of judgment for the wicked and salvation for the faithful.
- **The Suffering Servant**: In Isaiah 52:13-53:12, the "Suffering Servant" is described as bearing the sins of many, a passage often linked to Jesus Christ in Christian theology. This has eschatological implications for understanding redemption and atonement.
- **New Heavens and New Earth**: Isaiah concludes with a vision of a renewed creation, where God establishes eternal peace and righteousness (Isaiah 65:17-25; 66:22-23). This imagery resonates with the eschatological hope found in Revelation 21.

Isaiah's prophecies are rich with imagery and theological depth, making them foundational for understanding eschatological themes across traditions. How do you see Isaiah's visions connecting with your studies on the Book of Revelation or other prophetic texts?

J

Jeremiah: Jeremiah is significant in eschatology for his prophecies of judgment, restoration, and the establishment of a **New** Covenant. His writings, particularly in chapters 30–33 (often called the "Book of Consolation"), are rich with eschatological themes that have shaped both Jewish and Christian thought. Key Eschatological Themes in Jeremiah:

- o **The New Covenant:**
- o Jeremiah prophesies a future covenant where God's law will be written on people's hearts, and they will have a direct relationship with Him (Jeremiah 31:31-34). This is a cornerstone of Christian theology, often linked to the coming of Christ and the outpouring of the Holy Spirit.
- o **Restoration of Israel and Judah:**
- o He envisions a time when God will restore His people to their land and renew their fortunes (Jeremiah 30:3, 30:18). This restoration is seen as both a historical and eschatological promise.
- o **The Davidic King:**
- o Jeremiah speaks of a righteous branch from David's line who will reign wisely and bring justice (Jeremiah 23:5-6; 33:15-16). This is often interpreted as a Messianic prophecy.
- o **The Day of the Lord:**
- o Like other prophets, Jeremiah warns of a coming day of judgment for the nations and Israel's enemies (Jeremiah 25:31-33). This theme resonates with broader eschatological visions of divine justice.
- o **Hope Amid Judgment:**
- o While much of Jeremiah's message focuses on impending judgment, he consistently offers hope for a future where God's people are restored and live in harmony with Him.

- o Jeremiah's eschatological vision is deeply intertwined with his emphasis on covenantal faithfulness and divine mercy. How do you see his themes of restoration and the New Covenant aligning with your studies on eschatology and biblical canons

Joel: The prophet **Joel** is known in eschatology for his vivid and apocalyptic visions, particularly in the **Book of Joel**, which is part of the Hebrew Bible and Christian Old Testament. His writings emphasize themes of divine judgment, repentance, and restoration, making them significant in discussions of end-time prophecies. Key Eschatological Themes in Joel:

- **The Day of the Lord**:
- Joel repeatedly refers to the "Day of the Lord," a time of divine intervention characterized by both judgment and salvation (Joel 1:15; 2:1-2; 3:14).
- This concept has been interpreted as a foreshadowing of the ultimate end-times judgment.
- **Cosmic Signs**:
- Joel describes dramatic cosmic events, such as the darkening of the sun and moon and the appearance of blood and fire (Joel 2:30-31). These signs are often linked to apocalyptic imagery in the Book of Revelation.
- **Call to Repentance**:
- A central theme in Joel is the call for national repentance to avert disaster and receive God's mercy (Joel 2:12-13). This reflects the eschatological idea of turning back to God before the final judgment.
- **Outpouring of the Spirit**:
- Joel prophesies a future outpouring of God's Spirit on all people, regardless of age, gender, or social status (Joel 2:28-29). This prophecy is famously quoted by Peter in Acts 2:17-21, connecting it to the events of Pentecost and the broader eschatological hope.

- **Restoration and Judgment**:
- Joel envisions a time when God will restore His people and judge the nations (Joel 3:1-2, 16-17). This dual theme of restoration for the faithful and judgment for the wicked is central to eschatological thought.
- Joel's prophecies have been interpreted in various ways across theological traditions, from prefiguring historical events to symbolizing ultimate end-time realities. Given your interest in eschatology, how do you see Joel's visions aligning with other prophetic texts, such as those in Revelation or Daniel?

K

Kairos Time: Refers to the "right" or opportune moment in God's timing, which is significant for understanding biblical events and prophecies that unfold according to divine timing rather than human schedules.

> As opposed to **Chronos Time**: A concept of linear, measurable time, often associated with historical events in the Bible. In Greek mythology Chronos (Kronos) is often personified as the god of time. The concept of "Chronos time" generally refers to linear, sequential time, the kind of time that we measure with clocks and calendars. It is quantitative and continuous, moving forward at a constant, unchanging rate from past to present to future.

Ketuvim (Writings): The Ketuvim is the third section of the Tanakh. It contains a diverse collection of poetry, wisdom literature, and additional historical works including:

- Psalms, Proverbs, Job (wisdom literature).
- Song of Songs, Ruth, Lamentations, Ecclesiastes, Esther (*Megillot* or scrolls read on special occasions).
- Daniel, Ezra-Nehemiah, Chronicles (1 & 2 as one book)—historical and apocalyptic writings.

L

- **Literal**: In the context of biblical eschatology, the distinction between literal and allegorical interpretation refers to two different approaches for understanding prophetic and apocalyptic passages. A literal approach understands the text as describing actual events, places, and figures, often in a straightforward and factual manner. For example, a literal reading of Revelation 20:1-6 would interpret the "thousand years" as an actual, chronological 1,000-year reign of Christ on Earth, often referred to as the Millennial Kingdom.

  - **Strengths**:

    - Provides clear and specific expectations for future events.

    - Maintains the direct meaning of the biblical text.

  - **Challenges**:

    - Some passages contain symbolic or poetic language that may not easily fit a literal framework.

    - May lead to speculative attempts to align current events with prophecy.

- **Allegorical Interpretation:** An allegorical approach views eschatological passages as symbolic, metaphorical, or spiritual in nature. Instead of predicting literal events, the text conveys deeper truths or timeless moral and theological lessons. For example, an allegorical interpretation of the "New Jerusalem" in Revelation 21 might see it as a symbol of the perfected relationship between God and His people, rather than a physical city descending from heaven.

  - **Strengths**:

    - Avoids over-speculation about specific events or timelines.

- Emphasizes the spiritual and ethical teachings of the text.

  - **Challenges**:

    - Can lead to subjective or varying interpretations, as allegorical meaning is often less definitive.

    - Risks diminishing the historical and prophetic claims of the text.

- **How They Relate to Eschatology:**

  - **Literalists** often emphasize future, concrete fulfillment of prophecies (e.g., Christ's return, final judgment, and a physical resurrection).

  - **Allegorists** focus on the spiritual significance of prophecy, such as the ongoing battle between good and evil or the ultimate unity of believers with God.

These approaches are not always mutually exclusively interpreters blend the two, taking certain elements literally while understanding others allegorically. For instance, someone might interpret the "thousand years" literally but see the beast in Revelation as a symbol of oppressive powers throughout history.

Ketuvim (Writings): Ketuvim is the third section of Tanakh, A diverse collection of poetry, wisdom literature, and additional historical works. The books include:

- Psalms, Proverbs, Job (wisdom literature).
- Song of Songs, Ruth, Lamentations, Ecclesiastes, Esther (Mcgillot or scrolls read on special occasions).
- Daniel, Ezra-Nehemiah, Chronicles (1 & 2 as one book)—historical and apocalyptic writings.

M

Marriage in Heaven: The union between Christ (the bridegroom) and the Church (the bride), symbolizing the eternal relationship between Jesus and His followers, particularly following the rapture and at the end of time in the New Heaven and New Earth.

Metaphysics: Metaphysics is a branch of philosophy that explores the nature of reality, existence, and the fundamental principles that govern the universe. It asks deep, abstract questions like what is the nature of being and existence? What is the relationship between the material and immaterial (e.g., body and soul)? What is the essence of time, space, causality, and reality itself? Metaphysics often delves into concepts that go beyond empirical observation, addressing topics such as the nature of God, the soul, and ultimate reality. The Book of Revelation contains numerous metaphysical themes, as it is rich with symbolic and transcendent imagery. A clear example is found in Revelation 21:1-4, which describes the creation of a *new heaven and a new earth.*

- **Metaphysical Element**: This passage suggests a radical transformation of reality itself—where the old world passes away, and a new, eternal order is established. The "new heaven and new earth" implies the ultimate fulfillment of existence, transcending current physical and temporal limitations.
- **Philosophical Dimension**: It touches on questions about the nature of existence in the afterlife. For instance, how does the material (earth) interact with the divine (heaven)? What does it mean for sorrow, death, and pain to cease existing? What is the nature of existence in a realm where God dwells directly among His people?

This is a profound metaphysical vision of a perfected state of being, reflecting the culmination of God's redemptive plan and the ultimate destiny of creation.

Millennium: A prophesied thousand-year reign of Christ on Earth, marked by peace, justice, and righteousness, following His Second Coming.

- **Mores**: are the essential customs, conventions, and moral attitudes that define acceptable behavior within a particular community or society. They generally go without saying. They are so obvious or universally understood that it does not need to be explicitly stated. They are deeply ingrained social norms that guide how individuals interact and behave, often carrying moral significance. For example, mores might dictate what is considered respectful or disrespectful behavior in a given culture.

- **Mores in *Misreading Scripture with Western Eyes:*** In *Misreading Scripture with Western Eyes* by E. Randolph Richards and Brandon J. O'Brien, the authors explore how Western cultural assumptions can influence the way we interpret the Bible. They identify several areas where Western readers' "mores"—or cultural norms—differ from those of the biblical world. Some key examples include:

    o **Individualism vs. Collectivism**: Western cultures often prioritize individual rights and achievements, while biblical cultures were more collectivist, emphasizing community and family.
    o **Time Orientation**:
    o Westerners tend to view time linearly, focusing on schedules and deadlines. In contrast, biblical cultures often had a more event-oriented or cyclical view of time.
    o **Honor and Shame**: Western cultures are often guilt-based, focusing on personal responsibility. Biblical cultures were honor-shame societies, where maintaining family or community honor was paramount.
    o **Wealth and Poverty**: Western readers may interpret wealth as a sign of blessing and poverty as a lack of effort, whereas biblical cultures often viewed wealth and poverty in terms of communal responsibility and divine providence.

- **Rules vs. Relationships**: Western cultures emphasize rules and laws, while biblical cultures placed greater importance on relationships and social harmony.

These cultural differences highlight how our own "mores" can shape our understanding of Scripture, sometimes leading to misinterpretations. If you'd like, I can delve deeper into any of these themes!

N

Nation of Israel: During the Old and New Testament periods, the "Nation of Israel" referred to both a people and a land, but its political and spiritual identity evolved significantly over time.

- **Old Testament**
    - In the Old Testament, Israel began as a covenantal community chosen by God, tracing its origins to the patriarchs Abraham, Isaac, and Jacob (whose name was changed to Israel). The nation was formed through the Exodus, when Moses led the Israelites out of Egypt and into the Promised Land of Canaan. Key phases included:
    - The Tribal Confederation: After settling in Canaan, Israel was organized into twelve tribes, each descended from Jacob's sons.
    - The United Monarchy: Under kings Saul, David, and Solomon, Israel became a unified kingdom. David established Jerusalem as the capital, and Solomon built the First Temple.
    - The Divided Kingdom: After Solomon's reign, the kingdom split into the northern kingdom of Israel and the southern kingdom of Judah. Both eventually fell to foreign powers—Israel to Assyria (722 BCE) and Judah to Babylon (586 BCE), leading to the Babylonian exile.
- **New Testament**
    - By the New Testament era, the political landscape had shifted dramatically:
    - Roman Rule: The land of Israel, often referred to as Judea, was under Roman occupation. The Jewish people lived under Roman governance, with limited autonomy.
    - Religious Identity: The Jewish people maintained their religious practices and awaited the Messiah. The Second Temple, rebuilt after the Babylonian exile, was central to their worship.

o   Messianic Fulfillment: Christians believe that Jesus Christ fulfilled the Messianic prophecies, establishing a spiritual kingdom. The early Church, initially composed of Jewish believers, expanded to include Gentiles, fulfilling God's promise to bless all nations through Abraham's descendants.

Nevi'im (Prophets): Torah is the first section of the Tanakh- The second section of the Tanakh contains historical narratives and the writings of prophets who called Israel to faithfulness and warned of consequences for disobedience. It is divided into two parts:

- **Former Prophets**:
  o   Joshua, Judges, Samuel (1 & 2 as one book), and Kings (1 & 2 as one book)—historical narratives about Israel's early history and monarchy.
- **Latter Prophets**:
  o   Isaiah, Jeremiah, Ezekiel, and the Twelve Minor Prophets (e.g., Hosea, Amos, Micah, Malachi).

Ketuvim (Writings): Ketuvim is the third section of Tanakh, A diverse collection of poetry, wisdom literature, and additional historical works. The books include:

- Psalms, Proverbs, Job (wisdom literature).
- Song of Songs, Ruth, Lamentations, Ecclesiastes, Esther (Megillot or scrolls read on special occasions).
- Daniel, Ezra-Nehemiah, Chronicles (1 & 2 as one book)—historical and apocalyptic writings.

O

Ologies: The suffix -ology comes from the Greek word **logia**, meaning "the study of" or "the branch of knowledge about something." When added to a root word, it typically forms a term for a specialized field of study or discipline. The -ologies used in this book are philosophy, psychology, sociology, and theology In the context of the Christian Church, the term Orthodox has a rich and multifaceted meaning:

- **Literal Meaning**: The word *orthodox* comes from the Greek words *orthos* (correct) and *doxa* (belief or worship). It essentially means "correct belief" or "right worship." It conveys the idea of adhering to the true teachings and practices of Christianity as handed down by Christ and the Apostles.

- **Theological Identity**: In a broader Christian context, *orthodox* can describe beliefs and practices that conform to the core doctrines established by the early ecumenical councils (e.g., the Nicene Creed). In this sense, both Eastern Orthodox, Roman Catholic, and Protestant traditions might affirm orthodox beliefs in contrast to heretical or heterodox teachings.

- **Eastern Orthodox Church**: Specifically, *Orthodox* refers to the branch of Christianity that developed in the Eastern Roman (Byzantine) Empire. The **Eastern Orthodox Church** is distinct from the Roman Catholic Church and Protestant traditions, having formally split from the Roman Church in the Great Schism of 1054 CE. Eastern Orthodoxy emphasizes the following:

  - **Apostolic Tradition**: Faithfully preserving the teachings and traditions of the early Church.

  - **Liturgical Worship**: Highly structured, sacramental, and steeped in ancient practices.

- o **Theology**: Focused on the mystical union with God (theosis) and heavily influenced by the teachings of the Church Fathers.

P

Passover :(Hebrew: *Pesach*) is one of the most important Jewish festivals, commemorating the Israelites' liberation from slavery in Egypt, as described in the Book of Exodus. Its name comes from the Hebrew word meaning "to pass over," referring to the way the angel of death "passed over" the houses of the Israelites during the tenth plague. Key Aspects of Passover:

- **Biblical Origin**:
  - Found in **Exodus 12**, Passover marks the culmination of the ten plagues that God inflicted on Egypt to persuade Pharaoh to release the Israelites.
  - The tenth plague, the death of the firstborn, spared the Israelites because they obeyed God's command to mark their doorposts with the blood of a lamb, a sign for the angel of death to "pass over" their homes.
- **Celebratory Practices**:
  - The Israelites were commanded to observe the Passover annually as a memorial to their deliverance (Exodus 12:14-28).
  - Key elements included eating unleavened bread (*matzah*), roasted lamb, and bitter herbs to symbolize their hasty departure, God's provision, and the bitterness of slavery.
- **Significance in the Old Testament:**
- **God's Faithfulness and Deliverance**:
  - Passover represents God's covenantal faithfulness to rescue His chosen people, fulfilling His promise to Abraham.
- **Redemption and Atonement**:
  - The blood of the lamb, which protected the Israelites, prefigures God's redemptive acts throughout the Old Testament, tying into the broader theme of atonement.
- **Covenantal Identity**:
  - Passover became a defining event in the Israelites' history, shaping their identity as God's people and

reminding them of their divine calling to live in obedience and gratitude.

- **Theological Foreshadowing**:
  - Within Christian theology, Passover is seen as a type or foreshadowing of Christ, the "Lamb of God," whose sacrificial death brings deliverance from sin (1 Corinthians 5:7).

Perspicacious: having a ready insight into and understanding things.

Pentecost: the coming of the Holy Spirit upon the early believers, empowering them for mission and spreading the gospel.

Post-Millennium: 1. **Post-Millennium (Postmillennialism):** This is a theological perspective on the end times that interprets the "millennium" (a thousand-year reign of Christ mentioned in Revelation 20) as a period before Christ's physical second coming. Postmillennialists believe that Christ will return after the millennium, which is understood not as a literal thousand years but as an era during which Christian principles and the Gospel will spread and transform the world, leading to an age of peace and righteousness.

Preterist/Preterism: Preterism is an eschatological view that interprets many or all of the prophecies in the Bible—especially those in Revelation, Daniel, and the Olivet Discourse—as events that have already been fulfilled, primarily by the destruction of the Jerusalem Temple in 70 AD. There are two main types:

- **Full Preterism**: Believes all biblical prophecies, including the second coming and resurrection, are past events.
- **Partial Preterism**: Holds that many prophecies have been fulfilled, but the second coming and final judgment are still future events.

Preterism is an eschatological (end-times) viewpoint within Christian theology that interprets many or all biblical prophecies as events that have already occurred, particularly in the context of the destruction of the Jerusalem Temple in 70 AD. Key Aspects of Preterism:

- **Origin of the Term: The word "preterism" comes from the Latin praeter, meaning "past." It reflects the belief that certain prophetic passages have already been fulfilled in the past.**
- **Application: This interpretation primarily focuses on the apocalyptic texts of the Bible, such as the Book of Revelation, the Olivet Discourse (Matthew 24), and parts of Daniel.**
- **Types of Preterism:**
  - **Full Preterism (or Consistent Preterism):**
    - Claims that **all** biblical prophecies, including the Second Coming of Christ, the resurrection of the dead, and the final judgment, were fulfilled in the first century—specifically with the fall of Jerusalem in 70 AD.
    - Considered heterodox by most Christian denominations, as it denies a future, physical return of Christ and bodily resurrection.
  - **Partial Preterism:**
    - Argues that **many** of the Bible's prophecies were fulfilled in the first century (e.g., the destruction of the Temple and Christ's judgment on Jerusalem).
    - However, Partial Preterists affirm that key future events, such as Christ's second coming, the resurrection, and the final judgment, are yet to happen. This view is more widely accepted within mainstream Christian thought.

Preterism is one of several eschatological frameworks, alongside views like futurism, historicism, and idealism.

Pre-Mid-Post Millennium: Pre-Mid-Post Millennium refer to different interpretations of the timing of Christ's second coming relative to the "millennium" in Revelation 20.

- **Premillennialism**: Christ will return **before** the millennium to establish His literal thousand-year reign on Earth. This view can be divided into:
  - **Historic Premillennialism**: Focuses on a simple, literal second coming and millennium.
  - **Dispensational Premillennialism**: Adds ideas about a pre-tribulation rapture and distinct dispensations in God's plan.
- **Mid-Millennialism**: While not as common as pre- or post-millennialism, this term could suggest theories where Christ's return may coincide with or occur mid-way during the metaphorical "millennial" period. It's less a formal position and more a way of describing alternative eschatological timelines.
- **Postmillennialism**: Already defined above, where Christ returns **after** a golden age of peac

Pretribulation-Premillennialism (PTPM): A view in eschatology that asserts the rapture will occur before the Great Tribulation and that Christ will return before the Millennium—a thousand-year reign of peace.

- **Parousia / 2nd Coming of Christ**: **Parousia**, derived from the Greek word meaning "presence" or "arrival," is a theological term that refers specifically to the **Second Coming of Christ**. It describes the future event in Christian eschatology where Jesus will return to Earth in glory to fulfill divine promises and bring history to its culmination.
  - **Biblical Basis:**
    - The Parousia is mentioned in several New Testament passages, including:
      - Matthew 24:30-31: Jesus speaks of His coming with power and great glory.

- Acts 1:11: Angels declare that Jesus will return in the same manner He ascended into heaven.
- 1 Thessalonians 4:16-17: Paul describes Christ's return, the resurrection of the dead, and the gathering of believers.
- Revelation 19:11-16: A vivid depiction of Christ returning as a victorious King.

o Purpose:
- To judge the living and the dead.
- To establish the full realization of God's Kingdom.
- To fulfill promises of restoration, redemption, and eternal life.

o Eschatological Views, Different Christian traditions interpret the nature and timing of the Parousia differently:
- Preterism: Some aspects of the Second Coming may have been symbolically fulfilled in events like the destruction of Jerusalem in 70 AD.
- Futurism: The Parousia is a future, literal, and global event.
- Amillennialism: Often views the Second Coming as the culmination of history, without a literal thousand-year reign on Earth.

o Key Themes:
- Hope: For believers, the Parousia represents the fulfillment of God's promises and the ultimate triumph of good over evil.
- Preparedness: Many New Testament passages emphasize the importance of being spiritually prepared for Christ's return (e.g., Matthew 25:1-13, the parable of the ten virgins).

Philosophy: is the study of fundamental questions about existence, knowledge, values, reason, mind, and language. The term originates from the Greek words *philos* (love) and *sophia* (wisdom), meaning "the love of wisdom." It seeks to explore the nature of reality and human understanding through critical thinking and rational analysis.

- **Elements of Philosophy.** Philosophy can be broken down into several key branches or elements, each focusing on specific areas of inquiry:

  - **Metaphysics**:
    - The study of the nature of reality, existence, and the universe.
    - Central questions: What is the nature of being? What exists? What is the relationship between mind and matter?
  - **Epistemology**:
    - The study of knowledge and belief.
    - Central questions: What is knowledge? How do we know what we know? What are the limits of human understanding?
  - **Ethics** (or Moral Philosophy):
    - The study of right and wrong, good and bad, and the nature of moral values.
    - Central questions: What is the best way to live? What is the basis for ethical behavior? How should we treat one another?
  - **Logic**:
    - The study of reasoning and argument.
    - Central questions: What constitutes valid reasoning? How can we distinguish good arguments from bad ones?
  - **Aesthetics**:
    - The study of beauty, art, and taste.
    - Central questions: What is beauty? What makes something art? How do we experience the sublime?
  - **Political Philosophy**:
    - The study of government, justice, rights, and the role of individuals in society.

- o Central questions: What is the best form of government? What are the rights and responsibilities of citizens?
- **Philosophy of Mind**:
  - o The study of the nature of consciousness, thought, and perception.
  - o Central questions: What is the mind? How is it related to the body? Can machines think?

Philosophy often overlaps with other fields like theology, science, and literature, and it serves as a foundation for critical thinking in many disciplines

Psychology: is the scientific study of the human mind, behavior, and mental processes. It seeks to understand how people think, feel, and act individually and in groups, as well as how biological, social, and environmental factors influence them.

- **Major Types of Psychology:** Psychology is a broad discipline, often divided into specialized fields:
  - o **Clinical Psychology**:
    - Focuses on diagnosing and treating mental illnesses, emotional disturbances, and behavioral problems.
    - Includes therapies like cognitive-behavioral therapy (CBT), psychoanalysis, and others.
  - o **Cognitive Psychology**:
    - Studies mental processes such as memory, perception, problem-solving, and decision-making.
    - Examines how people acquire, process, and store information.
  - o **Developmental Psychology**:
    - Focuses on how people grow and change across their lifespan, from infancy to old age.
    - Examines physical, cognitive, emotional, and social development.

- o **Social Psychology**:
    - Studies show how individuals are influenced by their interactions with others and by societal norms.
    - Topics include group behavior, prejudice, conformity, and interpersonal relationships.
- o **Behavioral Psychology**:
    - Focuses on observable behaviors and how they're learned through conditioning (classical and operant).
    - Often associated with figures like B.F. Skinner and John Watson.
- o **Industrial-Organizational Psychology**:
    - Applies psychological principles to the workplace to improve productivity, employee well-being, and organizational effectiveness.
- o **Biopsychology (or Behavioral Neuroscience)**:
    - Explores the connection between biology and behavior, focusing on brain function, genetics, and the nervous system.
- o **Health Psychology**:
    - Examines how psychological factors affect physical health and well-being.
    - Addresses areas like stress, coping mechanisms, and lifestyle behaviors.
- o **Forensic Psychology**:
    - Psychological principles apply to legal issues and the criminal justice system.
    - Involves assessments, expert testimony, and profiling.
- o **Educational Psychology**:
    - Studies how people learn and how to improve educational processes.
    - Includes research on teaching methods, learning disabilities, and student motivation.
- o **Personality Psychology**:
    - Focuses on understanding individual differences and personality traits.

- Examines how personality develops and influences behavior.

Each type of psychology uses unique approaches to understand and solve problems related to human behavior and thought.

Q

Quaking:

The great earthquake during the sixth seal in Revelation 6:12.

The shaking of the heavens and the earth prophesied in Haggai 2:6–7.

The trembling of the earth on the "Day of the Lord" in Joel 2:10.

R

Rapture: The event in Christian eschatology where believers are taken up to meet Christ before the Tribulation period begins, as described in the New Testament.

Religion (Christian): The **Christian religion** is a monotheistic faith centered on the life, teachings, death, and resurrection of **Jesus Christ**, who is regarded by Christians as the Son of God and the Savior of humanity. Christianity emerged in the 1st century AD in the Roman province of Judea, rooted in the Jewish tradition but spreading beyond it to encompass a global following.

- **Core Beliefs of Christianity:**

  - **God:**
    - Christians believe in one God, who is triune in nature—Father, Son (Jesus Christ), and Holy Spirit. This concept is known as the **Holy Trinity**.
  - **Jesus Christ:**
    - Jesus is the central figure in Christianity. He is believed to be fully divine and fully human, having come to Earth to save humanity from sin through His sacrificial death and resurrection.
    - His teachings, miracles, and example serve as the foundation of Christian faith.
  - **The Bible:**
    - The Bible, consisting of the Old and New Testaments, is considered the authoritative scripture of Christianity. It contains historical accounts, laws, poetry, prophecy, and teachings central to faith.
  - **Salvation:**
    - Central to Christianity is the belief in **salvation by grace through faith in Jesus**

Christ. Salvation involves the forgiveness of sins and the promise of eternal life with God.

- o **Ethics and Morality**:
  - Christians are called to live according to the teachings of Jesus, including love, forgiveness, humility, and justice. The **Sermon on the Mount** (Matthew 5–7) outlines many of these principles.

- **Practices of Christianity**:

  - o **Worship**:
    - Worship often involves prayer, hymns, sermons, and the reading of scripture. The Eucharist (or Communion) is a central sacrament in most Christian traditions.
  - o **Sacraments**:
    - Depending on the denomination, sacraments like **baptism** and the **Eucharist** are considered sacred acts instituted by Jesus.
  - o **Community**:
    - Christians gather in congregations or churches to support one another spiritually and to worship collectively.

- **Christian Denominations:** Christianity is divided into several major branches, including:

  - o **Catholicism**: Focused on the authority of the Pope and the traditions of the Church.
  - o **Eastern Orthodoxy**: Emphasizes liturgy, icons, and apostolic tradition.
  - o **Protestantism**: Originating from the Reformation, with diverse denominations like Lutherans, Baptists, and Methodists, emphasizing scripture and faith.

Resurrection: The **resurrection of Christ** refers to the Christian belief that Jesus Christ was raised from the dead on the third day after His crucifixion, as described in the New Testament. It is a central doctrine of Christianity, symbolizing victory over sin and death, and is foundational to the faith.

- **Key Aspects of the Resurrection:**
  - **Biblical Basis:**
    - The resurrection is recorded in all four Gospels (Matthew 28, Mark 16, Luke 24, John 20), as well as in the epistles of Paul (e.g., 1 Corinthians 15).
    - According to these accounts, Jesus' tomb was found empty, and He appeared alive to His disciples and others over a period of forty days.
  - **Theological Significance:**
    - **Victory over Death:** The resurrection signifies Jesus' triumph over death and the grave, offering eternal life to all who believe in Him.
    - **Fulfillment of Prophecy:** It fulfills Old Testament prophecies (e.g., Psalm 16:10, Isaiah 53) and Jesus' own predictions of His death and resurrection (e.g., Matthew 16:21).
    - **Foundation of Christian Hope:** The resurrection assures believers of their own future resurrection and eternal life (1 Corinthians 15:20-22).
  - **Spiritual Meaning:**
    - It demonstrates God's power and faithfulness.
    - It marks the beginning of the new creation and the inauguration of the Kingdom of God.
  - **Eschatological Aspect:**
    - The resurrection is closely tied to Christian eschatology (the study of end times). It is seen as a foretaste of the ultimate resurrection of all believers at Christ's second coming (Parousia).

The final book of the New Testament that unveils prophetic visions of the end times, including the Second Coming, the final judgment, and the New Heaven and New Earth.

S

Second (2ⁿᵈ⁾ Coming of Christ (Parousia): Signifies the anticipated return of Christ to earth to judge the living and the dead. All so known as the Parousia, is a core concept in Christian eschatology (the study of end times). It refers to the future event when Jesus Christ is prophesied to return to Earth. This event will mark the culmination of history and the final judgment of humanity.

Seder: See Haggadah & Seder.

Seven Feast of Israel: See Feasts of Israel.

Sheol: Sheol is a term used in the Hebrew Bible to describe the realm of the dead, often translated as "the grave," "pit," or "the underworld." It is not a place of punishment or reward but rather a shadowy, neutral abode where the dead reside, regardless of their moral standing in life. Key Aspects of Sheol:

- **Biblical Context:**
    - Sheol is mentioned frequently in the Old Testament, often as the destination of all the dead, both the righteous and the wicked (e.g., Job 3:13-19, Ecclesiastes 9:10).
    - It is depicted as a place of darkness, silence, and separation from the living and, in some instances, from God (e.g., Psalm 88:10-12).
- **Characteristics:**
    - **Neutrality:** Unlike later Christian concepts of Heaven and Hell, Sheol is not characterized by judgment or moral distinction.
    - **Existence:** The dead are portrayed as shadowy, inactive "shades" (*rephaim*), without the vibrant life they once had.

- **Theological Significance**:
    - o In early Jewish thought, Sheol reflects a view of death as the inevitable end of human existence.
    - o Over time, beliefs about the afterlife evolved, especially under the influence of Persian and Hellenistic ideas. Concepts of resurrection, eternal life, and judgment (e.g., Daniel 12:2) began to develop, shifting attention away from Sheol.
- **Relation to Later Theology**:
    - o In Christian theology, Sheol is often compared to Hades, the Greek term used in the New Testament to describe the underworld (e.g., Luke 16:23).
    - o The doctrine of resurrection and eternal judgment transformed Sheol into a precursor to more defined concepts of the afterlife.

Sociology: is the scientific study of human society, social behavior, interactions, and institutions. It seeks to understand how individuals are shaped by society and how society, in turn, is influenced by individuals. Sociologists analyze everything from small-scale interactions, like family dynamics, to large-scale social structures, such as economies, governments, and cultures. Sociology is a broad discipline with several key elements or areas of focus:

- **Social Structure**:

    - o Refers to the organized patterns of relationships and institutions that make up society.

    - o Includes entities like family, religion, education, government, and economic systems, which influence individuals' lives and interactions.

- **Culture**:

    - o Focuses on the shared beliefs, norms, values, customs, and symbols that define a group or society.

    - o Examines how culture shapes identity and behavior, as well as how cultural change occurs over time.

- **Socialization:**

  - o Studies how individuals learn and internalize societal norms, values, and roles through interactions with family, peers, education, and media.

  - o Investigates how socialization shapes identity and behavior across the life course.

- **Social Groups and Interaction:**

  - o Explores how people form groups and networks, and how group dynamics influence individual behavior.

  - o Topics include small groups (e.g., families) and larger organizations or communities.

- **Social Inequality:**

  - o Examines disparities in wealth, power, status, and opportunities among different social groups.

  - o Includes studies of race, class, gender, ethnicity, and global inequality.

- **Social Institutions:**

  - o Analyzes the major organized structures within society, such as education systems, religious organizations, healthcare, and politics.

  - o Explores how these institutions function and influence individuals and communities.

- **Deviance and Social Control:**

  - o Studies behaviors that deviate from societal norms and the mechanisms that societies use to regulate behavior, such as laws and social sanctions.

  - o Looks at why deviance occurs and its impact on social order.

- **Social Change**:
  - Investigates how societies evolve over time, including the factors that drive change, such as technology, social movements, and cultural shifts.
  - Explores the consequences of these changes for individuals and groups.

- **Globalization**:
  - Focuses on the increasing interconnectedness of societies through trade, communication, migration, and cultural exchange.
  - Analyzes its impact on local cultures, economies, and global inequalities.

- Sociology provides valuable insights into the complexities of human interaction and societal organization.

Septuagint: The Septuagint, often abbreviated as LXX, is the ancient Greek translation of the Hebrew Scriptures (Old Testament). It holds significant historical and religious importance, particularly in Jewish and Christian traditions. Key Facts About the Septuagint:

- **Origin**:
  - The Septuagint was produced in Alexandria, Egypt, around the 3rd to 2nd centuries BCE.
  - According to tradition (as recorded in the *Letter of Aristeas*), 70 or 72 Jewish scholars translated the Hebrew Scriptures into Greek for the Jewish community living in the Greek-speaking world. This is why it is called the "Septuagint," meaning "Seventy."
- **Content**:
  - The Septuagint includes the books of the Hebrew Bible (Torah, Prophets, and Writings) as well as additional texts that are now known as the **Apocrypha** or **Deuterocanonical Books**, such as Tobit, Judith, and Wisdom of Solomon.

- **Significance**:
  - **For Judaism**: The Septuagint allowed Jews in the Hellenistic period, many of whom no longer spoke Hebrew fluently, to access their sacred scriptures.
  - **For Christianity**: The Septuagint became the primary scripture for early Christians, especially in the Greek-speaking world. Many quotations of the Old Testament in the New Testament are based on the Septuagint rather than the Hebrew text.
- **Differences from the Masoretic Text**:
  - The Septuagint occasionally differs from the later **Masoretic Text**, which is the authoritative Hebrew version of the Old Testament in Jewish tradition. These differences can be textual, linguistic, or theological.
- **Influence on Canon**:
  - The inclusion of the Deuterocanonical Books in the Septuagint influenced the **Roman Catholic** and **Eastern Orthodox** canons of scripture. In contrast, the Protestant tradition generally adheres to the shorter Hebrew canon.

T

Talmud: The **Talmud** is a central text in Jewish religious tradition, serving as a foundational work of Jewish law, ethics, philosophy, and theology. It consists of extensive commentary and discussions that expand upon the laws and teachings found in the Torah (the first five books of the Hebrew Bible). Key Aspects of the Talmud:

- **Structure of the Talmud**:
    - The Talmud is divided into two main parts:
        - **Mishnah**: A written compilation of oral Jewish laws and traditions, codified around 200 CE by Rabbi Judah the Prince.
        - **Gemara**: A commentary on the Mishnah, containing rabbinic discussions, interpretations, and elaborations, compiled between 200–500 CE.
- **Versions of the Talmud**:
    - **Jerusalem Talmud (Talmud Yerushalmi)**: Compiled in the Land of Israel around the 4th century CE.
    - **Babylonian Talmud (Talmud Bavli)**: Compiled in Babylon (modern-day Iraq) around the 5th century CE. It is more extensive and widely studied compared to the Jerusalem Talmud.
- **Contents of the Talmud**:
    - The Mishnah is divided into six sections (*Sedarim*), each addressing a specific area of Jewish law:
        - **Zeraim** (Seeds): Agricultural laws and prayers.
        - **Moed** (Festivals): Laws concerning Sabbath and Jewish holidays.
        - **Nashim** (Women): Family law, including marriage and divorce.
        - **Nezikin** (Damages): Civil and criminal law.

- **Kodashim** (Holy Things): Laws related to sacrifices and the Temple.
      - **Tohorot** (Purities): Laws of ritual purity and impurity.
    - The Gemara expands on these topics with legal debates, narratives, parables, and ethical teachings.
- **Significance**:
    - The Talmud is a cornerstone of **halakha** (Jewish law) and remains a central text for rabbinic study and interpretation.
    - Beyond law, it addresses philosophical, ethical, and spiritual questions, offering a wide-ranging exploration of Jewish thought and life.

Tanakh: The **Tanakh** is the canonical collection of Jewish scriptures, equivalent to what Christians refer to as the Old Testament, though the order and grouping of the books differ. The term "Tanakh" is an acronym derived from the first letters of its three main divisions: Torah, Nevi'im, and Ketuvim. Contents of the Tanakh:

- **Torah (Teaching or Law)**:
    - Also called the Pentateuch (Greek), The Law (English), The Torah consists of the first five books of the Bible. It is the foundation of Jewish law and theology.
    - Books:
      - Genesis (*Bereishit*): The creation of the world, the patriarchs, and the origins of Israel.
      - Exodus (*Shemot*): The story of Moses, the Exodus from Egypt, and the giving of the Law at Sinai.
      - Leviticus (*Vayikra*): Laws concerning worship, sacrifices, and purity.
      - Numbers (*Bemidbar*): The Israelites' journey through the wilderness.
      - Deuteronomy (*Devarim*): Moses' final speeches and the restatement of the Law.

- **Nevi'im (Prophets)**:
    - o This section contains historical narratives and the writings of prophets who called Israel to faithfulness and warned of consequences for disobedience.
    - o Divided into two parts:
        - **Former Prophets**:
        - Joshua, Judges, Samuel (1 & 2 as one book), and Kings (1 & 2 as one book)—historical narratives about Israel's early history and monarchy.
        - **Latter Prophets**:
        - Isaiah, Jeremiah, Ezekiel, and the Twelve Minor Prophets (e.g., Hosea, Amos, Micah, Malachi).
- **Significance of the Tanakh:**
    - o It is the cornerstone of Jewish faith and practice, containing God's covenant with Israel and guiding principles for life.
    - o It was written primarily in **Hebrew** (with some portions in Aramaic) and spans centuries of Jewish history and spiritual reflection.

Temple Periods: The "temple periods" refer to distinct eras in Jewish history marked by the construction, existence, and destruction of the First and Second Temples in Jerusalem. Here's an overview:

- **First Temple Period (c. 1000 BCE – 586 BCE)**:
    - o The First Temple, also known as Solomon's Temple, was built by King Solomon around 1000 BCE after King David established Jerusalem as the capital.
    - o It served as the central place of worship for the Israelites, housing the Ark of the Covenant.
    - o This period ended in 586 BCE when the Babylonians, led by King Nebuchadnezzar, destroyed the temple and exiled the Jewish people to Babylon.
- **Second Temple Period (516 BCE – 70 CE)**:
    - o After the Babylonian Exile, the Jewish people returned to Jerusalem under the decree of Cyrus the

Great of Persia. They rebuilt the temple, completing it in 516 BCE.

- o This period saw significant events, including the influence of Persian, Hellenistic, and Roman rule. Herod the Great later expanded and renovated the temple.
- o The Second Temple was destroyed in 70 CE by the Romans during the First Jewish–Roman War.
- These periods are central to Jewish history and theology, with the destruction of both temples commemorated annually on Tisha B'Av, a day of mourning.

Tertullian: Tertullian, whose full name was Quintus Septimius Florens Tertullianus, was an influential early Christian theologian and writer, often referred to as the "Father of Latin Christianity" and the "Founder of Western Theology." He lived approximately from 155/160 AD to after 220 AD, primarily in Carthage, a prominent city in Roman North Africa2.

- **Theological Contributions**:
    - o Tertullian was the first Christian author to write extensively in Latin, shaping the theological vocabulary of Western Christianity.
    - o He is credited with coining the term "Trinity" (*trinitas*) to describe the Father, Son, and Holy Spirit as three distinct persons sharing one divine essence3.
    - o His works, such as *Apologeticum* (Defense), defended Christianity against Roman accusations and emphasized religious liberty.
- **Moral and Ethical Rigor**:
    - o Tertullian advocated for strict Christian ethics, emphasizing holiness and separation from pagan practices. His writings, like *De Spectaculis* (On the Shows), reflect his moral rigor.
- **Apologetics**:
    - o He was a pioneer in Christian apologetics, using his legal training to craft compelling defenses of the faith against heresies and pagan critiques.

- **He was infamous for:**
  - **Association with Montanism:**
    - Later in life, Tertullian aligned with Montanism, a puritanical and charismatic Christian sect. This association led to his estrangement from the mainstream Church3.
    - Montanism's emphasis on prophecy and strict moral codes was controversial, and Tertullian's later works reflect these influences.
  - **Subordinationism:**
    - Some of Tertullian's theological views, such as the subordination of the Son and Spirit to the Father, were later deemed unorthodox.
- Tertullian's legacy is a blend of groundbreaking theological insights and contentious affiliations, making him a pivotal yet complex figure in early Christian history

Theology: Theology is the study of the nature of the divine, religious beliefs, and spiritual truths. Derived from the Greek words *theos* (God) and *logos* (study or discourse), theology seeks to explore and understand the nature, attributes, and works of God or gods, as well as the relationship between the divine and humanity. Theology often encompasses various disciplines, including:

- **Biblical Theology**: Focused on interpreting religious texts, like the Bible or Qur'an, to understand their teachings about God and humanity.

- **Systematic Theology**: Organizing and synthesizing religious beliefs into a coherent framework (e.g., doctrines like the Trinity or salvation).

- **Historical Theology**: Examining how religious beliefs and practices have developed over time.

- **Practical Theology**: Applying theological principles to everyday life, worship, and ethics.

- **Personal View of Theology**: Theology, for me, transcends mere academic exploration; it is beyond spiritual intelligence. My theology is a personal journey, one that shapes my relationship with God and influences who I am becoming. While I engage in Systematic Theology and take a structured approach to decoding end-time prophecy, these pursuits are part of a broader, transformative awareness and awakening. This journey leads me into a deeper connection with God the Father, the Son, and the Holy Spirit, while also embracing the concept of "Becoming Me" through the study and teaching of eschatology.

  I hold firmly to the principles of God's ontological participation and relationality, the Hebrew Hermeneutical framework for interpreting Scripture, and the enduring truths of *Sola Scriptura* and *Sola Fide*. Theology, therefore, is not merely what I study; it is the lens through which I grow, teach, and live my faith.

- **Time of Jacob's Trouble**: A period of intense tribulation prophesied in Jeremiah, specifically related to the judgment of the Jewish people for rejecting Christ as the Messiah.

Time of the Gentiles: The "Time of the Gentiles" is a biblical concept referring to a period during which Gentile nations have dominion over Jerusalem and, by extension, the Jewish people. This term is mentioned in Luke 21:24, where Jesus speaks of Jerusalem being "trampled by the Gentiles until the times of the Gentiles are fulfilled."

The Time of the Gentiles is generally understood to have begun with the Babylonian conquest of Jerusalem in 586 BCE. This marked the start of Gentile domination over the city, which continued through successive empires, including the Babylonian, Persian, Greek, and Roman empires.

The end of the Time of the Gentiles is often associated with eschatological events, particularly the Second Coming of Christ. Many interpretations suggest it will conclude when Jerusalem is fully restored to Jewish sovereignty and God's kingdom is established on earth. Some theologians link this to the end of the Great Tribulation, as described in prophetic texts like Daniel and Revelation`.

This concept carries significant theological and eschatological implications, often tied to discussions about God's plan for Israel and the Church.

Torah: The **Torah** is the foundational text of Judaism and holds significant importance in Christianity and Islam as well. The word *Torah* means "instruction," "teaching," or "law" in Hebrew. It refers specifically to the first five books of the Hebrew Bible (or Old Testament in Christianity): Genesis, Exodus, Leviticus, Numbers, and Deuteronomy. These books are also collectively known as the Pentateuch or the Books of Moses.

Content of the Torah:

- Genesis (*Bereshit*): Details the creation of the world, the early history of humanity, the patriarchs (Abraham, Isaac, Jacob), and God's covenant with Israel.

- Exodus (*Shemot*): Covers the Israelites' enslavement in Egypt, their liberation under Moses, the giving of the Law at Mount Sinai, and the establishment of the covenant.

- Leviticus (*Vayikra*): Focuses on laws related to worship, rituals, sacrifices, and holiness.

- Numbers (*Bemidbar*): Chronicles the Israelites' journey through the wilderness and their preparations to enter the Promised Land.

- Deuteronomy (*Devarim*): A series of speeches by Moses reviewing the laws and covenant before the Israelites enter the Promised Land.

- Significance of the Torah

    o Central to Jewish Faith: The Torah is considered the most sacred text in Judaism, representing God's direct revelation to Moses. It is read publicly in synagogues in weekly portions and is central to Jewish worship, ethics, and daily life.

- o Moral and Legal Foundation: The Torah provides the foundational laws (e.g., the Ten Commandments) and ethical teachings that guide Jewish life. These principles have also deeply influenced Western legal and moral systems.

- o Covenantal Significance: The Torah represents the covenant between God and the people of Israel, embodying their unique relationship with Him.

- o Inspirational Across Faiths: In Christianity, the Torah serves as the bedrock of the Old Testament and provides context for understanding Jesus' teachings. In Islam, the Torah (*Tawrat*) is recognized as a divine scripture revealed to the prophet Moses (*Musa*).

Tribulation: A seven-year period of suffering and persecution that will occur before the Second Coming of Christ, marked by the rise of the Antichrist and divine judgments.

U

Unveiling:

The unveiling of Jesus Christ's divine glory in Revelation 1:1.

The revelation of the mystery of God in Colossians 1:26–27.

The disclosure of hidden truths at the end of the age in Daniel 12:9.

V

Victory:

Christ's victory over death and sin in 1 Corinthians 15:54–57.

The Lamb's triumph over the beast in Revelation 17:14.

The ultimate victory of the saints described in Revelation 21:7.

Wrath of God:

The bowls of God's wrath poured out in Revelation 16.

The wrath revealed against ungodliness in Romans 1:18.

The call to flee from the coming wrath in Luke 3:7.

X

Xerxes:

Xerxes' role in the Book of Esther as a Persian king influencing Jewish history.

Historical speculations about Xerxes in relation to biblical prophecy.

Connections between Xerxes' reign and God's providence for His people.

Y

Yeshua is the original Hebrew name for Jesus, which means "The Lord is salvation." He is a central figure in Christianity, revered as the Messiah and the Son of God. Christians believe that Yeshua came into the world to fulfill God's plan for salvation, offering atonement for humanity's sins through His life, death, and resurrection.

In Judaism, Yeshua is acknowledged as a historical figure, but not as the prophesied Messiah. For Messianic Jews, however, Yeshua is recognized as both the Messiah and a fulfillment of Jewish prophecy, uniting aspects of Jewish and Christian beliefs.

Yom Yahweh (Day of the Lord):

The Day of the Lord as a time of judgment in Zephaniah 1:14–18.

The promise of restoration on the Day of the Lord in Joel 2:31.

The eschatological arrival of the Lord in Amos 5:18–20.

Z

Zechariah: Zechariah, the son of Berechiah and grandson of Iddo, was a prophet and priest who ministered during the post-exilic period, around 520–518 BCE. He was a contemporary of Haggai and played a significant role in encouraging the Jewish people to rebuild the Temple in Jerusalem after their return from Babylonian exile. His prophecies are recorded in the Book of Zechariah, which is part of the Twelve Minor Prophets in the Hebrew Bible.

- Eschatological Prophecies, Zechariah's prophecies are rich in apocalyptic imagery and messianic themes, making them highly significant in eschatological discussions. Here are some key elements:

  - The Coming of the Messiah:
    - Zechariah 9:9–10 foretells the arrival of a humble and righteous king riding on a donkey, a prophecy Christians believe was fulfilled in Jesus' triumphal entry into Jerusalem.
    - Zechariah 12:10 speaks of a figure who is "pierced," which is interpreted by many as a reference to the crucifixion of Christ.
  - The Day of the Lord:
    - Zechariah 14 describes a climactic "Day of the Lord," when God will intervene decisively in human history. This includes the gathering of nations against Jerusalem, divine deliverance, and the establishment of God's eternal kingdom.
  - Restoration of Israel:
    - Zechariah 8:3–8 promises the restoration of Jerusalem and the return of God's presence, symbolizing hope and renewal for the Jewish people.
  - Universal Worship:
    - Zechariah 14:16–19 envisions a future where all nations will come to Jerusalem to worship

the Lord during the Feast of Tabernacles,
highlighting the universal scope of God's
kingdom.

- o Zechariah's prophecies blend immediate concerns,
  such as the rebuilding of the Temple, with far-
  reaching visions of God's ultimate plan for humanity

Many of these definitions were taken or modified from Microsoft Copilot!

Index

www.ingramcontent.com/pod-product-compliance
Lightning Source LLC
Chambersburg PA
CBHW051135300726
48978CB00011B/285